Spies

RICHARD BEN SAPIR

Spies

DOUBLEDAY & COMPANY, INC., GARDEN CITY, NEW YORK
1984

All the characters in this book are fictitious, and any resemblance to actual persons, living or dead, is purely coincidental.

Library of Congress Cataloging in Publication Data
Sapir, Richard.
Spies.
I. Title.
PS3569.A59S65   1984   813'.54   83-45004
ISBN: 0-385-18910-9

For Warren Murphy,

a good man, a fine writer,
and a treasure as a friend

ACKNOWLEDGMENTS

Al Conti, T. Curtis Forbes, Eileen Slocum, Jack White, Ed Stein, Jim Thorp, The Preservation Society, Richard Marazeti, Aaron Sloam, Zeke St. John, the Newport Police, the Newport Historical Museum, Evelyn Cherpack and Henry Nicolosi of the U.S. Naval War College, Petropolis, David Phillips, Wayne Miller, Scott Sack, Mary Brownell, the Arlington Trust, Will Murray, Richard Senier, who knows everyone in the world and if he doesn't, he knows his friends, W. B. Murphy, Linda Sloss, Sandy Stott, Betsy John, Jane Danaher Richard, Elizabeth Chute, Dr. and Mrs. Joseph Sapir, Joseph Rosenberg, James O'Donnell, Reginald Phelps, David Brownell, who hopefully will be owed a dinner in Paris, Walt Lacey, Jordan Levy. Special thanks to my editors Lisa Drew and Anne Hukill, who did more for this book than any editors I've ever had.

Apologies to the half-dozen people I most certainly had to miss. Most thanks to P. K. Chute for advice, editing, and being there. Always for being there.

Spies

1

THE DEAD were dead and the war was supposed to be over. The bodies of the U-boat crew had long ago been retrieved, and with courtesy due a new ally given a little plot of land in nearby Newport, Rhode Island, where a West German vice-consul came every year to pay respects in a brief ceremony that got briefer with the years.

He talked of courage, the tragedy of misbegotten ideals, and hopes for peace. Then he went to one of the good restaurants on the Newport waterfront and took a public tour of the palatial mansions.

It had been the last submarine sunk off the American coast in World War II and for almost four decades no one questioned why it had been so reckless so late in the war, cruising near heavily fortified Narragansett Bay for nearly two weeks, sending out long radio signals, looking to pack up with other U-boats, and then, in an act of pure military futility, sinking a lowly collier bound for Boston while it was still in sight of land.

It was just too much to miss. The coast guard cutters *Atherton* and *Mobley* cruised out and nailed it to the sandy bottom of Rhode Island Sound between Block Island and Point Judith.

It was April. Germany surrendered in May, and then, in another spring almost forty years later, a scuba diver looking for lobsters off Block Island, poking around under rocks because they hid during the day, put his glove on something dark. It looked so much like a lobster, black with mottling. He tugged. It came up with a spitting mist of gray sand in the dark green Atlantic waters. It had no claws, and was as long as a forearm and as wide as an oarblade. It did not wriggle or squirm.

When he got it to the surface, he could see the black was hard rubber and the mottling, barnacles. It had been in the water a long time.

He could feel something inside. He could move it around. The rubber was a pouch, but nowhere did it have openings. No seams. A seamless piece of rubber he couldn't tear open with his hands, and couldn't even cut into with his diver's knife, which made only harmless little nicks as he slashed at it.

2

WITH FIRM footing on land and a hacksaw in his hand, the diver finally got through a corner of the pouch and saw why he had had so much trouble out in the water. Someone had laced the rubber throughout with wire netting. Inside were two thin books in waxy covers. They chipped easily with a fingernail. The pages were typed. The language was German. There were charts and numbers.

Everyone watching him cut open the pouch said it had to be from the sunken U-boat and therefore belonged in the U.S. Naval Museum at the War College on Route 114 in Newport because that U-boat was part of the Second World War. It was history.

"Like Gettysburg and the French Revolution, you know, ancient," said the diver when he delivered the pouch. He was twenty-two years old.

"Not that ancient," said the curator. He was sixty-two. He had fought in that war. He gave it to the intelligence officer at the War College for identification.

The young officer, an Annapolis graduate who had done sea duty, knew something was wrong immediately. The books themselves made eminent sense for something found near a sunken U-boat. First, the charts did divide the Atlantic coast into grids from Fort Lauderdale to Newfoundland, and secondly, it was the Doenitz code, established as separate from the main German code early in the war by Grossadmiral Karl Doenitz, commander of the U-boats.

But they were not for a ship, especially during a war. No ship would dare carry codes like that, not in a pouch that was laced with wire and sealed almost seamlessly. It had taken a hacksaw to get through it. The young officer could still see the blade serrations in the rubber; the wire ends glistened like silvery periods in a congealed black sauce.

A naval code always had to be where the captain could destroy it if the ship were going down. They were usually in an unlocked safe adjacent to a shredder. To lose a codebook meant compromising the communications of an entire fleet.

It was not for a ship, definitely not one at war. Yet it was a ship's code. And the striking thing about the pouch, the one thing the young officer saw was that there was no way to enter the pouch without hacking into it, wrecking it. Why? What purpose would that serve? Who would it serve?

Someone who absolutely had to know with certainty that no one else had seen its contents first and then put it back to watch him. It was for a spy.

The young officer had studied World War II, and he had a question now for the curator, something that bothered him. He phoned.

"Didn't we get all the spies during World War II? We got them didn't we?"

"During? We got them at the outset. It was one of the great counterespionage feats of history. I think the FBI rounded up over a thousand spies in the first weeks of the war."

"Outset, right? Not at the end."

"Had to be. Not one recorded successful act of espionage or sabotage during the entire war."

"That's what I thought," said the young officer. "But how do we know who we didn't get?"

The pouch was not going back to a museum. He was preparing its transfer to the FBI. That was his first intimation that this season at Newport was not going to be the vacation he had promised his wife, with the sailing, the horse shows, the tennis matches, the formal balls on vast lawns, and the America's Cup. Some of the background information about espionage and U-boats was still classified even though the Navy Department was trying to open up all files older than twenty years. But other facts he could take out of a public library.

Because of Doenitz's U-boats, the war that was supposed to be "over there" had really been over here, although newsreel camera-men and newspapers were not allowed to cover the carnage just off places like Jones Beach in New York, or Myrtle Beach in South Carolina. It would, as one high-level communication said, "devas-tate the morale of an American public already well shaken by Pearl Harbor."

History books listed Allied tonnage lost so casually that the young officer had to stop to realize that in America's first year of war, friendly tonnage sunk amounted to what was more than double the American battle fleet of today. In June 1942 alone, the Allies lost 144 ships.

From Fort Lauderdale to Casco Bay, it had been a shooting gallery and the classified documents showed the true desperation of those troubled hours.

The Navy was sure the U-boats had to have espionage assistance. Twice the FBI had heavily investigated the Newport area itself.

Still classified were the communiqués from Admiral Ernest J. King, the man now credited with ultimately destroying the U-boats, urging J. Edgar Hoover to redouble his efforts.

Hoover answered with countermemos describing manpower in-vested; informants and undercover agents infiltrated into so many levels of the Navy and Coast Guard within Newport itself that Hoo-ver had to conclude that it was virtually impossible for any espio-nage to continue.

A radio monitoring network had been set up between the Navy and the FBI here in Newport, exceeded only by that around Wash-ington. And all that was picked up from the enemy was normal U-boat radio traffic. Desperate pleas came from the British Admi-ralty to the United States Navy and the FBI to help cauterize the hemorrhaging in the Atlantic. Losses were "unacceptably high," "unreasonably devastating." Decoded messages talked of "far too accurate patterns of" the Doenitz wolf packs, the "unexplained nature of the magnitude of their successes."

Even Dwight D. Eisenhower, commander of Allied forces in the European theater, had added his name to those demanding an end to the "obvious assistance" being provided the Germans in the Atlantic.

Dead men, living memos, and then a living officer from that war came into the sunlit cubicle of the intelligence officer of the War College and stayed like a storm cloud that had to be respected.

His name was Admiral William "Screws" O'Connell, USN, retired. He was senior vice president of North American Technologies, Inc., a major defense contractor, and wore a dark gray suit that looked molded to his body. He had silver white hair, chill blue eyes, and a face weathered by the seas of the world.

He had no official position in the inquiry. That was what the commandant of the Naval War College had said. That meant the commandant was covered. Admiral O'Connell would not put his name to any communications, which meant the admiral was covered.

The young officer could deny the admiral access to classified material, which would have meant he was technically covered. He would also have offended a man who was a friend to the highest brass, and someone who gave out the sorts of jobs the brass liked to retire to.

The first thing the admiral asked for was the pouch. The young officer gave it to him.

The admiral held the pouch for a few moments, a slight tremor in his hands. He looked at the young man, his voice somber.

"We have them now. We always knew they were here." The young officer realized he had just stepped into a war that was not over yet.

The admiral sat down on a chair next to the officer's computer terminal, framed by prints of sailing ships, dreadnoughts, and propeller planes. The admiral talked as though to a partner. He was straightforward. There was no way, in his mind, the U-boats could have been so successful without espionage assistance.

"The Germans had a third-rate navy. Their subs were slow, not even first-rate machinery. Britain and ourselves were first-rank navies and all we could do was bleed and scramble and come on. Bleed and come on, until finally we pounded them out of the ocean."

The young officer nodded. The War College was filled with monuments to the great battles of World War II, Midway, Guadalcanal, the Coral Sea . . . all of them in the Pacific. All against the Japanese.

An entire war had been fought in the Atlantic, and except for the British chasing a German surface vessel into a South American port, there was not one battle that came to mind. There wasn't even a great commander at sea. An administrator, five-star Admiral Ernest King, won the battle of the Atlantic by ultimately putting together technological advances with overwhelming coordinated force.

But Admiral O'Connell was not complaining about lost glories. There was something else that was deeper and more searing. He didn't have to tell the young officer about this, but when he did, it became one Navy, from John Paul Jones to the computer terminal of an intelligence officer who was not going to spend a real vacation in Newport that summer.

"We knew they were there when we went out. We knew they knew our speeds, everything," said the admiral. He lowered his eyes into his memory. He was reliving it as a young junior officer. "I was on the *Reuben James*. They had fancy songs about it. We were sunk by U-boats. It was the beginning, early on, and losing someone was, well, heroic, or something. But it wasn't heroic. You don't know what a torpedo attack is until you live through it. We lost most of our men in that attack from the destroyer *Niblack*'s propellers' cutting up our own people in the water while trying to get the U-boat. We lost people because exploding depth charges drove seawater into their intestines through their goddamn assholes. It was a bloody mess of a war in the Atlantic."

The admiral had gone out again, and was sunk again.

"I don't know how I ever got it up to go out again, son. I don't know where I got it from."

"But you went out."

"We all went out again. We kept going out again. I'm not after revenge, son. It's just wrong that they got away with this, and no one now can tell us they weren't here. You have the pouch."

"Yes we do, sir," said the young officer. He felt good saying that. The admiral was familiar with all the communiqués the lieutenant commander had uncovered. But there was one he was missing.

"I'm sorry," said the junior officer. "I thought I got everything."

"No," said the admiral. "There's no way you could have known about it. The fucking FBI has it, and if you don't know about it, they ain't gonna tell you."

"Can we get it?"

"We got it," said the admiral, and the next day he came in with a photograph of a message. The photograph was glossy and brittle. At first the young officer wondered why they hadn't just photocopied the message and then realized they didn't have photocopying in those days.

"This was hand-delivered," said Admiral O'Connell, "from Winston Churchill to Franklin Delano Roosevelt. Hand-delivered."

But the note had no routing on it, no names of a Prime Minister or President. The language was from another age, with a sense of European battlefields and the destiny of mankind weighing in the balance. It had been decoded and routed, but even the original routing was missing. What was left was just two bald decoded paragraphs from a desperate Great Britain.

> It is our opinion that you are facing a group of superb judgement, quickness and flexibility, something far superior to anything the Hun has shown us so far in this war.
>
> We conjecture that this group must be the reflection of a single mind, certain of his mission, and with the sound good judgement to effect exactly what he wants and the wisdom to attempt nothing more. Do not look for the strutting fanatic, or paid criminal. You are facing something far more dangerous. The enemy who thinks.

"Can we get a written source for this?" said the junior officer.

"I never could myself, and I don't know why."

"Do we really want to send out something like this for substantiation?" asked the young officer.

"Make 'em shoot it down," said the admiral, and the young officer knew why the older man had gone out again. He knew he was going to win.

3

THE SECOND World War came sailing across the desk of Unit Chief Todd Oliver in the form of a memorandum supported by more than two hundred pages of documents, some still classified after more than thirty years. It came from U.S. Naval Intelligence and was directed to the Federal Bureau of Investigation with auxiliary or information copies sent to more than ten other intelligence units from the Central Security Services to the Net Assessments Board. Even the Intelligence Resources Advisory Committee had been informed.

Todd Oliver at thirty-four had not become the youngest GS-14 in the FBI because he missed such things. When the memo had arrived at his carpeted office in the J. Edgar Hoover Building, the first thing he did was calculate who at each of the routed groups would read this document, and what he would think of it.

Then he wondered what his supervisor would think they thought. He already knew what his supervisor thought. The package had come from Cobb with a small yellow hand-written note, probably the most important fact in the whole document. It was not signed, and it was meant to be thrown away. It said: "What is this shit?"

Apparently the memo had been sent to the Newport resident agent, who assumed it was an E-65, the label for espionage, who sent it to the Providence Field Office, which directed 65 work through the crucial eastern corridor; they for some reason did not think it was a valid 65, and sent it on to the Bureau. They did not append an opinion to it, just forwarded it when they got it. No one, no resident agent, field office agent, or Cobb, had established a Bureau position on it.

Todd riffled quickly through the two-hundred-plus pages. He was going to establish a position, but after a cup of coffee and the New York *Times*. It would be irresponsible for a GS-14 unit chief not to be apprised of the greater world.

This also gave him the delicious chance to read about a fellow graduate of De Paul Law School who was going to jail. He had already been through four years of trials, lost his wife and all his real estate holdings, and then, in a desperate gamble, attempted a drug deal and was caught. The man had previously been earning what must have been a half million dollars a year and gone on vacations whenever he felt tired or bored.

Todd remembered a profile piece on this hot lawyer where the man had boasted that "if a case doesn't excite me I don't do it. I like risk, it's where the cherries are. It's where lif· is. I also happen to make a lot of money."

The man had owned two Ferraris. They were also gone. It was a continuing story Todd had looked for first every day, and one that never failed to bring just a bit of joy into his small neat office. It made everything he had achieved with his De Paul degree so much more valuable.

Fortified, Oliver finally began his page-by-page reading of the document. His supervisor had sent it down to him because Cobb thought it was an attack on the Bureau. He thought so because of all the auxiliary notification, namely, the ten intelligence agencies also notified. Everyone else who had access to this would probably think the Navy had gone overboard because there seemed to be no clear and present danger to the country. The danger was decades old unless, of course, there was some evidence of new links to E-65 sources. And there weren't.

Therefore the Federal Bureau of Investigation was going to investigate, Todd concluded. Probably one full and documented week. Maybe two.

"How do you come up with that reasoning?" said Supervisor Cobb over the phone.

"I'll explain it in person," said Oliver.

Oliver had the clean athletic features of someone who ran three miles a day, with dark brown eyes, soft lips, and the quick smile of a young executive. He tailored his conservative suits like a young executive too. His mandatory side arm was holstered at his belt in the small of his back where he could reach it when he absolutely needed it, namely, when he changed his pants.

Supervisor Cobb wore rimless glasses, overly starched white shirts, and he had a large corner office. He carried a .38 Police Special in a shoulder holster as though he were actually going to use it. He made himself out to be just a regular agent wanting to do his job.

The facade worked well, and Todd respected him for it. If you didn't know better, you would assume Cobb's purpose with the Bureau was really chasing some bank robber or kidnapper across a North Dakota field at 4 A.M. And, *Shucks, ma'am, I was just doin' my job when they kind of came out and made me a supervisor and stuck me behind this big old desk here in Washington.*

"The problem is this, Bill," said Oliver, who knew Supervisor Cobb liked to be called Bill, just as though he were in a field office again with the comradeship that was supposed to engender. "The Navy is preclaiming we are trying to protect our World War II record by covering up now because of our failure then."

"What is that shit? What is preclaiming?" said Cobb.

Oliver, who had been standing, sat down in a chair at an angle to Supervisor Cobb's large wood desk. There were color pictures of both the director of the FBI and the President on the wall behind him. Oliver put the entire memo package on the desk.

"If we take the position that we are dealing with a couple of code-books from a war we already won, and don't do anything, we validate all those auxiliary notifications. Now do you see what I am talking about?"

"Possibly," said Cobb.

"There is no strong technical reason for the likes of the Intelligence Oversight Committee to be notified of this case, other than as witnesses to possible current flaws in the Bureau's approach."

"I don't know if they would really try to get away with that. What have we done that they would need witnesses for?"

"Nothing yet," said Oliver. Cobb had touched the crucial point. "But what happens when we memo back that we are too strained on real and present dangers, like the 65s that are ongoing in that area, the real 65s, that technological hemorrhaging we haven't been able to stop."

"That we're too busy with real spies to chase their imaginary ones, you mean?" said Cobb.

"Right," said Oliver. "At that point, it makes it look as though we are covering up for J. Edgar Hoover's failures. That we are really looking to protect our record, and if we are, everyone should know the Bureau needs an overhaul."

"And they come back with another request for an investigation, making our latest refusal look like part of an ongoing forty-year cover-up. Saying no today makes us look guilty then. And we'd still have to do something if they pressed, only this time it would have to be bigger and more extensive to show we weren't covering up."

Cobb had caught it all. He always did. He wasn't made a supervisor because he could put bullets into a target down at Quantico Barracks.

"They're in the driver's seat, and we are the wheels," said Oliver. "If we respond with a full week's investigation, maybe two, we give them what they are going to get anyway. They are waiting for us to do that."

"That's what I thought," said Cobb. "I just hate to give these bastards the time of day on this . . . this . . ."

"Shit," said Oliver. "But once we give them the week or two weeks with full documentation, they are left hanging out there, having wasted two good weeks of our time. And they look like they have always been unreasonable, even during the war." Todd was smiling. He added that the Navy therefore ended up vulnerable. But Cobb shrewdly noted some lieutenant commander was the only one hung out on a limb, and of course he wasn't behind it. No lieutenant commander was going to take it upon himself to notify the intelligence universe.

"Right," said Oliver.

"All right, you go," said Cobb.

"But, Bill, I've got crucial situations that can go either way for the Bureau," said Oliver, who had already done his annual overtime to qualify for his extra five thousand dollars this year.

"You always have crucial situations pending. Anything that comes across your desk becomes vital to the Bureau. You're good at that," said Cobb. He smiled as though it took the sting out.

"I really hate to leave the Bureau so vulnerable," said Oliver.

"Todd, we are so strained on real 65 people, I don't have anyone to send."

"Does it have to be Newport?"

"Todd, the Navy is in Newport, the complaint is in Newport. There is no statute of limitations, so it is still a crime."

"Couldn't we meet here?"

"The complaint is in Newport. Enjoy the city. It is supposed to be beautiful this time of year. Sit around with the Navy, and jerk them off. I'm sorry, you've earned your fringe overtime already."

"Bill, if you think that I could weigh the fact of the fringe—"

"Not at all, Todd. Just joking. This is just some shit we've got to do."

"Because that is just not a factor in these calculations," said Todd. He wanted to make that point clear.

Cobb winked and nodded assent. Todd accepted it. Both of them knew they were lying.

Back at his office, Todd tried to get some verification for a note without a sender and without a recipient rumored to have been transferred from the British Prime Minister to the American President during the height of the war. When he finally found it, the message was in a photograph. It had the initials "JH" in a corner. Hoover himself. But there was no verification that it had gone from one head of state to another.

Now he was sure he knew why Cobb was incensed. It was Hoover's presence in this. The Navy was attacking Hoover. Cobb had served under the founder of the Bureau. There was reverence for the founder even though Cobb told "Hoover stories," joking about the old Bureau, how if a clerk got pregnant Hoover would demote or dismiss a section leader. Tales of how some men seeking promotion would bring the director funny gifts. One even brought a pig. Cobb would laugh and refer to Hoover as He Who Was, and would talk of his preference for Notre Dame graduates—Irish Catholics could be trusted. But with all the ridicule there was that core of deep respect, and new men better not attempt to share the jokes about Hoover. They were to be listened to, but not repeated.

Todd Oliver now understood without question his mission in Newport. He understood what the supervisor could not say openly, or even hint at lest some congressional hearing down the road would have Oliver testifying against him. He was being sent to Newport to protect the reputation of the founder of the FBI, who was for Cobb and so many who had served under him the embodiment of the Bureau. No matter how Cobb would laud the qualities of the man in the field, especially to Oliver, he had not sent one of them on this assignment.

He was to defend a reputation of a man now dead, concerning a war now won, against an enemy still living. The enemy was not of course the Third Reich or Adolf Hitler. It was the United States Navy.

Going through the sheets of ship losses, the cries for help from both sides of the Atlantic, Todd could feel the desperation of a bloody Atlantic war.

But there was another fact now. After the war, the FBI began briefly conducted foreign operations, one in Germany specifically to determine any espionage penetration of America. There was none. It was after this that the historical record gave the American FBI performance during the war that perfect rating. Under, of course, Hoover.

By early afternoon, Todd's clerk located Operation Paperclip, which was just what he was looking for. In that, the OSS, later to give its duties to the new CIA, went into the bowels of the Third Reich to dissect the corpse, and in doing so, they had debriefed Grand Admiral Karl Doenitz, commander of the U-boats, the man who had surrendered Germany. They got nothing. There was nothing about espionage help.

By four-thirty in the afternoon, Todd's clerk had located and retrieved the file on the man who had debriefed Doenitz. He was, according to his file, not deceased; he was professor emeritus of German literature at Harvard in Cambridge, Massachusetts, an hour-and-a-half drive from Newport.

The FBI position was not as vulnerable as it had looked at the outset. If all went as it should, Todd Oliver would return to Washington in a week, with the Bureau's reputation even shinier than when he left. He would return carrying the cloth.

GS-14 Todd Oliver was out of his office at 5 P.M., and at his home in nearby Reston, Virginia, with enough light out to start a barbecue in back of his house, which still held that now miraculous 6½ percent mortgage and had quadrupled in value. Agents who moved from field office to field office couldn't get a mortgage for twice that.

Nor did agents in the field have a wife like Anne, whose stunningly perfect blond good looks always seemed to get admiring glances. Nor were their wives successful real estate agents, building solid retirement capital. They had dumpy wives, rack-dress, baby-making, stay-at-home wives, who at retirement would merely be old. When Todd retired with Anne, they could count on an income literally triple what his own father had made during his best years. He didn't even have to become assistant director of the Bureau. He could, if he wanted, retire at his current GS-14 although that was highly unlikely. He had achieved, by age thirty-four, what man, he was sure, had been looking for since he came out of the trees into thick-walled caves. Safety.

Of course there were a few minor problems. Very minor. And he would have had them anyhow, without the security. There were the down periods. He would have loved to talk to someone about them, but he didn't dare risk seeing a psychologist. While the new Bureau wouldn't hold it against someone officially, it wasn't that new. Hoover wasn't that dead.

Others must get depressed, like him, too. He was sure he wasn't the only man who had difficulty enjoying lovemaking with a wife of many years.

Of course, Todd should have enjoyed it. Anne had a body like a *Playboy* centerfold and a perfect blond face that belonged in a magazine too. Others would envy him, he was sure.

When he made love to her he would separate himself to get a better look at that perfect body and beautiful face so he could know how really lucky he was to be in bed with this woman. Really lucky.

She's beautiful, she's beautiful, she's beautiful, he told himself and then shut his eyes, imagining she were someone else so he could climax.

"That was good," said Anne.

"Yes, good," said Todd. They always said that.

He did not fall asleep quickly. He tried not to think, so he would fall asleep. He remembered the memo without source or destination, the Hoover-initialed one, about looking for the "enemy who thinks." He wondered what in hell he thought about. Did he think about not thinking? It was very hard sleeping. He felt one of those down times coming again.

4

THE THING you had to know about Charlie, the first thing, was that he had seykhl. That Yiddish word for brains didn't mean just book learning. Bob Goldstein's son had three advanced degrees and been married two times to women Bob wouldn't have banged on Guam during the war.

But seykhl wasn't not book learning either. Charlie read all the time, and knew things, knew that when Bob's son was enumerating some grand social theory about human events, it had more to do with ball bearings and trade routes than grand human aspirations.

"I would expect that from a hardware store man," Bob's son had said, and while Bob had gotten angry pointing out that that little hardware store on Broadway had made his son a fancy professor, Charlie only smiled and made peace, because that was the second thing about Charlie.

Charlie Drobney liked to be left alone. He had Sondra and Brandon, his daughter and grandson, with whom he liked to stroll on the Cliff Walk. He had his Boston Red Sox and he had half of Drobney-Goldstein, and that was it. So when someone who had never purchased so much as a screw from Drobney-Goldstein—although Bob was sure he had seen him around Newport—wanted to speak to Charlie immediately, Bob had answered, "I can handle it."

"It's personal," said the man.

"I said I can handle it," answered Bob.

"Can I reach him somewhere?" asked the man.

"Listen, I don't mean to be rude or anything," said Bob. "But I do know everyone Charlie knows, and I'm sorry, but I don't know you."

"Will he be back?"

"Was that you on the phone just now?"

"It really is personal, very," said the man.

The man may not have been any older than Bob, in his late sixties, but time had really worn on him. There were men who had lived a long time and kept on living, but this man looked as though he just kept on breathing somehow. His hands shook. His gait was slow, and his face was riven by liver spots. Bob ordinarily would have felt a need to be more courteous to him, but he wasn't going to extend himself for someone who wouldn't even give his name.

"Tell you what. You leave your telephone number, and I'll have him phone you."

"Thank you, no," said the man.

"You want to leave a message?" said Bob.

"No," said the man. "Thank you."

"Do you know Charlie from the Midwest?" said Bob. Charlie had come from Michigan, and maybe, just maybe, they had known each other there. Bob didn't know any of Charlie's hometown friends. Charlie still talked with a hint of Midwestern twang.

"Thank you," said the man.

Bob Goldstein looked at the one full-time salesman, and the schlepper, who hauled things. Bob shrugged.

"I've seen him around," said the salesman. "I think he's retired Navy."

"I couldn't help the man," said Goldstein, turning his eye to the new display of power mowers in the front window. Tourist buses were letting passengers off in front of the store, but few would ever enter Drobney-Goldstein.

They didn't do a tourist business, but by the end of this summer when the finals of the America's Cup races were held seven miles out in the Atlantic, the tourist crush would be so heavy, Drobney-Goldstein would have to rent out their lot to visiting cars, because they would take the open space anyway.

Bob Goldstein watched the man walk up Broadway, placing the rubber-tipped cane at each right step. When Bob was a young man he had thought he would rather be dead than so frail, but as he grew older he had changed his mind.

Charlie had understood that, saying a different age made a different person, and no man knew what another felt. It came up when no one but a Jew could feel and understand what the Holocaust meant to a Jew.

But, strangely enough, Bob felt Charlie did understand. He had seen the anger and frustration well up in Charlie's face when they both saw a picture of the gas ovens of Buchenwald in a magazine. "The verminous idiots," Charlie had said of the Nazis. "What reason was there for that? What purpose was there for that?" And Bob knew, as only a friend could know, Charlie had meant it. Charlie was the executor of Bob's will, and vice versa. Bob would trust him with anything. He was the one person in the world that Bob could leave something to do, and know it would be done, and with seykhl. If you had Charlie in your life, you had a treasure.

It was Charlie who had really saved both their lives. There was a time when many hardware stores were going into heavy appliances, and Bob Goldstein had a grand plan for making Drobney-Goldstein a department store.

Charlie hadn't come right out against it. He just laid out what would happen when they expanded, the staff needed, the loans needed, and in detail, such logical detail, he showed they would be at a greater risk. In other words, they could own a big department store that might go broke as opposed to a comfortable home center with a regular business that was secure now; it would never go under nor increase profits by much.

"Yeah, but with a department store we could make millions," Bob had said.

Charlie agreed. "But that's not your objective."

"Sure it is," said Bob.

Charlie shook his head. "No, you don't understand your objectives. That's what you think are your objectives."

"Yeah, so tell me, if I don't know already."

"Your objective, Bob, and this hurts to say, is to earn the respect of your wife and son, and, Bob, if ever there is something you're not going to get from those people, it's that. You'll kill yourself, and you won't get it."

He was so right. And it did hurt. There was nothing Bob Goldstein wouldn't trust that man with, except perhaps Charlie's lunch.

And so when Charlie returned to the store about 2 P.M. eating a dark muffin, Bob snapped it out of his hand and threw it into a wastebasket.

"Salt," said Bob.

"How do you know?" said Charlie. He was a neat man who wore pressed chinos and white shirts, and parted his full gray hair on the left, which always looked as though it had just been trimmed. His body was neat, the platform office where he worked was neat, even his smile, which was honest, seemed somehow always in place. So was everything in the small storage room right behind the store. Charlie had calculated floor space to storage space and come up with a formula so arcane Bob would have sworn it couldn't have worked if Charlie weren't the one doing the figures. Which meant, of course, that arcane or not arcane, it worked. Planning was Charlie's domain. Sales was Bob's.

"Salt, it has salt, you have high blood pressure, you shouldn't eat salt. That's how I know."

Charles Drobney shrugged. He was five foot seven, a good three inches shorter than Bob, and less expansive. Bob had dyed his hair black and wore jewelry displayed in an open shirt, and chest hair that called the virile black hair on his head an open lie. Bob had blue eyes, Charlie, brown.

"How does that prove it has salt? Do you have a mass spectrometer hidden somewhere on your person?"

"It has salt, it's in the garbage, that's it."

"You don't know that and you can't know that," said Charlie, and then smiled because both of them knew that Bob had been right.

Charlie had the Boston *Globe* under his arm, and he gave Bob the sports section. Bob followed Charlie up to his platform. It was a good day for the Boston *Globe* because the baseball news and horse racing news were on separate sheets, and Charlie wouldn't have to wait for Bob to place his bets before he got to read what was happening to the Red Sox.

"Somebody came for you today."

"Who?" said Charlie.

"Didn't leave his name," said Bob as Charlie booted up the Digital computer for the inventory.

"What do you mean, didn't leave his name," said Drobney. "Twenty-two 2-inch power mowers?" He was looking at the screen.

"Didn't leave his name. Wanted to see you. I think he phoned before. Mowers are moving well."

"And he didn't leave his name, and he wouldn't talk to you?" said Charlie.

"Right," said Bob.

"Fuck him," said Charlie, pleasantly.

"You gotta be polite," said Bob, who, Charlie knew, was the only one in the store who would blow up at an abusive customer, especially if he was abusing the salesman or the schlepper because he thought an employee was there to take abuse.

Drobney looked at the screen, shaking his head. "We'll be discounting by July. They're selling now. It's May. They'll sell in June, maybe."

"We can always sell power mowers," said Bob.

"I don't want to be holding them by next year. I think the Japanese may be coming up with something new. I don't know," said Charlie.

"They're moving," said Bob. He gave back the paper, dropping it on the shelf that housed the computer.

"How do you do that to a newspaper?" said Charlie.

"What?" asked Bob.

"Look," said Charlie.

Bob looked. Charlie took the paper, opened the paper, stretched the sheets, closed the sheets, then folded the sheets, then adjusted the paper at right angles to the computer screen and slapped the paper as properly settled and put away.

"You want it like that, I'll do it like that," said Bob, reaching for the paper. Charlie slapped the hand away.

"Leave it alone."

"I desecrated your paper," said Bob, clasping his hand to the jewelry on his chest as though he were horrified by his own great crime.

"Get out of here," said Charlie.

Bob got up, turning on the small radio. He knew the Red Sox were coming on and Charlie did not like to be disturbed for any reason during a Red Sox game.

So when the man with the cane returned to the cash register, Bob did not tell him Charlie was in. Drobney could work while listening to the Red Sox. He preferred the radio to television; it was the right medium for the sport. A radio lets you imagine the right moves, lets you remember how the game was to be played and felt. There were no replays of mistakes, or balls caught because someone stuck a five-hundred-dollar, scientifically cupped glove in the way of their flight paths. Balls had to be caught with fingers moving gloves when Charles Drobney had played, when the grass smelled like grass and was mowed, and the balls bounced weirdly from the holes that weren't repaired in front of second base, and it was not unusual for a catcher not to be able to read and write, and pints of whiskey were routinely sneaked into dugouts along with brass knuckles.

"Not now," came Goldstein's voice from behind the cash register. "Later this evening maybe, but not now."

Charlie could not hear the man's answer. It sounded mumbled.

"You can tell me anything you have to tell him," said Goldstein.

Bob's voice was loud. The man did not leave. Charlie looked over the three aisles of hardware and home appliances. The man had a cane. He was bald.

The man turned. Drobney saw him full-face. He squinted. Did he know the man? Somebody who wouldn't give his name.

He looked closer. The hair was gone, and the jaw had lost its strength through the folds of age.

No, thought Drobney. *What's he doing here?* He took a sip of water and left the platform as quickly as possible without looking as though he were rushing. His legs felt heavy and did not move down the platform stairs well. His mouth was dry and suddenly the overhead fluorescent lights that had been installed twenty years before felt uniquely strange and harsh.

Charlie arrived at the counter smiling and reached out to shake the man's hand. Bob blinked, surprised, and lifted an ear to make sure the Sox game really was on in the back of the store.

"It's okay," said Charlie. "I know him. Thanks, Bob."

He put an arm around the man's sleeve and moved him to the back of the store, right underneath the radio. He wanted to turn it up higher, but that would have looked suspicious.

He moved just a bit farther back, behind the paints, near the mixing machines. There he could see anyone coming up the other aisle. He talked in a whisper, but with as much calm as possible. The man was panicked enough already.

"I'm Commander McFeester. Do you remember me? I tried phoning you at home, but you weren't there."

"Fine. What is your problem?" There was no point in mentioning he should not have come. He was there.

"They say there's going to be a big investigation. Lots of old brass are saying the U-boats had to have help to do what they did. Some people are telling how they remembered people saying there were signals at night off Block Island and Point Judith. I'm scared. I tried reaching you at home. You weren't there. I couldn't get through on the phone here, so I came here."

Commander McFeester had made a very human mistake. He had interpreted the magnitude of his fear for the immediacy of his danger, thought Drobney. He was more afraid to wait than he was of coming to the store, which did not really have to be a danger unless the commander made it so.

The fear was contagious. Drobney felt his breathing coming hard.

"All right," he said very softly and very calmly. "Do you know of any reason why this thing is coming up again?"

"I think they found something. Codebooks or something. I can find out."

"No," said Drobney.

"I did just what you said. I got out of the Navy right away. I had a career. I gave it up. I did everything. Please."

"You are all right. There is nothing to worry about. Don't come here again. Go home."

"You will keep your promise? Nothing will happen to me?" said the old man, his body beginning to tremble.

Perhaps McFeester had always been like this on the inside, and the years had not changed him so much but had taken away his ability to hide it. The man always had a bit of an impetuous streak, kept in check only by his fear.

"You will be all right if you go home. You have got to do absolutely nothing."

"And you'll keep your promise?"

"Of course. I have, haven't I?"

"This is different. This is big."

"You don't know that. Go home."

"I'm active in retired naval things," said Commander McFeester, and the tears let go.

"You've got to stop crying. I'll wait here with you until you stop."

"I don't mind them seeing me cry. I just don't want to lose everything."

"If you are crying, I can't get you out of this store. Now stop. You've been safe for almost forty years. Do what I say, and no one will ever come after you. But you've got to do what I say."

"Thank you, thank you."

"Shhh," said Drobney. "Don't be so thankful." When McFeester had calmed down, he told him to just go along with whatever was said and walked him to the front register.

"I need fifty dollars from the register," said Drobney. Goldstein nodded to the salesman, who rang up a NO SALE and a fifty-dollar withdrawal.

"I'm sorry. I forgot," said Drobney, giving McFeester the fifty dollars as he opened the door for him, guiding him out.

When the door shut, Bob asked, "What took so long?"

"He had to tell me why he needed it back. Old people are funny," said Drobney, starting back toward his platform. He heard Bob mumble, "For fifty dollars he had to make it a federal case?"

"He thought I'd be embarrassed."

"I hope I never get old like that," said Bob, pushing back his dyed hair with his hands.

Drobney smiled. He went back to the platform. The Red Sox were using up relievers.

It was back again.

He looked out over the three wide rows of hardware and small appliances. Outside, the buses were backed up now along Broadway. It wasn't warm enough yet for the good sailing out of Newport. The wharfs were two blocks down on Thames Street, where new shops and restaurants with quaint wood shingles and names of the sea had replaced the bucket-of-blood bars that had once served the fleet anchored up Narragansett Bay. The fleet was gone now. The Eastern Shore Command, where McFeester had served, was gone now, and Charles Drobney was still here, only older and he could not think.

His head felt light and he took an Ismelin pill for the blood pressure. *It must be going through the roof,* he thought. *This is not happening,* he thought. It is not happening. He looked back at the computer screen. The inventory status of the power mowers was still there. It wasn't a dream. Only he had to tell himself it was a dream, a bad dream of youth, and it had never really happened, like nightmares that could feel so real it took time to get over them in the morning.

He was good at deceiving himself when he had to, he thought. When he was young, long ago. And, at sixty-seven, too, he realized, with the glass of water in his hand. It was not a dream. It had never been a dream. It had just been gone for a while.

The Red Sox had two men on in the second and Charles Drobney ordered ten more twenty-two-inch Briggs & Stratton mowers. It was not a dream and had never been. The Ismelin's peculiar taste came back up his throat. He had not followed the pill with enough water.

He glanced back at the front windows. Green garden hoses, stacked to look like barrels, set off red-handled tools. Bob had a flair for display, thought Drobney, and he wanted to cry. He was sixty-seven years old and it had all come back again, only now he could not plan. Had that gone? He had been so good at that sort of thinking before. He had been trained for that. He remembered how he had taken care of McFeester using the best possibilities, given the situation. On tactics, he never lied to himself. He was also younger.

It was a grand spring day in Newport, and it was a weekday in May. The Allies were meeting in Reims, France, with the remnants of the Nazis. Hitler was dead, by his own hand, the papers said. And Charles Drobney had sat in the front of the store behind the cash register, waiting for that one moment of maximum advantage he knew would come.

Broadway was quiet. Victory garden seeds were on display in the front window under the neat black-painted GOLDSTEIN'S HARDWARE and the small starred flag that showed Mr. Goldstein had gone to war. Mr. Goldstein had insisted on that before he shipped out.

"Right in the window," he had said, "and a gold one if I don't come back."

Rubber garden hoses were not available anymore for cash, ration stamps, or a night in bed. A 1941 Mercury, the last model produced before the war, cruised down Broadway on new tires. *Black market*, thought Drobney. He always thought black market when he saw new tires on anything but a military car.

And then the bells were ringing, and his moment had come.

It sounded like Trinity Church at first, but then the sounds were also coming from the Catholic church up the street. Loud bells, persistent bells, yelling bells everywhere. A woman driving a car with a radio antenna pulled over, jumped out, and kissed the first sailor she could grab.

Germany had officially surrendered. Criminals had kept it fighting, but then criminals had started the war to begin with. *Criminals and gutter fighters,* Drobney thought. The bells had rung, he had been told, after the First World War, and he had been sure that after this one, they would be ringing too.

He was right and they were still ringing when he arrived at the low gray huts of the Eastern Shore Command and couldn't even find someone to announce him. It didn't matter. Walking in while the bells were still ringing would be even more effective.

Lieutenant Commander William Farley McFeester was celebrating with an open bottle of Canadian Club on his desk. Enlisted men with paper cups in their hands were hoisting salutes to every branch of the Navy and even the Army.

McFeester had the clear eyes and forceful jaw of the war poster behind him, the one with the officer warning that loose lips sank ships.

Drobney waited until McFeester saw him. And then he smiled. McFeester's jaw almost fell off. Drobney didn't move. The sailors caressing a full bottle of Canadian Club hardly minded that their commanding officer had left.

"Jeesus Chrrist almighty," whispered McFeester. His eyes were wide and his voice sounded as though it had been pulled out of a jail cell. They stood in a hallway outside his office.

"I'm not leaving," said Drobney. He knew McFeester had thought he would never see him again. There had been no contact for the last half year. Drobney was counting on that too.

"Do you want to get us hanged?"

"I'm not leaving here until you retire."

"I'll meet you at the usual place."

"No. I am staying here until you cut your own request to retire."

"You're insane. We're going to hang."

Charles Drobney smiled. He was not insane, of course. He knew his man, and his situation. What was McFeester going to do, call the Shore Patrol to have him arrested? As for its being dangerous, only

Charles Drobney or McFeester could make it dangerous that day by saying what they had been doing for the last five years.

Drobney could have come on another day, but this day, with the bells ringing and people cheering, gave him the most pressure on this impulsive and frightened officer. Drobney had used those precise flaws to get the man to betray his country in the first place. He would use them again to make his own future as safe as possible.

Drobney smiled. The bells were still ringing, and McFeester was terrified. He dragged him into a men's room.

"I'll pay you. I'll pay back everything. Right to you."

"I don't want money."

"I'll pay back double. I'll do it. Double."

Drobney just looked at him.

"Are you crazy?" said McFeester. "What the fuck do you want? The war is over."

"I am not leaving here until you resign."

"Why? Dammit," said McFeester, slamming a urinal handle and sending a gush of water into wet cigarette butts and a pale round deodorant bar.

"You can do whatever you want. I am going to your office and joining your party, and I won't leave your office until your resignation is cut."

"Why?" said McFeester. "The war's over."

But Charles Drobney knew McFeester was not the sort of man who had to understand the motives of others. He had always been encased in his own world.

"You're bluffing," said McFeester. Drobney left the men's room and was heading toward the joyous noise, when McFeester caught up to him.

"I'll cut my retirement tomorrow."

"Now," said Drobney. "I don't want to have to come back. Do it now and I'm gone forever."

"Okay. Will you tell me why?"

"When you resign, don't contact me and I promise you this. You will never be caught. All right? You won't see me, and you will be safe. If you do it now."

Lieutenant Commander McFeester nodded. And an extremely vulnerable position had been made as secure as it was going to be. Left in the United States Navy, an officer who had found he could make extra money selling out his country might well do it again. That would expose him to capture, and having been captured for one espionage crime, he would more than likely hand up a previous one to reduce his sentence or escape a firing squad.

Out of the Navy, McFeester posed less danger to Charles Drobney, who had calculated that his own sentence would hardly be different if he surrendered at the end of the war or if he waited for them to come for him. He did not want to hang—that was his first objective—nor, having escaped that, did he ever want to return to Germany.

And there was no point in leaving Newport because running would open other dangers. If they were going to get him, they were going to get him. He calculated his chances of escape as modest. There were too many factors out of his control. How many of the records of the German General Staff might be captured intact he did not know. Nor did he know who would tell what for a carton of cigarettes or a truckful of coal in a defeated country. So many things could unravel. And he had been taught, in tactical matters, not to lie to himself. Giving oneself either hope or despair was the amateur's way to plan things. And one could see what that sort of thinking would accomplish. In six years, the amateur who had run that country had brought it to ruin beyond imagination.

So Charles Drobney waited to be caught, and after a few years he began to realize no one would ever come for him. There were new enemies and new wars and the fleet moved out, and he discovered people he loved, and who loved him, and what had happened so long ago during the Second World War became a bad dream that good doses of days following days tended to wash out of his system.

And then an old frightened man came through the door again and brought it back as though it had never left. Charles Drobney was in jeopardy again, only now he was sixty-seven years old and he could not think.

Instinctively, he looked up to the register for Bob, thinking that this was just the sort of thing with which Bob would know how to help. And just as quickly, he looked back down at the terminal. Bob, who could understand anything, was not going to understand this. Not after Auschwitz and Buchenwald. Even Charles Drobney could not understand that insanity. It didn't matter that he had contempt for the Nazis himself, most of all when he had agreed to his mission.

The one man in whom he wanted to confide was the one man Charles Drobney did not want to find out.

And then there was Sondra, his daughter. Thank God she had not come in that day to do the bookkeeping because she would have known something was wrong.

Sondra had the tendency to divide the world into forces of light and forces of darkness. She loved him and if he were caught she would have to understand, very painfully understand that her father had served the ultimate force of darkness.

She would make allowances for him because she loved him. And Brandon, his grandson, was too young now to care.

But the world would change. All the little hellos would have the hidden chill of that crime behind it even if it were forgiven.

The very weather of his life would change, and so would Sondra's, even though most people would still be polite. He might not even go to jail now. But his life would be over.

He had lied to himself again. He was not ready to surrender if they came looking for him.

5

HE WAS alone, he had everything to lose, and he was old in a world that had changed more in the last forty years than it had in the previous three thousand.

And, feeling helpless, he realized he had just made a tactical estimate. He was helpless in many respects.

There were more advanced electronics in the home appliance aisle of Drobney-Goldstein than the Third Reich had used to start the Second World War. The great espionage invention then was the thirty-pound shortwave radio they boasted even a woman could carry. Today governments had chips that could fit under a fingernail and read a hairsbreadth from outer space.

There was a world today that, should it come after him, would technologically make him a caveman at a traffic light. But his own vulnerability did not necessarily make him that much of a target. Most people made the mistake of defending against their fears instead of their enemies.

Just how important was this investigation? He didn't know. What did he know? A frightened old man said the codebooks, which probably were for his unit, had been found. And that had led to the rumors of investigation.

Charles Drobney glanced at the computer screen. He saw he had just ordered ten power mowers. What was he thinking of? The spring rush was past. He lowered his order to three.

Like most hardware men, he had learned to dislike the big-ticket items. The markup was relatively small compared to the staples such as screws and nails, which accounted for a major profit of any hardware store.

He took a sip of water. The Red Sox had just lost a three-run lead. Usually they waited until August to start their drive toward putting them out of contention. They were starting early this year.

Time. The one advantage he had was time. Time let loose ends settle into the dust of the scenery. Possible witnesses died. Records were thrown out and, most importantly, with time the necessity of capturing an enemy lessened because there were new enemies. Even the emotion diminished with time.

Knowing nothing more than he knew, he had to assume his capture was just not that important. Until, of course, something appeared that might show him otherwise.

There were dangers, however. Ironically, it was the rumors of the investigation that might prove a problem. He always had little use for rumors. But now they might hurt him. Newport was a city of rumors.

He had determined that, considering the strangeness of this new world of espionage and counterespionage, he was going to make no moves because it was movement that attracted attention.

But there was something he could do to minimize the danger of the rumors, and if he did it quickly and did it now, it might be the one correct move to give him the best position should an onslaught begin.

As soon as the Red Sox game was over, Charlie called the schlepper to put a small bedroom television set in his car and gave him an invoice for it. The television was the only electronic entertainment item Drobney-Goldstein sold, under Bob's assumption that he could sell it as an impulse item. But the $149 proved to need more impulse than Newport had given them last Christmas.

Goldstein saw the invoice as soon as the schlepper passed the register.

"What is this?" said Goldstein.

"No problem. I'll take it," said Charlie.

"Hey, screw them. They're no better than anyone else," said Bob, slapping the invoice. "If they want it delivered, let the schlepper do it. He's paid for it."

"I'm going home anyhow. It's a few blocks. It's almost on the way. You need the schlepper."

"The Avenue is no better than anyone else," said Bob, referring to Bellevue Avenue, where the great Newport mansions were, on the ocean side of the city. In Newport no one called the mansions or the wealthy who lived in them anything but "the Avenue." Everyone in the city knew what that meant.

"I don't think the Avenue is any better," said Charlie. "You know that."

"Let me tell you about the Avenue, a lot of them don't pay until the end of the year," said Bob, letting his voice fill with dramatic indignation. And then he read the address on the slip.

"And anyhow, these people don't even use us. I don't remember ever selling to them."

"I'll leave it in the car. The schlepper can take it out tomorrow. I'm going home," said Charlie.

"If you're going home, deliver it. It's nearby."

"Okay," said Drobney.

"But nothing special for them."

"It's nearby," said Drobney.

"Right," Bob said, making sure the salesman and schlepper and whichever customers were in the store had heard the Drobney-Goldstein policy line that every customer was as valuable as the next, and none was extra special.

Other stores might assemble in expectation for the Avenue as though awaiting royalty, but not Drobney-Goldstein. It served all of Newport, all of it. And Robert Goldstein was as happy to sell two screws to a customer as he was to sell a portable RCA to the Avenue, even though, and the customer should know this, there was a tremendous deal this day on portables.

It was a short drive to Bellevue Avenue. Newport was not a big city. The Avenue was shaded by great trees and walls, and only the mansions opened to the public as tourist attractions had names on their gates.

The one Charlie wanted was called the Hickories and had no name on its great massive iron gates set into the gray stone walls.

If you did not know who lived there, you were not wanted there anyhow. Someone had once mentioned it to him, and he had never forgotten it. This day, the gates were open because truckers were hauling in white- and red-striped tents. Like a little army, the work-men were pounding in spikes and raising the tents along a lawn vast enough to bivouac a regiment. The main house of the Hickories rose on a massive grassy crest like an alabaster palace reigning over its own walled world.

The driveway curved under an ornate entablature set above four Corinthian columns. Drobney parked his Buick Skylark behind four hand-polished foreign cars and hoisted the package the schlepper had made for him from the backseat.

It was not the lost strength of youth that bothered him, but the constant threat that any sudden movement could create a strain or pull that would take months in healing. The portable set was heavier than he had thought. The package had a rope handle, taped so it would not hurt his hands.

He hauled it up wide pink marble steps to an ornate brass and iron door and with effort used the lion's head knocker. For a large polished piece of brass it made surprisingly little sound, and then he realized it was not to call anyone. There was a small buzzer to his right, set into a black marble arch, that actually notified people someone was outside. He put down the portable TV box and walked over to the buzzer and pressed it twice. Then he went back to the center of the door and looked up. It was at least twelve feet high.

The door opened ever so slightly and ever so quietly like locks in a canal. A dark-haired man in a Nehru jacket appeared in the crack of the door. His white gloves poked outside as though saying hello by themselves.

"I am delivering a television set to Mrs. Wheaton," said Drobney.

The man pointed a white-gloved finger to the left.

"What?" said Charlie.

"Servants' entrance. Deliver there."

Charlie went back down the steps with his package to a cement path along the right side of the house. He walked beneath windows shaded by peach and gold drapes, past little bushes set into marble bowls, back to the rear of the mansion.

He put down the package and his shoulder still hurt. An old turnbell was set into the middle of a dark door and it rang with a brass chortling. The back of the house stretched out to lawns larger than several baseball fields. With all the manicured bushes and even, clipped grass expanse, it looked as though it were waiting for a horde of people. It looked empty. *An empty lawn,* he thought.

The door opened and a round-faced woman with dress and face dusted with flour was standing there.

"Yes?" she said.

"I have a delivery for Mrs. Alexander Wheaton," said Charlie.

"Okay, leave it here. Do I have to sign something?"

"It has to be demonstrated to her."

"I don't know, come in," she said and nodded at a chair by one of the long copper-covered tables. This was the kitchen. He was to wait. A man in overalls sat at a small flyleaf table by one of the windows. He was eating a chocolate cream pie with a glass of milk.

Drobney longed for a glass of water, but the cook had gone off somewhere. She came back with a wide-hipped woman wearing a tartan wool skirt and a severe white blouse.

"You're the delivery man?" said the woman.

"No. But I am delivering something to Mrs. Wheaton."

"Well, you have. What's the problem?"

"I have to show her how it works."

"You can show me, I'm her secretary."

"She wanted it demonstrated herself. It's a personal sort of television set. Small, that somebody else wouldn't be turning on for her," said Drobney.

"You're partners with Bob Goldstein, aren't you?" said the woman.

"Yes," said Charlie.

"I'm Amy McAllister. My family always uses your store. I don't know if you remember me. I am with Mrs. Wheaton, her personal secretary."

"I think so," said Charlie. "I think I remember you."

"You know, when you work on the Avenue you get so separated from the city. We just got back from Palm Beach two days ago, and we have the Renaissance League Ball coming up, and we're behind on everything. Quite hectic. Are you hungry?"

"I'd like a glass of water," said Charlie.

Mrs. McAllister nodded to the cook to bring one. "You say Mrs. Wheaton wants you to show her that?" she asked.

Charlie nodded. He did remember her now, about seven years younger and much thinner. She had gone off to Russell Sage College in Troy, New York, and, according to her parents, was looking for a job that could keep her in Newport. Apparently this was the job, and because it was on the Avenue, Drobney-Goldstein had never seen her again.

The cook brought him the water in a plain glass he was sure was used only for servants and deliverymen. He drank it slowly. Mrs. McAllister went off to inform Mrs. Wheaton.

Mrs. Alexander Wheaton was at tea with Aunt Jane and the very same people she had had tea with just the week before in Palm Beach, but this was her first week back here in Newport, so it had to be done again. Even the conversation was the same, how someone actually might be having an affair with the hired captain of her yacht.

"They say quite crudely, but quite accurately, 'Don't screw the crew.' And you know how I hate that word," said Aunt Jane, who was Miss Jane Baggswell Wheaton.

Aunt Jane had also hated the word just as much when she used it back in Palm Beach when everyone was setting off to return to Newport and wondering who would sail and who would fly.

Mrs. Alexander Wheaton said nothing. She knew Newport despised scandals on the one hand and yet on the other pounced on them like feasts, devouring scraps and passing gizzards of despair around the table like cannibals.

She never liked gossip because she never felt that people should live in any one particular way, which was a requirement of good gossip. When Claus was tried for attempting to murder his wife, Mrs. Alexander Wheaton felt only sad that now she probably never would get a chance to be alone with that handsome, charming man.

The problem for Mrs. Alexander Wheaton was that while she never cared about other people's private lives, Newport cared very much about hers.

She had married Alexander Wheaton in a society that welcomed new men but rarely new women, especially those without family or money.

But since Alexander had always treated her well, and his family had accepted her when they really didn't have to, she felt obliged never to embarrass them.

She couldn't get herself to condemn Aunt Jane's gossiping. That was Aunt Jane's way.

Even after Alexander had died, Elizabeth Boswell Wheaton,

Bunny to her friends, was still Mrs. Alexander Wheaton. She was part of Newport, but not of it, always at the right parties and the right places not because Bunny belonged there, but because Mrs. Alexander Wheaton did.

She longed for so many things a Mrs. Wheaton could never have, going into a bar and drinking with people there, running nude under the sun, inviting anyone for dinner just because she liked him. She remembered a very attractive, pleasant man she had met on a flight back from Athens.

She had felt his leg next to hers. They didn't have to look to know they wanted each other. They didn't even have to ask.

They were soundless in the first-class cabin as the flight attendants stayed behind their screens and the two other passengers slept. They were quiet when they were done.

"Would you like a cigarette?" he said.

"No," she said.

When they landed at John F. Kennedy International Airport, he asked to see her again. He asked so very nicely, like someone in a fresh rainstorm who knew a wonderful place to spend a somewhat dry afternoon.

"No," she said. "I'm sorry. I can't."

She could only laugh sadly. She could not tell him they would never accept a Denver accountant in Newport, even a handsome one, even one who asked to see her again so nicely. She could have him for love, but not for lunch.

"That's just what I can't have. Thank you for the flight from Greece," she had said.

There were those who were accepted and those who were not, and there were incredibly precise rules even though few would be so rude as to define them, or allow that there was something other than extraordinary charm that made one a member of Newport society. It wasn't even called Newport society, or, as coldly as in the Gilded Age, the 400. Now it might be referred to as "our friends."

But outside of it was just as outside of it as before.

Bunny Wheaton enjoyed the sort of stunning pure blond presence that gave a feeling of health and sunlight. The cheekbones, ice blue eyes, and natural suntan that hinted of a past of freckles, and the perfect sparkle of a smile that had sailed into invincible time, surviving longer because of the perfection of its line.

She was sixty-five and could still get a young man to turn his head, especially when she had an opportunity to wear shorts and show her legs.

She was pouring tea, as was proper, for Aunt Jane and Mrs. Drake when her secretary brought in some relief.

"Excuse me, Mrs. Wheaton, but the owner of the hardware store has come here personally to demonstrate something you asked for."

"I don't know about that," said Mrs. Wheaton softly as she continued to pour the tea. Mrs. McAllister waited.

"A tradesman?" said Aunt Jane.

"Yes," said Mrs. McAllister.

"My God," said Aunt Jane. "What next?" And she remembered someone saying they were walking across lawns now.

"You know, he may have even come to the front door and expected to be admitted," said Mrs. Drake.

"Doctors do now," said Aunt Jane.

"I would never let my doctor through the front door," said Mrs. Drake.

"Well now, dear, if you were that sick, why would you care?" said Aunt Jane.

"I am never that sick," said Mrs. Drake, and someone else said all doctors nowadays expected to be let through the front door. Mrs. Wheaton wished she could have let the tradesman in to show her anything. A demonstration of an eggbeater would have been preferable to tea again.

But she smiled and gave that very slight sort of helpless look that said she did not know the man, unfortunately, and Mrs. McAllister was to take care of the matter. This meant he was to be dismissed.

She couldn't even see the weather from this overstuffed parlor, jammed so tight with Wheaton glory it felt like clutter. The mansions were like giant marble hotels, with more care taken in gilding the ceilings in the ballrooms than in making the bathrooms convenient. Which was why no other Wheaton complained when it was decided that Alexander's wife should have the Hickories.

It had to be occupied by a Wheaton because it contained the family history, some of which hung from the walls in massive gilded paintings of the Wheatons, from the railroad builders and admirals who made the princely fortunes, to their descendants, who learned to live and act like the royalty of the nation that was not supposed to have royalty.

Mrs. McAllister was back again and this time spoke apologetically. "He says you specifically ordered the instrument. And you spoke to him. His name is Charles Drobney. He said the mention of his name might remind you. He is a reliable merchant in town."

"What do you have to have demonstrated? Everything is so complicated nowadays," said Aunt Jane.

"You can learn to use things, if you want to," said Mrs. Drake.

"There are gadgets for everything nowadays," said Aunt Jane.

Bunny Wheaton almost dropped the teacup. And then she smiled. "Why yes. Absolutely, yes. I did. I remember now. Yes. I'll see him later, thank you."

At 5 P.M. when early tea was over, Charles Drobney was told to follow Mrs. McAllister to the upstairs drawing room and bring his package with him. It did not get lighter as he lugged it up a back staircase behind the stolid and wide presence of Mrs. McAllister. He was puffing by the time he got to the head of the stairs. Apparently there were routes for servants to keep them from the main hallways and out of sight because this passage led into an ornate hallway with pink marble flooring, spacious walls, elegant paintings, and gold-leafed moldings.

Mrs. McAllister opened large wood-frame gilt doors with small glass panels and ushered Drobney into a well-lit, ornate room that looked as though it had been furnished by a museum of the nineteenth century: carved and gilded tables, full plush sofas and sitting chairs, dullish oil paintings under little lights, and lamps of such stodginess and embroidery that if they were not in a drawing room of the Hickories, they could well be considered junk.

A stunning blond woman in a severe pink dress sat in one of the large chairs by a thirty-foot-high window facing the rear lawns. The cool afternoon light of Newport bathed her perfect sharp features, making the little smile all that much more precious.

"Mr. Drobney is here, Mrs. Wheaton."

Charlie put the package down at his feet and crossed his hands in front of him, waiting in respectful silence.

"Thank you, Amy," said Mrs. Wheaton, and that soft signal was enough for Mrs. McAllister to remove herself, closing the doors behind her.

"Hello, Elizabeth," he said.

"Hello, Charlie."

"It's been a long time."

"How have you been?" she asked.

"I've been all right," he said.

"Good. You look good, Charlie."

"There's something that happened, that I feel I have to tell you about, so you'll know how to handle it." He felt his face flush and it was very hard to look at her. She was still beautiful. So beautiful. Sometimes he had imagined her growing old, and every time he did, her face collapsed, even though when her picture appeared in the papers at charity events she still looked quite beautiful. He had assumed it was the rough newspaper print that blotted out lines and age.

But the rich did not age like everyone else. There was sun and rest in her face, and the lines ever so skillfully kept to minimum damage by cosmetic schemes of the best professionals. But her voice had changed over the years, with that level sure crisp accent that could almost be English. She probably wasn't even aware she didn't speak like a Californian anymore, thought Charlie. That could happen when a person lived in a closed environment.

He was sure he, too, had changed in ways he did not notice. She had always been practical to a degree, and so beautiful, even when they had said goodbye with the tears in her eyes, calling him an "asshole," asking him what she was going to do. Where could she go?

"You're smart. You'll find something or someone," he had said. He was young, too, then. In full control, thinking he understood what was going on because he had calculated the various degrees of risk and safety, and had worked out the correct formula for surviving the war: contact only when necessary, limits on every move to keep its visible action to the minimum. He felt he was so smart then because he worked out these tactical necessities. That was the big difference of his youth.

The war was going to end in Germany's defeat despite the current Ardennes offensive, and the talk of the courage of the defenders at Bastogne saving the Allied cause. The Allied cause had been strategically won the moment uninterrupted convoy traffic reached Great Britain from America, securing the supply lines and the all but inevitable crushing of Berlin.

Only Adolf Hitler and newspapers seemed to be oblivious to those facts. Of course, reporters could be excused for lacking military training.

It was Christmas morning and he had said goodbye. There was no snow in Newport because it was always ten degrees warmer than the rest of New England. It was a sharp and cold rain that washed them that very dark afternoon on the Cliff Walk overlooking the Atlantic. Lovers often strolled there, and if there was one thing about Elizabeth, he was sure, she had lovers. He was just one of them saying goodbye. And the Cliff Walk was open. They could see anyone before they were overheard. "That's it. That's everything, Charlie?"

"Certainly."

"Do you still love me?"

He looked out into the mists of the Atlantic, mists created by the warmth of the Gulf Stream, which also cooled in the summer. Above them a stone watchtower stood guard over the shore, looking for U-boats, finally built after the major damage was done. He looked at the tower too. He did not want to look at her.

"Yes, and so what?" he said.

"That's you," she said. "Is that ever you." She shook her head even as she cried.

"It was a danger during the war, and I don't see how it would be less of a complication after it. A romantic involvement is not exactly conducive to safety, you know. Try thinking it through."

"So?" she said.

"So I intend to secure as safe a life as possible, and let me be brutally reasonable."

She made a motion with her head signifying he always was that way.

"If I loved you, I can love again. This is a fact. I can love. That's what you taught me. This time I'll love the right person."

"You're so smart and you're such an asshole, you know."

He was glad she cursed him. It made it easier. He didn't want to say goodbye again. It had been too hard the first time.

And looking at her almost forty years later, he suddenly realized it

might not have been made any easier by time. Although she seemed
to have gotten over every bit of it. She never held grudges.

"Well, Charlie, I must tell you, I am absolutely delighted to see
you and I hope that nothing really horrid has happened."

"There's something you should know about," he said. He felt
very old.

"Sit down, then. Don't just stand there."

"I should show you this. It's my reason for being here," he said.
He untied the larger knot of the twine.

"Oh, Charlie, how have you been? Really?"

"Fine. Fine. Listen, you may hear about something and I came
here to assure you that—"

"Charlie, now what is the matter with you?" He heard her walk
over to him, and saw her legs near the package and did not look up.
He felt her tap his shoulder.

"Just one moment, please. Stand up straight."

He rose, and as he did so, her arms were around his shoulders and
her lips on his, and they were warm, and she was kissing him, and he
was kissing back. There was not time in the universe to do it long
enough. He almost swooned.

"Now, good," she said. "What is the problem, Charlie."

He had trouble talking. "Newport is a rumor city," he said.

"Is it ever," she said.

"And you may hear of an investigation into some espionage ring,
investigating what happened here during the war, possibly."

"Oh, that. The war. It's over," she said with a little laugh in her
voice.

"Well, yes, the war's over, but there is a thing called a statute of
limitations, and espionage doesn't have it."

"Well that war is over. It never should have been in the first
place."

"The war is over, but if we do something foolish, we can attract
attention. Let time work for us."

"Charlie, I have forgotten that war and everything about it, and I
don't even want to remember it, and I have no intention of doing
anything that would remind me of it. The only nice thing about it
was you before it all began. Now, did you love again?"

"You won't do anything? You won't try to use some influence,
Elizabeth?"

"Charlie, I don't even want to talk about it. Now my name is Bunny. Did you ever love again?"

"I got married . . . Bunny."

"Use 'Elizabeth' if you feel more comfortable. I didn't ask if you got married."

"No, I never did."

"So I was the only one you ever loved. Well, Charlie, it serves you right. I have nothing against anyone, but Charlie, if there is a God in heaven, it served you right."

"Did you love again, Elizabeth?"

"Charlie, you don't want the answer to that one."

"No," he said, "I don't."

"I would have married you, Charlie. But you didn't want to marry anyone like me. I think from the moment we made love I was suspect because we made love. That's what I think, Charlie."

"Emotional passion and what we had to do would have cost everything. We had to end it once everything began."

"And when it was over?"

"You know. I told you. You have a good memory. It was for our safety, and it worked."

"If that's what you call working. I think you were jealous and you looked for just your sort of reasons."

He felt anger, compressed by rigid controls, within him, and then he laughed. Despite herself, Elizabeth laughed with him. She was still hurt. "What's so funny?" she said.

"It's been forty years and nothing has changed."

"Oh, Charlie," she said with warmth and sadness, sounding so Avenue, so British, "Chahlee, Chahlee, Chahlee. Don't things ever change?"

Charles Drobney shook his head. Nothing had changed. He loved her as much now as when he first woke up next to her so long ago when he was young.

They were quiet together for a moment. He looked down at his hands.

"I've got to go," he said.

"I know," she said.

He looked into her eyes. She was crying this time.

"May I see you again?" she said.

He shook his head. He felt her hand on his.

"We can't do that," he said.

"I know," she said and put her hands on his cheeks and kissed him. Then she nodded him toward the doors and the servants' entrance and went back to her seat by the window.

Charles Drobney found the door for the servants' passage and realized that saying goodbye had not gotten any easier in almost forty years. There was just no good way to say goodbye.

Only when he was out of the gates of the Hickories did he feel safe; he had really left and would not turn back.

The Avenue was on the Atlantic side of the tip of the curving island that made up Newport. It was just above the Cliff Walk he loved so much. From there Newport descended to its perfect harbor just a few blocks away.

They were very careful in the town to make the shops as authentic as possible, but they were all basically artificial. Ports were always places of seamy violence and desperation. When the whores and the sailor stabbings and the cheap gin left, it had become an artificial waterfront.

The afternoon fog was coming. Strings of pleasure boats were moored so tightly their decks seemed like a teak walkway across the perfect harbor. On one wharf a crowd was gathered around the British entry for the America's Cup races, a magnificent dark-hulled twelve-meter, hoisted up in a saddle after the day's trial run so that gentle brushes could cleanse it tenderly of the day's algae. The twelves always came up at night for brushing like fine horses. A large Union Jack donated by Pusser's Rum, one of the sponsors of the British campaign this America's Cup, was painted on a neighboring wharf.

It took Charles Drobney twenty minutes to navigate the cluster of the Thames Street cars to the yacht brokerage of M. Hiram Lederle and Son, Newport, R.I., Fort Lauderdale, Fla. He had seen the owner several times around Newport but only nodded to him after they were formally introduced at Christie's restaurant, when Charlie was with some people who dealt in boats. He had seen him once again since then, and they nodded again.

The man was reputed to be very wealthy, one of the success stories in a city where people did not rise from one stratum to another because the strata were not connected. There was the Navy, still a strong presence with the War College up Route 114, the Avenue, and the City, which was everyone else including business-men and politicians. And so someone might rise in his own area, but rarely move from one to another. A rich Newporter did not mean someone was part of the Avenue any more than a successful admiral would be part of the city council. Lederle, it was said, could move between all three rings that made Newport, although he was yet to be part of the Avenue.

Even Bob had met him once, when Lederle's son was campaign-ing.

"That guy could get along anywhere. I thought he was born with a bagel for breakfast," said Bob of the father.

The son had spoken at a UJA meeting on the American need for a strong Israel.

A big poster was pasted on the side of a gray-shingled, two-story frame office set back from the pier on an asphalt lot with several sailing hulls raised in drydock. The sign said LEDERLE FOR CON-GRESS. The sign was a year old. The son had lost handily in the Republican primary. People said the boy was just too weak. Rumor had it he was afraid of people. Drobney pulled into the lot.

Inside the brokerage, it was all wood and brass with the simplicity of an honest ship. It disguised the fact that most of the boats cost more than homes and a percentage point either way could mean thousands, especially since M. Hiram Lederle also owned a bank that financed these purchases, an insurance company that insured them, and many other things Drobney was sure big-money leverage could provide, about which he did not know.

Wood stairs led up one flight to a receptionist's desk, and Charlie climbed them at an even pace. A word processor sat on a polished mahogany stand. An attractive woman in her late thirties looked up.

"I've come to see Mr. Lederle. He said I should see him only. I'm Charles Drobney."

"Are you sure you can't be helped by anyone else?" she said.

"No, he's expecting me."

"I'm not aware of an appointment," said the secretary, without looking at a book. She wasn't really referring to an appointment, she meant she was unaware that Lederle even knew him.

She carried this off well. Drobney remembered her around Newport years before, being stunningly beautiful in her twenties. Her name was Tompkins, he thought.

"It is Mr. Lederle you want? Not a salesman?"

"Yes," said Drobney. "That's who I want."

She pressed a button on her telephone.

"It's a Charles Drobney, Mr. Lederle. Says you spoke to him before," she said. Her tone was icy smart, but the soft pads of her fingertips ran along the smooth plastic of the telephone cord. Her tongue played at the corner of her mouth. Drobney noticed she wore no wedding ring.

Was she having an affair with him, Charlie wondered. What a risky thing, he thought, to have someone so intimately involved in the comings and goings of one's business and at the same time be the one person who under the right circumstances might risk anything in the world to get revenge. Charlie could never understand why people would put themselves in such a vulnerable position where everything had to run right, or possibly come apart.

"Hiram," she said, her lips pursing the blood out of them, her eyes on some face in her mind attached to the voice on the phone. "Will you see him? . . . Okay."

She put down the phone, blinking.

"He'll see you," she said pleasantly, as though the world could not look in.

"Thank you," said Drobney. They were having an affair, he thought.

He opened the polished mahogany door with the brass fittings and saw M. Hiram Lederle sitting behind a very large desk in a blue blazer, his sea-reddened face like hard slate.

Pictures of sailing boats filled the room. An American flag hung just behind Lederle's head commemorating, according to a piece of framed paper, some yachting victory. He wore a simple unjeweled watch, a white yachting shirt. His hand was poised over a stack of papers with a pen in it. The white hair was thinning, showing scalp that had seen too much sun. He looked so much the righteous Yankee, rich as Hades and hard at work.

Charles Drobney shut the door.

"Hello, Harry," he said.

"What do you want?"

"Can I talk?"

"This is probably the safest place in Newport to talk. I have it checked daily."

If he had it checked for eavesdropping devices, he obviously was doing something he did not want others to detect. Business competitors? Charlie thought not. Not in the yachting or banking business. Probably the law for some reason. With all that wealth, still taking risks. The man had not changed. If one asked him what he wanted that money for, or what the difference was between three hundred million and three hundred and ten, he probably would think the questioner a fool.

"There is a problem," said Drobney, sitting down in a leather chair before Lederle's desk. He was close enough to read a small plaque given him by the Naval War College for some service.

"Yes?" said Lederle.

"There may be an investigation looking for an espionage ring left over from World War II."

"Why?"

"Because of something that was found."

"When?"

"Don't worry. Everything is under control. This is a city of rumors, nothing has to be done. Everything is all right."

"That's it? That's what you came for?"

"Yes."

Lederle smiled, tolerant, and almost warm.

"Well, thank you. Would you like to have everything more under control?"

"It's right the way it is, Harry. I just came to tell you not to worry. There's nothing you have to do."

Lederle's eyes flashed. The hands moved in a sharp gesture of someone trying to sell something off a showroom floor. The patrician Lederle of modulated self-assurance was gone.

"You're a funny guy, Charlie. I don't know what you want. Now you really have me puzzled. You don't want money, do you? . . . No, I guess you still don't. I can do things for us you wouldn't dream of. You have got one of the most influential men in this country whose self-interest is identical to yours, identical, and you're sitting back and saying no. For no reason. Charlie, you have never been in such a beautiful position in your life. Please, use it."

"You're safe," said Drobney.

"You don't want to be safer, right?"

Charlie did not answer.

"Do you know who is doing the investigation? Do you know why after all these years they are doing it? What sort of power is behind it? Who wants it? Who really cares? Who doesn't care? What do they know? What don't they know?"

"Harry, if everything is under control, why bother with anything more? You're safe, and the best thing I can do for you is to leave now and not come back."

"Charlie. I don't think you know what safe is. Please hear me out. I do not mean to be insulting. And I am not boasting. But even though you are calling me 'Harry,' I am not Harry Lederle anymore. I'm M. Hiram Lederle and it's not a front. I'm going to try to explain it. Old Harry Lederle would think that several hundred million dollars is several hundred times a million dollars. Well, it's not."

"I wish you well with your money," said Drobney. He glanced at his watch.

"No. No. Hold on. We are not talking about money now. Money is what you buy things with. A million dollars is money. Two hundred is cash, but hundreds of millions is power. Especially if you know how to use it. Especially. Lots of people let it sit there and live their lives off the interest on the interest. Some don't."

Lederle rose from behind the desk and Drobney saw he was wearing white slacks and Top-Sider deck shoes. His large body blocked the way to the door.

"Charlie, you are never safe until you have your enemy's balls in the palm of your hand. Tell me you have them, and I will feel safe. We'll say goodbye forever."

Drobney did not want a pushing match to get to the door. There was a good chance he wouldn't win anyhow. Lederle still moved with power despite being in his early seventies. Drobney tried to explain the overall picture.

"There is no strategic need for America to break this ring. It is not a danger. At most it is an old embarrassment, and old embarrassments are hardly the stuff of intense long-range investigations. There is no need for it. You just don't sustain large numbers of men for long periods of time at some task unless there is a perceived need."

"You don't know what they're thinking, Charlie. You just don't know."

"Therefore, if this investigation doesn't find something easily and quickly, it will dissolve. Anything we might do, something dramatic, some maneuver to find out something, is just the sort of thing they can follow. What they cannot follow quickly and easily is forty-year-old dust. The proper move is therefore to hold your position and do nothing."

"What about grudges? What about hatred? Hell, I've known men to follow others around the world for twenty years on a grudge."

"One person. But that is not how countries operate. Long operations just cannot be sustained indefinitely unless there is a vital national interest. That's a fact of the world."

"What about the Trojan War, Charlie?" said Lederle.

"You are probably thinking about the legends, not the war."

"Hell no. Historical fact. All the Greek city-states followed the King to besiege Troy for ten years because Paris had stolen Queen Helen, the face that launched a thousand ships. That's an historical fact. I've educated myself in the last few years, you see."

Lederle went to a small cabinet and took out two glasses of Waterford crystal. Drobney shook his head. He didn't want to stay longer. The sooner he got out for good, the better.

Maybe, thought Drobney, he would understand it as a businessman. The old shortwave operator had done very well for himself at business.

"That's the legend. It may even have been the announced reason, some form of moral outrage. However, Troy stood at the passageway of tin down into the Mediterranean, and was taxing it heavily. The Greeks needed the tin for bronze for weapons and implements. It was the Bronze Age. There are always legends surrounding every war. The fact is it was a war over tin, and that was why the Greeks were willing to perform a protracted siege. And you have your orders. I won't explain further. Good day."

"Charlie, Charlie," said Lederle, putting an arm over the smaller man's shoulder, keeping him in his chair.

"It's really foolish, don't you see, for us not to use what we have at our disposal, this thing you don't even understand, this power. What I am saying, Charlie—and I don't mean to insult you at all, I want you to understand that—is that I cannot afford to let my future, my safety, my well-being rest on a forty-year-old organization that in truth didn't work all that well then, and probably cannot work at all now."

Drobney looked at the hand. The hand left his shoulder.

"Charlie, you have no idea what I can do for us. The others would agree that we should use my kind of power."

"I'd like to leave. I told you our position," he said.

"Wait a minute, Charlie, the people who gave you power over me no longer exist. They're gone, Charlie. They lost the war, and do you want to know why? Precisely because they were a bunch of toady jerks in uniforms, thinking they were so fucking ruthless when they had no idea what ruthless is. If you want to see ruthless, look at the marketplace. They were just cruel back there. Ruthless is weeding out the weak from the strong not by some accident of race but by that coldest most accurate judge of all. The marketplace."

"I know you're rich, Harry, what is the point?"

"The point is, who would you want to get you out of trouble? Someone who has gone as far as a hardware store, or someone who is, Charlie, hear me now, I do not lie, close to a billionaire. You're the only other person in this world who knows that."

Lederle nodded on that one, smiling as though attesting a hidden sanctity.

"I will tell you more too," his voice lowered. His hands moved as though caressing a woman. "This morning I received congratulations from a cabinet member on my subscription to Bailey's Beach. I have been accepted for subscription. That means that in one year I will be a member. It would be easier, and I mean, Charlie, *easier* to get head from the Queen of England than to get into Bailey's Beach from where I started. If you have a title or three hundred years of WASP money, then you can get into Bailey's Beach. But someone who just came to Newport in 1938, never."

"Congratulations," said Drobney. What was he supposed to say? Although that did tell him why he hadn't seen Lederle on the streets but twice in the last two years. The Avenue lived behind their walls and in their special places, the Ida Lewis Yacht Club, the Clambake Club, and of course, Bailey's Beach itself, so exclusive they chose to give away half their beach to the public just to keep themselves fenced in.

There were other yacht clubs and other beaches, but those well-protected places were how the Avenue managed to live in Newport while being separate.

"They gave us nothing when we came here, Charlie. Everything you and I have we earned. Nobody gave us anything. They even cut off our money."

That seemed to bother the old shortwave operator still. He had been difficult at the beginning of the war when the money was cut off and, near the end, kept only in line by threats.

He had made a fortune in the black market and could not be stopped entirely no matter how risky that was, especially not since he wasn't being paid anymore. He had worried Drobney that he would get caught for his criminal activities and somehow implicate Drobney. Although that was unlikely because the punishment for espionage during the war was death, while black marketeering was a jail term.

The day after Japan surrendered that August following VE Day, Lederle had come to the store with an envelope filled with money even though Charlie had told him over the phone in guarded terms to just go his own way.

"This is my goodbye," he said. "I don't want to hear from you again. I got more friends in the law than you know of. Don't go somewhere and confess because jail cells are very good places to get killed, you know."

He wore a white silk suit and sported a Florida tan. He had the last model Cadillac built before the war. It was a white convertible. A diamond pinky ring flashed its advertisement in big bucks. The fingernails had a high gloss as though someone had lacquered them against any possible suspicion that this man ever had to do his own nails himself.

"Go. Goodbye," said Drobney from behind the cash register. He pushed the envelope back.

"I pay for everything. I don't want you getting ideas down the road that I'm good for a soft touch or old times. There are no old times. This is goodbye."

"Right," said Drobney.

"You can travel with that money," said Lederle. Drobney did not take it. "There is fifty-five hundred dollars in this envelope."

He knew why Lederle wanted him to leave town; Lederle had

decided to stay. When they passed on the street, they never said hello until they were introduced in Christie's restaurant by others.

The ironic thing about the payoff was that it had not occurred to Lederle that Charlie would not want to see him either. He could have gotten it all for free. Also, it was the worst time to come. Charlie had seen men in cars parked outside his boarding house fairly regularly and occasionally at the hardware store. He was sure he was under some sort of surveillance.

The years had made Lederle smoother. The pinky ring and lacquer on the nails were gone. But Drobney doubted he had changed.

This time Lederle was not gruff. He nodded as though he understood. He smiled with grace. He accepted, he said, but he did really want Charlie to think about what he might be able to do to help. He especially wanted Charlie to come to him if he needed any help. Or any of the others.

"Harry, don't worry. There is a tactical thing called *Panik vorwärts.*"

"I don't use that language anymore. I won't even let myself think it."

"German for 'panic forward.' It looks like a charge, it breaks through lines. It might even be successful for a while, like that monstrosity the Third Reich. But it is the worst thing an officer can do because he does not understand what he is doing, he does not understand his situation, and therefore, even if he wins for a while he must lose eventually. It is the one thing you do not want in a higher officer. Stay put. We are fine. Goodbye."

"What do the others think about what you're doing?"

"Goodbye," said Charlie, who had never told him there were others, although the former shortwave operator could have figured it out from the information being passed along. Yet this day Lederle had mentioned it twice.

And it occurred to Drobney forty years after it happened that the surveillance he was under seemed to end after Lederle had tried to give him the money.

Drobney left the brokerage during the rush hour, when many of the bars on the wharfs began heating up with evening tourist business. He drove through streets of old wood houses preserved with fresh insults of latex over their naturally sea-bowed planks. He might well be alive today because Harry Lederle, now M. Hiram Lederle to the world, did not know who else was involved.

He understood part of the reasoning for the attempted payoff now. Failing to find the others, Lederle could not eliminate him safely. One of the others might turn him in for revenge, assuming the others knew him. Therefore, Lederle had to try to buy him off.

And since there was no reason to believe Lederle had changed that much, Drobney had to assume he might be followed again. It didn't matter. There was no reason to believe the man would succeed now where he had failed before. There was nobody else left to see. Elizabeth was safe forever. And so, in all likelihood, was Drobney for whatever number of years that meant.

All their covers were as good as they were on the day they arrived in Newport from Germany more than a generation ago. They had built lives on them, all three of them. They held nearly forty years; they could hold past any possible need.

When he arrived at his white-shingled ranch house with the trimmed lawn and the flowers glorying in Newport's moist sea air (but not the soil, there were problems in that), he felt very tired and old. He saw Sondra's car and realized she had come to visit. His daughter had a problem.

6

MANY PEOPLE were thinking about Charles Drobney that day, but not all by name.

"I think he stayed in America," said Admiral O'Connell. "What was there to go back for? Germany was in ruins. And he was safe. God, was he safe."

"Are you sure it's a he?" said the junior officer.

"Whoever was running it. Pretty sure. I used to think I would read about him trying to surrender at the end of the war and being led to a police station with his handcuffed wrists trying to hide his face. I used to think of finding him in a jail and standing outside of that cell, you know. And getting a can of gasoline and some rags . . . Hello, Nazi, let's talk about torpedoes and ovens."

"Did you really, sir?" said the lieutenant commander.

The admiral nodded. "I wouldn't have done it, of course. But I thought about it, sometimes even when the war was over and I was afraid to go back to sea," said O'Connell. "Even then. The contempt they had for us. I just felt it. War's over. Have another schnapps, Otto. Try again next time. Bastards!"

"Well, at least now we know they were here. The FBI is sending help."

The admiral smiled. His face became a crafty mask of a man who not only could be exceptionally open to a junior officer, but also knew the way the world worked. "They are sending someone. They had to."

Todd Oliver wondered if the "enemy who thinks" might not turn himself in the day after Todd got finished proving he didn't exist. Of course that meant that Todd believed he did exist. Did he? No. But he had to respect the possibility. At Dulles International Airport, Todd walked outside the metal detectors, showing his FBI identification and getting a stub attached to his ticket to let the flight attendant know he was carrying a gun. When the metal detectors were first installed at airports as a protection against hijackers bringing weapons aboard planes, four agents, each carrying a .38 Police Special in shoulder holsters, walked right through the detector without a beep. Suddenly, the machine went off behind them. Looking back, they saw a teenager emptying his pockets of a set of keys. Accidents happened. Todd Oliver believed in accidents.

He notified the pilot there was an agent with weapon aboard, according to regulations, and also, according to regulations, refused a complimentary cocktail. He flew up to Boston next to a girl with acne and warm thighs.

Bob Goldstein knew something was wrong with Charlie. He was sure, but he could not prove, or at least not yet prove that it was more than a mere muffin's salt. His friend didn't leave early looking like that without salt. He had come from Tuesday's restaurant. He could have eaten their fried vegetables he loved so much. He was sure of it. Charlie had been eating fried again.

M. Hiram Lederle was sure he knew why the hardware store owner had refused his help. Here he was, Charles Drobney, in his store-bought clothes with the same Midwestern accent he was born with, giving orders to M. Hiram Lederle himself.

Drobney had done nothing of significance after the war, and probably not before either. The whole thing made him feel important again. But he was always a strange one, always refusing advice or help, timid at the outset of the war, and then at the end of the war when everything was lost, wildly incautious.

Charles Drobney was an American. Lederle was sure of that. One did not fake being as American as Charles Drobney. And yet, without a doubt, that man had to have been an officer in the German General Staff. And they never made any foreigner an officer. They were hard-pressed to take Germans other than Prussians in the General Staff. But Lederle remembered meeting Drobney back in Germany, seeing in him something he was sure no one in Newport had ever seen, even the man's wife. That cold, reserve, that pervasive stiff contempt that the General Staff had for the world. It didn't need a uniform to show. M. Hiram Lederle had seen it here in his office that day. And what on earth did they have to feel superior about? They had lost two wars.

It did not matter that a hardware store owner felt safe. In two days, M. Hiram Lederle would know what was really going on in this investigation. Drobney had gotten through the war because he was lucky. The man did not know how lucky he was.

Mrs. Alexander Wheaton prepared for dinner and thought how smart a man could be and still be so foolish, how intelligent poor Charlie was, and what an incredible baby. What an absolute child.

Many men were like that. They went about life under the assumption that love was another element in life that they should be able to handle, hopefully with ease. It was not quite as important as a job, but certainly more important than their car.

Nobody handled love, anymore than one handled the tides. You must try to make do in it as best you could, hopefully avoiding those that would destroy you.

Charlie had loved her. Therefore, he would love again, and therefore and therefore and therefore, everything so neat and tidy, and forty years later she was letting him out of the servants' entrance, knowing there were tears inside him.

What hurt her this evening as she nodded away the diamonds brought by her personal maid (this was not a diamonds sort of dinner) was that when she had seen him, when she knew he had come, she thought it was for her.

But it wasn't for her at all. It was to make sure she followed orders. That war was over. Nobody was going to do anything about that anymore. Men were working on yet another war. That was over.

Seeing him again had made her sad. She would have married him. She knew it would not have worked. It would have ended in divorce. He was wrong for her, and she for him. But she would have married him. She loved him. And he hadn't come back just to see her.

Sondra Drobney had to speak to her father right away. Not that he would agree with her. He rarely did. But if she could talk to him, just be with him, and hear his reasoning, it would ease the day's pain.

Dad was good for that. Few women she knew had fathers who could understand like her dad. Perhaps that was her main problem, judging all men by him. There were plenty of men in the world. Unfortunately, they all seemed very wrong for her or not available to her. And then again, perhaps the problem was she thought there was a Mr. Right. Then again, perhaps her problem was she thought too much. Or maybe she thought too much about thinking too much.

She was twenty-eight years old, and the mother of a five-year-old boy. She ran her own home, did an almost full-time job at the store, bookkeeping with Dad and Uncle Bob, and now she was running back to her father like she, not Brandon, was five.

She felt she should be able to handle this herself. But the problem *was* herself. She was mad at herself because she was hurt at something someone had said, at something she should have treated with contempt. And then she was angry at herself for being angry at herself. And worse, she realized how ridiculous this was.

Dad could use reasoning and end up with a practical solution. Unfortunately, she never agreed with Dad's solutions, which didn't make the world better. She felt the world should be better and people were put in the world to accomplish that.

Which was why she had joined the Renaissance League in the first place. That was where the incident happened. The League sought to protect and enhance this beautiful city she loved. The League's function was to care about Newport and so did she. She joined the League to work, and thus ended up petitioning homeowners to improve their property, attending tedious city council zoning meetings, calling the meetings, chairing the meetings, and eventually having the title of vice president. Sondra Drobney, it was known, was always good for the scut work. Sometimes during the winter she gaveled an empty room and went home.

But at this spring meeting where the incident had occurred, there were almost thirty people gathered at the old Bardwell House, a 1702 frame house that, in Newport tradition, had moved entire from one area to another, now residing at Gravel Point.

The meetings just before the Renaissance League Ball were always heavily attended because the ball on the Avenue was the reason most of the people joined the League, not the well-being of the city Sondra loved. The ball was in a few days. Side conversations from the audience dealt with only that.

Sondra's first problem had been she cared very much about what was on the agenda: petitioning the government to make its inside doors at the post office on Thames Street conform to its exterior architecture. And she tried to stay with that.

The recording secretary, a somewhat aggressive man who sat on her right at the head table, had another agenda. He kept passing her notes.

"Dinner?" read the last note.

She shook her head, and faced the audience of twenty-eight people in four rows of folding chairs. A woman in the front row made a strong point against the post office project.

"It is not pretty and it is not history and it is not fit for the attention of the League," said the woman. "Now, my family has been in Newport since before the mansions, even before the Civil War, and we have a sense of what is Newport and what is not. The Bardwell House is Newport. The ships are Newport. These homes on the Point, and, of course, the mansions are Newport. A post office is not."

Sondra could see heads nodding. The woman was good at arguing. In fact, she had refused several posts because she didn't want to give up her front seat, from where she could criticize. Sondra, on the other hand, made a special effort to understand what might be true about another person's view; she had trouble with arguments.

"Okay, that's a point," she said. "You're really talking about attractiveness as being a requirement for our concern, not the historical validity."

"What are we here for except to keep Newport attractive?" said the woman with a polite condescending laugh.

Another note came across from the recording secretary. Sondra shook her head again, very quickly.

"The post office on Thames Street, however, is a perfect example of 1930s architecture. Granted, it is massive and made of concrete."

"It's where I go to mail a package, not to appreciate the real Newport," said the woman.

"Well, it is a part of our history. It came from a time of the Great

Depression, a time when the Navy was more important to Newport than it is now, a time when that sort of architecture was considered a boon. It says something.''

"It says it should be torn down," said the woman, and everyone laughed.

Sondra Drobney knew she was losing again. Another note came across the table.

It read: "My place has clean sheets." The recording secretary was actually smiling at that one.

Sondra turned to him and said, "Stop bothering me."

His head jerked back, his mouth opened, and then he demanded to see her privately.

The woman in the front row began posturing with people who agreed with her, conducting her own meeting with the rank and file, and, as sometimes happened when Sondra chaired a meeting, it just dissolved.

"I want to see you privately," said the recording secretary through clenched teeth.

"Wait," Sondra said to the group. "What about the post office?"

"Do whatever you want, dear," said the woman, laughing, and everyone seemed to nod.

"It is thereby resolved that a petition shall be presented to the government office from the League regarding interior conformity," said Sondra. "All those in favor say aye."

She said, "Aye," a few people waved, one nodded, and it was passed, and the recording secretary was beckoning her over to the side of the room for his private conversation.

Despite her energy and drive, she was slightly overweight. Not fat, but not thin enough for a confident bikini either. She had soft brown hair and sweet brown eyes and delicate white skin. According to someone she didn't care to get close to, she looked "comfortable."

"I just want a minute," the recording secretary repeated.

She looked at her watch. She had to pick up Brandon soon at preschool. She followed him to the side of the room. When he spun around to face her, she was surprised to see his jaw was trembling.

"I just want you to know, Sondra, that I think you are being a bit absurd, to say nothing of insulting, to answer me like that in front of everyone . . ."

"Answer what?"

"My discreet note," he said.

"Oh, that. You were propositioning me, right in front—"

"I'm not finished, Sondra. There are times and places for things. Who you sleep with is your business, and frankly I don't care. I don't care. But when you have a five-year-old illegitimate kid banging around the house, don't you think you're being a bit stupid to play Miss Goody Pants now?"

Her body tensed. Electric shocks charged through her spine. She saw the startled recording secretary back off from her angered presence, but she was so furious that all she could say was "I can't, I can't believe you said that. I can't believe you just said that, you . . . you . . ."

And she was crying, and she didn't want that stupid bastard to see she was crying. "Stupid bastard. Stupid bastard," she said, knowing that wasn't the word to use in this argument.

People were looking at her, the recording secretary was apologizing, and she left, crying. She wasn't even sure why she was crying. There was just so much hurt in her that some of it had to come out in tears. Stupid, stupid bastard, she thought. Herself. Not him. For feeling bad. But she was hurt. She was so deeply hurt. For her son. For herself. For her place in Newport.

And he was such a stupid bastard and she knew it. Several times on her way to pick up Brandon, she parked the car to just cry in rage, and then she knew that a friend wouldn't be good enough for this anger and pain, at something so senseless. It had to be Dad.

Brandon seemed to sense something was wrong and at first tried to make things nice for her, which made her feel worse, and then he became difficult.

She did not stop at her apartment off Broadway, but brought him over to Dad's, the house she had been born in, the neat white ranch on the small, well-kept grass lot with the big backyard where Brandon could play while she made him supper.

But Dad wasn't home, even though Uncle Bob said he had left early. She saw he had not prepared himself dinner, so she made dinner for him and for Brandon while she waited.

When she heard Dad's car pull up into the driveway, she wanted to run out to him like she did when she was five. She waited until he came in and Brandon ran to him and got a big happy kiss and then went back to the table to eat his food.

"Are you okay?" said her father.

She shook her head and smiled.

"We'll talk later," he said. They ate dinner together, all of them, and then walked several blocks to Bellevue Avenue where the Cliff Walk began at the Elms, the old Astor mansion now open to the public. It was a good evening and the afternoon mists that seemed to breathe around Newport because of the Gulf Stream had gentled, so that the family could see and feel the great Atlantic beneath them.

Up ahead on the edge of the cliff workmen had left their tools on a large stone and concrete structure. It was one of the old submarine towers, Sondra knew. The city had been terrified of a submarine attack in that vital harbor during the Second World War and posted people constantly as lookouts. But no sub ever came closer than the one sunk off of Block Island. Her father had been a civil defense warden in the war. She believed deeply that that had been a just war. She did not feel the same about Vietnam.

When they turned to stroll back up the walk and go home, her father said simply, "This is a good day."

She knew he meant because she and Brandon were with him. Later, when Brandon went to sleep in her old room, she went to her father's study, where he had a cup of decaffeinated tea and she opened up a light beer.

The study was packed with books on history, many of them about World War II. It was where he said he tried to figure out how things happened.

When mother was alive he spent considerable time here to escape her harping and fighting, which became more severe with her drinking. When she went into the hospital for her last drying-out, she never left because they discovered she was in the late stages of an especially virulent cancer.

When she was a teenager Sondra did her schoolwork here; both she and Dad found it a way to avoid Mother. She often wondered why he didn't leave, especially after she grew up. She knew he never loved Mom. But he was always polite to her, always solicitous of her, and when she reached the pitch of yelling, would retreat here to the study, where now Sondra, too, was taking refuge.

"It's the illegitimacy thing again," said Sondra.

He nodded.

"A stupid nerd," said Sondra.

"That seems to be a requirement," he said. There was a gentle smile.

"I'm angry that this city still has such stupid, backward people."

"So it really isn't Brandon's birth. You want stupid bastards to approve of your life. Good luck, honey."

Sondra felt a little laugh. He was right the way he put it, but it wasn't quite that.

"I feel sad that there are people like that in the world, Dad. I feel sad for Brandon, and what he might be made to feel. Maybe you were right. Maybe I shouldn't have had Brandon."

"No," said her father.

"Have you changed your mind?"

"No," he said. "My opinion was based on what we knew. We did not know Brandon then," he said.

She was making another point when the tears started to come. She remembered how Mom had gone into one of her screaming fits when Sondra said she was pregnant but did not want to marry the man. She didn't think he would be a good husband.

When she came to Dad for his opinion, and it was his that counted most next to hers, he was hard on her.

She was wrong, he said, about the world becoming more understanding. It was just that it appeared that way now. And how would the child feel? And how would she feel about raising it? How would she feel about what others said? He knew she had cared about that.

He was not suggesting getting rid of the fetus, but if she did, he felt that she would have time again, in all probability, to have a child in wedlock, which, no matter what anyone said about it, was infinitely easier in this world.

He was right. He was logical. But she wanted the baby that was in her. It was hers. It was life. She was a mother. She didn't want to give it up, because it was not only hers, it was her. Unfortunately, she did not want the man who put it there. He was someone who was good in bed, not too good in life. He seemed like so many men that she only found out about after she was involved. She had the baby and moved out. Mom forced it. She made a big scene about not having that disgrace in the family. Dad couldn't help because he had already given over the house to Mom. The only thing he had ever kept for himself was the study.

Dad came to the hospital every day. Mom arrived once, smelling of some whiskey, crying that she had been a bad mother, and wanting forgiveness, and Dad had to remove her.

Thereafter there were several drunken phone calls in the wee hours with Mom either apologizing or condemning until Dad insisted that Sondra get an unlisted number and keep it away from Mother.

She wondered why he never left Mom. She wondered whether she questioned that because she might have an Electra complex, be in love with her father in an undaughterly way. But a therapist helped her distinguish her real love from her fancied love.

Uncle Bob thought Dad didn't leave Mother because he really loved her no matter how hard everything might seem from the outside. But Sondra knew Bob Goldstein was describing himself, not Dad. Dad never loved Mother. She knew that.

In the funeral car, they were alone.

"Well," she had said. "I guess that's it."

"That's it," he said.

And then her tears for the funeral, for the dying of her mother, came very strong on her. She cried during the burial and did not like herself for that because everyone would think it was because of losing her mother, when it wasn't; it was because she finally realized her mother would never be what she needed or wanted. This was the death of what Mom could have been.

She did not return then to the house where she grew up but kept her apartment. She returned for moments like these.

"I still stand with my reasoning, but thank God you made the decision and not me," he said. "Thank you for everything. You are the best, Sondra Drobney, and you'll never be like me."

She was crying when she heard that because she knew she had gotten everything she had come for.

"You really don't care about the world, do you?"

"There are two people whose opinions matter to me. Yours and Bob's, and the rest of the world can go do whatever it does."

"I think there is a better world out there. And I'm going to make it better. I am not helpless."

"Amen," said Charles Drobney, smiling, agreeing with not a jot of it, which also didn't matter for him either.

She finished her beer and took Brandon home, and the next day, fortified by the love she had shared with her father, went forthrightly to the post office to see about changing the door on the inside of the second floor to conform to the others in that hallway.

And of course she met trouble. She had expected it from those people.

"I spoke with you two days ago, and mentioned that I would be in to discuss this, that I felt sure the League would approve of my personal feelings, and you said if you were here, you would talk to me today." Thus spoke Sondra Drobney to Special Agent Wannaker of the field office, Newport, FBI.

"I'm not the ranking agent," said the FBI man. He wore a holster under a sports jacket.

"Well, I thought you were. I am mistaken. May I speak to the agent in charge?"

He smiled. "You were not mistaken. I was the ranking agent. This is now a two-man field office."

"Oh, is this something good or something bad? Do we have more crime or are we more important?" she asked. She tried to be pleasant. She hated that in herself, trying to be pleasant when she didn't feel like it.

"I just work here, ma'am," said the agent.

"Then may I see who is in charge?" she said pleasantly. She forced a smile.

"Yes, ma'am," he said, and in a few moments returned outside with an attractive dark-haired man with beautiful dark eyes and a soothing smile, wearing a light business suit, who seemed to listen to her explanation of the door. Immediately she noticed a wedding ring. His name was Todd Oliver. He was a unit chief, and even though he was busy, he thought he might be of help. At least he could find out where she might be able to go for help.

She explained about the door. She had him step back a pace or two. She felt he was staring under her clothes. She liked it because he was hiding it. It wasn't an invasion. It was an admiration. She was sure he didn't know she knew. She became more flamboyant in her gestures, almost posing, almost flaunting. She laughed a bit more at passing comments than normal. She noticed the ring a lot somehow. It kept coming up at her face. Then she realized it kept coming up at her face because she kept staring at his hand. He put it in his pocket.

He listened to what she had to say about how—even though the door to the FBI office was prettier than the others—it lacked authenticity precisely because it was wood, and beautiful.

"You mean to say you're here to suggest we make our door ugly?"

"No, authentic. I guess I am not making my case, but this sticks out, don't you see?"

Why was she looking at his pants? She laughed and looked away. She wasn't like that.

"So basically you want them to conform?" She felt that gaze again.

"Yes," she said. He had a beautiful presence. It wasn't rigid and sharp like the other agent. It was deeper, somewhat like her father.

Of course she couldn't know. All they were doing was talking about the door, and she was enjoying a small admiration bath. There was nothing wrong with it. This wasn't going anywhere; he was married. She wanted to get a door adjusted in a government office that might require a long march of years and years of letters and counterletters, and he might be gone by the time the door was put in. Back to his wife.

Why did she think back to his wife? Nothing was happening. She felt his eyes go down her waist. She pretended not to notice and just casually threw her weight onto one leg. Even as she did it, she thought of herself as a tease.

She laughed. He smiled and mentioned government regulations for field offices, not an impossible presence to overcome but a viable, methodical function.

"What does that mean?" she said.

He had to think a moment on that one. She wondered whether to tell him he had a nice smile. She wondered if he knew it. She brushed back her hair.

Of course her chest extended with that movement. She told herself she was using this charm possibly to improve Newport, this city she loved. She knew that was absurd.

He was just the sort of man she wanted to want her, and since she never got involved with married men, this was harmless. And if her ego was boosted by his blatant interest, she didn't care. This world was filled with enough things to put you down so that if someone politely was undressing you with his eyes, the least she could do as a civic-minded citizen was to enjoy it.

"It is not impossible," he said, nodding to the door.

"Okay, good. So where do we stand?" she said. Why did she think there was something special about him? Because he didn't flaunt a gun? Because he came out of an FBI office and acted not as a policeman but an executive? Because he had good looks, and was polite?

"You have to file properly, actually satisfying the GAO, the Government Accounting Office."

"I see," she said.

"Uh huh," he said.

Suddenly a woman was out in the hallway calling him back into the office. It looked incredibly crowded. There was an important call. It shocked her out of stance. She straightened up.

"We're not finished," she said.

"I'm sorry. I have to answer that call, Ms. Drobney."

"I think you should understand Newport."

"Yes, if I have time." He was halfway in the door.

"Lunch tomorrow. I can show you what we're dealing with," she called after him. She thought he said yes. So did the woman assistant. Sondra gave her title with the Renaissance League, vice president. She gave the suggested time and restaurant. Unless she heard otherwise she would be there. She was very official with the woman. This was official business. After all, that was why she felt she had to explain Newport.

Back at the store, Uncle Bob, who followed the local gossip, said the new man in the office was probably here because of some old codebooks found off Block Island.

"We usually have a one-man office," said Bob.

"Is this a convention up here?" said Charlie. "I could always get an office and a door and keep it locked." All three were on the platform.

"You want an office, we'll put in an office," said Bob.

"He was a unit chief," said Sondra. "He's not just an agent."

"Good. I hope they really go after them and don't pull a McCloy," said Bob, referring to John McCloy, who, as American high commissioner in Germany after the war, commuted sentences of too many Nazis, in Bob's opinion.

"He didn't seem FBI. He was a very nice man. Why does someone join the FBI? Do you ever wonder?"

"They like to carry guns. I don't know. I like the FBI. I have a second cousin who was with the Bureau. He was in under Hoover. That was the real FBI," said Bob.

"I don't think authority figures are valid anymore. I don't think this man is the sort who would work well under an authority figure," said Sondra.

"That's a lot of time you're spending on that door you're trying to get changed," said Bob.

"I just met him for a minute. You get a feeling about someone, you know," said Sondra, and seeing Dad was engrossed in the inventory review again, she gave him a little punch to get him back in the conversation.

But he was busy. He took an Ismelin and said he felt like going home early, just for a walk. Sondra wanted to get work done and Bob had a customer.

Charles Drobney decided to rest the next day also, spending it with Brandon. About 2:30 P.M. as he was dozing in the afternoon, Brandon woke him up with a little tug to tell him that the FBI had come to arrest him.

7

TODD OLIVER returned inside the office for the phone call while
his clerk, a GS-9 he had picked up in Boston along with a government pool car, dealt with the local woman who, he kept thinking,
must have a pillow of a body, just enough softness for interest. He
would have put her at more than a marshmallow and less than an
apple.

His wife, Anne, was a sleek mannequin of a woman, he thought.
Not apple or marshmallow. Fast-dry plaster. But she was a woman
he wanted to be seen with.

This brown-haired, plush, laughing woman was someone you
might want to have fun with. Other men wouldn't particularly ad-
mire you for being with that one. Ms. Drobney. She had dimples.
The brown eyes were nice.

The press relations officer out of Boston was on the secure line.
Oliver squeezed himself between the desks while talking. This was
an RA field office. A small single room occupied by a resident agent.
It was designed for one desk and one secure file cabinet and one
telex, and now not only had another desk and another secure file
cabinet, but a typewriter stand and two more people. There was just
less than a muscular thigh's room between two plain green steel
desks. The RA was looking out the window at the harbor.

The press relations officer from Boston was saying there had been
an inquiry about the two codebooks from the Providence *Journal,*

and the PRO Boston had gotten confirmation from Bureau that Unit Chief Oliver was handling that. What was the situation?

"Well, how did they find out?" asked Oliver.

"I don't know."

"Are they going to do a story?"

"They never say," said the press relations officer. Oliver had clearance himself to speak to the press. There was a 243-page procedure manual for dealing with the press, which covered subjects ranging from court cases to investigations of Congress itself. There were so many items that even if it were not a rule to get clearance from a main station press officer, most agents would do so anyhow. The Press Relations Manual was almost as large as the Espionage-65 Procedures Manual, and that manual had to deal with defending America's technological explosion.

"There was a German submarine sunk off Block Island late in the war. The codebooks are believed to be refuse from it. Right?" said Oliver.

"Yes," said the press relations officer from Boston.

"Then it's refuse," said Oliver.

"Are we investigating?" said PRO Boston.

"Tell them you'll look into it and get back to them."

"When?"

"One week." Oliver hung up. "I think we have a leak somewhere," he said to his GS-9 clerk.

"Not necessarily," said the agent, who could not help overhearing what was four feet from his ears. "This is a gossipy little community with lots of retired naval officers. Someone always knows something, and someone is always talking. During the Claus von Bulow trial this place was a madhouse."

"That wasn't a federal crime was it?" said Oliver.

"No. I'm talking about the gossip," said the resident agent.

"Thank you," said Oliver. He knew the resident agent resented him. He had to. He was a typical one-man field officer, keeping in touch with perhaps twenty police departments, his bank of informers, the U.S. attorney's office, and doing his own typing to boot on top of regular sixty-hour weeks.

Here a unit chief breezed into his one-man office with his own clerk typist and the authority to pass judgment on the RA's line actions from a comfortable nine-to-five job.

And while this wasn't like the old days under Hoover, where RAs could be moved around at whim, they could still be moved around. By people like Todd Oliver.

Promotions ground dismally along, the work was often hazardous and almost always disruptive of family life, and yet Todd knew some men actually preferred it. The one thing Todd knew about the work in the field, he had learned in his first year with the FBI. He didn't want it.

He decided to make a minimal peace with the man, who, in his own way, might cause some unnecessary difficulty.

"Hopefully, I won't be here that long," said Todd. "I am sorry to inconvenience you."

"That's all right," said the RA. He offered a short sharp smile. Supervisor Cobb claimed he missed this sort of life. Supervisor Cobb was a very good liar.

The GS-9 clerk had Todd's agenda. The Navy wanted a meeting in the morning to assist in the investigation, possibly to explain information not clear in previous communications. It would be at the Naval War College up Route 114 at 9 A.M.

Also, the former OSS man had been located. He was Professor Gardner Tobridge, a professor emeritus at Harvard, and was either available at Cambridge, or at his farm in western Massachusetts. He had extensively debriefed Doenitz.

"There are no hotel rooms available in Newport," she said.

"Did you tell him who I am?"

"Yessir," said the clerk. "This is an America's Cup summer."

"Don't they hold those races in September?"

"I don't know," said the clerk.

"The trials go on all summer," said Wannaker. "Couldn't help overhearing. They've been booked up for this summer for a year now."

"Okay," said Oliver. He thought he saw Wannaker smile.

"You have a noon luncheon with Ms. Sondra Drobney at the Black Pearl."

"What for?"

"You agreed to it and I made it tentative."

"I can't make that. That's a local problem," said Oliver. He leaned over around the clerk to speak to Wannaker.

"Do you think you might make that lunch?" said Oliver. "I guarantee no unit chief will double-guess you on that one." He gave the RA an extra large smile.

"I can't. I'm sorry," said Wannaker.

"I'll get you an air conditioner," laughed Oliver.

"Don't need one. This is Newport. Ten degrees cooler in the summer. Ten degrees warmer in the winter. We have the Gulf Stream out in the Atlantic. Best natural air conditioner in the world."

"How important is this League?" asked Oliver.

Wannaker shrugged. "Lots of groups in Newport, the Renaissance League, the Preservation Society, the—"

"Thank you," said Oliver. "If I have time, I will make that lunch. Would you care to attend, Ms. Cotter?"

"Thank you, no," said the clerk.

It was 1 P.M. and he assigned the clerk the rest of the day to get him a hotel room. She got one in Middletown, adjacent to Newport.

When Wannaker had to drive to Portsmouth to investigate a missing-child case that the local police thought might be a kidnapping, Oliver opened the file on Operation Paperclip, the American autopsy on the mechanism of the Third Reich.

He didn't care that Newport was supposed to be gossipy. There could have been a leak. It could have been Wannaker. It was not unknown. Pay off an old debt. Collect a favor.

Oliver did not want press coverage until the Bureau could look good through his work. He preferred to examine materials alone, not that he would ever accuse another agent of being untrustworthy regarding the press.

He had culled the file down to its high points back in Washington, specifically the dissection of German Intelligence, Abwehr, and what was left of it after Allied Intelligence and Adolf Hitler had mangled its innards.

Especially useful was the old debriefing report on Grossadmiral Karl Doenitz, picturing him as an arrogant committed Nazi with an unrealistic view of his own fleet. He had maintained after the war that his special code had never been broken, when indeed it had. There was even the reference to intercepted messages. Nowhere was there an admission from this boastful admiral that he had succeeded in some form of espionage. And he had shot his mouth off to a fine fare-thee-well. This from a young OSS captain, Gardner

Tobridge. Professor Emeritus Gardner Tobridge of Harvard was going to get a substantial visit from Unit Chief Oliver, along with the clerk typist taking notes. *One week and home,* thought Oliver.

Thus, when he met Admiral O'Connell the next morning he was feeling safe. Ostensibly it was a meeting with a lieutenant commander to review the Navy's request for an investigation. But it was really the retired admiral, a vice president of North American Technologies, Inc., who was behind this.

They met in a small office at the War College with pictures of sailing ships and boarding parties, and seamen lined in front of cannon and mizzenmasts. On the desk was a computer terminal.

The admiral did the talking. Todd tried to get him extricated, but couldn't. He tried to get him officially involved, but couldn't. Admiral O'Connell seemed to know all the moves.

The Navy wanted an investigation that Todd tried to portray as something so massive it could weaken the whole counterespionage structure along the coast. The Navy countered that now there was proof spies existed, and Todd's response to that was there was only a pouch containing old materials that he was investigating at their request.

"This is a damned spy pouch. It is not for damned ships, Unit Chief Todd Oliver," said the admiral, slapping the hard rubber. "You tell me how Grand Admiral Doenitz knew enough to change to a special code for U-boats if he didn't know the main code was broken. And how did he know? He had his own damned spy system, that's how he knew. And this pouch proves it."

"I take it you have considerable expertise in espionage, Admiral," answered Todd.

"I know a fucking ship's code when I see one."

"And that code is not for ships?"

"The pouch is not for ships. I see you are planning to successfully miss these people again."

At this point Todd listed manpower invested by the late J. Edgar Hoover in a thorough search of not only this area but various installations along the East Coast and proclaimed that that was an awful lot of effort in order to miss people. He had a good righteous voice. Nothing sermonizing, but rather the dry, reliable, enduring public servant being outrageously abused by unreasonable demands. It was good enough for a congressional testimony.

The meeting lasted five hours. During most of it, the admiral and Oliver went head to head. The lieutenant commander, the representative of the Navy, the only one who had any official risk in this, sat on the side. It was a classic bureaucratic maneuver. The admiral could pound away safely, without any official responsibility. Accuse anything. Demand anything without accountability.

He would have made a good lawyer too. Todd could almost hear the espionage network crackling along the entire East Coast from the way he dramatized monumental tonnages lost, the slowness of the U-boats, their need for surface time, which would have made them more vulnerable, and the changing convoy tactics, which somehow they always knew.

The losses were impressive. So was the case.

At the end, O'Connell said very dryly, with a low and angry voice, head set as though he was ready to kill or die, "You may think this is another investigation. But, Agent Oliver, I have thousands of dead sailors in the Atlantic. I want the men who put them there. I want you to get those men who put them there. I want them and I will want them until the Atlantic gives me back those men. For your sake and your career, Agent Oliver, you will get them."

"Is that a threat?" said Oliver.

"Absolutely," said the admiral. And then he smiled, got up, and left the room, with only Oliver and the lieutenant commander remaining.

"Do you have any useful information?" said Oliver to the young officer, stressing the "useful."

The lieutenant commander shook his head.

"Thank you," said Oliver, so drained from the encounter he could barely drive the car back into downtown Newport, where there was no parking available.

Wannaker was at the office when Oliver returned. He had news. The vice president of the Renaissance League had waited for him at the Black Pearl. She had phoned three times. The third time she had asked whom she was supposed to talk to about the door, about the Bureau's physical presence in the city if it were not Oliver.

"I wasn't sure what you wanted," said Wannaker.

"What happened?"

"She wanted to know who your superior was, since she obviously was being bucked upstairs, she said."

"And you told her?"

"Public record. Supervisor Cobb."

"Fine," said Oliver without anger. It would be no problem.

He was still dizzy from the admiral. Even though he had known it always had to be more than some lieutenant commander behind a call for a new investigation, he did not realize the extent of the power behind it. Admiral O'Connell represented a major defense industry. And he was not alone. He had support both inside and outside the defense establishment. And that could well mean right up to cabinet level.

But first things first. Damage control with the local lady. He found the address for Drobney in the phone book, and Wannaker told him he could walk it. Todd didn't feel fit to drive in the mess on Thames Street anyhow.

He walked up a very steep hill, with high frame houses on small lots, cramped into small streets obviously laid out before central planning, which probably had been cow paths that colonists followed.

The salt air cleared his head. He crossed a large avenue into an area with lawns and stone houses. It was a good thing, he thought, some E-65 specialist had not been sucked into this. The poor man probably would have drained every field office on the coast for it, without ever realizing this had nothing to do with espionage. It was an old assault on the Bureau itself through an attack on the integrity of the late J. Edgar Hoover. There would be an investigation, one that had to be considered reasonable and thorough in the light of current evidence, balanced against national importance vis-à-vis current manpower facing real and present dangers through the nation and the world.

It would be the sort of bland, even report that, if it should be assaulted by the Navy, would only show them to be the ones attempting to protect their record, not the Bureau, which had invested a full week of a modern unit chief's time to review all the evidence.

Painfully, Todd Oliver would be shown to be forced to draw the conclusion that even though America had suffered enormous losses near its own shores, there was no evidence now to indicate cause by a functioning espionage presence. In other words, regretfully the

Navy did all its bleeding on its own. There were no spies. Never had been.

He located his street, looked down at the address on the piece of paper, looked back up at the white picket fence and immaculate lawn with woodbark mulched flowers and the white-shingled ranch house with the trim windows, the door without a number, and then noticed the name on the mailbox next to the door. Drobney. He had come to the right place.

He walked through the gate of the white picket fence and rang the bell. Hopefully, he would be safely ensconced in the Hoover building within a week. The more the admiral blew, the more the Bureau would have to close in around him and the more the Navy would appear unreasonable. If Todd could get O'Connell to threaten in public, it would be a final triumph; of course, the admiral was too shrewd for that.

A little boy came to the door. He had red hair and was tall enough to reach the handle on the screen door, which he opened with authority.

"Hello, I'm Brandon Drobney. Who are you?" said the boy.

"I want to see Sondra Drobney," said Todd.

"Mommy isn't here," said the boy.

"Is your father here?" asked Todd.

"I don't have a daddy here. I have a mommy. Who are you?"

"I am an FBI man," said Todd, taking out his identification and holding it down to the boy's level. The young brown eyes widened with excitement.

"A real FBI man?"

"Yes," said Todd.

"Can I see your gun?"

"I'm only supposed to show my identification. That's what real FBI men do. Is anyone home I can speak to?"

"Granpa."

"May I speak to him?"

Brandon Drobney nodded and ran into the house, yelling, "Granpa, Granpa. The FBI is here for you. An FBI man is here to arrest you."

8

CHARLES DROBNEY woke up with Brandon telling him what he had thought he would hear before the end of the war. It had taken him a good two months not to believe that every stranger was not there to arrest him. Of course that was only fear. He knew how to handle fear. He had been trained for that.

"Thank you, honey," he said to Brandon and kissed him on the head. He told him to stay in the kitchen and finish his coloring book.

"What colors should the flowers be?" asked Brandon.

"Green for the leaves, yellow for the blossoms, here," he said, putting his finger on a daisy leaf. He kissed the red hair again and went to the door. A pleasant-looking young man in a suit was waiting there alone.

He wondered how they had found him after so many years and assumed instantly there had to be something that was not apparent during its time but stood out when looked at over years. There were forgeries like that, so accepted during their own times and so obviously wrong at a distance of centuries. Also there were so many new electronic things, so many things he not only didn't know, he could not even imagine. And here it was, when of course it was far too late to do America any good.

"Yes?" asked Charles Drobney. "My grandson says you've come to arrest me."

The young man laughed. "I'm sorry, sir. I just told him I had come to see you. I would have run in after him, but as you know I can't enter your house without your permission. I hope it didn't give you a shock."

"Can I help you?"

"Yes, I am looking for Mrs. Sondra Drobney."

"May I ask why?"

"Certainly, she is a vice president of a local organization—"

"The Renaissance League thing," said Drobney.

"Yes," said the FBI man.

"She is at the store. Drobney-Goldstein," said Charlie and pointed out where to walk down the street, and then turn left to Broadway. He couldn't miss it.

Charles Drobney thought he didn't look like an FBI man and he assumed they must have changed like everyone else. They used to wear a virtual uniform of neatly shined cordovan shoes and a fedora. When he had seen several of them in Newport during the war, wearing hats when they didn't need hats on a beautiful spring day like this, he had instantly shut everything down for two critical months, when the U-boat fleet fell back to the Caribbean to do their hunting there. Later, he read in a history book it had been their most successful time of the war.

Sondra Drobney saw the tall man with the dark curly hair and dark eyes wearing the very bankerly business suit and realized she may have been wrong.

She had not expected Agent Oliver to come to the store. She was sure from speaking to the other agent that Unit Chief Oliver felt she was some sort of local nuisance, and that a missed luncheon appointment was some bureaucratic detail that did not require a personal apology but could probably be handled by a computer letter of some sort. She could feel in Agent Wannaker's voice a certain weary and grudging politeness covering a real disregard for her concerns over the door and the quality of Newport itself. A reflection of that new agent in charge.

She had been infuriated. She had phoned his supervisor. She had been told to write a letter. She had written the letter immediately. Uncle Bob, who usually liked to say, "Stick it to 'em" for almost any situation, had commented, "Are you sure you want to send this?"

It was rather pointed. It had escalated the door into the one factor that made the FBI role in democratic America different from that of the Nazi Gestapo and Russian KGB. It elevated the missed luncheon appointment into an act of deceit. The appointment was mentioned; luncheon wasn't. It had been mailed five minutes ago, and he would surely arrest her if she took one of the Tru-Form steel crowbars to the blue postal box at the corner to get the letter out now.

"Hi," she said. "I didn't expect you. I thought you had forgotten me. Us. The door, you know."

"I didn't and I am sorry. There has been a mix-up. I just arrived in Newport and there's still confusion with the office staff." He smiled.

Sondra said that was okay. Had he eaten?

"I forgot to."

"You never had a weight problem," she said. Thin people could forget to eat. She was wearing a vertical-striped shirtdress this day. It covered seven pounds like a major fog.

"Uh, no. I haven't."

"Listen, we have sort of a problem," she said. She smiled.

He listened attentively. She suggested they get out of the store so they wouldn't have to talk with Bob around. She would get a wrap.

As she passed the paints Bob Goldstein whispered, "He's married."

When she passed him going back she stopped to explain this was a function for the Renaissance League; the man represented the FBI.

"I know. He showed me his identification when he asked for you. He's married."

"I love you dearly, Uncle Bob, but there are relationships between men and women other than romantic." She smiled tolerantly.

"He's still married."

She gave up with a sigh. He kissed her on the cheek; told her to be careful. Sondra knew Uncle Bob still thought of her as a vulnerable little girl. He had been the one who said he could force Brandon's father to marry her.

"I don't want him, Uncle Bob," she had said.

"Break his fucking head, I can get people to do that. Bleed him with lawyers. He's a scumbag."

"That's why I don't want to marry him."

"You sound like your father. Can't argue with him either."

What Sondra remembered fondly was not the wild threats Uncle Bob had made, but that he cared. The suggested violence itself she had found repulsive. But Uncle Bob had been there for her. And that was what was important.

When the man left Newport suddenly, Sondra hoped there had been no threats involved. But she was relieved he had not stayed to cause trouble or even be in town, possibly boasting he was Brandon's father.

She took the FBI man down Broadway toward the harbor, trying to explain. He looked somber and reasonable. She told him what she had assumed and then, regretfully, what she had written. She was surprised at how well he was taking it. What she did not know was that she was presenting him a no-lose situation if he should need it.

"Just write a letter explaining how you see the situation differently now. We aren't monsters," he said.

"I would be more than happy to do just that," she said. Her face was alive with everything she said, he noticed; all the nuances showed. Anne's always remained cool, the lipstick never smudged from a line that could have been drawn by a draftsman. Anne also never would let her hair be too free except by design. This woman had a few loose delicate brown curls around her soft white neck. Todd Oliver thought of burying his face in her neck, even while he showed respectful concentration on the history of Newport.

He wondered what would happen if he did that to her neck. The minute she mailed off that second letter, he had established by her own hand that her first evaluations were hasty. Therefore if she were to accuse him of anything such as suddenly grabbing her, throwing her into a doorway, and burying his face in her neck, he could respond that she was unstable.

There was something very pleasant about this woman in a warm sugary oatmeal sort of way. She was not, of course, Anne. And never could be. Anne would sooner gnaw her own hidden palms than bite a showing fingernail. If he were with Anne, the conversation might not be so animated, and the feelings not particularly warm. But he would feel compensated by knowing he was with a stunning woman, and was envied by other men. They did not have to know what went on in his bedroom. No one could ever criticize him for being married to Anne.

"What are you thinking?" she said.

"I was thinking how you could evaluate a second-floor post office door as relevant to the history of Newport," said Todd.

"Oh, I thought your mind was wandering," she said.

"No," laughed Todd Oliver tolerantly.

"Would you like to see Newport? Would you like to see what I mean? It won't take long."

Todd Oliver looked at his watch. He still had an hour until 5 P.M. This was a duty.

They walked down Broadway past Thames Street, which ran along the crowded harbor. She told him that during the height of the America's Cup season, when the summer started, there were so many boats in port, some people claimed you could walk from one end of the harbor to the other on expensive teak.

This day they couldn't see much because of a cool fog that had settled in. It was the Newport fog that would often come in the afternoons.

They walked across America's Cup Avenue to a place where clapboard homes boasted dates from the 1700s. Most tourists did not come here. It was called "the Point" and had once been the home of rum distillers, an angle in the triangle trade in which slaves were brought from Africa to the Indies and were exchanged for the molasses that was made into rum in Newport. Many great old Newport and Providence fortunes were made from that. Ironically, now the mayor of the city was a black man.

From the Point there was a bridge extending to an island where a boxy brick hotel sat like a sharp-angled fort. It was called Goat Island and there had been a torpedo factory operating there during the war.

"Just think. If it blew up from sabotage, the whole city might have gone."

"There was no successful sabotage in all America during the Second World War," said Todd.

"I guess you're proud of that," said Sondra.

Todd shrugged and smiled benignly. He wondered if she had soft delicate secret folds on her body.

"Rumors had it that during Prohibition Charles Lindbergh himself installed airplane engines in the rumrunner's boats, but I don't believe it," said Sondra.

"Why not?"

"Well, I disagree with my father on most major issues, but I agree with him on one fact. If the rumor is really juicy and delicious, it's probably not so. Gossip is so unreliable because it's entertainment."

"Sounds logical. How does your husband feel?"

"I'm not married," Sondra said.

"Oh," he said. "I met your son. I assumed you were married."

He lied. He knew she wasn't married. He didn't know how he knew but he wanted to be certain.

"No," said Sondra. "I'm not married."

He was imagining what she would feel like if he put a hand on her lower back, where, he knew, there was a curve under that blousy dress, when suddenly he felt her grasp his hand to guide him along the street. Skin on skin. He yanked it back.

"I'm sorry," she said. "I just wanted to show you something." She was startled by his suddenness, as though he had been attacked.

"That's all right," he said behind his mask of a face, his desk-bound face, a face that had routed along a thousand memos, ten thousand, countless memos, now very safe in front of his feelings.

She kept a small space between them as she brought him up Touro Street past the first synagogue in America and explained that it was founded by Jews who had escaped the Inquisition. Because of their experiences in Europe, they built an escape route underneath the synagogue, but George Washington told them they would never need it here. They read his letter every year, with a bigger attendance than on Yom Kippur, a very important Jewish holiday, Sondra pointed out.

There was also another synagogue in Newport where those Jews went who felt the Touro Synagogue had become too much of a public monument.

Farther on, Touro Street ran into the beginning of Bellevue Avenue. The first grass tennis courts in America were here, and the Tennis Hall of Fame was here. The Naval Academy had once been here. The Navy was always big in this port city; in fact, it was one of the three rings that made the city.

She pointed up the Avenue toward treetops in the distance. "That's what we call the Avenue, where the mansions are. One ring is made up of the wealthy, the other the city, and the third is the Navy, and occasionally they overlap. They're separate, though." He nodded. He was getting her sense of the city.

She liked the feeling of the Atlantic everywhere in this island city. She liked the old wood homes where 200-year-old planking bowed with time and sea, and brass plaques boasted of age. She liked the way the fog came in on afternoons and how the mists seemed to hang in the Atlantic sometimes for days. She liked the harbor and its noises.

She liked the way the grass struggled in bad soil but flourished in the salt air, and she liked how history never ended here, how people put brass pineapples on their doorways in remembrance of old whalers back from Hawaii who had once put out the real thing on their doorposts to signal when visitors were welcome.

She liked the lobster boats and the men who ran them, and their families, whom she knew. French generals who had served in the revolution were buried here. And she was born here, as was her mother.

"I love this city," she said. "That's why I care about your door. It's not the door. It's a little piece of a place I love."

He wanted to ask if she ever loved a man, instead of a place. When she grabbed his hand again, to cross a street, he let her. She was taking him to a large stone tower.

"I'll let you in on a secret. Lots of people think this is an old Viking fort," she said. Todd glanced down at a plaque that implied such. She brought him inside. It felt cramped. He was surrounded by stone. "This isn't a fort. Would you want to fight from here?"

"No, I wouldn't," he replied. "I feel closed in."

"Of course you do. It's a single tower. It can be easily surrounded. If you want to see a real fort, look at the harbor. Old Fort Adams is designed against an attack—men can be moved around inside it, cannonballs will glance off it. This isn't designed for men to fight from."

"You're right. You're very smart."

"No, Dad told me that when I was a little girl, and he said people's imaginations always seemed to be stronger than their reasoning. Look, where are you going to store food here? Forts have storage, food space, water space, movement space, they just don't stand up like some stone phallus."

"What did the Vikings use it for?"

"The same things the Phoenicians and the Romans and the lost people of Atlantis did on the East Coast along with Vikings, and everyone else they like to think were here once."

"I don't understand."

"Indians built all these structures along the East Coast but it's just not as exciting as thinking the Vikings or Romans did it." He looked around the tower. It did lose some magic, thinking it was just Indians who had lived here.

"My son Brandon gets dizzy when he looks up like that," said Sondra. "Do you have children?"

"No," said Todd. Anne had had two fetuses taken care of that he knew about. The first time, she had said it would interfere with her career, but then the second time, when pressed, she asked him if he would really want to sleep with a woman with stretch marks. When he said yes, she said she didn't believe him. Besides, she said, there was always time for children when it was more convenient.

"No," Todd said again. "I've been married a few years but I don't have a child."

"They are wonderful. You cannot imagine what they are until you have them. It's a chance to love."

"I'm not against children," said Todd. He smiled briefly.

He felt closed in. But he wasn't sure whether it was the pervasive stone around him, or Ms. Sondra Drobney. He looked at his watch. Five o'clock. Time to go.

"I didn't marry Brandon's father," she said. Todd didn't want to know that. He didn't want to know that in this small cramped stone tower. He made an obvious gesture of looking at his watch.

"I am glad now I have Brandon, and I do not have to get divorced."

"I met your son," said Todd. He looked at his watch again.

"Isn't he nice? That's not a fair question for a mother, is it?"

"No," said Todd. It wasn't. He had to go, and she reached for his arm.

"The Elms is open for tourists, it's really beautiful. You can't visit Newport and not see the mansions. The wealthy really have done so much for the city. I am liberal myself except when it comes to our society people. They're special. I mean they are grand. It's rare these days, but they are still that way."

"I do have to go," said Todd.

"Well, thank you," she said, "for going on the tour with me."

"I enjoyed it," he said. "And I really would like to see the mansions sometime."

"When?" she said.

He shrugged. He was very official, very Washington, human, yet a person going about the government's business. He would, he said, let her know. He did have a rather full schedule of Bureau obligations. It was, in so many words, goodbye.

"Goodbye," said Sondra, "and thank you. I'll get that letter off to your supervisor. The second one."

But she did not stop thinking about him, how he seemed so sad in a way. And when she mentioned what a hard rigid life the FBI must have, Dad said people were often happy in jobs that she might not like.

When she had to inform Mrs. Wheaton's secretary of the final roster of Renaissance League members, she put down a guest for herself, just to make the deadline.

She phoned the FBI office and got Todd's clerk typist.

"As vice president of the Renaissance League, I have been invited to attend an affair in the mansions he said he wished to visit. I know that Unit Chief Oliver wants to know about the city in relationship to your office and I had, just tentatively, scheduled him to go to the Renaissance League Ball as a guest of the League."

The clerk typist took down the time and place and said she would forward the invitation to Unit Chief Oliver. Todd Oliver saw his clerk typist drop the message in his in-basket. He ignored it.

He had the professor on the phone and was setting up a meeting, at which the conversations could be transcribed, when he hit a home run by accident.

"Now just a minute," said Professor Tobridge. "I don't know what's happened since the end of the war, and all you fellows are into microchips and satellites and things like that, but the Second World War was not what you think it was. Now you say you have some codebooks that belong to submarines, which raises old allegations about spies."

"That's what I want to talk to you about. Your debriefing of Grand Admiral Doenitz."

"You can't get the files?" said the professor. Todd wondered if the professor wanted to avoid being seen with an FBI man. Attitudes had changed on campuses since the Second World War.

"I can get the files but I would like to present you with some questions for an overview, in a current frame," said Todd.

"What?" said Professor Tobridge.

"Two submarine codebooks were found that raise new questions about old claims about spies."

"German spies," said the professor of German literature.

"Yes," said Todd.

"Who served *der Grossadmiral?*" said the professor, apparently assuming some shared mirth in that reference.

"Yes," said Todd.

"No," said the professor. "No. No. Very doubtful, although he would have loved for us to believe he had pulled off something like that. A boaster he was. He contended even to me that we never broke his code. He wouldn't believe we could. Of course we broke both his and the main German code."

"Didn't he change his code because he believed, or possibly had been warned, that the main German code had been cracked?"

"Oh gracious. Doenitz? No. No. He didn't like Canaris, the head of the German Abwehr, because Admiral Canaris wasn't Nazi enough for him, or whatever. You don't understand what went on over there during the war."

"So it wasn't some spy system that warned him?"

There was a chuckle at the other end of the telephone coming from some Harvard office. "I would be extremely surprised if that were the case, coming from Doenitz or the Abwehr."

For all practical purposes the investigation was over. He phoned Washington before the RA returned.

Todd could feel Cobb bubbling. Todd sounded dry and routine, building up the Navy's case and then pulling the one pin that held all the circumstantial facts together. Grossadmiral Karl Doenitz, who not only would have known, but in the opinion of the old officer would have likely boasted of it, did not indicate he ever had access to such support.

"It seems no matter what you say, you have to say J. Edgar Hoover did one hell of a job here," said Todd.

"By the way, we have a confusing letter here absolving you of something we don't have any record of you being accused of," said Cobb. "From Newport."

"The door," said Todd, picking up the clerk typist's note from the in-basket.

"Yes. I guess I got the apology before I got the complaint. The apology came express. What are you being accused of?"

"I'm not sure, but she wants our exterior to conform to community standards. It seems as though we have a door that differs from the other doors on this floor. We have a reason for that. We had to have a special door installed so conversations couldn't be picked up outside the door. But I didn't tell her that."

"I see. Just an old busybody."

"A nice person, she showed me some of the sights in Newport. She wanted me to understand why a door was important. From her point of view she is right. I wish we could help her."

"Good job up there, Oliver."

"Thank you," said Todd. "I think I will affect some community relations though. No point in leaving the poor RA with some briars."

"She seems to have already apologized."

"That's because she thinks she's getting a chance at the door," said Oliver. He heard a chuckle at the other end of the line. He had a friend now, as much as one could have a friend in Washington.

Should the admiral go at him personally with accusations of whitewash, Todd Oliver would be securely tight in the bosom of the Bureau, having done his job for his country, his Bureau, and the memory of He Who Was. As for the troubles this RA caused him, Todd could ignore them. The man was where he belonged forever, sixty-hour weeks and very little likelihood of rapid advancement. As of now, no likelihood of any advancement.

Todd Oliver phoned Sondra but got her father, who told him Sondra had an apartment and an unlisted number. She did not live there. He had gone to the wrong house previously.

"May I have the number? She's expecting my call."

"Yes," said Mr. Drobney. "Of course."

When Todd got Sondra on the phone he told her he would love to see a Newport party as an escort of the vice president of the Renaissance League, but he could not guarantee her a door, unfortunately.

"Oh, that's all right," she said.

9

It was a night of laughter, stars, and music, and the party hadn't even begun.

Todd could feel it a quarter mile away down Bellevue Avenue as he pulled his car to the right, behind a slow-moving line of cars headed toward the open gates of the Hickories. He could see trees strung with lights above the walls. The ornate roof of the Hickories blazed like a palace ready for a coronation, and the music came softly above it all, above the hum of joy from that magical place behind the walls that he and Sondra Drobney were soon going to be allowed inside of.

He wore a dark evening suit, not a tuxedo, as Sondra had instructed, with a crisp white shirt, black-draped, perfect on the shoulders.

Sondra wore her brown hair up very tastefully. Former frowziness became delicate wisps of light brown curls playing over her pure white neck. Her breasts rose splendidly in her dark red evening gown, graced by a single strand of pearls she had inherited from her mother.

"I still can't believe I am going to a party that begins at 11 P.M.," said Todd.

"I know, isn't it exciting?" said Sondra. "For them it begins earlier. They have dinners among themselves. For someone like Mrs. Wheaton, they just know who is supposed to have dinners for whom. Once we're inside I'm told we're just like anyone else."

"Of course we're just like anyone else," he said maturely.

"That's horseshit, don't you think?" laughed Sondra.

"Yeah," Todd answered and he, too, was laughing.

"There'll be four hundred people there. It's the same number as in the society 400, and the same number that their ballrooms hold. These mansions were made for these parties."

"So we'll be part of the 400."

"Four hundred and five. We're part of the five." Todd laughed at that and then they were at the gates of the Hickories itself.

He did not expect to be nervous. He had met several attorneys general at the Bureau and was often called upon to explain to congressmen and senators the Bureau's position on certain events.

But when a uniformed young man took their car and they followed a line of other people, every man in black, every woman in formal dress, slowly shuffling toward the receiving line, he sensed here was grandeur that belonged in marble palaces. He had seen similar processions in film clips of White House dinners—he even knew Secret Service positions for the President's bodyguards on these receiving lines—but being here with the women in jewels and fine gowns, the soft music playing at a distance behind the red- and white-striped tents where the popping of champagne corks came like the flock call of happy birds, he felt the mansion, and the grounds, and the music become part of him. He could sense he really belonged and felt very much in place like some dream of a royal Persian court out of the mists of the past where suddenly he spoke the language and knew the customs.

A waltz played behind pink marble pillars and two-story windows were opened to make the vast lawns part of the ballroom, part of a perfect gem of an evening.

He felt Sondra squeeze his hand. He was going to drink champagne and dance this evening, serving his country through community relations.

"I'm glad you're with me," she said.

"So am I," said Todd.

At the beginning of the receiving line were the relatives of Mrs. Alexander Wheaton, who, since she had married Alexander Wheaton, was responsible for the Renaissance League, which he had helped found. Sondra explained that the relationship of the Wheatons to the League was like British royalty to their government. They lent prestige.

"You know, I can't tell who the few workers of the League are and who is Newport society," whispered Todd.

"They can," said Sondra.

And then they were next to the first Wheaton in the line, Miss Jane Wheaton, aunt of the late Alexander Wheaton, who was so glad to meet, according to someone whispering in her ear, "Mr. Todd Oliver and Miss Sondra Drobney. So really glad you could come." An upper-class Newport accent exuded those deep regal vowels of the British with just the slightest flavor of neighboring Boston. But it was softer than Boston. Todd could hear the money and influence resonate from the larynx. Mrs. Alexander Wheaton, a stunning blonde from California, Sondra had told him, had been in Newport so long her accent was indistinguishable from her aunt's.

Mrs. Wheaton wore a severe black evening gown with diamonds so large a Newport mansion was the only setting in which they would not appear fake. She wore them not as a captive of wealth, but easily as an adornment to her exquisite presence, the true jewel being that sunlight of a smile in a healthy tanned face.

A stout woman in a lighter evening gown stood behind Mrs. Alexander Wheaton whispering names. She was her personal secretary, Mrs. McAllister, and she acted like an aide-de-camp.

"This is Sondra Drobney, who is a vice president of the League, and one of the more enthusiastic workers," said Mrs. McAllister.

"Oh yes," said Mrs. Wheaton. "Mrs. McAllister tells me you are an historian of sorts, also."

"Very amateur, Mrs. Wheaton," said Sondra.

"We appreciate what you are doing, and I am so glad that you could come tonight," said Mrs. Wheaton as though Sondra's presence made a difference.

"And this is her escort, Todd Oliver from the FBI, who has been so gracious to agree—am I correct?—to have the FBI office conform with the rest of the post office," said Mrs. McAllister.

"We are looking into it," said Todd, "but I can't promise."

"How splendid. We appreciate your joining us in the spirit of this lovely city," said Mrs. Wheaton.

"Thank you," said Todd.

Mrs. McAllister did not mention that Sondra was the daughter of the tradesman who had delivered a package a few days before because it would, in a small way, make Sondra Drobney not quite as acceptable as the other guests. And that would be rude. There was a Newport grace that prohibited rudeness, something that had grown as the great fortunes diminished.

At the turn of the century, a party on this scale could be done with one's servants, who numbered thirty or forty. But now, staffs had been reduced to three and four and sometimes even two and the parties were all catered from the outside. One did not give this sort of party with any less than thirty servers. For one thing, the champagne might be delayed. And if there was one mark of a Newport party it was good champagne always present. Even a Wheaton party could be ruined if the champagne were slow or, worse, used up. The earth might stop spinning on its axis, but in Newport, until it did so, the champagne would always fill the bottom of the glasses.

Todd and Sondra joined the small table where other League volunteers sat. Little sugar cakes made in the form of the Bardwell House were in the center of each table, and clear crystal glasses only waited to be filled. Todd noticed this was a superior brand of imported champagne and estimated they were drinking up to three years of his salary.

He and Sondra toasted and drank and because the glasses were filled again they drank again, and they became as giddy and light as the vintage. He took her by the hand and led her from the tent to the lawn and across it to where crystal chandeliers lit marble floors behind open doors two stories high, the main ballroom of the Hickories. And they danced. He could smell her hair and feel the wonderful contagious joy of people exhilarating in the moment.

It was a time without a future or a past, that eternity of now with only the champagne, the music, Sondra, and the feeling of marble floors beneath their feet. He could have been one of these Newport socialites since birth and an agent in a previous life, a forever away, as was tomorrow. It did not matter that Sondra was not as beautiful as Anne. She was here. And she was happy and she was with him, and tomorrow she would not be any obligation. This was one night that on the morrow would be written off as duty, and then he would be back with Anne. This perfect light and formal night would be gone, like any other dream, disappearing with the opening of the eyes.

They were laughing at everything when Mrs. Wheaton, who had been visiting all the tables, came over to theirs.

"I'm so glad you are enjoying the party," she said after getting the proper gushes of approval.

She sat down next to Todd, and a glass was set down immediately for her, and filled. Sondra could tell by the ever so slight sharpness of her head movements that she was a little tipsy. She put a hand on Todd's arm and was serious.

"Young man," said Mrs. Wheaton. "Tell me who decides what you do."

"My job, sort of. FBI work is the kind of work I do," said Todd. He wondered if he would think that was stupid in the morning. But when Sondra smiled he felt perhaps it was the right answer for the time.

"Yes, well, everyone knows you're here because of some very old code things left over from a war that is over. Now wait, I know you can't say why you are here, so don't say anything. Who decides that you come down?"

"We have procedures."

"If you discovered a British general from the Revolutionary war, assuming he could live that long, would you arrest him?"

"No," said Todd. Everyone at the table was laughing, everyone knowing that for this moment—because Mrs. Wheaton had stopped at their table with them, and at none other so far—they would be talked about in the morning. Somehow they became better because of her presence with them.

"Why wouldn't you arrest him?"

"Well, the British are our allies."

"Well now, aren't the Germans? Isn't that war over?"

"Yes."

"Then why don't you just enjoy our lovely city and let the war that's over be over? It was a terrible war, no one wants to remember it. Mrs. Auchinwell says that it should never have happened, and I don't think it should have happened either."

"It was inevitable," said Sondra.

"Who says?"

"I do."

"Well, you're not a general, are you?" said Mrs. Wheaton.

"I read *Mein Kampf*. It had to happen."

"It was an ugly book by an ugly little man," said Mrs. Wheaton. "Don't you think he was an ugly little man, Todd?"

"I do," said Todd. That was safe.

Mrs. Wheaton sipped at her champagne, put it down, then took a larger sip.

"We all do. And it's good the world is rid of him. Now, who is your boss?" Todd gave her Supervisor Cobb's name.

"And who is his boss?" Todd gave her the name of the director of the Bureau.

"And who is his boss?" Todd gave her the name of the attorney general. There Mrs. Wheaton could finally make contact.

"I know him. He is a lovely man. He was on the same board as Alexander. And he is absolutely the sort of man who doesn't waste time. Alexander said that many times. Many, many times. The sort of man who doesn't waste time. Now, do you think he wants you to waste time here? Do you?"

Mrs. Wheaton finished her glass on that question. It was filled again.

"I'm sure he doesn't," said Todd, suddenly quite aware of how he had to set limits with this powerful woman.

"And isn't investigating a war that is history a waste of time?"

"I'm sorry, Mrs. Wheaton. I can't discuss my work."

"Oh drubble, everybody knows. You're just causing old wounds to be opened. The one thing everyone wants from a war is for it to be over. And that one is over. I am sure our attorney general would like that too."

Todd allowed a silent very small smile.

"Don't you think so?" said Mrs. Wheaton to Sondra.

"No. That wasn't just any war. That was murder that was unlike any other war. They threw people in ovens and drove them into ditches to exterminate them. I don't approve of any war, but that war was different. It was a horror to the whole human race. None of them should be let off."

"I see," said Mrs. Wheaton, apparently hurt. "Well then, that's how you feel. I don't feel that way, and I am sure your young man doesn't feel that way either. Do you, Todd?"

Todd gave another short smile.

Mrs. Wheaton got up, with a small waver in her legs, and went on to the other tables, getting people's opinions in support of letting bygones be bygones, which, of course, everyone was happy to do when honored with a request from Mrs. Alexander Wheaton. There were exceptions: her aunt, Jane Wheaton, and Mrs. Eileen P. Allcott, who thought the Germans were beasts. "With a beast, nevah," said Mrs. Allcott. "They were all beasts."

"Well, you don't know them all," said Bunny Wheaton.

"Well, Bunny, you never take a position on anything," said Mrs. Allcott.

"I don't like to judge people," said Mrs. Wheaton.

"I am not judging. I am just saying they are what they are. And the world knows it."

"You don't know any Germans, how can you say that?"

"I do," said Mrs. Allcott.

"You don't," said Mrs. Wheaton.

"Well, there we are, aren't we?" said Mrs. Allcott, who had never forgiven Elizabeth Wheaton for not condemning Claus von Bulow even before the trial.

"There we are," said Mrs. Wheaton, and her voice cracked slightly with hurt.

"At least I am pleased," said Mrs. Allcott, "that you are at last taking a position on something, even if it is an horrendous one."

The party ended at 4 A.M. with a light breakfast of eggs and breakfast meats and sweet rolls and, of course, more champagne, and, most of all, with everyone still there, which made it a Newport success. Alexander Wheaton would have approved.

Todd held Sondra's hand as they walked to where uniformed young men were bringing up the cars.

"I guess it's over," she said.

"Is it?" he asked. He saw a stand of elegant elms, large and graceful, pruned undoubtedly since they were seedlings, ruffle their leaves in the pleasant Atlantic breeze that had made this place that magical city by the sea.

"The car turns into a pumpkin at dawn," she said.

"It was like that," he said. "It was a fairy tale."

"There's a path by the sea."

"I'd love to walk it. I'd love to be with you . . . some more."

He thought she would not answer. He thought she might return to being the Renaissance League lady and he the government official. Perhaps everything was turning into a pumpkin. The world was a pumpkin, and light-strung trees and marble floors and champagne popping in red-striped tents on park-size lawns would all become in the morning an interdepartmental memo and a crowded field office he was leaving. Then there was the door she was not getting.

"I'd love to go," she said.

"Good," he said. He wished he had more champagne. They were buzzing with it. They drove to the nearby entrance of what she said was "the Cliff Walk." Before the First World War it was where the servants went to be alone.

He felt her hand, very good in his as she guided him down the wide path. The white moon throned itself over the Atlantic, allowing gracious light upon the darkness of the unending water, with a perfect rhythm of the earth, splashing the American shore beneath them. He felt her move to him and her face was raised, and he kissed her.

It lasted no longer than it should, and they walked farther down the path, which descended beneath the cliffs upon which the great mansions were built.

"The servants used to make love down here. They didn't have any other place."

"I do," he said.

"So do I, and if I were never going to see you again, and we had this night, I would end it at my place."

"Do you think it's wrong?" he said.

"It's not wrong, nothing is wrong tonight. Nothing is wrong."

"I am leaving tomorrow," he said.

He was right, she knew. She wanted him. She wanted this fulfillment of the perfect night. She wanted him with her clothes off, and she wanted him badly. She was ready the moment he kissed her.

"No," she said.

"Why not?" he said.

In a world of reasons for anything there was not one good reason, and less as she felt his touch.

"No," she said.

"What?" he said. She felt him kiss her ear, and she moved her face to get more of him, holding him to her as his head lowered, kissing her neck, and then she felt his lips on her breasts.

"No," she said. "Please don't." She didn't move. She had to move away. She had to move before he kissed her nipples, and then he was doing it and she wasn't moving at all.

"Please don't," she said again.

And then he stopped. He was trembling. And then she told herself she was doing it for him, because it was the right thing to do. You didn't end all that champagne and dancing with the great "no" of life.

They did not take off their clothes. She stepped back to where there was grass rising and, very carefully, with his help, lowered her undergarment, and then felt him come to her, quite stately, like the dance, and with all the rhythmed pace of the great Atlantic they joined, with Sondra kissing his cheek and ear, and him kissing hers, and she felt she could smell the moon of life itself. She was still kissing him when he was spent, and he stayed with her.

Slowly they went back up the Cliff Walk in an ending that fit the evening too. He left her at her father's house, with a kiss. They had said nothing since they started the love.

It was a perfect evening. Sondra lay in bed not wanting to sleep because even though he was off to some motel in Middletown he hadn't left her at all. Of course, in the morning, the pumpkins had to be dealt with.

Todd woke up the next morning with his mouth sticky sweet from the champagne and his mind working on how to reduce the negative effects of the night before. Namely, to get away with it.

The first thing he would do would be to have his clerk type a letter to Ms. Drobney at the Renaissance League. The Bureau itself would commend her and the community on the work it was doing. The Bureau would acknowledge its own presence in the community. The Bureau would, in that light, study further adjusting its door in the Newport field office to local community standards, namely, 1930s federalism, for the post office. The Bureau, and here came the important part, was grateful for a chance to experience the formal Newport ball at the Hickories the night before. It had given, as she had promised, a new and fuller perspective on the meaning of Newport. One can hear about things, but to experience them is entirely different and he and the Bureau were grateful not only to Ms. Drobney but to the entire Renaissance League.

Good, he thought. That would take care of the party, and what he was doing there. Nicely. As for screwing the Renaissance League vice president after the dance, Anne didn't have to find out.

Now he knew why he had not acted on those sex thoughts before. Brushing his teeth, trying to get the fruity grape flavor out of his very thick tongue, he knew why. It was messy, and Jesus was it ever complicated.

Anne called that morning. She had tried to reach him the night before but there had been no answer.

A choice now. A: lie about the party. B: lie about only the sex. His head had about twelve pounds too much pressure. His tongue wanted to dissolve with the coffee. A holding lie would do. Say nothing. She didn't know anything.

"I'm sorry. What's up?" asked Todd.

"How long are you going to be in Newport?"

"I should be wrapping up everything in a day or two."

"I thought if you were going to be there longer, I might come up. Well, it is Newport, you know. They are doing condo conversions in a significant manner."

"Sure," said Todd.

"Or if you're coming home, I could go up later."

"My motel is in Middletown. You don't get a spot in Newport in the summer even if you're a cabinet member. And it's a madhouse. Tourists like mosquitoes. Double-density tourists. The boats are nice though."

"I don't care about boats."

"The most beautiful boats on the East Coast," said Todd. Was he pushing it too far?

"No. If we ever get a boat, it will be when we can afford a captain and a crew. Will you be home tomorrow?"

"Tomorrow or the day after."

"Okay. You didn't get a chance to see exactly what they were doing with the condos?"

"No," said Todd.

At the office, with the resident agent and clerk typist less than a telephone cord away, Todd got a call from Sondra, who wanted him to understand on the spot, not later at another time, that she was not that kind of woman.

"Like last night," said Sondra.

"I understand," said Todd, pushing the receiver tightly to his left ear, so that the sound would not carry.

"It happened, but I don't do that with everyone. And, well, I thought you might think that."

"No," he said. Did he think that?

"You can't talk freely."

"Correct. Yes. That is our position," said Todd. The RA was looking at him. Todd locked eyes. The RA turned away.

"But I think it was beautiful," said Sondra. "Better than that. Gloriously wonderful. Glorious. What do you think?"

In trying to find an answer that would give nothing away, Todd stumbled through some phrases that could be taken either way. But in a short moment, he came up with an answer that he realized later was the truth.

"Yes," he said. They had banged upright in the open air against grass-covered rock like two rutting dogs and it was strangely wonderful. Glorious. And somehow cleaner and purer than his marriage-sanctified, community-approved rituals in his Ethan Allen Vermont Colonial double bed at home.

He said it again: "Yes."

"I wanted you to know how I felt. I wanted to know how you feel."

"Well that really doesn't matter, you know. There is a prevailing prior commitment which of course takes precedence. And that is a final thing, you know."

"I knew that. I don't want to marry you."

"Oh, good," said Todd.

"I don't want to take another woman's man. I would never break up a marriage. I want you to know that too."

"Fine," said Todd. His voice floated out quite chilled. He showed his staff that he was interested in the next file, and that this was a boring business.

"I wanted to phone you also because you were almost done, you said, and I didn't just want you to go like that without knowing how I felt. You are going soon, aren't you?" she said.

"Somewhat," said Todd, getting the clerk's notes, preparing for the Harvard professor interview.

"Are you going and when?" she said.

The hangover was gone. Todd thought a moment. "No, I can't go into what has to be done here, but it will take at least two more days."

"Lunch?" she said.

"I don't think so," said Todd. "Something later, if we can."

"Dinner at my place. I'll leave Brandon with Dad."

"I think that would be workable," said Todd, and he hung up.

The clerk was organizing the dictating machine for the trip to Cambridge, Massachusetts.

"I don't think I want to move into that just yet," said Todd.

"Should I cancel the meeting with Professor Tobridge?"

"Yes, I think it would fit in within the next few days, if he would oblige. I want to be certain on this."

"Very good," said the clerk typist. Todd could never had made the meeting with the professor and been back in Newport in time for dinner.

That night he found that making love with Sondra Drobney was not always the same. It was good, but different. He mentioned it.

"It's never the same when it's good," she said. "Only when it's bad."

"You've been around."

"Not that much. Have you?"

"I used to think so," said Todd.

10

BOB GOLDSTEIN was delighted. He thought Charlie should have had an outside activity long ago instead of just walking and reading. Boating was great.

"And I'm glad this time you're going to buy from Lederle. It doesn't hurt to do business with a man like that. I was disappointed that you didn't get Sondra's boat there." Goldstein had said yes for Charlie to an eleven o'clock appointment at the Lederle brokerage on Bannister's Wharf.

"Who called?"

"Lederle's," said Bob.

"His secretary?"

"Yeah."

"Okay, thank you," said Drobney, and spent the morning waiting to go to Lederle's. He thought he might phone and cancel. Yet if he didn't show up, Lederle might go ahead and do something, if he hadn't already. What that man used for a thinking process was beyond him. If he were worth almost a billion dollars as he claimed, why was he still worried about whether someone was listening in on him?

Lederle has to be seventy-two, and he was still climbing. He was a classic case of someone who would make an ideal tank commander and should never be allowed to run a war. He was shrewd for tactics but never understood strategy, namely, what was the purpose of the tactics, namely asking yourself if you win, what are you winning?

It was very possible that M. Hiram Lederle had never asked himself why he wanted to be a member of Bailey's Beach. That kind never seemed to ask the why of things. Excellent cavalry officers, but anyone who ever put one of them in charge of a war should be hanged. A cavalry officer never seemed to understand that battles had purposes other than the battles themselves. They never seemed to understand the why of things, which of course could be of benefit in battle, but a detriment in running a war.

Unfortunately, there was going to be very little he could do to control the almost billionaire M. Hiram Lederle. Nevertheless, he had to see what he wanted.

Charles Drobney drove down to Thames Street in the heat of the tourist crush and parked in the lot next to Lederle's brokerage. It was 11 A.M., precisely. There was no reason to be late or early.

Lederle's secretary wore a light yellow sweater and was waiting for him outside the office, bubbling over about Newport traditions, how Mr. Lederle himself preferred to show a Chris Craft Dayboat to a Newporter than sell a hundred-foot yacht to someone from California. "We should look after our own, shouldn't we?" she asked.

Her name was Harriet Tompkins and the Tompkinses had been in Newport since 1685, but, of course, were not rich.

"There is nothing like the Newport air, is there?" she said.

"No," said Drobney.

Lederle was on the deck of a small powerboat at the end of the pier looking every bit the casual New England sailor with his light blue rugger, white scuffed Top-Siders, and white slacks with the wind blowing his thinning white hair over a sun-freckled scalp. Only the eyes were black.

It was low tide. The boat was way down. Charlie didn't feel safe climbing down the ladder. He thought it was a very small ladder and the iron was slippery and he was wearing street shoes.

"Jump, I'll catch you," said Lederle.

Charles Drobney turned and, holding the cold steel bars of the ladder, climbed down to the boat's railing.

"You've got to trust me," said Lederle. "Just jump the last foot."

Drobney was not about to jump a foot. At sixty-seven, he would break a leg jumping a foot, if not twist a ligament that wouldn't heal for a year.

Lederle reached up and with a powerful motion pulled Drobney off the ladder down onto the deck.

"There," he boomed. The secretary was laughing approvingly at her boss's vigor.

"How do I get back up?" said Drobney.

"How does he get back up he asks," yelled out Lederle to the secretary. "Wait for high tide," Lederle answered for the secretary's benefit.

Not laughing, Charlie sat on the cushions in the back, his hands in his lap, very much like an old dog on a porch waiting to see what the world would do to him before he wasted a move of a muscle. Bones and skin and two eyes, watching it all.

Lederle wanted Drobney up front in the little half cabin so he could show him the controls. Drobney went, making himself as comfortable as he could in a corner. He glanced at his watch.

"Well?" he said, when Lederle pulled the boat out into the channel marked by buoys through the yacht-packed harbor.

"Wait until we are out into the bay. Lots of electronic eavesdropping in the harbor. Husbands, wives, lawyers, legal agencies. The signals are all over. Where there's money, Charlie, there are people who will pay anything to know what money whispers." Lederle smiled. Drobney did not return it.

Drobney watched Lederle wave to people as they engined their way past the long wood pier of the Ida Lewis Yacht Club, and then Fort Adams, which guarded the harbor. During the war a net had been strung from Fort Adams across the entrance to Narragansett Bay to keep submarines from getting in and attacking the fleet anchored up the bay beyond where the torpedo factory was operating on Goat Island. The fort was still there but Goat Island had been turned into a resort with a Sheraton Hotel.

The net, of course, was useless, because no U-boat was going to attack that fleet. It would have been a flamboyant risk of a valuable submarine to achieve a purposeless victory. The U-boats were not in the Western Hemisphere for a naval battle but to cripple the supply line from America to the Continent. Shipping was what the U-boats were after, not its protecting vessels. America could always produce more of them than the U-boats could sink.

The sea air was good, but the boat was small enough to pick up any wake or chop of the bay. Drobney felt banged around. Up ahead he saw the high tower of a sports fishing boat tugging the dark sleek hull of the French syndicate's contender. The Europeans were beginning their trials now. Lederle pointed to the French twelve.

"You know what makes those boats so beautiful, Charlie? Other boats are feminine. Those twelves, dammit, are men. They are dangerous in the water. That's what everyone comes for." Lederle's voice had the rich round cadence of the wealthy. He smiled like any Yankee millionaire born to the water and sharing his wisdom with a guest.

Drobney did not smile back. He knew what anyone could know about the twelves who did not race them. It was not men and women boats, but a safety factor differential. Where other boats had safety factors of at least 6, which meant all the parts could take six times the stress listed for them, the twelves, in a craze for speed and maneuverability, sailed with a safety factor of 1.5 or 1. A wrong gust of breeze could snap a mast. A race could be lost because of a wrong choice of sail on a certain day.

The America's Cup series was so much like war. You could be in the middle of it and only guess what was going on. As for onlookers, even if they were told what the tactics were, most wouldn't know what they were looking at. So much like war, thought Drobney, looking over this bay he knew so well. He doubted most of the syndicates that raced these boats actually understood why they were doing it in the first place. So much like war.

"America is so strong in this race. You know why, Charlie? Technology, they say. But I say we put the best manhood in the water, a will to win. That's what makes nations great," said Lederle, slowing the engine and turning for the serious discussion.

"Does this mean we're friends now because you share your views of yachting? I am not interested in your global wisdom. Why did you do something so unnecessarily foolish as to make contact with me? What could have inspired you to do something so foolish?" said Drobney.

"I want to keep you safe. I want to help you. And I gave you your chance, and you failed."

"Really? How?"

"You haven't kept the crew in line. You said everything would pass over if everyone kept quiet. I let you have your little command. You played commander. And it's coming apart."

"Really? How?"

"I had the distinct pleasure of attending the Renaissance League Ball. Of course, I did not know everything that went on at that ball, every corner of it. But what did disturb me was what others noticed, which led me to find out things. I have not survived by letting things handle themselves."

"Get to the point," said Charlie.

"I know about Mrs. Wheaton. I want you to tell her to keep her mouth shut. She has been conducting a very obvious campaign to have this investigation by the FBI quashed. She doesn't know what she is doing but she is making scenes, Charlie."

"And you want me to . . . ?"

"Tell that bitch if she doesn't keep her mouth shut, someone is going to put her away in her own mansion."

Drobney was quiet. He watched the pleasure boats trail out into the Atlantic after the jewel-sleek hull of the twelve. Gulls waited by the little powerboat as though they were going to get fish heads.

"And tell me, Harry, with what should I threaten Mrs. Drake-Hume, Mrs. Allcott, Mrs. Grayson, and the other ladies of the Avenue? I mean, if I am threatening Mrs. Wheaton, why exclude the others from your charms. Is that how you are making your way to Bailey's Beach?"

Drobney laughed contemptuously. Suddenly, with power and speed, Lederle's large hands were at Drobney's throat, the thumbs squeezing off air.

"You will do what you're told, little man. I've had enough of you." Lederle's face pushed close to Drobney's and the two eyes locked. Drobney felt darkness close around the edges of the world, and then he did the only thing he could do, he smiled. He let a smile cross his face as he looked into M. Hiram Lederle's face, smiling as his head pounded, and the air went out of his blood.

Lederle let him go.

"Jesus Christ, Charlie, you would have let me kill you, wouldn't you. You crazy bastard." Lederle supported Drobney with both hands until he could get him up on a small stool.

"I still may die, Harry, if I don't take my pills. Do you have some water?"

"Brandy."

"No. Water."

"I'll look. I never knew you were a lunatic."

"If you don't have anything constructive to say, let's go back now."

Lederle found a bottle of carbonated water.

"I can't drink it. It's got salt in it," said Charlie.

He took two Ismelins with a bottle of orange soda whose label did not list salt.

"If you had succeeded in killing me, you would have done yourself in. You don't know who will turn you in, you don't know who will go at you. You can be certain of one thing, my death is your end."

"Why are you so fucking stubborn, Charlie? Give up the command. Let me help. I'm a goddamn billionaire. I'll give you a million dollars. Do you want a million dollars, Charlie?" pleaded Lederle, his large hands palm upward. "What is this shit? What do you want?"

"Stay in place. Everything is fine."

"Charlie, I know Bunny Wheaton was one of us. The woman is notorious for never taking a position on anything, and suddenly she pursues this thing like she has pursued nothing in her life. I am not just talking about her going on at length with the FBI unit chief sent into town. I am talking about her phoning people. Making noise."

"I regret this woman's actions unsettle you, Harry, but our position is still clear. Stay in place."

"She came to Newport in 1938, Charlie. I came here then. You came here then. So did the others."

"And all of a sudden you are going to conduct some study to find out who came to Newport in 1938. You don't think that will attract attention? Harry, will you please let the FBI investigate in its own way."

"I can keep the others in line for you. I can keep her in line for you. I can make you safe."

"Thanks for the water," said Drobney.

"Would you take one hundred thousand dollars if I just gave it to you in an envelope? Just take it. In an envelope, like you found it lying on the ground, Charlie?"

"Our business is not doing business," said Drobney.

But before they passed Fort Adams on their return, Lederle let Drobney know the woman's life was in her hands. He was shockingly crude.

"Tell our Mrs. Wheaton if she doesn't keep her mouth shut, I am going to shoot off her tits."

Charles Drobney did not dignify that threat with an answer. Harry Lederle was still in the man no matter what he called himself now, how he spoke or dressed or acted in public. Drobney looked away to the shoreline of mansions like a dozen Parthenons set along the magnificent cliff.

The tide was up when they docked.

Charles Drobney did not go directly to Elizabeth but spent the next two days making sure he spent time with four other women customers, visiting their homes, on one pretext or another. When he did arrive at the servants' entrance of the Hickories, his blood pressure was 200 over 130, and he was balancing between an overdose of Ismelin and a stroke.

"Mrs. Wheaton said the other TV was broken. I don't know how. I think perhaps it was that I didn't explain fully how it worked. I've got another one just in case the set was really broken as she said," stated Drobney. He stood in the entrance with the package at his feet.

"Oh, I'm sorry. Did she call you?" asked Mrs. McAllister, looking worried.

"Yes," said Drobney.

"She is not feeling well. I wonder if you would just wait here a moment. I am not sure she is seeing anyone."

Drobney waited. He was not sure delaying the visit, seeing others, and bringing another portable television would definitely throw off Lederle. All he could hope for was that it might support a doubt, and that doubt might delay a precipitous action. Lederle could not have survived without some caution.

Mrs. McAllister returned, speaking in hushed tones.

"She will see you, but please be brief. As a favor to me."

Apparently, he looked as though he was in need of help because Mrs. McAllister carried the television package for him. She commented on seeing Charlie's daughter at the ball, and how lovely she looked, and what a good job she did for the League.

They took a different passage this time, and the plain gray door opened to an expanse of plush pink, deep rugs, diaphanous drapes, walls of gracious fabric, and a large canopied bed. He was in her boudoir. He hesitated, and then entered.

Elizabeth, in her nightgown, lay perched in the bed with a silver ice bucket containing an open bottle of champagne. A single pink rose rested on an ivory end table. Her eyes were puffy and red, and her hair needed a brushing. Her confident smile lied. She had been drinking heavily.

"Amy, I will see to this alone," said Elizabeth.

But Mrs. McAllister, soberly trying to sustain propriety for her mistress, said she would like to see how the television operated also.

"Oh, Amy, don't be such a drudge. I am a grown woman, and this is a grown man, and I feel perfectly proper being alone with him for this brief moment."

"I would like to stay," said Mrs. McAllister softly.

"Don't be such a bully. Don't be such a mother. One mother is enough for anyone. Don't you think so?" she said, looking at Drobney.

Thank God, thought Drobney, *she didn't call me Charlie.*

Mrs. McAllister gave him a somber look before she left that let him know she expected him to leave as quickly as possible and to protect Mrs. Wheaton's interests even if champagne made her a bit careless at this moment.

"Oh, Charlie, I am glad you are here. Everything is going so well. I have spoken to the senator and to Puggy Wentworth over at the Justice Department. Both of them agree that this investigation is silly. Do you know that? And do you want to know something else? Sit down."

"Elizabeth," said Charlie, standing by the bed. "You have got to stop this."

"Wait, Charlie. Wait. Do you know, the FBI itself didn't want to do this investigation. Thought it was silly. That is what I hear from important people. Important people, Charlie."

"Elizabeth, you shouldn't be making these inquiries."

"You don't understand. Everything is being taken care of. The top people think like I do. They really do. I don't even know who got this thing started in the first place."

"Elizabeth, listen to me."

"I'll listen," said Elizabeth. She drained the champagne goblet and held it out for Charlie to pour a refill. He did so somewhat clumsily. She offered him a sip from the glass. He shook his head. She reached for the pink bell cord. Drobney grabbed her hand.

"What are you doing?" he asked.

"Getting you a glass."

"You will not drink with a hardware store owner."

"Oh, Charlie, why are you doing this to me?"

"Elizabeth, I am here because some very dangerous people know you are making inquiries. To those very dangerous people you have exposed yourself."

"I saw your daughter with the FBI man. Do you know that he is the one investigating us? Did you know that?"

"It doesn't matter. Ignore it. That's what I am saying. Let it be. Do nothing. Never mention this again to anyone at anytime," said Drobney. "If this room is bugged, and it might be, we are both dead now. Do you know that?"

"Do you think it's bugged?"

"No, because I think he expects you to be reasonable. You are endangering yourself, Elizabeth. All your social contacts are not working."

"How do you know?"

"What am I doing here, Elizabeth? How did I find out, Elizabeth? How does a hardware store owner find out people are beginning to suspect you?"

The confidence went with tears into the champagne. "Oh, Charlie, why are they doing this to us? If I were a real Elizabeth, this would never have happened to me. I'm beautiful. I'm lovely. Why can't they let me alone, Charlie?"

"Elizabeth."

"This does not happen to an Elizabeth."

"Shhh. Shhh," said Drobney. He patted her hand reassuringly. She yanked it away.

"You know who gets this shit thrown in her face? Always thrown in her face! Gusti Kroeninger. Gusti Kroeninger is just your friendly little Bavarian fuck."

"Elizabeth."

"Charlie, I know. Don't tell me no. I know. Elizabeth Boswell is beautiful and marries Alexander Wheaton. Gusti? Well, she is a pretty lay. 'Did you see the girl I screwed?' That's Gusti. Gusti is the one who gets it all taken away from her, Charlie. Gusti at a more golden age gets arrested, huh? They are not making me a Gusti Kroeninger again, ever. That's what they're doing to us, you know."

"Elizabeth."

"Call me Gusti."

"Elizabeth, that is a name you can't even think anymore."

"Charlie, why does this have to happen to us. I'm so scared. I'm so alone. I don't have a friend in this world."

"Elizabeth, I know this is hard. Stop phoning. Stop talking to people about this. Be quiet. And stop drinking."

"Hold me. Gottzy, hold your Gusti."

"I can't."

"Am I too old?"

"You're never too old," said Charles Drobney, looking only at the eyes and only at the tears. And she put out her arms, begging. And he was crying too. He could not hold her now. He put his arms around her. He held her and he rocked her and he kissed her cheek and tasted the salt from the tears.

"Gottzy," she whispered. "I love that name. It's better than 'Charles.' Gottzy."

"Elizabeth."

"I am not Elizabeth Boswell. If I were, I would not have any problems. None of them. I am Gusti Kroeninger. Gusti Kroeninger, drunken Gusti."

"Shhh," said Charlie. He rested on top of her, his cheek to hers, comforting her, he in his store chinos and she in her chiffon.

The deadly problem was that if she were still Gusti Kroeninger, he would not even have had to come here. She would know what to do. Gusti Kroeninger knew how to get along in an unfriendly world. Elizabeth Wheaton had been taught by forty years of protective wealth that unpleasantness in her life meant that the world was not working correctly. Too many people had been too willing to remove the burrs and thorns of reality for her for too many years now. They had made the natural feelings of vulnerability a vestigial attitude.

"Do you dream about Gottherd Hauff? Do you ever, Gottzy?"

"Yes, sometimes. Rarely, now. Not since my daughter was born. No, I don't, I guess."

"I dream about Gusti. It's a nightmare. Is Gottherd a nightmare to you, Charlie?"

"No," said Charles Drobney. "Gottherd Hauff was not a nightmare to me."

"Why not?"

"Because he was a good boy, I guess."

"He was American, you know. He was so American, and Charles Drobney wasn't. Isn't that funny, Gottzy."

"That's funny," said Drobney with great pain and sadness. She felt so good pressing into him, so good to give comfort. He kissed her ear and he knew he shouldn't.

"I ruined that good American, eh Gottzy?"

"No, it wasn't you. Did you think all these years it was you?"

"Yes. You loved me. Didn't you?"

"Oh yes, I do. I do."

"How did we get into this thing. How did you, you so American, little virgin pure boy, get into it."

"I wasn't a virgin," said Charlie. "Did you think I was a virgin?" He could feel her chuckle. "I really wasn't," he said. He felt her kiss his cheek. "Really I wasn't." She bit his ear.

"You know," he said, lying fully dressed in his store-bought chinos on the pink silk bedclothes with his arms around his love, "it's a good thing you didn't order champagne for me, people might start to suspect we're intimate."

He felt her body convulse with laughter, and his tears became laughter.

"You know, we can be killed. Really," he said.

"If you must die, this fun is worth dying for, Gottzy. You know, I think now maybe I was happier as Gusti Kroeninger. I think I was."

"Elizabeth, you were always happier with what you were not."

"That's not so."

"It's true. When you were in America, you wanted Germany. When you were in Germany, you wanted America."

"That's not true. All I ever wanted was to be with someone I loved, under the good sky, with no worries."

"That's not an all," said Charles Drobney. "They were the happiest days of my life, ever. Joyous. There was only one thing wrong."

"What was that?" asked Elizabeth Wheaton.

"I thought they would go on forever. You think when you have them, they are eternal. The world makes sense then."

He was kissing her, and he tasted the champagne in her mouth, and felt her hands work up to his head, and then down his chest, unzipping his fly.

But he was on too many units of Ismelin and it had taken its toll.

"I'm too old," she said. "You don't want me."

"You're never too old. I am on medication."

"Then hold me. It's still beautiful, Gottzy, my Gottherd. Hauff, my Gottzy."

"Gusti, I can't protect you anymore."

"I know."

"But I have not lost my mind. I do know how to think."

"You always did."

"I will be happier, I will sleep better, if you do what I say. Please, dear. Please, darling. Please. Please. I beg."

"Give me a night."

"I can't. The longer I spend, the worse it will be."

"Give me an hour. Just hold me for an hour."

"Will you stop making calls then?"

"Yes."

"I want the hour too."

"It's as good as then," she said.

"It's always as good as then," he said, and he was crying.

The hour was over like the good days they both remembered when she had shown him how incredibly blue the sky over Bavaria was, when he was sealing the fate of his life, and Germany was sealing the fate of millions.

"I never looked at the skies," he said and, getting a promise from her that she would reach out for no one anymore, gave her a last kiss. It was better than the first. On the first kiss, he didn't love her.

He lifted himself from the bed filled with the presence of her perfume, and the love he had, and the sadness on her face.

"Goodbye, Elizabeth," he said.

"Goodbye, Charlie," she said.

And then he left by the servants' entrance.

As she watched him go, she thought how poor he looked, how humble he looked, and thought that perhaps he was wrong about the situation. After all, he didn't know important people.

It was he who needed protection, poor dear.

She rang for more champagne, and with two glasses she was ready to get a definite promise from the state's junior senator that they were going to stop all this nonsense about spies in Newport.

11

MRS. ALEXANDER Wheaton was shot to death in her bedroom without ever getting to Bailey's Beach or the Ida Lewis Yacht Club or the Clambake Club, without even beginning anything of the season except her ball, which was, of course, a success.

The first thing everyone said was "No." The next thing everyone said was "Why?" And what they did not say is "Is it one of us? One of our friends?" After the Claus von Bulow tragedy that would have been too much.

No, they were told, it wasn't. Dark People. Two young men. No one knew whether it was one of Bunny's lovers. But Bunny never did that in Newport. Some people said Bunny did have her fun at times, but she knew where and when. Someone else said, "Yes, anywhere, with anyone." But that was just a witticism.

She had been a proper wife to Alexander, and had been a Wheaton as well as anyone from California could be a Wheaton, and she never caused trouble. If she were to cause anyone touble, Alexander's aunt, Jane Wheaton, would have been the first to notice, but Jane had said she always felt the girl had been proper. She learned well and was studious, though she liked the outdoors a bit too much, but Alexander had not made a bad choice, or at least not as bad a choice as it appeared at the beginning. Not to say Alexander could not have done considerably better. But she was exquisite—one had to say that—and he could have done worse.

The searing question that emerged was had Alexander really

made a mistake. Some were now beginning to wonder. After all, why was she killed, and who had let the killers in? Could they enter any home? Did servants have to be warned? Should there be people with weapons protecting the homes?

At Bailey's Beach, the scandal of the season came with the first good warm bathing water. M. Hiram Lederle, a decent sort of local yacht broker, who always seemed ready to help people, was asked what he thought of it all.

"Very sad," he answered. He was on subscription, and people often treated that like a trial, but everyone knew one really had to be totally out of place, and rude, not to be made a member after subscription. He really could have taken a position on this tragedy. After all, everyone else did.

Mrs. McAllister could not stop crying as she tried to tell the detectives what had happened.

"They wouldn't stop. They wouldn't stop. They wouldn't stop," she kept saying. She was trying to describe how Mrs. Wheaton's chest had been shredded by two young men, no more than twenty-five years old, who shot these little guns at her. "They didn't even have a loud noise. Just crack, crack, like goddamn little plates breaking. Oh Jesus mercy. They wouldn't stop."

The little guns were .22s, she was told. One of the detectives got her a glass of water.

"I didn't know who they were. They just looked as though they belonged. They just walked in like that. Through the front door."

"Were they her lovers?"

"I never saw them before."

"Where were you?"

"In her bedroom. I had been organizing some thank-you notes for letters for some people in Washington."

"And you had been on vacation?"

"We just came back. She begged them to stop. They were shooting at her, my God, just shooting away at her chest like it was work and she said, 'Enough, enough.' "

"She said, 'Enough, enough' as they were shooting?"

"My God yes. You could see the nightie pop up as the bullets went in. My God. Jesus. You could see the nightie pop up. Like jumping beans popping up from her. God."

"What did you do?"

"I tried to run away. I wanted to get out of there."

"Why didn't you?"

"They were using the door to leave. God, she just kept begging them, telling them, 'Enough, enough.' She knew she was going to die. She knew that. And they didn't stop."

"And what did you do?"

"I tried to phone for an ambulance, but the telephone lines were down and it's such a long driveway. Oh God, they wouldn't stop."

"Did she die right away?"

"Nooo," sobbed Mrs. McAllister, and she collapsed in tears. The detectives waited for her to recover.

"What happened?" they asked finally, telling Mrs. McAllister apologetically they had to ask. Both detectives knew her parents, one had even known her and dated her when she was younger.

"She lay there on the bed, and her chest just kept pumping her life out of her," said Mrs. McAllister, staring at nowhere, her mouth filled with her own tears, her eyes so very wide, and her body so very rigid. They were in the kitchen because she was not going back up to that room.

"And then she mumbled, and I went over to her and listened. But I didn't want to get her blood on me. I didn't want her blood on me, so I didn't get close."

Mrs. McAllister was sobbing again, heaving, tearing, banging her fists against her knees. "I didn't want to go near her."

"What did she say?"

"Foreign it sounded like. I don't know."

"What exactly. The sounds."

"Dremel something nesht . . ."

"Yiddish, Polish? What?"

"I don't know. I don't know. I don't know. I don't know. I don't know."

Mrs. McAllister was given a sedative, and Mrs. Wheaton was taken in a black rubber bag from the elegant pink bedroom to the morgue. Both detectives knew that .22 bullets traveled around the body. The coroner could be removing them from an ankle or skull. The only thing unprofessional about the hit was that the two did not put the bullets in the brain. Everything else—the escape, the businesslike attitude, the coldly coming right through the front door and then into the bedroom, knowing where it was, knowing where the phone lines were, and knowing what the traffic was going to be like on Bellevue Avenue at that time of day—was purely professional. There was also another aspect of a professional job, one that Mrs. McAllister could not understand, the reason why they didn't kill her even though she might be able to identify them at some trial. It was a professional job and there was virtually no chance they were going to be caught, let alone brought to trial. This just did not happen with professional jobs. They were out of state by now, maybe even the country. Mrs. McAllister would have only been in danger if she had tried to stop them. And she hadn't, which was why she was alive now, and so wracked with guilt.

Because of that guilt, Mrs. McAllister agreed to undergo hypnosis to re-create the words Mrs. Wheaton had spoken.

The sentence recorded on tape sounded like: Dye—himmul—nished—sindblow—genunguh.

The most probable translation was: "The skies are not blue enough."

The language was German.

Charles Drobney passed out in the rear of his hardware store and was rushed to Newport Mercy Hospital three blocks up Broadway.

It was not, thank God, a stroke. Bob Goldstein himself rushed him to the hospital because he wasn't going to wait for a damned ambulance.

He got Charlie to his car and to the hospital within three minutes, screaming for oxygen and a doctor and he did not stop screaming until there was help with Charlie. There was no politeness about this, no propriety. Bob Goldstein was going to get Charlie the fastest help possible if he had to put a screwdriver into someone's head to do it.

Nurses were telling him that yelling would not get help faster, but he knew they were there that quickly because he was yelling. When a doctor arrived Bob stayed with Charlie. The doctor, a young Texan, wanted Goldstein to leave. Then Goldstein promised to be quiet. They gave Charlie an intravenous and put him in a semiprivate room because there were no private rooms.

Bob waited as Charlie drifted in and out of sleep. When Charlie's eyes were focusing, Bob told him everything was going to be all right.

"How are you feeling, friend?" said Bob.

But Charlie didn't answer. He seemed locked inside himself. "Everything's okay. It's okay, Charlie. It's okay. Don't worry about anything. I'll take care of everything. You know that, huh?"

Charlie's doctor wanted to know what had brought this on, and Bob honestly told the doctor he knew of no binges or special worries that would raise Charlie's blood pressure like that. Charlie would take an occasional muffin with salt, but that was it as far as Goldstein knew. They had just chatted that morning about the Red Sox, the shooting on the Avenue, and that the Australian twelve looked awfully good this year, according to everyone.

"This is serious. His pressure has gone through the roof."

"Will he survive?"

"He is so close to a stroke," said the doctor. "He hasn't had one yet. A miracle."

"Which means?"

"Either way," said the doctor. "We can prevent a stroke here, but what brought it about is what we don't know and if we don't know it, how the hell are we going to treat it? Has he been taking his pills?"

"Yes, as far as his daughter and I know."

Charlie was resting comfortably when Bob looked in. He thought he saw tears in his friend's eyes, but he wasn't sure.

"Please," said Bob in a whisper. "Please don't leave me, Charlie."

He phoned Sondra and was very careful to explain Charlie was out of danger now, but she should get to the hospital right away. He had passed out. And he was under sedation now. He could take Brandon, but he was going to wait at the hospital with Charlie.

"I'll get the sitter," Sondra said. She phoned Todd, and her voice was shaking. "I can't make it for dinner," she said. "Dad's in the hospital. I don't know when I can see you."

"I may be leaving this evening. I'm not sure now."

"I want to see you."

"When?"

"When I know."

"I will be here all afternoon. Phone here. Let me know how he is. All right? How are you feeling?"

"Scared. Sick."

"Phone me," said Todd.

He didn't know what to say. He shouldn't have asked that question. Wasn't the affair over? Wasn't the case over? Wasn't everything over? Maybe nothing was over. Why was he thinking about her at all? The Newport *News* had called. The Providence *Journal* had called, and then the Associated Press called, and there were calls in from Boston and New York and Washington. Someone had put together the codebooks, Elizabeth Wheaton's last words in German, and the Wheaton fortune.

By the afternoon editions, there were Nazis in Newport and the Boston Field Office press relations officer was screaming for something out of Newport or Washington because this was major national news.

"It's gonna be bigger than the von Bulow murder," said RA Wannaker. "You couldn't get a table at Tuesday's during his trial."

The word from Washington was that there was no way they could get press cooperation for quiet on the spy angle now. There had to be some kind of statement. Washington bucked it to Boston, which sent it right back to Todd Oliver. RA Wannaker went happily out to lunch. The clerk typist worked through lunch answering calls, taking down names and numbers, promising someone would get back soon. This gave Todd time.

They got a three-way secured hookup between Cobb in Washington and the press relations officer with clearance in Boston. Sondra was trying to reach Todd again. She gave a message to the clerk that said if she wasn't at home she would be at the hospital. Todd signaled he was not to be disturbed.

"We can't 'no comment' this thing much longer," complained the press relations officer in Boston.

"Why not?" asked Oliver.

"You are there for the codebooks," said PRO Boston.

"I am investigating," said Oliver.

"Didn't you just finish?" said Supervisor Cobb.

"I did," said Todd.

"Then we announce it," said Supervisor Cobb.

"We say there's no connection then?" said PRO Boston.

"This is a local murder. We don't investigate local murders. It is not a federal crime to kill someone unless in so doing you deprive them of their civil rights. This is not a civil rights case either," said Todd.

"You're there investigating spies in Newport, or possible spies that the Bureau missed, a sixty-five-year-old woman is shot fatally, speaks her last words allegedly in German after she makes a pest of herself saying there should be no investigation, and we say what?" said PRO Boston.

"Where did you get that hearsay?" asked Todd.

PRO Boston yelled, "From the fucking Boston fucking *Globe* this afternoon. With our 'no comment at this time.'"

"I see your difficulties," said Todd.

"Are you calling this investigation finished?" PRO Boston sounded furious.

"I don't think so now, no," said Todd.

"Are we going to look into that killing?" asked PRO Boston.

"We have not been invited by the local police. It is a local crime," said Todd.

"We are allowed to request to look into it if we think it is pertinent to other investigations," said PRO Boston.

"It is press speculation that connects it. Nothing that I have been informed of by the RA who coordinates with the local police specifies any relationship to the current investigation," said Todd.

"Do you really want to call it closed?" said PRO Boston.

"No. But look, how do we know about this killing? I believe it sounds like a professional job. That's what the first edition had this afternoon, here in Newport . . . that it was a professional killing . . . professionals. That's what they say," said Todd.

"Not the *Globe*," said PRO Boston.

Supervisor Cobb broke in: "I cannot believe I have two agents in Newport and we are getting our information from the newspapers. Are we the FBI or a clipping service? What's going on here, Todd?"

"I'm trying to work out our position, sir," said Oliver.

"Well, who isn't?" said Cobb.

"If it is a professional job, then that's hardly spies. They used .22s, didn't they? It was professional, wasn't it? That is something that is certainly not some Nazi submarine coming up out of the sea with people with Lugers and such," said Todd.

"What are you getting at?" asked Cobb.

Todd said, "I think there is an indication in the way she was murdered that this was professional. Therefore, it could very well be some other motive. You see?"

"Some other motive because the sort of people who killed her kill for other motives," added Supervisor Cobb.

"Yes," said Todd. "That's it. That's what I think."

PRO Boston asked, "Which is what? What's the press position?"

"We're looking into it."

"Do we think it is connected to the codebooks?" asked PRO Boston.

"We are looking into it."

"So," said PRO Boston. "We are continuing an investigation. And we have not ruled anything out or anything in."

"Yes," said Oliver. "An FBI investigation."

"All right."

"Good," said Cobb.

"And while we are officially investigating," said Todd, "I think we ought to look for something on the hit men."

"That's a professional hit. How many of those do we nail?" asked PRO Boston.

"Not to a prosecution but for information. Of course, if we do luck out with prosecutable information, then of course we have the hit men," said Oliver.

"And they are ours," said Supervisor Cobb.

"Are they ever. And hit men are not spies," said Oliver.

"Yeah. Look, I think there is some Navy Department element in this also," said PRO Boston.

"I will handle that. It's a big thing. Goes back to the Second World War," said Oliver.

Supervisor Cobb stepped in on that. "Haven't gotten over that Krauts sailed their ass off. It's a ton of shit. I'll tell you from the word go. Right, Oliver?"

"Absolutely. There is an old admiral behind it and he's getting pissed off and getting other people to be pissed off and you're absolutely right, it's a ton of shit."

"All right, so that's where the shit comes from," said PRO Boston.

"That's where it comes from. But I have something from the old OSS that says the possibility of spies is highly doubtful. Impossible, if we can use that word. So we are all right. In the end we are going to be all right," said Oliver. "I want to get it more fully, though."

"You don't have it fully?" asked Supervisor Cobb.

"Just a statement that he debriefed the German admiral who

would have sent the codebooks, and the old bastard didn't have a crew here."

"Good," said Cobb. "Nail it."

"Going to get it full with clerk typist and a tape recorder and then maybe you as the press relations officer for Boston might want to use him," said Oliver.

"Probably," said PRO Boston. "But make sure you get your answers first and make sure there aren't going to be any questions that foul us up."

Supervisor Cobb wanted Oliver to stay on the line and PRO Boston to get off. PRO Boston requested another person for the press situation.

"Take him from New York," said Cobb.

PRO Boston wanted to know if Supervisor Cobb had anyone else. In the FBI, getting someone from the large New York Office meant a wild card. NYO often sent just the people who didn't fit in as smoothly as others. Therefore, NYO personnel were invariably the best and the worst.

"If you want someone now, it's NYO," said Cobb.

"All right. New York is fine. Thank you," said PRO Boston. He clicked off the line. Supervisor Cobb had special information about procedures in Newport.

"Oliver, we are getting some lines from cabinet-rank people coming through the Justice Department and all that. If you do investigate this shooting, and it looks like you will now, there are some people who want to talk to you," said Supervisor Cobb.

"In what way?" asked Oliver wearily.

"No, nothing like that. Nothing like giving you instructions or anything. If you are going to talk to people in that society element there in Newport, there are names of several people who want to talk to you."

"Are you serious?" asked Oliver.

"They want to be called on. They want to be involved. I told the attorney general that we couldn't leave people out of it if we were going to investigate, and he told me it wasn't that. They knew the woman and they had opinions. They are powerful people in that society."

"They call it the Avenue."

"And, Oliver, I am glad we have you there at this time. Sometimes you may get the feeling that I don't altogether think of you as a real agent because I come from the RAs and hate this bureaucratic horseshit. But, we are all Bureau."

"I always assumed you knew the job I did, sir," said Oliver in a flat voice. But it felt good.

The secure three-way ended. Oliver told his clerk to have all calls automatically answered by the Boston press relations officer, and that she should go to lunch.

When she was gone he phoned Sondra. She was at the hospital, and the call went up to her father's room.

"I'll be here tonight," he said.

"I'm going to be here at the hospital and then I am going to my apartment with Brandon. Brandon will be with me."

"Oh."

"Do you want to come?"

"Yes."

"Thank you."

"I want to come."

"Okay. I've got to hang up."

There was a knock at the door of the office. "Come back later," Todd called out.

"Is that you, Oliver?" It was Admiral O'Connell's voice.

"Is that you, Admiral?"

"Yes."

"Come in."

Admiral O'Connell was wearing a dark blue suit that had to cost a thousand dollars the way it set to his body, breathing executive power. Admiral O'Connell pulled a small plain wood chair next to Oliver's desk. His large frame did not fit with comfort, but he sat down anyway. He put an elbow on Oliver's desk. Oliver waited. Admiral O'Connell locked his eyes with Oliver's. Oliver did not move. The admiral did not move.

"Hello," said Oliver, finally.

"Hello," said Admiral O'Connell. "I just flew back up from Washington."

Oliver nodded.

"I heard all these rumors that you were completing your investigation and it was a ghost hunt. That's what I heard."

"Well obviously I haven't completed it. I am here, Admiral."

"So am I. I will be at the naval commandant's headquarters at the War College. I'm his guest. I am staying awhile."

"I wish I could enjoy it like you, sir, but I have to work," said Oliver. He gave the admiral a smile on that one.

"Fuck you, too, sonny," said Admiral O'Connell. Todd Oliver felt good all over.

The admiral left the office.

"Dad, what is a Gusti?" Sondra Drobney sat by her father's bed. She asked him the question when he seemed to focus. He had said the word twice.

She was crying. She had been praying. She hadn't prayed since her mother had tried to teach her by explaining one got things from God by praying and then doing what you were told to do.

She had stopped praying at twelve, but now she was praying again that her father not die. And then she thought if God were indeed good or even existed He wouldn't believe hypocrites like her. She just couldn't lose him. She couldn't live without Dad in her life.

She knew someday it would happen. Someday it would have to happen. But not this day. Maybe a hundred years from now. Maybe even next year, if next year weren't so close.

Somehow in her prayers she tried to explain to a God she did not altogether believe was there that Dad never had much of a life. Always seemed to do the decent thing. Never hurt anyone. Never went anywhere, and God shouldn't take anyone who never traveled, as though there were now some code of justice that one shouldn't die if he only spent a life in a hardware store, faithful to an unloving woman, and never traveled. God would not let people die before a trip abroad.

"Gusti?" said Drobney weakly, still in the dull haze of sedation. He felt Sondra hold his hand. She had asked the question.

"Yeah, you were saying that. What is a Gusti?"

"I said that?" said Charles Drobney, and it was getting dark again. Sondra Drobney ran out of the room because it suddenly looked as though the life was draining out of him.

All of it. To the last wretched moment it was going to come back to him, the tricks to get back to America. It was all coming back to him, and that awful deal he had so proudly made with the colonel.

And he thought he would never have to remember again how he had become a spy, how beautiful Gusti was, how young she was, how young they all were so long ago in that lunatic asylum he had found himself trapped in called Nazi Germany.

12

WHEN CHARLES Drobney examined the torturous "ifs" of his life, the most painful "if" of all was that if he hadn't batted only .188 in the old Class D Piedmont League for the Kinston (North Carolina) Aviators, he never would have left America, and none of the rest would have happened.

He would have remained Gottherd Hauff, so very American, or "Dutch" Hauff as they called him in the Piedmont because nobody wanted to bother with "Goddahd," as they sometimes called him.

Mostly the other players were farm boys. They lived on buses that smelled of rubbing compounds, whiskey, tobacco spit, and resin bags that hadn't had anything left in them for the last two seasons.

He was twenty-one years old, he remembered, when he was told he had no future in baseball. Twenty-one and done in Kinston, North Carolina. So long ago when he thought he was so shrewd.

The world was a game for young Gottherd Hauff and all you had to do was figure out the right percentages, figure out people. He was good at that. So that when the problem of his batting came up, he just didn't hand in his Aviator uniform, he listened to the manager to find some way to talk him out of it.

"You're a pretty good fielder, Hauff. But .188 in the Piedmont is not going to get you to the majors, and you're a pretty smart fella. Some of these bums can't make a living elsewhere."

"I think if I can get used to the pitching—"

"In Class D ball, you're either going up, or you're coming down. Hauff, you're going nowhere."

"I'd like to give it a try at least to the end of the season."

"We already have your replacement."

"I've seen that guy. He bats worse than I do."

"Yeah, but he's got potential. You know this is a farm club, Hauff. He's got speed and power, and maybe we can do something with him. You see, your problem is that you've gotten everything out of your body you're going to. You know everything. It's just that you can't do everything. You know the pitching as well as you're ever going to know it."

"I can help manage."

"Except you don't get along with everyone. We got a lot of Southern boys and you're from Michigan, and I hate to say it, Hauff. You've got a reputation as a nigger lover."

"I know where that comes from," said Gottherd. "We saw the Birmingham Barons play and I said there had to be a half dozen players on that team that could start in the majors right now, if it was just pure ball playing that counted."

"Not what I heard. You said they were the best damned ballplayers you'd ever seen and all of us were lucky they didn't let Negroes— you said Negroes, Hauff—that they didn't let Negroes play pro ball because half the majors would be Negro."

"All right, niggers, niggers, niggers," said the young Hauff.

"Shit, Hauff, at .188 you could be the imperial whatsit of the goddamn Ku Klux Klan. And what the hell do you want to be an assistant manager for? Shit, if I could get another job like you, I wouldn't want to be manager. If I could do something else, do you think I'd be here?"

But he couldn't do something else. He had never cared for school that much, so his grades were mediocre, and any college scholarship for baseball was impossible now because he had played professional ball. And there just were no jobs around.

It was 1937, and the world was still in the Great Depression. His father, and many Ford workers who had come over from Germany after the Great War, were being told they could return there with the help of Ford because there was plenty of work in the new Germany.

His mother was delighted. She had never felt fully at home in

Dearborn except among other Germans. His father wanted work. His mother wanted to go home.

Gottherd didn't have a job, didn't have an education, and thought at the time that if he didn't like Germany, he could always get back. There was always something he could connive. There was never a tight spot he couldn't negotiate. It was the confidence of youth, a firm conviction rooted in unshakable innocence.

The Ford Motor Company paid their way, and they sailed on the German-American Line from New York City to Bremen, on a ship of many returnees, not all of them happy.

In Stuttgart there was a small apartment for them, food was available but neither plentiful nor luxurious, and everyone was in a uniform of one sort or another. Even the newspaper sellers wore their own special uniform.

His mother put the picture of Adolf Hitler on the mantel right next to her picture of the Pope.

"Our Fuehrer will be made a saint. You'll see," said his mother.

"And what will happen to the apostles? Will they be forbidden because they are Jewish?" his father had answered.

"The only problem we ever had was not being German enough," his mother answered.

"I was on the Western Front. I had more than enough of being German. I was more German than I ever wanted to be."

"You see, you give Gottherd bad ideas. You are the one, Rudiger. The bad ideas come from you. And you take this wonderful gift and you see all the bad things."

"I came for work. A man without work is not a man."

Gottherd did not need his father to dislike Germany. In fact, at that time the boy had little respect for the older man. His father was the typical Schwabian, appearing slow to outsiders but keeping his shrewdness to himself. He made judgments but he rarely shared them with the world. He did his job, minded his business, and was more than grateful to be left alone. During the Great War, he had worked on trucks. At Ford in America he worked on trucks. At Ford in Germany he worked on trucks. Once Gottherd had asked his father if he liked working on trucks.

"It's a job," the old man had said.

In America Gotfherd had been a bit ashamed of his father. In Stuttgart his father seemed to fit in. They were all like him.

But Gottherd wasn't. He hated the uniforms, hated the constant droning propaganda, hated the mannerisms of respect, hated soccer. The worst was the uniforms.

And he hated the hate these people seemed to live on. His father said the anti-Semitism would pass, that it was something minor that the Fuehrer was using. Gottherd didn't care. He thought these people didn't even have enough intelligence to be embarrassed by their stupidity. Of course, at the time, he felt that even if the madness were not temporary, it was their problem and not his. His problem was getting away from there, and what was making everything so unbearable was the growing suspicion that he could not get home.

Home was Dearborn. Even Kinston, North Carolina, was more home than Stuttgart. The problem for Gottherd Hauff, as for most Americans who had come young from Germany, was that he was an American. Granted, he spoke German without an accent because that was his first language until five years of age, and then the language in his home. But he didn't belong in Germany.

He tried to get special assistance money from the American embassy, but he didn't qualify, being a German national also. He had been born in Germany. He went to the German-American Lines and offered his services free for passage to America. "I'll clean anything, do anything, work anywhere. I'll hardly eat."

Unfortunately, he was not the only one making that offer; they had a long waiting list and only so many one-way positions that could be filled.

He thought of espousing some forbidden political slogan, but that might get him jailed, not deported.

When he heard about a place that offered free passage back to America for those who spoke English fluently, he would have crawled there. He was surprised not by his mother's hysterics, but by his father's selling his gold wedding band to get him a one-way train passage to the Aero Klub in Wilhelmshaven, where the interviews were being held.

At Wilhelmshaven he found himself in a stuffy room with forty people and a rumor that only twenty were going to be accepted. And he was younger, at twenty-one, than most of them. Worse, there were several engineers in the crowd, and this had something to do with engineering, he had heard.

A man introduced as Dr. Pfeiffer entered and everyone stood up. Dr. Pfeiffer had one of those silly little moustaches so popular in Germany, like a mistake of a razor, that fluff of hair that went with tight collars and eyeglasses and suits that looked uncomfortable. Dr. Pfeiffer wore a Nazi party pin on his lapel, called a *Marmeladenplatte.*

He took the opportunity to enlighten the group as to the historic importance of the moment.

England and America, he assured everyone, would never be at war again with Germany because the new Germany understood that race was the deciding factor in human events and therefore Aryan peoples would join together. It was unnatural that they had been separated in the first place.

This separation had been fostered by the demons of history, the Jews, who had stolen, of course, the great technology of the Aryans and brought it to America. What Dr. Pfeiffer and his group wanted to do was merely take that technological information that was really German and use it for all Aryans by throwing it against the menace from the East, communism.

Gottherd didn't need any more of a hint. When the time came for his interview, he told Dr. Pfeiffer how impressed he was with seeing the world racially. He understood now the simple basic truths of human events, denied him these many years by the decadence of the West, the slander of the American newspapers, controlled of course by Jews, and the machinations of Wall Street, Freemasons, and the communists.

Years later he would come to realize that all movements so capable of mass murder, so willing to destroy whatever was in the world, had that same simple solution to the problems of living. The solution was always simple, and those getting in its way were always demons.

But at the interview, all Gottherd could think of was how much he could push a lie to assure himself that free passage back to America. He went as far as saying he had two years of engineering at Lou Gehrig's old school, Columbia, but had been expelled from there because of his profound National Socialist convictions. New York was a very Jewish city, as the Herr Doktor understood. Columbia was in New York. Need he say more?

The good Herr Doktor in his wisdom preferred someone well grounded in racial beliefs over someone with a few more years of schooling. One could always add the schooling. The training for this mission was really in America's behalf because Germany was fighting America's battle, although America didn't know it.

Besides, since there was no war, gathering technical information was not spying, even if that information were about bombsights and guns. One did not spy on someone he was not at war with, and especially not someone whose real interests were the same. They would actually be doing America a favor.

Gottherd nodded sagely when he heard this nonsense. He would have agreed that the sun was a form of Limburger cheese, if the good Herr Doktor said it. The training lasted four weeks. The curriculum kept changing, sometimes in midlecture.

Basically they were learning about secret inks, three kinds, one being a common pain reliever that when dissolved made an invisible ink; the use of codes; and the miraculous shortwave radio developed in the new Germany that weighed only thirty pounds, the Argenten.

Everyone sat in the same class and everyone knew everyone else. Everyone planned also to meet in America. Gottherd knew he had only one decision to make, and that was when to turn everyone in. He knew they were spying no matter what they called it, and he didn't believe the FBI was as doltish as the good Herr Doktor made out. They had caught Dillinger and Gottherd didn't see anyone in the classroom as smart as Dillinger.

Besides, he was sure someone else had to be smart enough to go right to the police. And he didn't want to be the one turned in. He didn't want to go to jail. He decided early on that his first stop in America would be the police. He felt somewhat guilty.

The last test was for "nervous tensions." The good Herr Doktor thought that was the one thing that he could not allow in his people. Besides, for the awesome sum of five hundred dollars a month, the Third Reich had the absolute right to expect its employees to be above nervous tension. And for that, there was a test the good Herr Doktor was sure they would pass.

The test occurred on a cold drizzly day outside of Wilhelmshaven at a gray barracks manned by sailors. Apparently, the whole German secret service was run by an admiral.

But at this navy base, there were several army officers, air force officers, and SS officers. Gottherd was glad he was getting out of Germany because if he could begin recognizing some of the uniforms, he knew he was there too long.

Dr. Pfeiffer gave another one of his speeches about courage and nervous tension.

Gottherd was the first selected. A sailor put a soldier's pot helmet on him, and then marched him alone to the center of a large field one hundred yards from everyone else. Sailors back at the reviewing stand were erecting steel barricades in front of the officers.

The sailor told Hauff that no matter what happened he should hold his head steady. The ground was muddy. Gottherd noticed the sailor's shoes were shined sparkling black. The sailor very carefully took what looked like a potato masher from a steel box. The bell had a wooden handle, but the tube was solid. It had what appeared to be some sort of bump on the top.

"This is the pin," said the sailor, pointing to the bump.

"When I am behind that metal screen, and not before, you will pull this pin. You see?"

"Is that a hand grenade?" asked Hauff.

"Yes," said the sailor.

"I've never seen one up close before."

"There is one safe place in this field for you. And that is your own willpower to remain steady because you will pull the pin and put it on top of your helmet. If you are nervous, you will not be able to balance this flat end on your helmet and it will fall off and kill or maim you."

The sailor gave the handle to Hauff. He was grave.

"Why are you smiling?" asked the sailor.

"Nothing," said Gottherd. "I laugh at death."

"You'd better be careful."

"Of course I will," said Gottherd and removed the smile.

"Careful now," said the sailor.

"Fine, you just say when."

"Not now. When I am behind the steel barricade."

"Sure, sure," said Gottherd. He was certain the good Herr Doktor was enjoying this.

The sailor scurried with the box in front of him back to where all the officers had disappeared behind the screen. For a few seconds, Gottherd toyed with the idea of pulling the pin and then sticking the handle in his mouth and laughing. But then that would be failing the test for nervous tension because then it would show he knew he had nothing to be nervous about. Nobody was going to give him a live hand grenade to put on his helmet.

So, he pulled the pin, which came out with a short tug. He put the hand grenade on its flat end, careful to balance it. And waited. He was expecting Dr. Pfeiffer to run out from behind the barricade any second, when the world caved in around his head. His eyes blackened for a moment, he was on his knees as though a mountain pushed him there and his ears were ringing. Sirens were going off in his skull and he was getting up on his feet, and there were people around him and the world smelled of gunpowder and his nose was bleeding.

Dr. Pfeiffer was chortling and patting him on the back, and telling the other officers that his group had the mettle to withstand the steel of combat and the fire of battle.

"That was a live grenade," Gottherd was yelling. His mouth was moving. His throat was trying to make sounds, but he didn't hear himself. "That was a live grenade, you idiots. You idiots."

His voice was a whisper far off but it must have been heard because Dr. Pfeiffer was telling him not to ruin a splendid test by a sudden loss of will.

"You idiots, people can get killed by those things. Who let you people use live grenades? What's the matter with you?"

"Attention, Hauff, or you will not be considered passing."

"Not passing, for what? You think that 'Katzenjammer Kids' magic ink shit's going to work?"

"Invisible ink. Quiet, Hauff. You are under orders. That is an order."

"I'm through. You people are dangerous. I just thought you were a bit stupid, but you're dangerous. You can get people killed." His teeth felt like they had been polished with ball bearings. He could focus better now.

"As of this moment, 2:37 P.M., you are dismissed from Abwehr Group Pfeiffer," said Dr. Pfeiffer.

"Why do you think this operation is stupid?" asked an officer in simple blue uniform with a red stripe down his trousers. He had that strong sort of Prussian nose but a face so quiet it was almost clay. He tapped soft leather gloves over his sleeves.

"He is a young boy who has failed his test for nervous tension," said Dr. Pfeiffer.

"Because we're being told we're helping America, and we're really spying. What are we being paid five hundred dollars a month for if it's not spying? What are the secret inks for if it's not spying and how the hell do you know you are not going to be in a war with America? How do you know that?"

"You have failed your test," said Dr. Pfeiffer.

"I don't give a shit. I don't want to get killed, and you dumb fucks would do just that. I should have known that anybody as stupid as you are would use a live grenade. Crazy bastards."

"Why do you think we are stupid?" asked the officer.

"Don't talk to him. He is a failure and dismissed," said Dr. Pfeiffer. Upon this order, the officer just turned and gave Dr. Pfeiffer a look of bland contempt and the doctor bowed apologetically.

"Why?" repeated the officer to Gottherd.

"Well, first of all, what happens if there is a war? The one time you people want a spy system to work is during a war, and you're setting it up so that it's the one time it may not work. What's going to happen to all your wonderful nonspies the minute they find out they can hang for this fun and games that isn't spying?"

"I am glad," said Dr. Pfeiffer, "that we have discovered your lack of nerves. The test is a success."

Everyone seemed to defer to the officer, and when he nodded for Gottherd to follow, two sailors pushed Gottherd after him across the field. The officer signaled them to leave, and nodded Gottherd to follow.

"Am I under arrest?"

"Not for anything I heard."

Gottherd shook his head to get the ringing out, but when he shook it, it hurt. He kept blinking his eyes and the officer told him not to shake his head.

Somehow a brownish Mercedes-Benz touring car appeared, and the officer motioned Gottherd into it. He gave him a handkerchief. "Your nose, it's bleeding."

A bottle of red wine and two glasses came into the backseat from an orderly.

"Drink, don't gulp," said the officer. "Just sip."

The wine was good. Gottherd noticed there was some blood on the handkerchief. His blood.

"You might have a mild concussion," said the officer.

"Why are you being so kind to me?" said Gottherd.

"What makes you think I am being kind?"

"The wine. Your handkerchief."

"That's courtesy. Don't mistake it for kindness. I am interested in where you learned about spying."

"I don't know anything about spying."

"Did you study anything about it at Columbia? Any military history?"

"No, I was an engineer," lied Gottherd.

"And you left after two years because the Jews kicked you out?" The officer must have read a report. "I just wanted to leave."

"They were powerful in the engineering department?"

"It was New York, you know."

"And you love Germany?"

"Just let me go."

"Where are you going?"

"I don't know. I don't know. I just want to get away."

"Fine. Where would you like us to take you?"

"What do you want from me?"

"First, for you to sip your wine and then, in exchange for a bit of honesty, I will get you one of the finest meals in Germany, and then deliver you anywhere you want, within reason."

"How about America?"

"That's why you joined, yes?"

"Yes."

"You're not a German at heart, are you?"

"No," said Gottherd.

"Good. Now, why did you surmise that at the outbreak of war the Pfeiffer group would misfunction."

"What do you mean?"

"Share your thinking process with me. Sip, Hauff."

"Well, it's logical, isn't it? I mean, here you have everyone knowing everyone else, and then everyone being told there's going to be no war, and you're not spying. All you need is for one of us to panic for everyone to get dragged down with him. And I am sure there would be more than one."

"True."

"Common sense, right?" said Gottherd.

The officer smiled. "No, not common at all. Tell me some more of your thoughts. What do you think of the great racial alliance of Aryan peoples?"

"Great talk, but look, most of the German-Americans who come here like Hitler anyway. What about the Germans who left here and stayed in America? Just common sense they wanted to be Americans, not Germans. We German-Americans will be the first out of the trenches at you if there is a war."

"How did you get stuck here? Did you believe in the new Germany?"

"I came with my father."

"And you want to get home?" said the officer.

"Very much," said Gottherd. His head still rang.

"Just what did you do in America for a living?"

"I was a baseball player."

"That's a sport like cricket, yes?"

"Yes. I didn't make it."

"Tell me, were you ever a policeman at any time?"

"No," said Gottherd.

"Did you ever run a business? Direct people?"

"No."

"Where did you get these observations of people from?"

"It's obvious," said Gottherd.

"And no military training whatsoever? Correct?" said the officer.

Gottherd did not know it, but when he had mentioned that the spy system would suffer its greatest vulnerability at the outbreak of war, he had tangentially touched on a basic military theory of war, that in every battle there was a crucial moment. The crucial moment for a spy system was, in the case of a war, the outbreak, at which time the German one was virtually guaranteed to misfunction. At the time, Gottherd Hauff had thought he was only being logical. He did not have the professional's eye to examine just how well he really thought. The officer did, however.

"I think I can show you how you can get home, and work for us at the same time. I can show you, Gottherd Hauff, how both of us can serve each other."

"I don't even like Germany."

"I don't want your love, Hauff. I want your service."

"I'm not going to spy for you."

"Let me worry about that, Hauff. Allow me to introduce myself. I am Colonel Hasso von Kiswicz of the Generalstab. Have you heard of the German Generalstab?"

"Oh yeah. You were the guys in the Great War who, if you lost a battle, would go out and put a bullet in your heads."

"Not quite that, but there can be a situation in which it is the proper decision, perhaps the only one, besides being the honorable thing to do."

"I would never put a bullet in my own head. I could be two hundred years old and dying of cancer and I wouldn't do it myself no matter what."

Von Kiswicz laughed and personally poured him some more wine. He told Gottherd he was going to teach him to think.

"I already think," said Gottherd.

"Yes. You do," said the colonel.

13

GERMAN SPIES in Newport? Meeting U-boats? Scoffing at capture? Killing again because one of their own kind—a wealthy socialite—was about to let the beans out of the bag or something?

"Come, come, Agent Oliver. I should hope you would know better than that," said Professor Gardner Tobridge from his office with a window facing the red brick and green-ivy and white-trim Harvard Yard.

Todd held up his hands, signaling he didn't want the professor to start talking until the clerk typist set up both a tape recorder and a court recording machine. He wanted it all down.

Todd knew who this man's friends were, what he owned, and what people said about him confidentially since he was twenty-eight. That was the year he was accepted by the Office of Strategic Services and had to undergo an FBI clearance.

Professor Tobridge was now seventy years old, a professor emeritus of German literature at Harvard, a Yankee millionaire owning great parcels of western Massachusetts, who had been part of Operation Paperclip, the gigantic intelligence effort at the end of World War II to gather up all German officials and records so that nothing of the Third Reich would escape.

Professor Tobridge, like many in the OSS, had come from the Ivy League. The OSS liked its men from Harvard, Yale, and especially from Brown University, and because of that, the OSS, Office of Strategic Services, became known as Oh So Social. Hoover liked his

FBI men from Notre Dame, and this social rivalry showed in the first clearance on Professor Tobridge: "No communist or Nazi links; typical Yankee millionaire; lots of land, lots of stock; brown bags his lunch and will never be at risk for money problems; bookish but not homosexual."

Professor Tobridge apparently had not changed since 1941 except in body. Although he still had the clearance of a four star officer, he would have looked like a vagrant if he weren't in an office overlooking Harvard Yard. He had a partial shave, apparently from saving razor blades, wore a pair of eyeglasses held together by a rubber band, a dark jacket, and a strangely grayish shirt that, when new, might have come from a mail order catalogue.

He had made time for Agent Oliver and his clerk during his lunch hour. Lunch was a package of saltine crackers he was willing to share. Oliver knew Professor Tobridge still had the same family land worth approximately fifteen times what it was when he was a millionaire in 1941.

Oliver was not unaware that the old man did not start talking until he saw Oliver's Bureau identity card, and actually checked the picture against Oliver's face.

"We talked before and the shooting that occurred down in Newport doesn't change anything," said Professor Tobridge.

"I'd like to ask the questions, if I may," said Todd.

"Certainly," said Professor Tobridge. "You know, every time the newspapers get a hold of something like that, you're really shocked how much people forget, or perhaps never knew, about what went on in the Second World War. I had always thought that because of the extensive news coverage this would be the first war that people really understood and remembered. But I guess it wasn't, was it?"

The clerk typist set up her recording machine, backed up by a tape recorder.

"You mean about spies?"

"My Lord, yes! There was an excuse for that sort of thing at the beginning of the war when there was so much hysteria, but you know, after the war, to believe that the Germans had a spy system successfully bubbling away here is like thinking cavemen could fly jets."

Whoopee, thought Oliver. "Could you wait a moment and let me start with a question," he said calmly.

Professor Tobridge nodded. He washed down his last saltine with a glass of water, apologizing for eating in front of them, but this was his lunchtime. Oliver saw the clerk suppress a smile.

"Recently," said Oliver, "two codebooks were found that the United States Navy believes might have been intended for spies assisting Grand Admiral Karl Doenitz's U-boat command."

Professor Tobridge folded his saltine paper and threw it into a wastebasket.

"Moreover," continued Oliver, "the U.S. Navy contends two things lead them to believe a very effective spy system operated in America, probably based in Newport. First, the high incidence of Allied tonnage sunk; second, the U-boats alone used a different code from the basic German code, which the Allies had broken. They believe this was a result of Doenitz's having his own spy system."

"Doubtful and virtually impossible," said Professor Tobridge. "Oh, the Herr Grossadmiral would have loved for you to believe he had something like that. We broke his code too. The man was such a damned show-off, which was why he was held in contempt by the German General Staff and loved so much by Adolf Hitler. No, Doenitz would be the last sort of person to be able to effect a successful spy operation. I might add we were looking for just that sort of thing in Paperclip because the Navy said it had to be there. We didn't find it then. And I doubt anyone would find it now."

"And the codebooks?" said Oliver.

"It's very possible they had been convinced they had people ashore, or were trying to reach them, when they were actually already in prison. Your FBI records would bear this out. The German intelligence system was an enormous mess in America. I think you people broke the whole thing in the first few weeks of the war."

"Those were the ones we picked up. What about some possibility of one we didn't pick up? After all, how does one prove there is no needle in the haystack?"

"By owning the haystack, for one. You see, in Operation Paperclip, we cooperated, of course, with the British. Well, I remember one of their fellows, as a matter of fact someone I had known at Oxford, saying, 'It is good to visit our chaps again.' He meant that the British practically ran the German secret service, the Abwehr."

Todd could have said like the Russians had run the British secret service after the war. But he didn't want the British downgraded while he was using them. Professor Tobridge did that.

"Of course, the Russians used the British. But then again, we may be running the Russian secret service. One never knows till afterwards. We may be running the KGB, you know."

"I doubt that. They're so good."

"That's just when people aren't. When you hear about them, they are not. The ones you have to fear are the ones you don't know about."

"Why not from Nazi Germany?"

"Well, they did have many intelligence arms, but what you don't understand is that spying then and spying now are as different as a jet plane from a Roman spear. We started our own espionage system only after Pearl Harbor. Sounds shocking today but it's true. There was contempt for spying, even among professional soldiers, and especially in Germany."

"Explain."

"Adolf Hitler himself did not like spies and forbade them to operate in America or England before the war. He allowed it only in the East."

"What about the ones we picked up?"

"Ah," said Professor Tobridge, "Exhibit A. They were trained by a Dr. Pfeiffer in Bremen, whose only experience with spying was that he was a Nazi party member. Since Hitler had thought America was of no account except for technology, he allowed this Dr. Pfeiffer and his cronies to attempt to steal America's technology. And they did get some of it."

"Could they have been used as German spies against our Navy, helping Doenitz's submarine force?" asked Oliver.

"None of them survived. Some of them didn't even know they were spying."

"Explain, please," said Todd, glancing at the clerk getting it all down.

"Dr. Pfeiffer, as it turned out, told them all nothing would happen to them because if Germany and America were not at war, they weren't spying. As soon as war broke out, many turned themselves in wholesale. Then you had the professional Nazi who went around not only spying but passing out Nazi literature to boot. And I think they all used German steamship lines to return to America after their indoctrination in Germany. You got them all by steamship records."

"But they did have Admiral Canaris of the Abwehr. Could he have had some system even though he was penetrated by the British?"

"Canaris?" said Professor Tobridge, letting his glance fall on papers on his desk. He shook his head. "The man was a toady to Hitler, and kept his spy system alive by giving Hitler reports on Roosevelt's sexual life, and that of Churchill's wife. Dirty stories. You should be familiar with that. Didn't Hoover do that for American presidents?"

"So, basically you have described an organization of high incompetence where we knew everything it was doing. Therefore, knowing what they were doing, you could say you doubt or strongly doubt a spy group from Germany existed in America during World War II."

"Strongly doubt."

Todd nodded. Good. He had one last point, hardly even needing refutation because it had so little substantiation. But if the Navy felt it necessary to include it, he would have the officer from Operation Paperclip knock it clear out of the park. It would set the tone for the report. He had little doubt now what Professor Tobridge would do about that superspy enemy in the photograph of the note.

"What would you say to an unsubstantiated contention that America faced a—" Todd looked down at his notepad, " 'a group of superb judgement, quickness and flexibility—' "

"From the Germans, no," said Tobridge.

"Let me finish," said Todd.

"By all means," said Professor Tobridge. He surreptitiously picked up a student's paper and began perusing it with a wandering eye. Todd didn't mind. Neither the tape recorder nor the clerk typist would mention that.

"Okay . . . 'a group of superb judgement, quickness and flexibility, something far superior to anything the Hun has shown us so far in this war.' "

Professor Tobridge dropped the paper and fixed his eyes on Oliver. He brought his bony old hands in front of his face like a church ceiling. Oliver, reading his notes, missed this. The clerk typist did not. But she could not warn Oliver.

" 'We conjecture that this group must be the reflection of a single mind, certain of his mission, and with the sound good judgement to effect exactly what he wants and the wisdom to attempt nothing more. Do not look for the strutting fanatic, or paid criminal. You are facing something far more dangerous. The enemy who thinks,' " said Todd, adding before he caught Professor Tobridge's eyes, "No routing whatsoever. We don't even know what department."

"British warning, wasn't it?" said Professor Tobridge. Todd noticed the sudden absolute coldness in the professor's face.

"No routing on it at all. Yes, but we don't even know what department."

"You wouldn't," said Professor Tobridge.

"Why not?"

"Why should they share it with us? Do you know who the source could have been?"

"No," said Todd.

"And they didn't want you to then, and probably don't today. For all we know, it could be the man who is Chancellor of Germany today. The British had people in the highest places. And they didn't want to risk sharing those valuable people with an ally of just the last half century. The British have been in this a long time, so they not only would not let you know their source inside Germany, but probably not even the department of their Intelligence which controlled that source. Churchill himself probably didn't know who the source was."

"But it's still unverified," said Todd. "This thing has no routing. It could have been written by anyone with a typewriter, and then photographed. That's why we have routing. To validate things. Show where they came from. We can't know someone wasn't making up a source in Germany. Without procedure you just don't know what you have. That's why you have procedure in the first place. Do you see?" said Todd.

"I think if you check out that sort of note you will find it was hand-delivered by one high-ranking government official to another. Maybe the highest. Was it? I would guess even Churchill. Churchill to Roosevelt?"

Todd nodded assent. He didn't want to say yes because that would appear on the tape. The note was becoming a major problem. "Still in all, we have the evidence that the Germans were incapable of a successful espionage activity in support of their U-boats. You debriefed Admiral Doenitz. You described the Abwehr."

"The 'usual people,' 'the Hun,' " said Professor Tobridge, using a phrase from the note. He was smiling. "Absolutely. And that's what this source was warning us about. He knew there was serious and damaging espionage in America, and warned us to look elsewhere, not to feel complacent because we had thought we had rounded up everyone."

"Isn't it possible that this source, or the British, just wanted to make a point? The note is dramatic. Some admiral possibly just wanted to justify the U-boat success?"

"No," said Professor Tobridge. His face was grim. "They were fighting for their lives. And the note was quite specific. When they referred to an 'enemy who thinks,' it didn't mean just someone who was intelligent, or thought, although he undoubtedly did."

Todd sat back. The tape recorder was running. The clerk looked to him. It was too late to stop.

Professor Tobridge spoke evenly now, almost as though it were a simple lecture. "When British Intelligence referred to an 'enemy who thinks,' it meant something very specific. The German General Staff, or Generalstab. Those bastards could have pulled off an espionage network, they could have pulled it off brilliantly. Yes, they could have done it. That note from some source that still may be in Germany knew the General Staff had something going with espionage, but could not penetrate it. Forget the Hitler folk, it said. 'You've got the General Staff on your hands.' "

"Are you telling me that Operation Paperclip failed to debrief the German General Staff, missed a whole spy network?"

"We debriefed them. We weren't looking for espionage. These were professional soldiers with old-school ethics. I didn't think they engaged in espionage until you read me that note moments ago," said Professor Tobridge. He narrowed his eyes. "I am sure there was one specific thing they wanted. They were always specific when they did things. One thing they knew they had to have. Knew what they wanted and didn't play games. That's how they would do it. No cumbersome network either. In and out. Done. Perfect."

"Excuse me if I have difficulty following you, but you described in some detail the inability of these militarists to conduct successful espionage. Now you are contradicting yourself, saying they could have done it brilliantly," said Todd. As a lawyer, he knew that if he couldn't get useful testimony, he could at least neutralize it.

"One of the great misconceptions, especially here in America, was that the German General Staff, which by the way no longer exists, were a bunch of booted uniformed warmongers filled with arrogance and parade-ground pride. That might be accurate for a German field officer . . ." said Professor Tobridge, his voice trailing off as he scanned an adjacent wall for a book. He found it and with quick joy had it down on his desk.

"They were the absolute opposite of what most people think Prussians were in many respects," said the professor. He showed Todd a paragraph in Gothic print.

"I don't read German," said Todd.

"It says, 'To Be, Rather Than to Seem'—hardly boots and medals, eh?"

"Well, I would imagine, yes," said Todd.

"I would have to say of all military planners, they were unique. Don't think Nazi or some German officer that you are familiar with when you think General Staff, or Generalstab, as they called it," said Professor Tobridge, explaining further.

"The German General Staff shunned glory and the parade grounds, and rarely would any of them ever command an army in battle. That was what made them different from all other armies, where officers could lust for their own command someday while doing staff work."

Oliver had been imagining them as bureaucrats, until he realized that none of them could become heads of their departments, command troops. They were always advisors. What a brilliant way to thwart ambition. Of course he did not mention it. He was trying to think of another question to turn this one around. But Professor Tobridge drove on:

"The General Staff had been formed after Napoleon taught the Prussians that they didn't understand war, and they set about learning war. They learned it like few men ever did. Quietly and methodically, they devised techniques to understand what happened to men in war, and what happened in wars.

"They were the best judge of military men the world has ever seen. In fact, one of their chief jobs while serving with officers who commanded troops was to observe them and select proper leaders, leaders they themselves knew they could never become.

"They didn't believe in wasting men or movement. Many of them came from the landed aristocracy, frugal, proper men of high honor, more like the American Yankee than anyone else in the world."

No wonder he likes them, thought Oliver.

"Or at least how we like to look at ourselves, eh?" said the professor. "However, the General Staff was of the old school. They didn't approve of spying themselves. On the other hand, they were perfectly willing to smuggle Lenin back into Russia during the First World War to get the Russians out of the war, so who knows what they would do in a pinch."

The professor's position was that the one memo that Todd Oliver thought would have the least effect turned into the one best supporting the Navy.

"A man who thinks," said Professor Tobridge. "Look for a man who thinks. They knew Hitler was going to lose his war, and they warned him of it and he hated them for it. I spoke to Doenitz. Damned fool didn't know he had lost the war till American tanks were in his bedroom. He succeeded Hitler in those last days, you know. Probably thought of it as a promotion."

"Are you connecting that wanton killing in Newport with a man who thinks?"

"That?" said Professor Tobridge. "Oh, no. The man you want is probably back in Germany now tending his horses. You'll never find him."

14

IT WAS his innocence as much as anything that made him suscepti-
ble to the colonel. Not innocence of the horrors of war. Everyone
knew about the hell of the trenches in the Great War.

Gottherd Hauff had been innocent of the thinking that went into a
war, innocent of history as seen by good professional soldiers, innocent of the character of someone whom he had been taught in
Dearborn schools to see as some brute under a spiked helmet. And
innocent, too, of his own nature.

How did the colonel know he could reach the young man? Hauff
was an American. He did not like these Germans particularly and
thought the Nazis were a very bad joke.

"If they're so fucking wonderful, why do they keep talking about it
all the time? I'd believe the Germans were the master race if they
would shut up about it for a while."

The colonel laughed at that one. That was one thing about the
man Drobney would always remember. The colonel could laugh,
especially at himself or Germans, and Prussians.

Growing up in America, Gottherd had accepted that Prussians
were rude, arrogant bullies. This man appeared different, especially
in a country increasingly being filled with real bullies in jackboots.
Perhaps that was what had disarmed Gottherd Hauff. Then again,
von Kiswicz was in an excellent position to sell. Gottherd Hauff
needed supper.

Von Kiswicz was not a snake about it. It was a simple arrangement. Anytime Gottherd did not like what was going on, he could return to Stuttgart. If everything went well, he would return to America.

"To spy?"

"We are not paying for a vacation, Hauff."

"I'll take your meal," Gottherd had said. "But I am not agreeing to spying."

"I owe you the meal. I said I would give you the meal. I am aware you do not like us. You don't want to get back to America so badly because you are in love with the Third Reich," the colonel smiled.

"So why are you doing this?" asked Gottherd. The colonel didn't seem like a fool. He caught lies very well.

"Considering many ramifications, you look like a good choice at this time."

"That I don't want to spy doesn't mean anything?"

"It means you say you don't want to spy."

"Do you think I am going to change my mind?"

"I think you do not have all the facts yet. I think you are extremely intelligent. All I want is the opportunity to deal with your intelligence."

"I like flattery," said Gottherd.

"Gottherd, you know I wasn't flattering you," said the colonel. "Now, I owe you the best meal in Germany. What do you want?"

"I don't know fancy restaurants."

"I have found that the best meal in any country is what a person wants the most at any moment. So, what do you hunger for?"

What Gottherd wanted more than anything was steak, corn, and ice cream. He wanted an American meal.

They could not get him the corn. The ice cream was too sweet and the cut of the steak was strange. Back in Stuttgart he had been eating German food at his mother's.

Gottherd Hauff noticed how much more respect this man had in this country than his father. How people would defer to him, make way for him, and on his own estate an hour east of Berlin, his farmers would take off their hats when they spoke to him.

Yet, von Kiswicz did not posture superiority. He would often walk into the fields with the workers, step through the damned pervasive manure and human waste that they like to fertilize with, and would listen with respectful attention to everyone. He had that sort of grace Gottherd thought from movies belonged only to the British aristocracy. There was a sense that he could look upon any disaster with a detached calm, and good humor.

The colonel took him in as a guest in his own house, although Gottherd sensed that Frau von Kiswicz was against this. There was also a purpose to this. In his own estate, no one would see Gottherd Hauff or wonder what a colonel was doing spending ten-hour days teaching the boy.

At the von Kiswicz dinner table, the sparest, simplest meals were served on the most opulent china. Gottherd would have preferred to eat in the kitchen because then he could have filled himself with bread.

Gottherd had his room, his own orderly, and was in for a grand surprise. He had always felt history was boring, but when this man taught it, it was more exciting than the World Series.

It was a game in which they scored in nations. There were logical reasons for things. There was cunning. There was chance. There was how things worked and how they could work.

For a young man who knew when to put a left-hander in against a batter, understanding the mechanics of defensive military positions and their reasons, most importantly their reasons, was no great jump in thinking.

He had never been one to hate another team, even a pitcher who threw for the head. There was a reason for that. The pitcher didn't want the batter digging in.

So too in war were there reasons for things, but the most astonishing thing for the young man brought up on the courage of Valley Forge, and the sad glory of Pickett's charge at Gettysburg, and the grit of the Marines at Château-Thierry, was the new way of looking at America.

America was not the innocent democracy put upon by the evils of the world or, as Dr. Pfeiffer had tried to suggest, some racially mixed dolts, but, as the colonel said, "the monster." And he did not say it with contempt, but respect. You could look at the New York Yankees like that.

It was not that America was evil. It wasn't. The colonel never engaged him in an argument over the moral merits of a country. They simply were irrelevant to understanding the mechanics of war, as a pitcher's private life was to his fast ball.

In later years, there would be time for the young man to realize he had been breached at what he never realized was his most vulnerable point, his willingness to look at things rationally. The colonel did not have to know that Gottherd's admiration for many black players or his disdain for anti-Semitism had nothing to do with morality.

Somehow he knew Gottherd, and when he referred to Gottherd's intelligence, he had meant that reasoning power devoid of morality. To those who didn't know better it might look evil or good, when it was really neither.

In later years the young man would have all the time to understand fully what a fool he had been; the colonel, too, because perhaps the colonel, being an older man and having lived through a war, should have known better. But Gottherd was young and the game was fascinating, and neither of them in that little wood-lined study with the sabers of old Prussian cavalry days lining the wall bothered with the right and wrong of things.

Perhaps the colonel's upbringing had taught him that to ignore every war was either moral or immoral, that if there were no good guys or bad guys you were left with only fools killing each other. But that understanding was for a more painful time, a time of growing up.

In the study, which smelled of oiled wood, the mud of the fields still on their boots, the world laid out in maps and munitions, Gottherd felt the exhilaration of competition. He could look at America's strength as the "Monster," the same way one called the Yankee's batting lineup "murderer's row." Of course the New York Yankees did not kill people. But then again, nobody was dying on the maps either.

"During the Great War," the colonel explained, "we knew we were in trouble when you would make airfields by pouring drums and drums of gasoline onto the grass and burning it off. God in heaven—a supply situation with virtually no limit."

For the first time Gottherd, who had grown up in Detroit, where cars were manufactured, learned to appreciate America's ability to organize and carry out a war operation industrially.

But the biggest surprise was his learning a new way to look at the American Civil War; a textbook example of the use of new tactics, weapons, and how great generals used them. Whether the purpose of the war was to end slavery was not even mentioned, of course.

It was an entirely different Civil War from the one Gottherd had learned in his Dearborn classroom. He wondered what the Southern boys back home would say if they knew that it was not Lee who was the great general of the Civil War, but Ulysses S. Grant, who even Gottherd, coming from the North, believed was only a lunging butcher with a cigar in his mouth.

While Lee was competent tactically, which meant knowing how to fight an individual battle well and where to move what when, it was Grant who understood the war itself. Grant understood strategy, a knowledge beyond any single battle, something the German General Staff had come to realize when it first began to study war.

Battles were part of a war, and might decide a war, but they were not the war. And therefore the crucial battle of the United States Civil War was not Gettysburg, as dramatic as that might have been, but the Battle of the Wilderness, which few Americans bothered to study. There, Lee won a battle against Grant, but instead of retreating as all previous Union generals had done after being beaten by Lee, Grant took his large remnants and pursued, driving Lee inevitably toward Appomattox and surrender.

On the other hand, at Gettysburg Lee lost the battle, but was allowed to regroup, to continue the war.

"What often seems simple in retrospect is more than likely genius at the time. Because until then everyone believed that if you lost a battle, why naturally you retreated," explained von Kiswicz.

What war required more than anything, Gottherd was learning, was thought. And he liked that. He liked the concept of assuming the enemy was perfect until he showed you how to destroy him.

"How do you find that out?" asked Gottherd. He was curious.

"First, you do not lie to yourself," said the colonel, and that day he stopped his lecture to take Gottherd around to the stables so that he would have his mind clear for what he was about to say.

They rode for a half hour, the colonel having taught Gottherd to ride so that even during exercise he could continue the lectures.

"You may not understand this now," said the colonel, "but many strategic mistakes, tactical mistakes, come from lying to oneself. They come from unreasonable hope or despair.

"Either one is a lie. Most people and even some generals do not know what they know or do not know, but fill their heads with their own ambitions, wishes, fears."

"Is that what you mean by understanding a war?"

"Partly. Only partly. Listen. Listen closely even if you don't understand right now. This is how you make decisions. There is rarely such a thing as a perfect tactical decision in a war. Everything we look at now is not how it was or will be. Now it is safe and we have time. In war, there is confusion, partial information, and a strong possibility that every heretofore logical move can lead to complete disaster."

"Sounds like life," said Gottherd. He was joking. But the colonel did not laugh.

"There is a way, however, to reach a proper decision," said the colonel. "And that is really the product of understanding your purpose, your limitations, and precisely what little you do know. It is a reasoning process devoid of both hope and despair. In total, it is a way of thinking. We called it *Takt.* It does not mean tactics, it means the process of correct decision making. It is not clairvoyance and it is not courage. Do you see?"

"I think so," said Gottherd, who had always been taught that hope was a virtue and despair a sin. "But what exactly is wrong with hope?"

"For personal comfort," said the colonel, sitting so erect in his saddle, "nothing. For a leader it can prepare the foundations for the worst disasters. Hope is a distortion. It is what you wish is so. It is not necessarily what is so, that lovely luxury that people use to make themselves happy."

"But without hope people can give up."

"At certain times that is a proper course, for war. To fight on when it is useless is murder. It's not war. No leader has a right to get his people killed uselessly. And hope will do that surest. Hope leads to attempting what is realistically prohibitive."

"And despair?"

"Surrender. Despair usually follows hope. People convince themselves something will be easy, and when it is not, it becomes impossible. They give up, when actually the task may have just been arduous."

"Without hope and despair, what's left?" asked Gottherd.

"What is left is the little you know about what is happening, and therefore what you really can do about it."

"Limits," said Gottherd.

"Exactly," said the colonel.

Gottherd sat comfortably on the colonel's favorite mare. The ever-present odors of Prussian fertilization didn't bother him anymore. He didn't even notice them.

In Kinston, North Carolina, Gottherd had been too slow for the Aviators. But something in the theory of war seemed easy to Gottherd Hauff, and when it was difficult, the difficulty was not an obstacle but a fascination. He always knew he could figure something out.

He knew he was doing very well when occasionally another Generalstab officer would visit and ask questions, and von Kiswicz at the end would say, "Two months' training," "Three months' training," or whatever Gottherd had completed. He also knew some of his answers had gotten him notoriety.

Many Prussians had Polish-sounding names and this was because they had taken those names at a time when the Poles were the preeminent power of central Europe. Now of course the Poles were the objects of ridicule as racially inferior Slavs.

To this, Gottherd had commented, "Racial superiority is not so much a matter of blood, Herr Oberst, but of calendar." The colonel laughed at that.

Sometimes Gottherd was allowed in the colonel's den for drinks with other officers, provided he told none of them what he was doing.

A proud moment came when it was assumed he was a junior officer, a relative of the colonel's.

He knew he was accepted when they told jokes about panzer leaders, actually old jokes about cavalry officers.

Why did a panzer leader never commit *Panik vorwärts*? Because to panic would require the time to bother with a rash assessment in the first place.

But Gottherd knew there were places, needed places for good cavalry officers, whose daring and courage and often tactical brilliance could swing battles. The place for them however was not in charge of everything.

Panzer leaders were grand leading tanks under the command of a field general. Unless, of course, as the visiting officer said, they had been elected Herr Kanzler.

And here was the first time Gottherd heard criticism of Adolf Hitler. It was not the last, and there were no direct criticisms, rather, little snide remarks about their corporal who thought he was a military genius.

As for what was called "the Jewish Problem," Gottherd knew only that von Kiswicz's father-in-law had owned a department store with a Jew and had bought him out in 1933. It only mattered to von Kiswicz that the partner had been paid a fair price; otherwise that would have lacked rectitude.

He never heard von Kiswicz comment on what was happening to Jews in Germany, but then he never heard him comment on Jews either. It seemed somehow to be a problem between Nazis and Jews, neither of which he was.

But Gottherd was still bothered by this.

"So it doesn't bother you, but you don't run the country," said Gottherd. "These guys are lunatics."

"Gottherd, this . . . this new social movement of our . . . leader . . . is another government. We have had several governments. They have been different. The Generalstab remains the same. This one has an advantage. We are allowed to rearm. Germany should have that right along with any other country."

"Why? I don't see why? If I were running the British or French armies, I would invade Germany the first time one extra tank appeared off a production line."

"I see I have taught you well. Yes, that was the best time."

"Probably still is," said Gottherd, and the colonel laughed. Gottherd was aware of the problems of rearming and the feeling among Generalstab officers that Hitler seemed reckless.

He had taken back the Rhineland, and while it was territory seized from Germany at the end of the Great War and rightfully German, Gottherd knew Germany was so ill-prepared that if a policeman fired a shot at the German Army, they were under orders to return to the borders established by the Versailles Treaty. No one fired.

By the time anyone did fire, Hitler had several countries under his belt, and the strongest military machine in the world. And this young man would no longer be Gottherd Hauff.

A change was taking place in Gottherd at the von Kiswicz estate in

Wenksbrücken. The seasons were not quite the same as in Dearborn, the snow not harsh, the summers not as sweltering, and he missed that. But he was not as unhappy as he had been in Stuttgart. He felt in a way somehow at home, a belonging. He was still not ready to spy, but another profound change was taking place. With the colonel he lost that bit of immigrant shame he had felt as the son of a couple who spoke with an accent in America.

For the first time, he felt truly proud of his German heritage, not German-American, but German. He was now as proud of von Moltke and von Clausewitz as he was of Lou Gehrig.

He felt it would be as grand to plan a war with the colonel as to play in the World Series. Although he would not want to fight one against America.

"That's understandable," said the colonel. "Of course, you were born in Germany, and you are a German too."

"Yes," said Gottherd. "And it would not be as though I hated America. I would just be an opposing officer."

"A professional soldier would understand that," said the colonel.

"Yes, I think he would," said Gottherd, who had been training for nine months now, and secretly hoping the colonel might ask him to join a unit as a staff officer. He had still not agreed to spy. That was something else. But then again, the colonel had not mentioned it again. The colonel had something else for him.

He was given an orderly-driver, who, of course Hauff understood, was to watch him, an open-air touring car, and, sitting in the backseat, a blond girl who spoke perfect English in case Gottherd wanted to hear that language again. She was from California. He wore a Generalstab uniform, with the rank of lieutenant. It was not official, but it would make moving around less difficult in Germany. He had even taken a liking to its fit and posture, and the formalities that went with it. He was on a two-week leave.

The girl noticed the uniform immediately. "I thought you were an American," she said in English.

He kept that little mystery to himself and only smiled. She was so beautiful, with that fresh blond milkmaid look the Nazis liked to boast about, and so few of them had. Her hair was cut short and curled, and she seemed so happy with everything.

"Can you speak English?" she asked. She wore a light print dress and Gottherd could see her ankles and calves were golden tanned.

He didn't know what to answer exactly. He wanted to ask what her business was. He wanted to close his mouth because he was gaping. He just didn't think women were actually that beautiful, not women he knew, not women who weren't in the movies. Frau von Kiswicz had a face so common it looked as though it had been issued by ordnance.

And this young lady just kept smiling. At him.

"I speak English," said Gottherd.

"Well, I think you do. Come on in. They promised me this car and someone charming and I thought I'd see."

Gottherd felt himself being looked up and down.

"My name is Gottherd Hauff," he said.

"If worse comes to worst, we can enjoy the food. Two weeks with our own car and money. What luck, eh? Which place do you want to see?"

Gottherd shrugged.

"Well, get in the car," she said, patting the seat next to her. Her name was Gusti Kroeninger and she, too, had come over with her parents, and Bavaria, she assured him, was the only place to see. The people were nicest there.

"You're not a Prussian, are you?" she asked.

"No, I'm from Dearborn, Michigan," said Gottherd.

"Were your parents Prussian?"

"No."

"Good. I don't like Prussians. You must be very smart. They don't let others into the Generalstab that easily unless they are very smart. Are you very smart?" asked Gusti.

"I am smart enough to know not to talk about my work." He did not tell her he was not an officer.

"You sound so Prussian," she said.

They drove south, headed toward Bavaria. Dinner was a roast duck with sugared potatoes at one restaurant, costing just a few marks, and then across the street in the small town was a coffee shop where one got the real dessert. This was whipped cream loaded on layers of chocolate, with sugar crisps burned to brown.

Gottherd was not thinking about dessert. He was wondering if someone who looked so beautiful and so innocent actually went all the way and did that thing. He would have been thrilled just to kiss her and, perhaps later, get married. He ordered two rooms next to each other just in case of incredible good fortune. She told him the expense was ridiculous and ordered one room. The clerk did not ask to see the wedding license. He just nodded to the Herr Oberleutnant.

Gusti had to remind Gottherd this was not America. This was Germany. People didn't have to pretend to be married to get a room together. Unless of course he wanted a separate room?

"No," said Gottherd. The word did not convey the full absoluteness with which he meant it.

Gusti just took off her clothes and sat on the bed. Exquisite. A body like a drawing. A smile like an angel. Bare as brass and twice as happy.

Gottherd stood there.

"What are you waiting for?" she asked.

"Like that? You're undressed?" he said. What did he mean? He didn't even know.

"You're a virgin, aren't you?" she said.

"No. I'm not. I just don't think that this is the way to do it, that's all."

"How would you suggest?" she said.

"Well, I am not a prude, but—"

"You are a prude. You are a mud pie. A mud pie prude."

"You don't have to taunt me to get into bed with you," he said.

"Then what are you waiting for? Are you going to make me beg you?" she said. She looked so damned innocent, he thought.

Of course, what was she guilty of? He just had never expected someone so beautiful to be so willing.

His boots did not come off fast enough. He would have cut them off if he had a knife. He ripped off his shirt and climbed out of his undershorts on the run and leaped into the bed laughing. Gusti was laughing with him. She tried to escape as a game, but he caught her around the middle and rolled over on her. She wriggled out. Then she wiggled on top.

She did things Gottherd had only heard about, in locker-room boasts, but then it had been dirty. Nothing she did was dirty. Nothing about her and the loving was anything but fun. Passionate, yes. Passionate to groans. But it was fun.

They kissed everywhere. He thought she was leading until he found out he was. It was warm. It was strong. It was violent, and when it was over, it was just plain beautiful to be in her arms, kissing her.

"That was wonderful," he said.

"Yes," she said. "Where did you learn that?"

"What?"

"You were wonderful, Gottherd," she said.

"Really?" he said.

"Yes."

"I don't know what I did for sure."

"That's always the best," she said.

They had a bottle of brandy that they drank that night and ate fruit and candies with it and joked and made love two more times, and Gottherd thought there never was such fun in the world, and he was not altogether wrong. Each time had its own feeling. The once it just sort of happened and was lazy with easy movements that suddenly took them both to climax. Another he was playing with her lovely body when he realized he wanted her again, and she wanted him and why not? It was just plain good to do.

The next morning they had wine and fruit and sausages for breakfast.

When Gottherd got a Nazi salute from a policeman and did not return it, she said, "Good."

She did not like the Nazis but she felt she could live with anyone. They didn't really matter, she said, if you grinned at them. She thought it was terrible that Jews had to wear yellow stars, but then again she wasn't running things. She thought perhaps Berlin Jews deserved that sort of treatment but not Bavarian ones. And what surprised her most was that so many were still left in Germany.

"I think the whole policy is stupid dirt," said Gottherd. "On no level does it make sense."

"You Prussians are so cold. You would say don't kill your grandmother because her blood will make the floor messy. That's your reason," she said.

"I'm not a Prussian. I would say I am an American."

"Well, so am I," she said.

"Why do you keep saying I am Prussian? Because of this uniform?" he asked.

"No. You walk like one. You talk like one. You hit your gloves on your sleeve like one."

"I don't know what else to do with gloves," he said.

"Oh, I do," she said, her eyes suddenly sparkling. And she whispered it.

"Have you ever done that with men?" asked Gottherd.

"You are always so concerned with what I've done with others."

"Not really," said Gottherd with coolness, to cover a total absolute falsehood.

They drove the next morning with a picnic lunch into the Bavarian hills. The skies were dancing blue, a sparkling blue, the bluest blue, and yellow flowers dotted the meadows and the warm mountains. The snow was gone, and there was birth in the air. They walked into a meadow as the orderly waited in the car, and in the meadow he made love to her that morning, as the driver kept the farmer out of his fields so the lieutenant and his woman would not be disturbed.

Gottherd did not think about the next day, or getting back to America. He had Gusti. And she was fun. She wanted to run nude through the field. He stopped her. She wanted to make love pretending they were lord and peasant girl. He agreed. But it had to be out of sight of others.

She wanted to cover them with chocolate cream and then lick each other off. He refused. Whipped cream would be easier. Nothing was wrong anymore.

They stayed at inns, at hotels, dozed one night in the car, and one dawn, as she snuggled into his shoulder, and he smelled her hair, he knew that he was not going to be without this woman. He didn't care what she had done before. He was young enough to believe that love changed character and that wonderful times of love, the glory of the earth, could be repeated.

They had all the fourteen days, and every one of them was a jewel, every one of them was a beginning of a new life, and then they were over.

And Gottherd was determined it was not going to end. After all, Gusti loved him too. And he was sure that the reason she had known other men was because she hadn't loved like this.

He wanted more of those fourteen days. He did not realize he could never have one more of them again, but would have all of them forever.

When they returned to Wenksbrücken, Gottherd told the colonel his intentions.

It was after a dinner at which Frau von Kiswicz seemed happy with his company for the first time. She spoke a lot to Gusti. They left the women together.

"I want to marry her," said Gottherd.

"I see. Are you going to leave? What are your plans?"

"What are your plans, Herr Oberst?"

"We have a mission for you that hopefully you will never have to put into effect because we hope never to be at war with America or Britain."

"But we might be," said Gottherd.

"If certain things happen, yes."

"I had hoped possibly you might have something else for me," said Gottherd.

"If we did not need you so desperately for this specific mission, I would this very evening recommend a commission for you and personally sponsor you for the Generalstab."

Gottherd felt a pride almost to tears. Spying itself had lost its sting. But he still had reservations about Nazi Germany.

"This propaganda for the masses is embarrassing. These orgies of horns and uniforms they call parades. These storm troopers allowed to wear uniforms. The SS." He was only repeating what he had heard from some guests, naturally like the colonel, part of the Generalstab.

"The Nazis are not Germany, Gottherd. We are Germany. Germany was a bunch of little feuding degenerate states. We made it a nation. Our Bismarck made Germany. This . . . leader . . . with his corporal's fantasies will be gone when we are done with him. Germany will not tolerate him for that long. He will get in line, or he will be gone. You'll see. He is a man who risks too much, too often. He does not have time on his side. All right. You have heard it. It could be called treason. But I will not betray Germany."

The colonel was so sure that Gottherd became sure. He came to believe that what he had seen on the streets of Stuttgart was merely an ugly external, sure to pass like acne on a teenager's face. The rest of the world might believe that was Germany. He knew better. He knew this man, Colonel von Kiswicz, and he trusted him. It was inconceivable that the colonel would underestimate Chancellor

Hitler. After all, that would be a form of hope, and incredibly dangerous. Irresponsible to both the Generalstab and Germany itself. Therefore, it had to be so.

"Colonel, I am a bit embarrassed, but I must deliver an ultimatum. I not only want to marry Frau Kroeninger, but since I do not know how long I will be away, I want her to come with me."

The colonel pointed out the obvious dangers of being in love with an accomplice, the tactical limitations of caring so much for another person, and the problems when people fell out of love.

"Do you know what people do at the end of a romance? They often hate with such ferocity that they care not what happens to themselves, Hauff. Do you really want to endanger everyone's survival by incurring passion?"

"Yes, with her. Not without, Colonel. I think I am in a commanding position. You have invested almost a year in me. You are a full colonel, so let me assume I am very important. You might be able to force me, but what you need is my cooperation, not subjugation."

The colonel tried to reason some more, but it was not reason Gotthard dealt in. He wanted Gusti, and he did not want a life without her.

Frau von Kiswicz did not want the girl in the house, so Gotthard was given a house with Gusti on the estate. Gusti was quite intelligent. Like many women, she could figure out what was going on in a family much better than a man. It was like witchcraft. Gotthard never did understand how she could find out so quickly, but she told him that the colonel had married Frau von Kiswicz because her family had money, and he needed it for the estate. The colonel had two girlfriends in the village and three bastards.

"Did you go to bed with him?" asked Gotthard.

"Why do you always ask questions like that? It ruins everything."

"You did, didn't you?"

"I won't tell you."

"You did."

"You make so much of sex."

"My God," said Gotthard, and Gusti broke down into hysterics, shaking her head and demanding that "Gottzy"—she was calling him Gottzy now—look at his face in a mirror. Of course, she hadn't slept with him.

"It's not proper for a wife to do that, to ridicule."

"We're not married."

"We will, won't we? I assumed you would be delighted," said Gottherd.

"Let's see, yes?"

"See what?"

"See if we are right for marriage?"

"Right? We're in love. What's righter?"

"You're not enjoying yourself. You're such an American. You have to make every woman honorable. You really are an American."

She was so beautiful. He could watch her do her hair, or just sit pulling flowers, and think, *What a lovely creature. How could anyone be that lovely?* And then he would think of other men in her life, and he would feel the rage at what they would do, and worse, what she had enjoyed.

Everything von Kiswicz had done all became clear when they began studying another tactician. For months now he had been filled with names like von Moltke, von Clausewitz, von Schlieffen, von Scharnhorst, Beck, Delbrück, men who had replaced the myths of war with organized thought. Now he was introduced to a stranger. A Mahan, Admiral Mahan. And the book was in English.

"I don't need a translation into English. I have been reading everything in German," said Gottherd.

"The translation would be in German," said von Kiswicz.

And so Gottherd Hauff was introduced to the great naval theoretician Admiral Alfred Thayer Mahan, so much more appreciated outside than inside America. Every Japanese naval officer went to bed with a copy of Mahan next to him.

Mahan showed how sea power was land power, that one defended his own borders on the alien's shore by control of the sea.

The sea was the supply line for both an aggressive or defensive war. There could be no credible threat to Britain without threatening therefore America, and bringing in the "Monster." One could look at the Atlantic, controlled by the vastly superior British or American navies, and see strategic depth for Britain beyond Germany's reach.

Gottherd Hauff saw the strategic nightmare and saw the one solution. He spread out a map of the Atlantic, and then ran his finger from Casco Bay to Fort Lauderdale.

"This war will be won or lost here, because if it is lost here, it will be lost"—and then he put a fist down over Europe—"here."

Von Kiswicz nodded.

"But there is no chance of defeating a combined American-British navy in the Atlantic. Therefore you must be calculating an attack not on the navy but the supply lines. Diminish them here," said Gottherd with a finger somewhere around Baltimore, Maryland, "to give the time to effect a conclusion here," he said and the hand waved over Europe.

Von Kiswicz nodded again.

"So, what you really are talking about is an amount of time to be granted, not endless. There is no way Germany could win a total war on the sea."

Von Kiswicz nodded.

"So, here you are, a Generalstab officer, examining spies headed for America and you select me, correct? So there are two things we know. First, you do not approve of spying. I know that. So you must feel you have no choice."

Von Kiswicz nodded.

"Therefore, I would guess you are desperate. But I thought you did not expect a war with Britain or America."

"I said it was a hope."

"So much for that," said Gottherd. "Now, do you expect a war?"

"The situation is too fluid now to give any sort of estimate. Therefore we must prepare for the possibility."

"I don't like the idea of a limited time to effect an outcome on the continent. It is just too precarious. We must stay out of war with Great Britain."

The colonel only nodded. It was still a hope.

"There is another factor here, the second. Just how bad is our Navy?"

"With justifiable perception, they envy Great Britain. Unfortunately, they also want to fight a war like Great Britain. Given their own way, they would be building more battleships instead of U-boats."

"So there is a distrust of the Navy's strategic understanding."

"If we have a war, it will be a naval war. All wars between continents are naval wars. Only the conclusions are drawn on land," said the colonel.

"Therefore, your presence at a navy base. Therefore me. But why the strategic training? Well, I would guess you are extremely limited in what you have available to spy with."

"To a degree."

"But also, you must have someone who understands the strategic picture because whoever you send will have an extreme amount of freedom of choice, so he must know what is important and what is not. Therefore, I must believe we are starting almost from scratch because I would imagine a spy would ordinarily have a very limited specific mission."

"I would imagine," said the colonel.

"You don't know?"

"I know we found someone smart enough to know the Abwehr is not going to be good enough. Gottherd, thinking is thinking. We both know how to do it. We will figure out the mechanics of espionage together."

So it was done. Agreed to and done. Gottherd was still bothered by the fact that the espionage would be directed against America. But it was only one fact of many. And with his new way of looking at the world, it became minor. Yes, he was still an American. But he also felt like a Generalstab officer. He also felt that little twittering challenge in his stomach when he thought of the vastness of the American fleet, and what possible ways he might figure out with the colonel how to diminish its effectiveness to give the German land forces their one chance for a conclusion, should the Austrian corporal, Herr Kanzler Hitler, be allowed to stumble into another disaster of a world war.

And there was Gusti, and the certainty that now she would be his. Only later would he realize that he had successfully begun to lie to himself. But by then they were calling the disaster World War II.

He was allowed to say goodbye to his parents in Stuttgart, and he, of course, wore the uniform. His mother was exquisitely overjoyed by "her little officer." His father only asked if Gottherd knew what he was getting into. But his father was a simple Schwabian mechanic who only went where the work was. He probably had made a good infantryman, doing what he was told, not causing trouble, thought Gottherd. He tolerated the remark with good humor, and said, "Until we meet again."

Gottherd's father embraced him and whispered so his mother could not hear. "We're never going to meet again. None of us. Goodbye and God help you."

Back at the von Kiswicz estate, there were three months of learning the limits and strengths of U-boats, which were the only realistic weapon against shipping because Germany could never hope to control the surface against the British lion. The U-boat had been vastly improved since the First World War, when none of the commanders was sure when he submerged that he would resurface. Yet some of the reports virtually crowed about the naval situation.

"It has been improved to modest," commented Hauff.

"Fine commanders," said von Kiswicz.

"And after them? If the sea war goes on more than a year, these fine commanders will be at the bottom of the sea. We can't afford losses. We must avoid naval battles. We just can't afford it."

"I agree," said von Kiswicz. "They must avoid the warships."

"Only transports. I don't care how much they lust for the carriers."

"I don't think you will be able to stop their doing that; they are a bit like cavalry officers after all."

The worst of them was an admiral who talked about nothing but seamanship and courage, and the Viking-Teutonic love of the sea.

He knew a lot about U-boats. The man was brilliant when it came to that. But when Gottherd found out the admiral was commanding all the U-boats, he said, "My God in heaven, who let that happen?"

The Fuehrer, he was told, had a very high regard for this man Doenitz.

"My God, I am done for," said Gottherd.

"Don't worry," von Kiswicz assured him. "We promised to supply information. I will always be between you and him. He will not know anything he absolutely does not have to know. I agree with your assessment. Another man of destiny."

"And who will be between him and those poor boys in the U-boats?" said Gottherd, knowing the strengths of British and American fleets.

"The water," said von Kiswicz.

In his one meeting with Grand Admiral Doenitz, Gottherd had

been introduced as an aide to Colonel von Kiswicz. The admiral had not even been told his name, and apparently did not notice.

One night the colonel took Gottherd into his den for drinks. He talked about his family; he talked about service; he talked about real honor, not the affectation of a uniform. Honor, he said, was what you did, not what you said. Honor was what you did when no one was looking. When you were alone.

"Gottherd, you will be most alone. If they catch you, they will call you a spy. They will execute you and perhaps call you a traitor. But I know you are an officer in the Generalstab. What they call you and what you are, Gottherd Hauff, are two different things. You will seem to be a spy, but you will be an officer of the Generalstab."

It was better than suddenly being a New York Yankee. The colonel saluted him. Gottherd Hauff clicked his heels as he returned the salute and it was done.

It was immediately clear they were going to be helped by Abwehr Group Pfeiffer. Flooding the field with incompetents would make Gottherd's group that much safer. Still, one could not underestimate the FBI.

"Running from the American police makes you feel like a criminal, yes?"

"No," said Gottherd. "Just another factor."

Von Kiswicz suggested that only Gottherd know everyone in the group. Gottherd pointed out that he wanted it as small as possible because in espionage the converse of warfare was true. The larger the mass, the more vulnerable.

"Do you still want Kroeninger?"

"Most of all."

"She is intelligent, I will give you that. It will be your love for her that will be your problem."

"Women are more perceptive about certain things than men. I am not talking about pots and pans either, Herr Oberst."

"So you will use her for other things. Good. She is shrewd. A happy girl, but shrewd in her own way. Bavarian."

There was a choice between Baltimore, Maryland, and Newport, Rhode Island. Baltimore because of the heavy shipping, and its proximity to Annapolis and Washington, or Newport because of the Naval War College.

The Naval War College was a combination of general staff and training for the higher officers. It was where the strategy for America's future wars was being thought out. Von Kiswicz thought that from Newport they might be able to ascertain the total Atlantic picture and thus decide on the best station. Maybe even stay there. Gottherd understood he could not penetrate all naval installations, nor was any particular station important.

What he needed was the best point at which to secure the best information on supply traffic across the Atlantic. It might be anywhere along the East Coast.

Newport was where to begin.

The group would have American names and forged American passports and would leave the Continent from France separately, except for Gottherd and Gusti, who would travel together.

Gottherd refused a weapon, saying, "If I have to shoot back at someone, I've lost. My battle is lost when the first shot is fired. This is a different battlefield."

The colonel approved of the thinking but insisted Gottherd know how to use a side arm. Gottherd took one day of instruction and was told that he would never be competent with a side arm without an extraordinary amount of work.

The absolute minimum personnel they could survive with, Gottherd reasoned, was three. Most crucial was the radio contact, but every message and moment of contact was also an area of vulnerability. One exposed one's position whenever a message was sent. Messages would have to be brief and would have to come at varied times to reduce the danger that would nevertheless still be there with every radio or personnel contact with a U-boat. Therefore he wanted someone who could survive on his own and detach himself, perhaps flee if he were identified.

Von Kiswicz found a man he believed had the right characteristics. His name was von Schaumburg and, like Gottherd, had been raised in America. He was not, to the colonel's knowledge, related to any von Schaumburg the colonel knew.

This worried Gottherd because if the man were pretending to be a "von," Germany was the most ridiculous place to attempt the masquerade.

"I cannot afford heel-clicking fools," said Gottherd.

"He is not a fool. You will have to keep a tight rein on von Schaumburg, but he has got the wherewithal within him to press an attack if you need it. He is crafty and tough, and with a tight rein will make you a good subordinate. Think of him as your cavalry in a way. I grant you, a risk. But you don't want to find yourself in America with someone who discovers great wells of temerity within him."

"There is no one else?"

"Gottherd, whom do you think we get to choose from? The graduating class of West Point? I am sorry, but now you understand why we had to take a chance on someone who said he did not wish to spy for us. I went with capability, and character, and of course some observations on how you decided things. Otto von Schaumburg is about as good as you are going to get."

Otto had been raised in Madison, Wisconsin. He spoke gruffly, and wore a Nazi party pin. He did not want to give up his "von" by taking an American name. He did not want to serve under a younger man. He was not against following orders, but this man, Gottherd Hauff, was at least five years younger.

"Your passport already has 'Harry Lederle' on it," said Gottherd. "I will entertain any reasonable complaint you have, but limit the nonsense if you want to survive."

The man who claimed to be a "von" looked at the colonel. The colonel did not respond.

"Of course, I follow your leadership. I look forward to making you a success, Herr Oberleutnant, and will be an obedient servant. I follow your command," said Harry Lederle.

"You will be our radio operator," said Gottherd. Harry Lederle got up and gave a Nazi salute. Gottherd returned a formal army salute. Lederle, at the time, gave the impression he was at Gottherd's feet.

Gusti, as a special favor, was allowed to choose her own name, within reason. It could not be flamboyant or of German origin.

Gusti took a week to choose among at least fourteen names, finally settling on Elizabeth.

"With a name like Elizabeth, the world will open for me. Elizabeths lead elegant lives. Oh, Gottzy, I am going to have so much fun. This is such fun."

"I am afraid, dear, I am not your Gottzy anymore," Charles Drobney told Elizabeth.

The colonel assured him that he would never endanger Charles

Drobney unnecessarily and, if the war went badly, he could be assured he would not be one of those surrendered.

"You didn't have to promise me that, Colonel. I never had doubts about that."

They shook hands goodbye and saluted, the last salute.

In America, Lederle became an immediate problem. He wanted to do too much too quickly. And he was also vocally anti-Semitic.

"I don't care whether you feel that or not," said Charles Drobney. "It attracts attention."

"I've found as much anti-Semitism here as I have in Germany."

"That only tells me that you are hanging around with the wrong people."

"Well, yes. It's good to hang around with our own kind, sir."

"That stops now," said young Charles Drobney, "and don't you ever call me 'sir' again under any circumstances. You know what we're doing."

"I thought you would like it, you know. Considering who you are and everything," said Lederle.

"I am Charles Drobney."

"Yes, Mr. Drobney."

With almost half the funds supplied by the colonel, Charlie helped Lederle purchase a little fisherman's house and a boat so that Lederle could go into the fishing business. There, Lederle would operate the shortwave, but never without Drobney's orders. No message was ever going to be sent without Drobney's approval. The boat gave Drobney physical access to the Atlantic.

Gusti, now happily Elizabeth Boswell, was given limited and specific duties. Like Lederle, she was not told anything she did not have to know. But unlike Lederle, she didn't ask. Her job was to find out personal things about officers at the War College, indebtedness, drinking habits, little character chinks. Nothing elaborate and nothing extensive. She was not to be so inquisitive as to be noticed.

"I've never had that problem, Charlie," she said.

When she didn't come home after a full night, he accused her of sleeping with another man.

She said that made it easier to get information.

"Then for the duration of this assignment, I will not sleep with you." He stared at that pretty doll face like an officer rebuking a private.

"If you're jealous, say so," she snapped back.

"No. It's not jealousy, it's just too dangerous."

"It is jealousy."

"Think what you want. Fuck who you want. I don't care."

But, of course, he did. He did very much. He moved out. It was strange being back in America. He was home. At Wenksbrücken he could feel like a staff officer. But he was an American. He wasn't a German-American anymore, he was a German and an American.

He told himself that the newspaper stories coming out of Germany were just the sensationalism of people who didn't understand the real Germany. The real Germany was not Adolf Hitler. Germany had basic interests that went beyond whoever happened to be the current leader.

He told himself there would be no war. Those first months back in America were hell. If he didn't want to live so much he would have done what he used to think Prussian officers did—end it all with a bullet.

Charles Drobney had to make a choice. He could run to the FBI now, and probably get a minor jail sentence at worst. But then what about his parents? They were still in Germany. Would they be punished? The colonel had mentioned they would be treated like the family of a Generalstab officer, which meant protection from the vagaries of the Geheime Staatspolizei (Gestapo). Was that a threat behind a promise of protection? And what about the colonel?

Did he want to betray the colonel? He was proud of what the Generalstab represented. Of course, here in America, Germany looked more like the property of Hitler and the Nazis than the upright tradition of von Moltke. In America, seeing the American flag on American ships, it was hard not to feel the old tugs of loyalty. Yet there were so many American ships, ships he had only thought about before, catalogued in his mind. It was exciting to think that here they were, the other side, range, firepower, and possible weaknesses. He had a strong desire to see if he actually could set up a system that might neutralize such a preponderance of power. It could be done but he had to be precise. They were going to use convoys again, and probably better detection devices. But it was still not impossible.

There was this feeling also that he had been trained for this; he would be good at this, he was sure. It seemed like such a shame not to try, despite his old loyalties. And besides, wasn't he a professional soldier now? Good guys versus the bad guys was what you told the ranks. Officers did not believe it.

The colonel didn't hate America, or Britain, or France. They were simply factors in equations.

The General Staff wanted time to conclude a decision in a European war. Drobney would not be fighting America itself, rather he would be keeping it from using its power abroad. That was the indisputable strategic mission.

And Lederle had begun to press him for a communication. They had received three over a period of two months and not responded. Was their unit dysfunctional? How long would the colonel wait? How long could the colonel wait? And what would Lederle do should the colonel become dissatisfied? Just about anything. Turn Drobney in? Kill him? Why not?

It was a change in seasons in Newport, a very mild spring when Charles Drobney knew he had run out of time. With all the information he had at hand, he came to the conclusion that he could successfully and safely perform the colonel's mission. It was a multipart decision. *Takt.*

He proceeded with a brief status report on the Eastern Shore Command already being set up to comply with Britain's request for convoy assistance, should Adolf Hitler invade Poland.

It was 1939, and young Drobney told himself there was still a possibility that there would be no war. For someone who was supposed to calculate accurately, he had discovered an inordinate ability to lie to himself. In that year of 1939, he was not alone, he would realize later. Most of the world had lied to itself.

He would understand later with great pain that to think about war like a professional soldier was not giving up innocence but exchanging it.

He would understand as a man the sins of the boy. And there would be no one he could turn to for forgiveness.

As he grew old, he would remember often in his study, with his wife churning a sea of hostility outside the door, those beautiful days in Bavaria and two young people under those special skies. More often, he remembered how crudely he lied to himself. Of course, he had only known that when he stopped. But only in the hospital did he let himself remember fully those dreadful little self-deceiving steps that led a good American, Gottherd Hauff, to become a traitor, Charles Drobney.

The nurse came in before dawn to check Charles Drobney's blood pressure again.

"Are you feeling better?" she asked.

"No," he said.

15

TODD SLEPT over at Sondra's house that night. She needed someone so badly, she didn't fully appreciate how much he needed someone too.

He was not at liberty to say whether his investigation had anything to do with the shooting.

"I thought perhaps that was why you might have gone to the party. Remember her talking about how you shouldn't be investigating the codebooks?"

"I can't say, Sondra."

That night they just held each other.

In the morning, the Navy launched its full attack. Admiral William O'Connell, retired, a veteran of the war in the Atlantic, had struck publicly with his theory about submarine warfare and the high tolls.

Nazis in Newport became, in some newspapers, a cell operating out of one of the mansions. No newspaper mentioned that Elizabeth Boswell, who had married Alexander Wheaton after the war, didn't live there during it. The photographs of the marble palaces were just too appealing. And Mrs. Wheaton in file photos was gorgeous.

Now, television newsmen, when they couldn't get background shots of the Hickories, stood in front of barred gates through which other mansions could be seen. Their voices intoned tense drama. They talked of shock. They talked of Claus von Bulow's being convicted of attempting to murder his wife. They began to mention that he might be more German than Danish.

If one listened to the television commentators, one could imagine local police taut with dramatic intensity desperately trying to unearth forty-year-old clues.

File shots of Nazi U-boat commanders grinning from turtleneck shirts were superimposed on flaming tankers. The navy lieutenant commander in charge of the investigation appeared on national television, repeating what retired Admiral O'Connell had said. Old embargoed footage of death on America's beaches was released.

The Navy thrust was that it had complained several times to the Federal Bureau of Investigation during the war and had been reassured by J. Edgar Hoover himself that investigations showed nothing.

"No, I would never suggest that it was an FBI sort of cover-up, just to protect its record," said the lieutenant commander. He had not been asked that.

On the morning news, Admiral O'Connell, himself a decorated war hero, a veteran of the bloody war in the Atlantic, also did not suggest that it was some sort of FBI cover-up. He did not suggest this on ABC or NBC. His cab had been tied up in New York traffic that morning, so he didn't have a chance to not suggest it on CBS until the midmorning news.

The FBI did not counterattack immediately. The Orlando Field Office had a tip on who did the shooting. Two Chileans involved in drug smuggling, and there was no way to get hands on them, much less admissible evidence. It was a professional job and it was drug-related.

There was a further complication in that Oliver had not notified the Bureau he had been at a party at Mrs. Wheaton's. He explained that it had been a routine community relations thing for the Renaissance League, of which Mrs. Wheaton was chairwoman for that year. Yes, he had spoken to her and she did seem to know about the investigation of the codebooks.

"All right. So you were there," said PRO Boston.

"We let them nail it into the wall as a cover-up, and then you let them know we have had a man here for more than a week," said Oliver.

"One who was at that party too," said PRO Boston.

"And look here, we are investigating and the Navy is actually getting in the way, by saying there has been a cover-up," added Oliver.

"Right. We didn't want to say anything about an investigation because we weren't playing publicity games. We were trying to do our work, and we certainly don't want to advertise we have a man in Newport just on that."

Supervisor Cobb entered the conversation: "Don't forget the drug link."

"I think we ought to leak that after we establish we are doing our job and are being hampered by the Navy running to the press. They hate the Navy as much as they hate us," said PRO Boston.

"Right," said Oliver.

"Did you see that O'Connell?" asked Supervisor Cobb.

Oliver suggested a public response. "We had a man in Newport, quietly, and we didn't publicize it, a man quietly looking into navy charges."

PRO Boston agreed. "You appear for an interview and solemnly say you have been looking into this for a week and you are busy and then the spokesman takes over for you. You are very official, and you are there for the cameras, and they are saying cover-up, and you're there. Physically there, mentioning how long you have been there."

"Good," said Oliver.

"How is it going, Oliver?" asked Supervisor Cobb.

Oliver replied, "I did the local police today, and tomorrow I see all the people who want to talk to me and those who don't."

"God," said Cobb. "All this because some rich bitch probably didn't pay her supplier."

"You know," said Oliver, "she wouldn't be the first rich person to deal drugs on a large scale, and then think they could get away without paying."

Supervisor Cobb summed it up: "The Navy is just trying to promote a revision of the Second World War. And they will use a drug case or anything to justify it."

"We can't say that, can we?" asked PRO Boston.

"No, dammit," said Supervisor Cobb angrily. "It's the truth, though."

"We can leak it," suggested PRO Boston.

"Don't do it out of Boston," said Oliver.

"Is the United States Navy going to look foolish when we tie in Mrs. Wheaton to cocaine or something. Right, Todd?" said Supervisor Cobb.

"It certainly is something I am not going to ignore from here," said Oliver.

"Right," said Cobb.

"Right," said PRO Boston.

"Okay," said Oliver.

The next day, Todd made the proper application to get the tax files of Mrs. Wheaton and made arrangements to see the lawyer handling the Wheaton estate. He was a New York City lawyer, part of the prestigious firm that handled the entire Wheaton fortune.

The lawyer phoned Oliver at the Newport office. Elizabeth Wheaton did not touch money. She received money from a trust. The family would not object to the FBI's examining any records, provided the information would be kept confidential.

"So she had no cash of her own?" asked Todd.

"What do you mean?" said the lawyer.

"Dollars in her pockets."

"What would she need them for?" asked the lawyer.

"To buy things."

"If she had to handle cash, I am sure she could always get it. Mrs. McAllister would have taken care of that."

Mrs. McAllister, who was in Newport and lived in the mansion as staff, met Todd in her office at the Hickories.

"I have been told you are interested in how Mrs. Wheaton got cash?"

"Yes, how much did she have?"

Mrs. McAllister thought about that a moment and looked puzzled.

"Each day, or what? I don't understand?"

"How much money was available to her personally?"

"Whatever she needed."

"What about her wants?"

"Yes," said Mrs. McAllister, as though that had been obvious.

"You mean she could buy a twelve-million-dollar ruby and pay for it with ready cash?"

"She wouldn't do it that way. She would look at it and then tell me that she wanted it, or if it were twelve million dollars, probably the lawyer would handle it. She wouldn't actually put her own hands on the money. Is that helpful? Is that what you wanted?"

"Uh, yes. Now, on her last words. Do you speak German?"

"No. I don't."

"So, you don't know whether she spoke German or not."

"Right."

"People told you it was German."

"Yes."

"And it made no sense, did it?"

"Actually, it did. That was something she had said to me in English, a couple of times. When they told me what it meant, I was so sad. I remember once on a beautiful day, gorgeous day, how the skies were absolutely perfectly blue and perfectly clear, and she said, 'No, they are not blue enough,' and I answered, 'If this isn't blue enough, what is?' And she just smiled and went back in the house."

"Did she have lovers?"

"Sir?"

"Did she have a lover? She was single for quite a while, a widow."

"No," said Mrs. McAllister sharply. "I do not wish to discuss that with you."

"How do you know there wasn't something in a love affair that prompted a jealous lover to kill her?"

Mrs. McAllister thought about that a moment.

"All right. She didn't have those kinds of affairs. They were more like little snacks she took. She was very discreet."

"All right, thank you, Mrs. McAllister. I may call on you again."

"Don't you want to know about her conversations with the senator and friends, trying to stop your investigation? I thought you would ask that, there being rumors about her being a spy and all that. I don't believe it. I will tell you right now, I don't believe it. She couldn't have been a German spy. They're saying because she spoke German while dying she was a German, but she wasn't."

"You know that?"

"Absolutely. She could not have been a German because she was so un-German you would not believe it. She didn't care what anyone believed. It didn't bother her. You could be a communist, or a Nazi or a hippie. She just did not care. She felt your way was your way, and she had hers. Live and let live. Is that German? You will never tell me that is German."

"Thank you, Mrs. McAllister."

"Never."

At the Drake-Hume mansion, Todd was asked to go around to the side of the building to the tradesmen's entrance.

"I am a special agent for the Federal Bureau of Investigation. I am here because Mrs. Drake-Hume asked the Justice Department if she could give evidence."

"Of course," said the butler. "She is expecting you. Just go around to the side, thank you."

"I am from the FBI," said Todd, so shocked he wasn't offended.

"And you are on time. Please, she is waiting for you."

Todd went to the servants' entrance and then into a hallway, led by another butler, and then into a small overfurnished parlor set before a larger overfurnished parlor. The room was dark, overcrowded with plush chairs of another era. He was told where to sit.

Mrs. Drake-Hume was in her midfifties, and wore a light green skirt with a gold chain around the waist. She sat behind a gold-trimmed leather-topped desk. Her husband, Albert, dozed on a couch, nodding off and then suddenly lifting his head. Mrs. Drake-Hume did not seem to mind his nodding off nor did she even appear to think it was in any way irregular.

"I am glad you are here, young man, because everyone is getting everything wrong, and I want you to get it right. Now, what have you been told so far?"

"I am just beginning my investigation."

Mrs. Drake-Hume remembered World War II most acutely in its absence of young men, the tennis and golf instructors being the first to go. She thought the suggestion of spies operating in Newport was impossible.

"Everyone knew each other," she said, creating a view of Newport that could only be fashioned behind the walls of a mansion. Unbelievably, she knew very little of the city, quite naturally thinking of it as always composed of her friends and their servants; since at that time all the servants were Irish and loyal of course, there could not have been spies.

Todd listened with a straight face. He was not, of course, going to use that information, even though Mrs. Drake-Hume stressed twice:

"Therefore, young man, there could not be any spies here. Never in Newport. Providence, possibly. Boston, yes. New York, God knows what they have there."

Mrs. Drake-Hume knew Mrs. Alexander Wheaton, and she knew she was a decent sort of woman who would have nothing to do with spies. This whole investigation was silly, foolish, and a waste of tax money. "Isn't that right, Albert?" she asked.

"Whauhhhh," said Albert, lifting his head briefly and then letting it drop.

"He's just taken his medicine. He always gets sleepy right after the medicine. But God help us if we run out."

"What do you mean?" said Todd.

"His nose starts running and he gets headaches, and three years ago we were aboard our boat without it and when we couldn't get a prescription, we thought he would die. Absolutely die. You felt your skin was coming off, didn't you, Albert?"

"Did it stop hurting after twenty-four hours?" said Todd.

"Why yes. How did you know that?"

"May I see the prescription?" asked Todd.

She rang for Hughes. The butler brought the bottle. It was a derivative of morphine. Albert was on heroin. He had suffered a withdrawal and was nodding off just like any other junkie except he was supplied by his doctor.

"Is there any problem getting this?"

"Of course not. You just make sure your physician orders what you need."

"And Mrs. Wheaton, if she wanted this, could she get it?"

"If she told her doctor, of course."

"Do you know of anyone taking medicines, oh, little powders that keep them awake?"

"Absolutely, and it is wonderful for losing weight, they say. But really, it is unsocial and who really wants to do that?"

"Doctors can get that too?" said Todd.

"Yes. Of course. If you tell them."

Why not, thought Oliver. If they didn't use a physician, they probably could have ordered it from a drug company they owned. There was no drug problem here on the Avenue because those sorts of laws just did not apply here when one had the right doctor.

Elizabeth Wheaton may have been killed by drug-connected people, but her death had nothing to do with drugs. And she certainly didn't need the money. She didn't even bother with money.

And the next day, as Mrs. Elizabeth Boswell Wheaton, widow of Alexander Wheaton, was buried, two Washington columnists let their readers know what unnamed sources were keeping under tight wraps. The spy "socialite" had been killed by drug dealers. Drugs in Newport were now competing with Nazis in Newport. Todd's side had struck back.

When Charles Drobney was finally moved to a private room, he asked that the television set be taken out. He didn't even want to watch his baseball games because the games were interrupted by the news. He spent two weeks getting his blood pressure down and avoiding newspapers. Sometimes he read poetry. Often he would visit with Sondra. He missed Brandon very much.

The boy was precious to him. He was at the same age Sondra was when Charles Drobney had begun trying to kill himself slowly with alcohol, and many other things; driving the car too fast, driving himself too hard.

It was at a time after the war when all the lying stopped. It could not go on any longer. Buchenwald and Auschwitz showed the world and Charles Drobney what he had served. In detail, massive and personal, Charles Drobney saw what he had seen on the streets of Stuttgart. The storm troopers, the gutter fighters, were not an aberration. They had been Germany. Those who struggled against the Nazis were the exceptions.

Bob Goldstein's wife had lost relatives. Decent Bob Goldstein, who kept asking what was bothering Charlie, asking if he could help. Every time he did so, Charles Drobney felt the sharp spikes of shame.

Von Kiswicz had never told him it would be like this. You had dinner with the winning general and discussed why you did not support this flank or committed that unit early or late.

Nobody ever told him he would have to know for the rest of his life he had helped keep a war going so that maniacs would have more time to make lampshades of people's skin.

It was a time of reflection on the Nuremberg War Crimes Trials and it seemed as if every day another page of the horrors was shown to the world and one day he saw Bob read a newspaper account about Auschwitz. The blood drained from Bob's face. The lips became tight. And Bob looked to him.

"The vermin," said Drobney. "The vermin. How could they do that?"

"Yeah," said Bob, and that only brought Bob's good feelings closer. Bob did not know that Charles Drobney had really meant not how could they do that to the poor victims so much as how could they do that to the professional soldiers' war that he had lied himself into believing in—how could they do that to him?

For the Nazis had as surely done a crime to Germany as it had to the Jews and the rest of the world.

And yet, he was, he knew, lying to himself again. He had done it. He had helped. He had escaped. All his logic, all his reasoning, all his proud tactics and strategy were so much grease on the skids to hell.

He even tried to make amends because there was no living with himself, once the lies stopped. And that was worse. He volunteered to read to patients at a veterans' hospital. And there he saw the people he had so accurately targeted.

And he had the privilege of hearing firsthand what it was like to be the victim of a torpedo attack. If they got off the ship alive, that is, if they were not dragged down in a coffin of a room, or trapped in dark water-filled passageways that suddenly changed conformation with each new hit, they might make it safely to the sea, where they could either breathe water or swim through flames.

Charles Drobney saw the burned oil still dark in the burn scars on young faces.

He heard the crewmen who, if they could get off the ship and should make it through flames, would then have to stay afloat in another hell. A sub attack meant a battle with their own destroyers cutting frantically through the waters trying to protect the other ships, and get the sub. Depth charges would go off crazily at different levels and those surviving in the water would have to jam a finger into their rectums to prevent the concussion of exploding depth charges from driving seawater into their intestines. The glory of war.

One young man, who had made it safely off a torpedoed ship with a life jacket, had been cut from belly button to armpit by the blades of a ship desperately maneuvering to escape a hit.

The scar was big as a rope, and he said he was lucky to be alive. He kept saying that to Charles Drobney. He was so damned cheerful. So decent. He had played triple A ball in Minneapolis when he was drafted. He had batted .374 and was fast.

"You would have made it in the majors. You were a natural for the majors," Drobney told him.

"It looked good."

"Better than good; you would have made it."

"Well, you know. Who knows. I'm alive. Lots of guys aren't."

"You would have made it, dammit," said Drobney. "Triple A pitching isn't all that different from the majors. Maybe you'll see one weak pitcher a team, but you would have made it. With .374, no way you weren't going to make it."

He must have been making a pest of himself over that and other things because the hospital told him they were sorry, but he was not really a help. He had to learn not to take the victim's plights so personally. They were sure it was his guilt over not having served. They suggested psychiatric help.

Of course, a psychiatrist was useless. Drobney's problem wasn't neurotic guilt. He was guilty. And besides, the psychiatrist would probably turn him in if he told the doctor of his real crime.

There were no amends and no forgiveness, just a life that dragged on by tedious days, with warnings about his drinking so heavily and driving so quickly and working so long.

And then he saw a helpless girl reach out her hand to him. His daughter needed him. His wife Catherine was drinking heavily also, and Sondra had no one but him. Was he going to destroy someone else by destroying himself?

Was he lying to himself again? Perhaps. But there was something he could do. He had been trained to think. The thinking was good. The logic was good. They were, after all, only tools. And they had obviously been improperly used.

He decided he would use his trained thinking to understand how wars came about, how the horrors came about, to force himself to understand every bit of it, with all the pain of looking directly into sunlight while the soul cried to look away.

He could never make up for what he did, but he might do some good. And instead of avoiding all things about the Second World War and the history that led to it, he read avidly. He read grand opinions of historians, and he read the details of as many reports as he could get.

He set up a room in his house for this. He knew he could bring a unique perspective, someone who didn't try to prove he was innocent. Someone who had been taught to think with neither hope nor despair.

He saw some patterns emerge in history when he applied the rules of strategy, specifically of knowing, first of all, one's realistic objective.

To his amazement, he realized most nations did not fight their real enemies, but their myths. They waged ferocious wars against their fears. Their real enemies were often something else entirely.

War was not, as von Clausewitz had written, an extension of foreign policy, but its breakdown. One only had to look at supposed objectives of nations to realize this. Borders changed sometimes only to create new problems.

The only thing that ever justified a war was survival. Other than that, objectives of war were actually ludicrous.

Then he began something far harder than looking into history and governments. He looked at himself. He realized then that he had no objectives in his life. He had been trying just to survive for so long, he didn't know what he wanted from the world when survival wasn't a factor anymore. He started realistically to examine what a person could expect out of life. What were the good things? What did more of something mean? Was it really better? And while he was asking himself what a good life was, one just seemed to happen with the years, through the few people and few things he allowed himself to love.

When Charles Drobney thought it might be safe, he tried to search for his parents—making international telephone calls from phone booths in Boston to any Hauff living in Stuttgart, and not being connected to the right Hauff or even finding anyone who knew a Rudiger or Maria Hauff. He went on by random phone checks to other parts of Germany, refusing to concede that his father had been right, that they would never see each other again, that it was goodbye and not *auf Wiedersehen.*

He gave up phoning, but only during his two weeks of recovering in his sixty-seventh year did Charles Drobney finally accept without resistance the conclusive fact that he would never see his parents again. They would have had to live through the war, and then go into their nineties. It was highly improbable. His grandparents, he knew, had died in their early sixties.

One of the nurses taking care of him reminded him of Gusti Kroeninger. She was so happy with life, but having problems with her boyfriend; well, with three of them. Drobney could listen thoroughly and after a short while, he told her what she already knew. The boyfriends weren't the problem; she was. She wanted them all to accept the others.

"That's right," she said.

"When you find a world where people's feelings coincide with your convenience, invite me."

She liked that, but she wanted advice. And so the man whose thinking had originally been molded by von Clausewitz and Beck and von Moltke told her to see how long she might string the three of them along, which would leave her with only those or one who could without jealousy be her boyfriend. It was the *Takt* decision. Unfortunately, it had one drawback.

"The one who leaves first is going to be the one you want the most," said Drobney.

"You know me," said the nurse, laughing.

"A thousand times and a thousand years ago," said Drobney, "a long time ago." Gusti was dead.

16

M. Hiram Lederle, for his serious physical checkups, went to Boston to Massachusetts General Hospital. He stayed two days at the Phillips House and heard once again in his seventy-first year that he had the body of a man in his early sixties. And since the doctor's name was Rosenblatt and he therefore would never be moving in circles of the Ida Lewis Yacht Club, Clambake Club, and never even by accident be at Bailey's Beach, Hiram Lederle added:

"And I fuck whatever I can lay my hands on too." He held out his forearm to the world. "I am like this."

"I take it you don't feel threatened sexually?" said the doctor.

"I don't feel threatened by anything. If I am afraid of it, I get rid of it. That's the secret of sleeping good, fucking good, and living long."

Charles Drobney left Newport Mercy Hospital with a warning to avoid stress and salt, and do more walking and relaxing, or the next time he might suffer a stroke and not be walking out at all.

Sondra drove him past the store, saying he wasn't to go in there again until his blood pressure was at least 140 over 100.

"But I find it relaxing."

"Uncle Bob won't let you in. He bought a blood pressure gauge. It's at the cash register, and you don't get in the door until your pressure is 140 over 100."

"You're kidding," said Drobney.

Sondra laughed.

"He would do that. He would really do that," said Drobney. "He really would."

"He threatened," said Sondra. "God, am I glad you're alive, Dad," she said, and just as she was laughing, she began crying, and Charles Drobney knew his daughter was happy.

She set up a small television in the kitchen and prepared him a bowl of salt-free tomato soup from a special packet. It screamed for salt. It tried to make do with a celery-pepper-vegetable-spice combination. But when your crackers were saltless, and your salad dressing was saltless, the one thing your taste buds cried for was real tomato soup with salt.

"How is it, Dad?" asked Sondra. "It's shit, right? It didn't taste that bad to me."

"It's all right," said Drobney.

"The chicken was worse, Dad," said Sondra and turned on the television. He did not remember her liking television that much, but it was a news show, midday.

"Do we have to watch it?"

"Todd's on."

"The fellow who took you to the ball?"

"Yeah," she said. She wasn't looking at him.

He watched her nod her head as the young man came on the television set to answer questions.

"I am still investigating. I cannot comment. I am still investigating."

"Dammit, why don't they leave him alone," said Sondra.

"How did he get in front of those cameras? Did the networks chain him there?" said Drobney. He looked around for a saltshaker to sneak a dash into his soup while Sondra was watching the television. The amount of good the salt would do for this soup hardly equaled any damage it might do to him. There was reducing salt intake and then there was obsessive. Sondra was obsessive. She had hidden the saltshaker.

"I am sorry. I cannot comment. I am still investigating," came Todd's voice from the television set.

"The Navy knows how to use the networks. It's just a bureaucratic fight. That's all it is."

Drobney quietly got up from the table and moved to the kitchen cabinet. There was usually a large container of salt there.

"I got rid of that too, Dad," said Sondra, without taking her eyes off the set. "Look at the look on them. They won't leave him alone. All he wants to do is do his job, and there are forces that won't let him," said Sondra.

She mouthed the words, nodding her head severely as once again he told the interviewer he couldn't comment and was just investigating.

Charles Drobney did not have any salt in the house. His house.

"I'm going to work."

"Eat your soup. Look at that. Look at that." Sondra shook her head. "The stress they go through."

"Are you serious about this fellow?" said Charlie.

"You'd be the first to know."

"And you might be the second," said Drobney.

To presume one branch of government was innocent to the ways of publicity while another was cunning and wise had to be a suspension of critical judgment. Every branch wanted to look like the victim of publicity while they did their work, which was what this fellow had done beautifully. Charles Drobney was sure he would appear, badgered by reporters, in front of the cameras a few more times, just investigating.

And why? To appear that he was investigating, of course. But why?

Was it possible he wasn't really investigating? Was it possible for some reason someone didn't want to catch them? Was it possible that after that brutal lunacy by Lederle there were still those who could believe there wasn't an espionage ring here?

Thinking about these things would do him absolutely no good. He tried to change the subject but Sondra wouldn't let him.

"I personally find him pleasant company, Dad. I'm glad he'll be here three more weeks. And I think I'll be sorry when he goes. But it's not a serious thing. I don't think I'd let it be. Do you understand?"

"It's taken me a long time in my life to realize you just don't maneuver love like that."

"I agree. And if I loved him, there would be no trouble, but we are very safe from that. He has obligations in Washington, and I am not about to start taking married men away from their wives. Do I shock you?"

"No," said Charles Drobney. He ate his soup without thinking.

"See, the soup isn't that bad," said Sondra, watching him eat, eyeing the spoon to make sure it all got in.

"It's that bad, honey," he said.

The next day he was back in the store, with a diastolic pressure of just under 100. It was good to be back.

"Oh shit, here goes the store," said Goldstein. "What are we not going to be able to sell now?"

Drobney glanced to the right aisle and the row of green power mowers.

"Them, for instance," he said.

"They're selling," said Goldstein.

"This July they've sold. I told you they sell in May. They sell in April. Sometimes if great fortune and accidents occur in the course of human events, mowers sell in June. In July they discount."

"I'm discounting."

"That's not selling," said Charles Drobney.

"It's not going broke either," said Goldstein and gave him a joyous hug. "Besides, we got a good price. I got a good price."

"In July, shmuck, everyone gets a good price."

"Go back to your platform and let me deal with human beings already."

"I'll see what's left of the store," said Charlie. It was good to be back. He almost cried. He almost kissed Bob. But he marched to his platform with a stiff face. It was a good homecoming.

He remembered how different the store was the first day he came. It was a cover then. He needed a job and almost any salary would do. He was hired as a schlepper and when he knew that word he thought he might have given away his German origins. But Goldstein assumed he knew Yiddish.

He quickly divined the logistics of a hardware store. There had to be a balance between inventory and overstock. Certain things could be kept forever, like Christmas tree lights, especially the ones without the price stamped on them, so that they could be increased in cost yearly to cover the 5 percent a bank would charge for its money at that time.

Mr. Goldstein, who had bought the store two years before and was new to Newport, as was Charles Drobney of course, liked to order flamboyant items. He was a good salesman and if anybody could sell bubbling bathroom racks, it was him. The problem was there wasn't nearly enough market in Newport for Bob Goldstein's passion for novelty.

Drobney found out he could not only argue with Mr. Goldstein, he could win. Goldstein respected logic. He respected someone who knew what he was doing. After a half year, Goldstein was hardly bothering to check the inventories, and in some cases deferring to his schlepper's wisdom. But he did not give Drobney a raise until Drobney pushed it. He was not in the business of giving away money. In 1941 Charles Drobney was raised to sixty-five dollars a week. He had started at twenty-two dollars.

Goldstein himself only made $125 a week, which was not small in those days. Goldstein never discussed his private life or his politics nor asked Charlie his.

And then on December 7 of that year, the Japanese surprised America and Goldstein surprised Drobney.

Goldstein had phoned with an urgent request to meet but Charlie had other things on his mind. He wanted to check on his system immediately.

This was not going to be a war just against Japan. Germany had to come in now if it were going to come in at all. If the American Pacific Fleet were destroyed at Pearl Harbor, as the radio information so carefully avoided saying, Germany would never have as good a chance again to go at American shipping that was supplying Britain with Lend-Lease.

Crippled in the Pacific, America would have to fight a two-ocean war. Britain's strategic rear was as vulnerable as it ever would be.

Charles Drobney knew these were the last moments of not being at war with America. Every chance to safely refuse espionage seemed blocked. He had secretly hoped he would be drafted, but Lederle had already branched out from just the fishing business.

He was a man who got things done. He was the man who got him a 4-F, at a cost of fifteen thousand dollars. With Lederle the point of contact because of the radio, he could not refuse the fix with the draft board.

And if he removed Lederle from the shortwave, and then information ceased or slowed, he would have to explain why. It was a position with no option but to proceed, unless of course, something happened to change Lederle, which was doubtful.

But now, during these emotional moments of this Sunday on which the shooting part of the war began, was the best time to find out where everything stood. Having calculated and determined there was no way but to proceed, Drobney saw no reason not to perform the mission properly and well.

He was also anxious to see how well his system would work. He was proud of the way he had set it up. Strategically it was the supply lines, tactically it was the Eastern Shore Command that controlled the formation of convoys. He had used Elizabeth first. She had been shrewd enough to know she only had to go with one officer in the ESC to meet them all. And she had proved even shrewder in her analysis of the nature of men than Charlie had expected. She said it was not a great thing, most women were.

"I want someone who will not suffer great pangs of remorse."

"Then you're looking for a fool," she said. He understood she was not talking about officers so much as herself.

"I promise you, you will not have much to do, if anything, once I get what I want," he said. They had already stopped living together for the duration, as he called it.

One young officer proved interesting. He was an ensign who was not an Annapolis graduate but who hoped to make the Navy a career, a difficult task without a war. Elizabeth thought he might be one who would not suffer great remorse. "How do you know?" asked Charlie.

"He is always talking about his future. He wants sea duty."

"What does that prove?"

"I never heard him talk of doing a good job at ESC, or whether it mattered."

"Maybe he doesn't talk about his work?"

"He does. Do you want me to find out how it is set up, things like that?"

"No."

"He has a streak of timidity. I don't think he would agree to being a traitor."

"Don't even think. I didn't ask that. You are not going to be involved in anything but telling me about the officer's character. That's all."

"Well, he doesn't have any. He joins the right clubs; he hangs around with the right people. He doesn't squander money, drink, or womanize. He is not married."

"Is he in love with you?"

"He likes to be seen with me because I'm beautiful."

"Expensive places?"

"The officers' club. Not expensive."

"I think you should start going to expensive places."

"I don't like this, you know."

"You get paid. You got back here. That was paid for too."

"I still don't like it."

"Just do this, and there will hardly be anything."

"That's it? Expensive restaurants?"

"And get him to buy you things. Showy sorts of things, if you can."

"You don't want anything else from me?"

"Exactly."

Harry Lederle's shady activities had proved invaluable at that point. Drobney had tried to limit Lederle's questionable money-making because of risk. But Lederle was just the man to be able to reach an assortment of loan sharks and, more importantly, to buy a favor. "Do we need money. Are we in trouble?" Lederle asked.

"No," said Drobney.

"I can be helpful, if you give me more responsibility."

"I just want the names."

Lederle also knew which ones resorted to more strong-arm tactics, and which ones were more subtle but just as devastating. Drobney wanted someone shrewd but not that shrewd. He chose someone who had been in the business awhile. Drobney did not want broken arms or something inventive or extraordinary.

He got the name and gave it to Elizabeth and told her to borrow fifty dollars from the man, who operated out of nearby Providence, Rhode Island.

Then, she was to have the young ensign pay it back for her

because she wouldn't have the money for a week. It was a small amount, and of course she gave the money back to the young ensign. But he had already gotten to know the loan shark. And the next time the sum was seventy-five dollars, and the ensign himself borrowed the money from that man in Providence that she found repulsive.

She was so beautiful, and it all seemed so small, and so harmless when it began for Ensign William Farley McFeester of the Eastern Shore Command.

When the sum reached three thousand dollars, Elizabeth, of course, did not have the money. Charlie did not want to know what she offered in exchange, but the important thing was that McFeester didn't have the money either.

He phoned McFeester at an officers' barracks and explained that they had a mutual friend in Providence and that things could be worked out a lot more easily than McFeester might think.

McFeester naturally thought Drobney was from the loan shark. They met in a diner off Route 114, and there was a strange exhilaration at how well it was working for young Drobney. He felt he was doing something as demanding as moving great armies. He was moving a single man.

"Listen, I have problems. You have problems. Maybe you can help me solve my problems."

It was all so agreeable. It was all so easy for McFeester, who was not so rash as to accept right away. But his problem was he had a loan shark in Providence making severe threats for three thousand dollars and someone in Newport who didn't want all that much for a third of that.

What Charles Drobney wanted was a chance to sell things to ESC, a salesman seeking inside help.

"I don't handle supplies."

"But you know people who do. I want to find out what you are paying for things you buy locally. Bids and things. You don't have everything shipped in."

"Can you make that much profit?"

"You don't have problems enough of your own, ensign, you have to worry about mine?" said Charlie.

The thousand dollars held off the loan shark in Providence. For another thousand, Charles Drobney wanted to know when certain ships were going to leave because, he said, he had other friends who made loans to sailors. The advantage he had over McFeester was that he knew where this was going, and McFeester did not. By the time the loan was paid off, McFeester was on Drobney's payroll and routinely providing information so sensitive that the young ensign was no longer in danger of just losing his commission, but his life.

Everything was in place that Sunday in 1941 when Bob Goldstein insisted he meet Charles Drobney at the store.

"Could we make it tomorrow, Mr. Goldstein. It is Sunday."

"You're not religious, Charlie, and this is real important to me. It's important to you too."

Mr. Goldstein was waiting for him, leaning against a barrel of tenpenny nails. The store was closed for Sunday, even with the disaster of Pearl Harbor. Goldstein hadn't shaved that morning. He was fingering a three-quarter-inch screw.

"I want to make you a partner," said Goldstein. "Fifty-fifty, even-steven, down-the-middle partner."

"Why?" said Drobney.

"A good question," said Goldstein. "I'll tell you why. I am volunteering tomorrow. I am getting in this war."

This surprised Drobney, who knew Goldstein as a passionate man but a reasonable one. He did not seem to be the kind to run into a war. It was then he found out how deeply Goldstein felt about some things. It was not because America was in a war, it was because Goldstein was in one.

"So I can embarrass the living shit out of any prick who says Jews don't fight but stay home and make money."

"And why me as a partner?"

"Do you remember the flood when I was on an overnight trip to Boston? You didn't raise the prices for a quick gain when everyone needed hardware to repair. You didn't do that."

Drobney remembered. It would have been foolish to charge exorbitant prices to make a few dollars during a time of distress, when a hardware store depended not on sudden windfalls, but on a clientele that came in for the screws and nails and light bulbs and other staples on which any hardware store made the major part of its profit. And knowing that Mr. Goldstein was trying to build that sort of clientele, the few extra dollars made during an emergency might well lose the entire future of the store. In fact, he was even thinking of taking out an advertisement on his own to announce the prices were the same because Newport, the City by the Sea, was not going to give up to the sea. Goldstein's was here as usual with prices as usual for its friends.

When Mr. Goldstein got back, he put in a sign proclaiming Charlie's decision.

"I remember," said Drobney. "You didn't need the few dollars, you needed customers."

"You see, Charlie, I want you as my partner because you think like a Jew."

"Is that Jewish?" asked Drobney.

"Sure," said Goldstein, unaware that this supposed Jewish shrewdness was simple tactics, quite basic and quite common to any General Staff officer who had been taught that one always knew one's objectives first.

If Goldstein were impressed with Charlie's thinking, the reverse also held true for Goldstein's decision to give up half the business. Charlie was impressed with the logic. Goldstein knew that someone had to run the store or he would probably lose it. An employee might well let the store go for a quick profit, if not steal outright. But the best chance of coming back to a store was to give away half of it. Not a stingy 10 percent, where someone might feel he had been cheated if the hours became too long, but an open and generous half.

"I give you my word," said Drobney, "that I will do my best and that I will not cheat you."

"If I need your word, I made a mistake," said Goldstein.

Those were just about the words Charles Drobney had said to the colonel when getting assurance he would never be surrendered by the General Staff.

He promised in his heart that if Germany should win he would somehow help Mr. Goldstein and his family from suffering from their racial laws if they had not been repealed by then.

He had little expectation of a German victory, however, even with the disaster of Pearl Harbor. Germany had a year and a half before the strategic imbalance would begin to show, even to a corporal.

Mr. Goldstein offered to have Charlie's name put right on the store, even first. "We'll both do it when you get back, Mr. Goldstein."

"I'm your partner. I'm Bob."

"When you get back, Mr. Goldstein," said Charlie. He didn't need his name on a sign.

He would rather be a partner than just appear like one. Besides, until the war was over, he would just as soon not have his name on a sign so big and blatant.

It was sealed with a handshake and a contract. Drobney only got to Lederle by nightfall. He wanted to see how Lederle felt. Some things had happened that might have changed Lederle's mind. For one, he hadn't been paid in six months. Drobney had refused a submarine rendezvous just for yearly funding. It was too risky. He wanted three years at once, and that only when intensive patrol activity lessened down the road. Lederle might not want to go into war without money, no matter how strongly he felt about inferior races and the triumph of Aryans over the darker peoples of the world.

Lederle was doing quite well in the Newport area. He already owned two boats besides the one Drobney had financed to give him legitimate access to the sea. He had others fishing for him and he owned a small apartment building in nearby Portsmouth.

They met in the fisherman's house in Little Compton that Drobney had purchased for him years before. There were several cases of imported scotch stacked in the bedroom. He was offering Charlie a bottle.

Drobney refused. He sat down. A roomful of scotch and there weren't even sheets on the bed yet or dust off the chairs. Lederle was in his undershorts. He was chewing on a cigar.

"I don't think we are going to be able to secure funds for a very long while," said Charlie. "Germany will definitely enter."

Lederle was a firecracker of joy. "The war can really be big. Did you hear what happened to the American fleet? Russia is dying, Britain is all but dead, and here goes America. Charlie, you want to talk of money, talk money. They're not going to be trusting these jerks in the Bund to run things. You know who'll run things. You, Charlie. Me, Charlie. On just the money of Rhode Island Jews, you'd be rich. Let me be minister of Jewish affairs, not even for New York City. One year, Charles, and then—" Lederle poured two glasses of scotch and clicked his, "and then the world. I am yours to command."

"Be careful," said Drobney, nodding to the scotch. He had noticed the bottles didn't have tax labels on them.

"If you can't be careful, be fast, eh Charlie?" said Lederle. "Your 4-F and mine are my gift to the fatherland."

Lederle was so enthusiastic he wanted to blow up a few naval war ships in Narragansett Bay to do something visible before the war was over.

"We've got to show them we're doing something. Maybe you know war, but I know people. They've got to see something, too, you know. What do you think?"

"I think they will be very pleased with what we are about to do. Just keep the radio contact within the limits I have ordered."

"Yeah, but now that a war's coming, don't you think we ought to increase the radio contacts, make ourselves more available?"

Charles Drobney did not answer. The intermittent contact with randomly varied days had been set up precisely for a wartime situation, when surveillance would definitely be heavier.

"Do what you're told," he said.

Lederle whispered with his fumed breath, "Heil Hitler."

He winked.

Drobney left the house feeling the December Atlantic winds around him, but what made him shiver was thinking about his radio operator's suggestion. The man was insane. If they should even manage to destroy the whole fleet anchored up the Bay, they would not make much impact on the war. The ships would be replaced, and, of course, with such an enormous sabotage, the FBI and whatever else America was using to fight espionage would infest the area so heavily that the unit might not be able to make any contact with U-boats.

Sabotage here in Newport would be the best way to make them strategically useless even if they were not caught and hanged. And Charles Drobney was not about to make flamboyant and senseless decisions. He would perform his duties with maximum effect, which naturally meant maximum safety.

It was prudent to reassure Elizabeth that she was not going to be endangered. He didn't want her surrendering herself with a plea for mercy when Germany came into the war.

She had her own apartment in Middletown off Route 114, and Drobney found her in it, still in a nightgown, and smoking a cigarette. But the apartment smelled of a recent cigar. There was a green pack of Lucky Strikes crumpled on a card table. Soon the green would go off to war, green being used for camouflage, as the cigarette makers would advertise, and the Lucky Strike would remain a red bull's-eye thereafter. Elizabeth had her legs drawn up under her chin. She was on her bed. Charlie did not sit down. Elizabeth looked at her cigarette as they talked.

"I know what you think I am, and I wish you didn't think that. Well, whatever I am, I don't hate America. I don't want to hurt anyone. I was never happy as that other person here, but I am Elizabeth Boswell, and dammit, I like it."

"Elizabeth, we can't get out now."

"Why not?"

"Because we can't."

"What if I turn myself in?"

"They might not hang you," Charlie said. "They might keep you in jail. Maybe."

"Dykes go crazy in there. You know. The guards are dykes, I've heard. I don't want that. If I turn myself in now, maybe I won't go to jail."

"You've already done your share. You'll go to jail!"

"What have I done? I've told you about the personal lives of a few officers and what they did. I didn't give you information. Are you getting even with me, Charlie?"

"No," said Charlie. He had to do this his way.

"Shit," she said, and put out the cigarette in the neck of a Coke bottle. "I believe you."

"I won't let them get you."

"How will you prevent that?"

"First of all, every time you do something, you risk getting caught. Just don't do anything. I don't think I will have much for you."

"And?"

"And if I get caught, I won't give you up. I'm the only one who can harm you besides you."

Elizabeth was quiet. She nodded her head slowly. She didn't wear a bra under her slip, and Charlie could see the beginning of her perfect breasts slope down underneath the pink material. Her thighs were flawless.

Suddenly, like a pert flower hit by a pleasant gust of breeze, she lifted her blond head and was smiling.

"Thanks, Charlie," she said, and she patted the bed like she had the backseat of the touring car.

"No," said Charlie. "That's over. We will be in a war."

"Don't be like that, mud pie."

"I do want to be able to reach you, so we must keep in touch. Just let me know where I can reach you."

"I'm not doing this because I want you to protect me, Charlie. Give me some credit."

"I won't give you any credit, Elizabeth, just stay where I can reach you."

"Oh, Charlie. Why are you such a . . . such a mud pie?"

Ensign McFeester, of course, wanted to use this as a chance to break and was told to just try it. Charlie would go to jail, but McFeester would definitely hang, after, said Charlie, they stopped beating him with hoses in some basement in Washington somewhere.

McFeester was in it for good. If Hitler did win, McFeester would have nothing to worry about, and if Hitler didn't, there would be no point to Charlie turning him in. "I'd go too. You see?"

"We're going to hang," said McFeester. "We're going to do it together."

But Charlie told him there was less risk than the ensign imagined. He didn't want him breaking into offices to find out about new equipment. Just keep on telling him the speed of the slowest ship in each convoy.

"You don't understand, Ensign McFeester. I want you to do the minimum, not the maximum. I don't want you doing any more. I don't want you caught. I want a minimum of contact between us and between you and your objectives."

"That's all. Just the slowest ship in each convoy?"

"That's all," said Drobney, who knew the slowest ship in any convoy was the fastest the convoy could move.

Charles Drobney remembered that day as he went back to work on the inventory, almost hoping for mistakes. He would hate to think at this moment Bob Goldstein had learned what to order and that he would not be needed. He was relieved to find that somehow they had inventoried a case of dynamite. He called Bob to the back of the store.

"What's this dynamite?"

"Some construction guy. Hasn't he picked it up?"

"No. I'm getting rid of it."

"We'll sell it," said Goldstein.

"Then people will think we have dynamite and more people will come in asking for it, and we'll end up stocking dynamite, and to pay for the insurance we'll start stocking major construction. It's not just dynamite, Bob. Where's your mind?"

A wicked joy sparkled in Bob Goldstein's clear blue eyes. "We'll sell it as a roach killer."

"I'm getting rid of it."

"We'll advertise. Yes, we have your roach killer/termite exterminator in stock. If you think Liquid Plumr is good, or Drano is better, Drobney-Goldstein has got something for your john to beat the ass off Ty-D-bol," said Goldstein in wild exhilaration.

Charlie was not going to give in to laughter. He was determined he would not joke about dynamite, but as the smile kept growing on his face, Bob got wilder, and Charlie was laughing finally. He hadn't felt so good since June just before a retired naval officer came in with the crime of his youth.

17

SUMMER CAME to Newport on the Avenue and everyone retreated behind their walls, which, of course, everyone knew were not safe anymore since the Wheaton episode. Everyone felt so exposed by the fact that strangers could walk right in and shoot people in their bedrooms that Mrs. Drake-Hume said as far as privacy went, one might as well walk naked among the tourists.

The yachting was good from the Ida Lewis Yacht Club and was made even more fascinating this year because the basic competitive boat of the club the Shield, a small imitation of the twelve-meter racers in Newport for the America's Cup. The Clambake Club was not as good this year as it was in previous years, but Miss Jane Wheaton said everyone said that every year, and it was still the finest eating in Newport outside of one's own kitchen.

And Bailey's Beach, of course, was Bailey's Beach, where now everyone knew what more and more were saying, that there never had been spies in Newport and there were none now. Important people with important friends at the Justice Department knew for a fact that poor Bunny Wheaton had been shot, possibly by accident or mistaken identity, by drug dealers. How this happened was still unknown, and might never be known. But it did not mean that Newport was a nest of Nazi spies.

More and more it was apparent to those who bothered to care about what had happened and who took it upon themselves to be responsible and find out the facts, as one could at Bailey's Beach, that some officers in the Navy were behind these accusations of spies.

However, the FBI would soon declare Newport as loyal and uninfested as it had been during the dark days of World War II. The young man from the FBI had been around and spoken to the right people. Everyone was sure he had gotten everything down correctly. After all, the Justice Department certainly wouldn't send around someone who couldn't, would they?

Todd's report was done and he was leaving, and Sondra pretended she didn't care. But she knew that wasn't so. She cared very much. She just couldn't do anything about it. She just couldn't reach him anymore. Everything was the same, but it was all different. He would come over to her house, and they would eat and they would talk a bit, and sometimes he would go right to sleep and sometimes he wouldn't. She thought he might have some feelings about his wife that he didn't share, but even those feelings didn't explain what happened. Something had come between them, and she couldn't figure it out. And when she had tried to broach this to him, he said with the same damn protective film between them, "No. Not at all. Everything is fine."

So it was fine. He was leaving and it was fine because she always intended it to be an affair and nothing more and that was fine.

She made an elegant dinner for the last night, paying fifteen dollars apiece for large lobsters down at the Gravel Point pier, bought a thirty-dollar bottle of Pouilly-Fuissé, and turned up the refrigerator to let it chill more crisply. She wore the slacks that he liked to run his finger around inside of, just beneath the band, and put on the perfume he said he liked, but which she thought he had just said because she was wearing it, which at that time was a nice compliment. She also sent Brandon to Granpa's for the night.

She had even put candles on the kitchen table.

"You're not eating your lobster," he said.

"I'm not going to," said Sondra.

"Is something wrong?" asked Todd.

"Everything is fine."

"You're sitting there like a mole underground, so solemn. I'll be back," he said with extra bouncy joy in his voice.

"What for?" said Sondra, who had been spending most of the day thinking, telling herself why she was not going to bring this up at the last minute.

"What's wrong?" said Todd. He put down the shell crackers and the pick. He had gone into the lobster with savage gluttony and perhaps that was what made everything so damned unbearable for Sondra. He actually was enjoying the lobster and the thirty-dollar Pouilly-Fuissé, and he would have thought it was a good evening, too. Even the rotten lay after dinner.

"Everything is fine. Eat your lobster and get out of here. Just don't phone again."

"Hey, what's the matter?" said Todd. "What happened?"

"Nothing happened. Eat your lobster."

"Are you angry because I'm leaving?"

"You already left."

"That's not fair, Sondra. If you perceived something was wrong, in whatever way you perceived it, don't you think you should have mentioned it to me?"

"I tried. You're too slick."

"I stand here, somewhat hurt, but mostly confused, wanting to know what's going on. Just tell me. All right? Is that so much to ask?" asked Todd, the prick.

"I hate that voice on you. That's your Bureau voice, your official voice. So fucking reasonable."

Todd looked so helpless. His beautiful dark eyes widened. His sweet face drooped. He was putting sweet reasonableness on her.

"Bullshit," she said. "It's all bullshit."

"Maybe I'd better go."

"Maybe you better go," she said. She didn't want to look at him. She didn't want to see the act instead of the man.

"What's the matter? Why are you angry?"

"You left me."

"You knew I had to leave."

"You didn't have to leave three weeks ago. You left then."

"I was here."

"Not in bed. Not really elsewhere either, but not in bed."

"I thought it was good," said Todd. The voice was mature. The voice was honest. He kept his head level and his eyes unblinking. No one was going to successfully assault that posture.

"I can't believe you felt that way. I won't believe you felt that way." She threw the napkin on top of the lobster. "Is that the way you make love to Anne?"

"Since you can read minds, why even talk to me?" said Todd. She was getting too close. How did she know? Anne never knew. Anne always said it was good and he always said it was good and that was the right way to conclude. Now this woman was making a turmoil in areas he had successfully kept under control.

"So I'm right?" said Sondra.

"You let this feeling of yours go three weeks, and now you're telling me I'm dishonest?" asked Todd. He was not going to lose to her in an argument. He was too skilled at that.

"I mentioned it," she said.

"When?"

"The first two weeks of it. You said it was job pressures and I didn't want to make you any more uncomfortable. You did change. I saw the pressure."

"There's always pressure in this job," said Todd.

"When you came here, it wasn't like that."

"It was new."

"It was getting better as we got to know each other. It's over. Todd, we have nothing to lose. What are you defending? What are you afraid of? You're never going to see me again. Ever. Tell me what happened to it. Tell me what happened to us, because I think what we had was beautiful, you . . . bastard."

Todd took a gulp of the good wine.

"Now let me understand what you are suggesting," he said. His voice was cold. "Because we are never going to see each other again, because I am leaving, because everything has turned to ashes, I should now bare my soul? Is that it?"

"You've won, Todd. You've won your argument. You win. Now will you tell me what you have won? I'd like to know. Most people win things they have no fucking use for. They spend lifetimes at it."

She lifted her arms over her head and, just as in old newsreels of surrendering German armies, dropped her hands to her head and paraded two steps toward the living room, then turned on Todd.

"What the hell have you won, Todd Oliver?"

"I thought you just surrendered."

"What have you won?"

"I have an excellent secure job, I have had a good time here, I am returning to that job, which in this none too safe world I am going to keep until a very comfortable retirement with a very desirable wife."

Sondra dropped her hands. She was numb. What was he talking about?

"Does that answer your question?" said Todd.

"Answer it? What are you talking about?"

"I am talking about, Ms. Drobney, what I have won in my life. You asked me what I won. I told you."

"Oh," said Sondra. She still didn't quite understand. She pulled her chair over to Todd's side of the table and pushed the lobsters away to keep them from dominating everything. They were awfully big. They had not been big enough to cover what had been lost, unfortunately. They were just very big expensive pieces of food.

"You feel threatened by something? Me? Us?"

Todd laughed, and the laughter cracked in his throat. "Us, no. Hell no. Not us. I never expected anything that nice."

"Thank God," said Sondra.

Todd smiled. "No. It was wonderful."

"But it changed?"

"Yes. But not because of us. I have a job that's not quite as easy as chasing a bank robber. I'm a GS-14, a unit chief. At certain times I undergo certain pressures that take over my life. It never bothered Anne. At least she never said anything about it."

Sondra had a sudden delicious thought: Was it possible Todd never had with Anne what he had with her? She didn't dare entertain it longer. She was not going to break up a marriage. She didn't do that sort of thing. Todd Oliver was a wonderful man she shared herself and her time with. This is how she had allowed herself to go on. She had always known it would end, but she wanted it to end clean and well, as she felt it had begun.

She took his hand. She could help. She knew it. He was trying to be open.

"Is there something you don't like about your job?"

"Every job has problems," said Todd. She saw how tight his neck was, and put a hand on the back of it, kneading the tension out of it.

"You don't like your job?"

"Sure. It's better than being broke and unemployed."

"Do you think that's a reasonable prospect? You're a lawyer."

"Well, no. Not broke broke."

"You know, my father—"

"Your father again," said Todd.

"I don't mention him that much anymore now. But the man does make sense even if I have too high an opinion of him."

"I'm not attacking him."

"I guess I was defending him, anyhow," said Sondra. She smiled and cocked her head. And Todd smiled. She knew he liked the way her cheeks dimpled when she did that. "In any case, the truest thing he said was that most people run their lives afraid of the wrong things. They defend themselves against myths. Not real enemies."

"I'm not a nation," said Todd. "Your father's history doesn't hold here."

"People. I'm talking about people. What are you afraid of? Why are you going to lose your job?"

"I am young for a unit chief. I've got a good career. I am going to keep my job. I am going to be at least an assistant director. Because I am good at my job."

She could sense the anger rise in him. On one hand he was afraid of losing his job, on the other, he was angry that he was so sure of keeping it. Something this absolutely contradictory had to contain the truth somewhere, and probably deeply, Sondra was sure. Nor was she going to force him to be logical because that was what he always used to keep himself safe. If he wanted to, she knew, he could win any argument with her. It was his strength and her weakness. But he had chosen to risk seeming foolish, and being contradictory.

She didn't stop him when he appeared to talk about something irrelevant. He had done this report, he said. It was a good report, considering the problems he and the Bureau faced now. Once the Navy publicly implied that the Bureau had tried to cover up their World War II record, there really wasn't much else he could do in the way of reports. "The report is bothering you?" she said.

"It's a great job I did," he said, but the voice was sad. "Sondra, I trust you. I don't think I really have trusted anyone like I do you, now. Maybe it's because I'm leaving. I don't know. Maybe it's because you care."

"I do," said Sondra.

"I know," said Todd. And he told her more about his wonderful report. He had it in his briefcase. It had just been typed up by his GS-9.

Sondra saw it was marked "Classified" and she wondered if she should be looking at it.

"Just don't tell anyone you saw it. You put 'Classified' on anything that isn't the toilet paper."

Sondra read the report. She looked up, surprised. "Why, the Navy . . . it's the Navy that wants to protect its reputation. I mean, here is a woman who was obviously involved in a drug-related incident and the Navy has jumped on this as proof that they have been right for more than forty years. It's awful. I think you're in the right. And look at this. Why, they have this retired admiral, in California, no less, who remembers sleeping with her, and her complimenting him on his organ. I mean, that is what they have come up with?"

"I told you it was a good report. Not everyone can—without telling a lie and using only facts—create such pure bullshit. That admiral out in California was willing to expose his personal life to show that she was sleeping around with navy officers at the War College in 1939 and 1940, and that professor who used to be with the OSS isn't really as sure there were no spies as the report makes out. I played down something."

"And the drug-related killers that your informants talk about?"

"That's real. It's just at this point it doesn't make sense. There is no drug problem there on the Avenue."

"I am sure they have drug problems like anyone else."

"Yeah, but you see, the very rich don't have doctors like everyone else. They can get their pharmaceutical companies to ship over samples. It may be a personal problem to them but it's not a law problem. They would not be doing smuggling or any of that sort of thing which involves them with the sort of hit men who did the job on Mrs. Wheaton."

"Money. Some of the people on the Avenue are not as well fixed as you imagine," said Sondra.

"The Wheatons are. She made more money that morning having breakfast than most people make in a year. Money was not a worry."

"Maybe a lover killed her?"

"She was into quickies and not in Newport. You don't hire hit men because something goes wrong with a quickie. You hire them, possibly, if you do hire them, because you're in love."

"I can see that," said Sondra. "So what do you think?"

"I think I have done a wonderful job protecting my Bureau and myself from public insult."

"Do you think she was a spy?"

"Not only do I think she was a spy, I think she was killed by a compatriot, and not only do I think she was killed by a compatriot, I think that with age, he has gotten senile because that was the first stupid move those people seem to have made since 1939.

"It's stupid because before that shooting, their existence was a possibility. I think even that prick O'Connell must have wondered whether they were here or not."

"Was he the admiral pulling strings and making those awful statements?"

"He didn't say we covered up. He went around to a lot of places repeating he wouldn't say it. He's a tough one. The killing was stupid because I was on my way home that day. That spy made me use all my wondrous bureaucratic powers over the last month to avoid seeing he was here. During the height of the war, Hoover went into this city like a storm. And we couldn't find a trace of him. The British went at them from inside the bowels of Germany and they couldn't get him. Now, when they are as safe as a worm in mud, they come out of hiding and bite us on the ankle. Any bureaucrat knows they are here now."

"So what are you going to do?"

"I am going to do what we bureaucrats always do. I am going to submit that report that lets us continue investigating fruitlessly if the Navy so insists. But it really ends here. I am not a good FBI agent. I am a good bureaucrat. That's what I'm good at. That's what they use me for, and when there is no need of this bureaucratic shit, the rest of the Bureau just doesn't have much use for me. They know I will outsurvive all of them, the RAs, in the field offices, everywhere. I am safe." And Todd Oliver realized his eyes were getting moist. But he was angry. God, was he angry.

"Are you happy like that?"

"Of course not."

"So what are you going to do about it?"

"I am going to be safe," he said, his voice breaking.

"From what? What would happen to you if you said you were mistaken. You believe now everything you told them was false before. You have new evidence. What would happen to you? Would you be shot?"

"Of course not."

"And if they fire you, what will happen?"

"They are not even going to fire me. I mean, that's how low I am. The FBI is not going to fire a man for doing his job. They don't do that."

"Then what harm can the truth do you?"

"I will be the man who misled and then exposed the Bureau. But they are not going to stamp down on me. It isn't done like that. The days of Hoover are gone. They would find me a less sensitive job out of Washington."

"Then what?"

"Then I lose the house. I probably lose the marriage. And I am off to Juneau."

"Are you sure—Juneau, Alaska?"

"No. Just any place far away," said Todd. "And I don't think my inside track towards fast promotion would survive."

Sondra did something her father had taught her to do but without telling him her father had taught her. She had Todd examine the real possibilities, the very best that could happen to him if he got everything he wanted from the Bureau and the very worst. And the difference was only where he lived and the money. And what was he going to use the money for?

"Anne is a real estate agent and she can always get more cash," he said, somewhat embarrassed, "so we can have more leverage for more cash."

When he laughed he understood.

"I know you don't like me bringing up my father so much, but he always said most people actually don't know why they do things. They are afraid of the wrong things," she said.

"I'm still afraid, but I don't know what I'm afraid of," he said, and he was laughing, even with the tears of anger in his eyes. They talked a lot that night. And they laughed a lot, usually at what he thought he had wanted most. He was so busy getting everything he really didn't want, he didn't have time before to stop and realize it. What a fool.

"People are like that," said Sondra.

"I'm sorry, though, it's your father's thinking that helped me."

"Why?"

"Well, I don't know. Maybe I'm jealous. Maybe I want you to talk about me like that. I don't care if I deserve it. I just want it."

"I do. To him."

"Do you really?" Todd liked that. "What does he say?"

"He doesn't say much."

"Fuck him," said Todd. "I would have liked to be resented."

"I think he does, a little."

"Good," said Todd. It was 4 A.M. when they started moving toward the bedroom, and they were friends. It was already very good. The bedroom only made it better.

In the morning, when he got up feeling good, he still felt frightened.

"Why are you frightened?" asked Sondra.

"Because I am not handing in that safe report. Those spies are here, and dammit, we don't cover that up."

"Good for you, Todd Oliver," said Sondra Drobney and gave him a kiss right there even though she hadn't brushed her teeth yet. He was dressed already and at the door, smelling so good with his aftershave lotion.

"I'm coming back," he said.

"To investigate?"

"I don't know who they'll send. But someday I'm coming back because I love you, Sondra Drobney."

"What? What did you say?" said Sondra.

"You heard me," said Todd Oliver, leaving her apartment, whistling his way into the glorious Newport morning.

The new FBI man had been gone for two days, when Bob and Charlie took their summer trip to Boston, leaving the salesman in charge. In the last few years each felt, but neither mentioned, that each annual trip might be the last. Charlie was sixty-seven and Bob was seventy-one, although Bob, of course, was in better health.

It was this unsaid thing that added just a touch of occasional manic concentration to the fun.

They always did the same thing, but it always was new. They laughed a bit harder than previous years when they entered the turnstiles at Fenway Park. Weekday games were getting rarer now than when night games had started in the early fifties. Now most of the games were played under the lights or weekends.

But the peanuts were the same, the darkness of the stadium surrounding the open bright field was the same, and the crowds were the same. The seats were the same, just as hard as they had been since the early fifties. They refused to buy cushions. They sat in box seats behind third base so Bob might make an occasional bet. Bob had to do something to occupy his time. Charlie was in his own world.

Charles Drobney was not in his hard seat, but he was on the field, always young, always strong, always fast, and always playing at the level he had dreamed of, which few outside of the baseball diamond would ever understand.

He could feel the snares of the skittering balls, spitting dirt on the base paths. He could sense the power of the pitches and know what it was to be alone against a fastball. In his life he had heard many strikes smack into the catcher's glove behind his ear.

He was with the men in the dugout. Even going to the water cooler, he was with them. He was on first base with two outs, and Lord was he running fast to second, where this time he was safe.

He knew what they were doing out there on the diamond. He had first seen a major league diamond when the Yankees came to play the Detroit Tigers and he screamed for Lou Gehrig, his hero. Lou Gehrig, the iron man of the Yankees. Lou Gehrig, a German-American.

Lou Gehrig, who had made it. Lou Gehrig, dead now these many years.

It was a beautiful game if one knew what to look for.

He noticed that every defensive player on the field came alive with every pitch. They went with the ball into the plate, so that when it was hit, they were following it. In the minor leagues, a player's mind might wander. No one could give away concentration and remain in the majors.

It was the beauty of it, to know it. Bob only came alive when the ball was hit, or when a manager came out to protest a call, or when a woman with especially big breasts walked by and he would say, "Don't tell me you don't see that?"

Charlie smiled lasciviously. It was the one unchallenged response he could give in order to get back to the game quickly.

A second baseman easily picked up a grounder in front of him and casually threw the runner out at first base.

There was a mild murmur in the stands. It looked so routine. But there was a reason the second baseman was just there. He knew to be there, and was fast enough to be there.

You had to be with him from the beginning to know that. Charlie would have made that play, but not like that. He would have had to take one more step to make that play, probably throwing himself off balance, and therefore looking more dramatic, and, to the untrained eye, better. But he had not been good. The good ones made it look easy. This second baseman fielded so well that he might have made it to the majors batting .188.

He was black. So many of them were. How many of them had missed the major leagues because of the color barrier, so impregnable before the war.

If, if, if. The horrors of it all. And yet, without those ifs he never would have had Bob for a friend, or Sondra for a daughter, or Brandon, naturally. Considering the hell of it, he had ended up a very fortunate man after all.

The seventh inning came too soon and he left his imaginary speed on the field for the reality of slowly, and with some aching joints, standing up for the seventh-inning stretch.

"This game is slow, Charlie; you would think the Yankees could do something better, huh?" said Bob.

"It's a good game," said Charlie.

"It's a good game if you like it, buddy," said Bob, and he threw an arm around him. And then the game was over and the players left with the routine jog of young men who would play other games all over the country until October.

"It's been nine innings," said Charlie.

"Thought it would never end," said Bob. "A three-to-two game."

He asked that Bob let the others go first, and that they wait in their seats for a while. When most of the stadium was empty and when only the grounds keepers were out on the infield protecting the bases from a stray fan who might want to steal one, Charles Drobney felt himself say goodbye to the field and the base paths and the game. And as Gottherd Hauff had been taught, like a good boy he said, *Thank you.* This in his head, one pause and then up the aisle, leaving a game he thought he could never leave.

Bob hugged him again going up the aisle.

"Hey, we're coming back," said the man who could miss a double play being set up, or a pitcher losing control of a batter.

"Sure, we're coming back," said Charlie. "We make it every year."

Having gone to Charlie's baseball game, they then visited Bob's girlfriend. Bob had known her for eight years and referred to her as his Boston lady. After Charlie's wife Catherine died, Bob's Boston lady would bring a friend for Charlie.

They were both in their late forties, and made up to look younger instead of beautiful. Bob could be disparaging of his Boston lady when he was away from her, but he was the essence of courtliness in her presence. Bob wouldn't hurt another person. Charlie was certain the gifts he gave her were really payments. She was not a prostitute, of course; Bob's ego couldn't handle that.

They ate at the Ritz Carlton and Bob had phoned earlier to order something prepared especially without salt for Charlie.

Both women tried Charlie's dish and declared the chef had done a miracle without salt. Bob said it was better. No one wanted to trade with Charlie. Charlie's date was named Maureen. She had been married twice and wore both rings.

He wondered whether Sondra would be going out on dates like this when she was in her forties. Sondra was an exceptional woman, of intelligence and love and honesty, and perhaps not quite as much self-esteem as Charlie would have liked to see in her. She had difficulty with men.

Sometimes he wondered if she didn't belong in a larger city where she would have a better chance to meet the sort of special man she needed.

While Bob and his girlfriend disappeared into a bedroom, Charlie and Maureen sat in the living room making an effort not to notice they had disappeared into the bedroom. Maureen talked a lot about food, jewelry, and the weather, and men, and the changing times of the world.

There was another bedroom in this apartment. That, too, was carefully not discussed, but it was really what sat between them while she made conversation about other things.

What was happening was that Charlie was not taking her to bed and he wanted to explain to her that he was not rejecting her. He did not want to patronize her while doing so, and he did not want her to feel he assumed she wanted to go to bed lest she be hurt by that also.

If he were younger, he thought, perhaps he would do the act. There had been times like that in his life, doing it because two people were there, and he had always felt somehow a bit empty and strange afterward. So did the women, he was sure. He hoped very much Sondra would not see her forties like this, without a man who loved her and a man she could love.

He wondered if it was not just the medicine that made him so sexually dormant, but that his time for these things had passed.

Maureen was one of those people who had successfully made her life impregnable to joy. Compliments and affirmations of her desirability were deflected by her with precision and experience. The rejection, however, the fact that they were not going to sleep together this night, went through uninterrupted into her already damaged self-esteem.

"You are very attractive," he said finally.

"Thank you," she said with the sort of terseness that let him know any attempt to alleviate any hurt was not only unappreciated but considered a form of hypocrisy on his part, and was treated as such. He got her another drink, and when Bob came out of the bedroom with his date, parading around in virile pride, Charlie gave him the signal to leave.

Bob had gotten what he wanted, and now it was Charlie's turn again. He wanted to leave. Sometimes they would spend the whole night in Boston, but even though Bob's son lived only a few blocks away, they would never phone to say they were in town. Bob would visit only when his wife Charlotte forced him to drive her.

It was not that Bob did not love his son, but the father, unfortunately, had come to accept the fact that he would no more get his son's approval in life than he had his wife's. She had made the boy the man she always felt Bob wasn't.

The problem was that Mrs. Goldstein had always felt she had married beneath her because her family were German Jews and Bob's father had come from Russia. Charlie could hear in Mrs. Goldstein the German attitudes toward the Slavs, although she translated this prejudice into occupations, as though only German Jews excelled in higher occupations, which was, of course, not so.

Bob had married her because he loved her. She had married him because she was twenty-nine and he was solvent. She never, however, approved of the hardware store.

Which was why on trips to Boston, after having avoided his son, who shared the mother's attitudes, Bob would start talking about upgrading the store, making it more than a hardware store, making it a department store.

"There is no department store big enough for you to change Charlotte, Bob. If it stretched from Boston to Newport, it wouldn't be big enough."

"Yeah, money won't do it. Sometimes I wonder why I married her. You know, I do love her. But why I married her, I'll never know."

"Maybe you believed that horseshit about what a man should be?" said Charlie.

"Don't shrink me tonight, Charlie, this is too nice an evening."

"I can't figure you out, Bob. You're impossible."

"No, sometimes, Charlie, I think you and your books have figured out the whole world."

"I've tried."

"I know," said Bob. "All you've come up with is that none of those people who say they know, know either."

"That's not all, friend. That's more than I started with," said Charles Drobney. And he knew Bob Goldstein understood.

They left Boston and headed south for Newport, the summer night very dark, speeding down Route 24. And they began to sing. They sang old favorites, glorious favorites, in voices that knew no bounds or limits and with the great mercy of a car roof and sixty miles an hour underneath them, sparing the rest of the world.

They sang most of the way back to Newport. Bob let Charlie off at his house.

"Goodnight, Buddy."

"You've got a lousy voice," said Charlie. "You make saying goodbye a pleasure."

"At least you didn't order something I couldn't sell," said Bob, and Charlie shut the door, chuckling. He watched Bob drive away a little too fast down the residential street, but he always did that. It was not until Charlie was at his door that he noticed there was another car in his driveway.

Inside, Sondra was with the FBI man, and babbling to Charlie about whether he could stay over that night because he had had a very hard day and she didn't want to force him to find a motel room at this hour, and Brandon was already asleep here.

"I don't know," said Drobney. "I'm feeling better. I don't need a nurse. You can use your apartment. I'll take care of Brandon. I did a couple of days ago."

"That was for one night. Besides, it's late. You should be in bed," said Sondra.

She was so caught up in the man's return, she was not open for reason. She hardly heard her father object. The agent was explaining how frightened he had been back at the Bureau in Washington, how he had overcome something. He wasn't specific about what he had overcome. He couldn't discuss that in front of Mr. Drobney. But the drift, nevertheless, was clear. He was back in Newport to look for spies.

Charles Drobney climbed the stairs to the bedroom he had lived in for more than a quarter of a century and tried to read himself to sleep from a *National Geographic*. Shortly he heard Sondra and her FBI friend tiptoe upstairs and go into her old bedroom.

The door down the hall clicked shut and then the bedsprings began to squeak.

18

UNIT CHIEF Todd Oliver, GS-14, sat in the Newport Field Office alone. He did not have an appointment, a memo to respond to, and especially he didn't have a meeting. He didn't even have a clerk typist to dictate to if he should have a memo or a report. They had taken that away already.

There was no fire to put out, no angry interdepartmental rumble that had to be soothed, and no liaison to be organized. There wasn't even an element of the Bureau to protect in any of this.

He looked for a paper to move. There wasn't one. The clerk typist had filed everything, typed everything, and left permanently for Boston. Transferred back. His Date-Minder calendar, which listed his appointments, was empty.

He had been stripped of all the bureaucratic protection, all the noise and flurry of action, the business of protecting GS-14 Oliver, who was made more secure usually by protecting the interests of the Bureau, of the department, and of his superior.

And gone most of all was policy, the golden umbrella that could be served until retirement, making everybody else conform to it with all the contradictions and vagaries of the Bible.

One could be busy interpreting policy until the last memo of the last department in the last cough of government, or the first pension check.

But there was no policy now. There was a job to do. Catch spies.

Bare, barren, blatant, exposed: catch spies. Todd Oliver had been shorn of every familiar protection.

And he was terrified. All the exhilaration and confidence of his new courage had disappeared at the stroke of 9 A.M. this first day back in Newport at the empty desk.

Supervisor Cobb said in so many words that if Todd Oliver was certain there were spies in Newport, Todd ought to go back and get them. Personally, Supervisor Cobb questioned that assumption, but Todd should leave no stone unturned that he himself—without a clerk, without other agents, without so much as Boston press relations officer assistance—could turn over. The Boston PRO of course would be there to screen Todd's comments, while Agent Wannaker, who would be in later, would probably go about his own business, unless, of course, the time came when he might be asked to testify if Todd made any slipups.

It had all been so exciting. There was the confrontation, the chance to back away from his beliefs, the standing up, the evening with Anne when she didn't even care that he had to return to Newport other than that he would not be able to go with her to several parties she was invited to, the face-off with Cobb, and most of all the return to Newport, to share it all with Sondra, and then 9 A.M., the first morning of the investigation.

Todd Oliver endured another very long quarter hour of terror until he asked himself what he could change now? And there was nothing he could change. It was done.

He would either get himself some spies or be shipped to Juneau, Alaska, or possibly both. But he could tell himself that morning, as he reviewed just how one would go about getting a spy or spies, that no matter what happened, he probably would have Sondra, and would definitely have himself. And he wondered if he had done all this for love, whether he hadn't acted emotionally and kissed away a bright career.

Maybe he had. But gone was gone, and somehow the loss made him free. He started to think.

By the time the resident agent came in, Todd had already isolated several areas that could not be pursued.

If the RA was no help before, he certainly was not going to be of assistance now that Todd had really lost power with the Bureau.

Somehow RAs always seemed to sense who was in power and who wasn't, thought Todd.

Besides, two men or even ten could not perform a massive enough canvas to find who was in the Newport area during the Second World War and who had access to naval information.

It was a war city then with a fleet based here. Fifty thousand? A hundred thousand? For anything less than a current national emergency a canvas was out. He did not have the personnel to throw at this thing. He didn't, in fact, have much.

Only one thing kept surfacing as something he could do. He could somehow exploit weakness. The very fact they killed the society woman showed they suffered from some lapse of judgment, probably due to fear. While the professor at Harvard, the former OSS man, said that would be an unlikely move for someone of the German General Staff, still in all they had done it. In one dramatic move, which even he could not miss when he wanted to miss it, they had said they were there. It was a brutal and obvious killing.

Why? The killing could have been made to look like an accident. But it wasn't. It was flagrant. Did that mean something? he wondered.

Maybe there was something more to the killing? Was it possible that this was a rather large ring, that this was a demonstration to others, that the very horror of shooting up her chest was a warning? Could this be more vast than he imagined, stretching even into higher levels of government?

Something that big would have had to come apart someway by now, thought Oliver. He got up from the desk and went to the window, looking out at the morning harbor with the crowds just filling the wharfs and the small powerboats making a trail behind one of the twelves being towed out from the harbor into Narragansett Bay.

He opened the window and felt the salt air.

If it were a big group, it would have had to have lots of patching up to do. No, it couldn't be too big. No espionage unit could be big and survive. The bigger the unit, the larger the chances were it would be caught. Each member multiplied its vulnerability. It would have been caught already.

Nowadays, according to the briefings on the 65s, it was all one person and one controller or contact.

But this was the Second World War. They had groups then.

The killing, if it were a demonstration, as he suspected, was for a few people, done by someone who felt he didn't have enough control over the remaining ones. That is, if he thought at all. How did Todd know that?

He made himself a cup of instant coffee in a Styrofoam cup. They were out there and they were coming apart. Suddenly he felt he might really be able to get them. Even for a demonstration to keep people in line, that killing was a wrong move. That brought him back. Someone in there wasn't as smart as he used to be.

He had no way of knowing, of course. This was all conjecture, but he was sure someone in this city or hereabouts couldn't take the pressure.

When squeezed, he would kill.

Todd Oliver would need a different holster, something he could get to faster. But he didn't want to frighten Sondra. She would notice that. She was very sharp. Anne wouldn't have noticed if he wore a bazooka around his pecker, provided it didn't clash with the underwear. He probably wouldn't need a gun. Agents rarely fired their weapons on duty. But it was good to have one reachable, especially since he had decided to fix the bastard who had shot off the lady's chest. Todd silently turned over the possibilities of squeezing him—leaking stories to the newspapers about getting close, letting rumors go about someone about to tell all. It just might work. He tried to explore other possibilities but he kept coming back to that.

The parking lots near the wharfs were filling. Off on the left, from a long jetty out to a rock outcropping, people were being rowed out to small sailboats. Todd suddenly realized that he had been structuring his investigation without writing down one word. It could have looked as though he had been standing at this window for over an hour. Over an hour? Todd looked down at his watch.

It was ten-thirty. Wannaker had just gotten off the phone.

"Excuse me, Agent Wannaker, I was wondering where I might get a shoulder holster that would give me faster access to my gun. Nothing obvious, I'm not a cowboy," said Todd.

"You're in trouble with the Bureau?" asked Wannaker. He wore a blue rugger and an open sports shirt and was well tanned by the

Newport sun. It was the season now when Newport was cooler than the hot cities. Todd could wear a sports jacket to hide the gun.

"No, I just want to know where I can get a holster," said Todd. He smiled. Wannaker's lean bony face did not smile back.

"Shit, your clerk typist has been removed, you're back here at the one-man RA office looking for a better holster, and you're telling me you haven't fucked up with the powers that be?"

"I am continuing on the—"

"Hey, this isn't the Hoover building. This is the real FBI, Oliver. This is where we work. You don't have to be afraid of me. I am not looking for your job, I have a job."

At this point, GS-14 Todd Oliver was not going to get any more strung out by being more open.

"Okay, I fucked up with the Bureau."

"What did you do?"

"I got them hung out on a position about no spies here, assuring them that's what I thought, and, I assumed, what they might want to hear, and then I came in with something that left all of them out on a limb. I reported I believed the spies were here."

Wannaker shrugged. Todd expressed surprise that it did not seem like a major event to the man. A major event was drinking instant coffee, which he hated, said Wannaker. They both went to a restaurant and got two cups apiece to go, and back to the office again. Todd told Wannaker his conclusions, his course of action, and wondered whether Wannaker had any suggestions.

"Sounds good to me, but I'm no 65 expert. I refer all of them to Providence. But those are all technological things. That's all it is today. You're talking about war people who did wartime spying. When ships are leaving and that shit," said Wannaker. Todd nodded.

"Then you're as good as anybody, I think. These people aren't the KGB and they don't have to make contact with home. I would do it just like you're doing it with a few exceptions. Playing with the newspapers for leaks is dangerous. Don't do that right away. I have someone you can use if you have to. But playing with newspapers is trouble."

"Okay," said Todd.

"If one of them kills again, like you're thinking, Newport is beautiful. It's an island. They have to escape by boat or bridge, and our local police can seal them in. And it's not a big community either."

"What do I do first?"

"You've done it. This is Newport. I guarantee by this afternoon everyone will know that the FBI man looking into the spies is back. The pressure has started already."

"And what happens if that doesn't work."

"I swear five detectives to secrecy on the fact that you are close to breaking the case. That's why you came back."

Oliver smiled. Since man could talk, no five people could keep a secret.

"But what happens if he doesn't feel squeezed enough?" asked Oliver.

"Then I will put you in touch with a reporter you can trust. And you take a little risk."

"And if that doesn't work?"

"You go home. You've got nothing else," said Wannaker.

"I don't know where they are going to send me."

"This isn't a bad life if you like work. But you've got to like it," said Wannaker, whose first name was Ralph. "And I want to thank you. With you back here, I'll be able to face my police departments."

"They won't think you're fronting for some bureaucrats now, Ralph," said Todd.

Before noon there was a mysterious call from the United States Navy. Admiral O'Connell wanted Todd Oliver to meet him at Fort Adams, which was still guarding the harbor, although the last time it might have done some real good was during the Civil War.

O'Connell was standing on a parapet, red-faced, white hair whipped by the harbor breeze, and when Oliver finally climbed up the stone stairs, and emerged slightly winded, O'Connell snapped to a salute.

"G-man, a thousand dead sailors, ten thousand dead salute you from their Atlantic graves."

Oliver was perplexed by this. "Yeah?" he said.

"Welcome back, Oliver. You have really won my respect. I thought you were just another damned bureaucrat out of Washington to protect your damned agency's reputation, but you've got my salute, son. And I want you to know you've got a friend at North American Technologies. We can always use good people."

Todd Oliver suddenly thought of a very appropriate answer. "If you ever offer me a fucking bribe again, I will nail your ass to the wall, Admiral. I don't need a cushy retirement offer for me to do my job. I am a graduate of De Paul University Law School, not Annapolis."

"I wasn't saying that."

"You fucking well were."

"All right, I was."

"Then we're cutting the shit," said Oliver.

"Right. We're cutting it," said the admiral. "Can I help?"

"Yes," said Oliver.

"With what?"

"Everything," said Oliver.

"And, Oliver, I didn't go out into the Atlantic and get my ass shot off for a retirement job," said the admiral.

"I didn't say that," said Oliver, sensing that first delicious taste of the moral high ground and the wonderful weapon it could really be.

"But let me add," said Oliver, "that Hoover didn't avoid catching spies during the war either. It was a tremendous record."

"Let's get 'em now, G-man."

"Admiral, why are you calling me G-man?" asked Oliver.

"I thought you guys liked it."

"No," said Oliver.

"I would if I worked for the FBI," said O'Connell with a shrug.

At the commandant's home at the Naval War College, the admiral, Todd, and the lieutenant commander sat down over the information in a well-lit room with a spacious view of the stone buildings of the campus and the large arching bridge built for aircraft carriers to be sailed under, just before the fleet moved out, making the great height of the structure unnecessary.

The admiral offered Todd a drink. Todd declined. The admiral lit a cigar. The lieutenant commander brought out the old two-hundred-dred-plus-page collection of memoranda. Todd isolated the unrouted memo from Great Britain. The lieutenant commander admitted he thought that might have been the weakest bit of evidence.

Todd explained about the British espionage system, why it could have no source, and then he said one word: "General Staff."

"German General Staff?" said the admiral quizzically. "I'd expect them to be running a tank into Newport, not a spy or a ship. What the hell would they want a U-boat code for?"

"I am not sure at this point. But whatever this spy system was, it was probably organized by the German General Staff, according to our analysis," said Todd.

"The General Staff were the strategists, military thinkers," the lieutenant commander explained to the admiral. The lieutenant commander had studied the war. The admiral had been too busy fighting it to study the German army element of it, and then after the Second World War all the tactics had changed when it appeared the next war would be against Russia. There was a gap in his knowledge.

O'Connell still disagreed. "I don't see what a General Staff would be doing with the Navy anyhow. I mean, this was a naval thing. The whole thing was a naval thing, dammit. Those codebooks weren't designed for people who were going to get an atomic bomb, dammit; they were sea coordinates that were in there. The damned Navy. U-boats."

"Their Navy didn't have the political influence ours does, sir," said the lieutenant commander. "The General Staff might have stepped in, especially since sea power is land power. They read Admiral Mahan, too, sir. Quite extensively. As much as the Japanese did, sir."

"I am thinking about that memo, and they referred to knowing just what to do and no more. I'm thinking," said Oliver, "and I don't know military strategy, but might not somebody who is so sharp say to himself, 'Listen, we can't win this damned war on the sea, but what we can do is maximize what we do have'?"

Admiral O'Connell mulled that over. "They did make damned effective use of those submarines. The tonnages sunk were awesome. They never had a great fleet. Never came at us ship to ship."

"Maybe they weren't looking for a naval battle," said Oliver.

"That would make sense strategically," said the lieutenant commander. "Just go for supplies to Europe. That would explain why you didn't have your great naval battles, Admiral. They weren't fighting battles. They were fighting the war."

"Damn," said the admiral. "That's how an army man would want it fought. That's just what they were doing. What else do you know about these General Staff spies we're looking for?"

"I don't think they're as smart as they used to be," said Oliver. "Calculating people don't shoot up women's chests."

"They threw people in ovens," said the admiral.

"That was the Nazis," said the lieutenant commander. "The General Staff tended to look down on them, and most everybody else. Hitler ended up executing many of them. They were the ones who tried to kill him."

Todd didn't care about that. And neither did the admiral.

"Okay, we've been looking in the wrong places. We've been looking at Doenitz and the Abwehr. That was the link we looked at," said Todd.

"We should be looking into the General Staff," said the lieutenant commander.

"Exactly," said Todd. "Doenitz may not even have known exactly what he had here. I suspect that from the man who debriefed him."

"Someone had to know quickly," said the admiral. "They homed in on convoy traffic immediately. I just don't see them shortwaving Berlin and then back again, not enough time."

"What about submarines? They worked this coast. Messages to subs. Landings of subs," said Todd.

The lieutenant commander looked to the admiral, as though getting clearance. The admiral nodded.

"Of all the submarine landings on American shores, and they were numerous—they would come ashore in some cases to buy fresh bread and fruits—that's how open this shore was for a while— of all the landings, there was not one recorded in the Newport area."

"And you held that back so as not to damage your case for spies?" said Oliver.

"Well, yes," said O'Connell. "I didn't think you were on our side then."

"Now, what else haven't you told me?" asked Oliver. He saw the lieutenant commander look at the admiral. O'Connell nodded.

"Nowhere, anywhere in all the records of the U-boats, was there ever listed a land contact point for spies," said the lieutenant commander. So much for direct contact.

"Of course not," said Oliver. "They're not going to send a message addressed to 'our spy.' Look at the codebooks. Sealed rubber surrounding them. U-boat codes."

"The reports on the radio monitoring mentioned only U-boat radio traffic. That was all they found. And for that time the monitoring was extensive," said the lieutenant commander.

"Is there some reason why one of those submarines really wasn't land-based? It seems sort of obvious, the spies called themselves a submarine."

"No, you can tell a land-based position from a moving one," said the lieutenant commander. "No problem there."

"Then?" said Oliver.

"Sure," said the admiral.

"How?" said Oliver.

"After a while when the position doesn't move, you know. That's how we knew then. Today we can tell in an instant."

"What if their messages were always limited."

"They'd have to miss some information. Communications then isn't what it is now. There would be no way they could get all the information on every convoy consistently and not stay on the air long enough for us to know they were a fixed land-based position," said the admiral.

"So they would miss a few. Perhaps they would even miss many," said Oliver. "We're dealing with people who were fighting a war, not a single battle. They had an overview. What was the strategic purpose? Limit supplies. Don't go after anything that would expose them. If a message wasn't clear, and some sub wanted them to stay on longer, they just wouldn't answer. So long as they stayed under a certain time on the air, they could continue to disguise their station as a sub. I am sure they knew what their limits were."

"I think you're right," said Admiral O'Connell. He thought about what Oliver said a moment, then looked to the young officer, who said softly:

"He's right, you know. That's how they did it."

"A pouch you couldn't enter without the recipient knowing, a submarine that wasn't; they really did think," said the admiral.

"And let me add this," said Todd. "If you are dealing with someone who is that precise, disciplined, and controlled as the General Staff spies were, then the Newport area would be the last place any of those sub commanders would dare land for food and drink. I think that absence of recorded landings proves that Newport was their base."

"They're still here," said O'Connell.

"Where they always were," said Todd. "Except now they're not as smart as they used to be."

The investigation as Todd outlined it would occur on two fronts. First, there would be pressure here in Newport, where they would try to force the ring to make another mistake, a constant squeezing of a quarry that showed it responded to pressure. And secondly, there would be another investigation into possible espionage rings, this time with a focus on some General Staff boat link.

Since Todd had limited support, could the Navy take care of Germany?

"We have plenty of contacts there," said Admiral O'Connell.

"Good, you might want to talk to all those U-boat commanders, figure out which was the U-boat that didn't have a commander anyone knew. Something like that."

The admiral suddenly looked gloomy. "Ninety percent of their U-boat commanders were killed."

"So you got them. What was the bitching about?" said Oliver. He thought that was a bit funny, if not offensive.

"I never said we lost the war," said O'Connell. "We just bled more than we had to. Much more. As for the prospects over there, we are looking for someone who knows of a U-boat that isn't among the 90 percent which are at the bottom of the Atlantic."

"Look anyhow," said Oliver.

"I didn't say we wouldn't," said the Admiral. He smiled. He offered Todd an evening drink. It was 6:30 P.M. They had been working out strategy for more than five hours now, and Todd had lost track of the time. And there was still so much more to do.

"They're still here," said O'Connell.

"Where they always were," said Todd. "Except now they're not as smart as they used to be."

The investigation as Todd outlined it would occur on two fronts. First, there would be pressure here in Newport, where they would try to force the ring to make another mistake, a constant squeezing of a quarry that showed it responded to pressure. And secondly, there would be another investigation into possible espionage rings, this time with a focus on some General Staff boat link.

Since Todd had limited support, could the Navy take care of Germany?

"We have plenty of contacts there," said Admiral O'Connell.

"Good, you might want to talk to all those U-boat commanders, figure out which was the U-boat that didn't have a commander anyone knew. Something like that."

The admiral suddenly looked gloomy. "Ninety percent of their U-boat commanders were killed."

"So you got them. What was the bitching about?" said Oliver. He thought that was a bit funny, if not offensive.

"I never said we lost the war," said O'Connell. "We just bled more than we had to. Much more. As for the prospects over there, we are looking for someone who knows of a U-boat that isn't among the 90 percent which are at the bottom of the Atlantic."

"Look anyhow," said Oliver.

"I didn't say we wouldn't," said the Admiral. He smiled. He offered Todd an evening drink. It was 6:30 P.M. They had been working out strategy for more than five hours now, and Todd had lost track of the time. And there was still so much more to do.

19

SONDRA WAS sure her father wouldn't object. She was asking as a mere formality. Out of respect.

"You won't mind if Todd stays here regularly, would you, Dad?"

"Here?" he asked.

"Yes. I mean, I want to be here with you to make sure you get the right foods during this time, and, well, you know, be here if something happens to you."

"I appreciate that."

"I am not hiding that I sleep with Todd. You know that."

"He did stay here the last two nights," said Drobney. He was reminding her that she had failed to get his permission then.

"It was late and I didn't have the heart to send him back to Middletown. We are grown-ups."

"It comes sort of suddenly to me. Could I have some time to think about it?" asked Drobney.

"Sure," said Sondra. She wore a green bathrobe with blue embroidery. She put the coffeepot down in the middle of the table and sat down.

"I told him it would be all right," she said. "I was sure it would be all right. I just didn't see what objections you could have. Mom's the only one who ever minded those things," whispered Sondra. They had been talking quietly because Todd was upstairs sleeping.

"I like to be informed," said Drobney.

"It just happened. He is so good with Brandon. Brandon likes him, really likes him. And he's neat, Dad. If there is one thing, he is neat as a pin. He is disgusting he is so neat. And you'll like him if you talk to him more."

"Sondra, I deserve the right to have time to decide."

"Okay, Dad. I see that. What should I tell him?"

"Say I need time to decide."

"He's got his bags here," said Sondra. She looked up with a naughty girl sort of look from her brown eyes. "I'm sorry," said Sondra.

"Then perhaps you should stay at your place," said Drobney.

"I can do that, but I think I ought to be here for you."

"I'll be all right," said Drobney.

"Come on, Dad. You're just out of the hospital. Someone should be here."

The question was how strongly he should object. How strongly would he object if he, Todd, were a postman or a banker? It would have been mildly uncomfortable, but not something he couldn't get used to. Times had changed since he was a young man, and he was more broad-minded on the subject.

"It's just so sudden," said Drobney.

"I'm sorry," said Sondra. "I am. I just assumed you wouldn't mind because we've been talking about these things—"

"I do mind."

"In what way?"

"I should have been consulted."

"Okay. You're not going to discuss this. All right?" said Sondra.

He could feel the hurt in her voice. He wanted to give her what she wanted, but that would fix the FBI man too close.

It did not necessarily endanger him more, although that was a good possibility. It was the very tension of it, the little remarks that might slip from anyone, even her young man who was upstairs at this very moment, asleep in the bed Sondra had used since junior high school.

Charles Drobney ate his cereal in quiet and he could smell the very diesel oil of the panzers, feel their tremble into the ground. Everything came back from that one lesson von Kiswicz had taught him physically.

He felt he was really Gottherd Hauff again, so proud in his uniform as he and the Colonel approached the panzer park at Galsbrugen.

They looked so fearsome lined up tread to tread, big dark steel bodies with the iron cross insignia. Yet, by this time he knew tanks. As fearful as they were, as powerful as they were, as effective as they were, they had limitations. Everything had a limitation, he had been taught.

He was proud of his officer's uniform and the red stripe down his trousers that showed Generalstab.

He was surprised at the prevalence of the Nazi insignias at the panzer park, dominated by the large blood red flag of the Nazi party with the swastika in the center.

"They look like *Sturmabteilungen* with all the swastikas," commented the Colonel, referring to the street fighters of the Nazi party, the rowdies and gutter brawlers that the political movement had used in its early days. "Nevertheless, these are real cavalry, the best in the world with all their benefits and drawbacks. The best."

Neither Gottherd nor the colonel gave the Nazi salute but offered the standard salute, with the click of the heels.

A deep small hole was dug in the ground by two privates. One of them got in the hole. His head was two inches beneath the packed clay surface of the panzer park. An officer signaled and one great beast growled out of formation and bore down on the hole. It rolled over and then rolled on.

The enlisted man climbed out with streaks of reddish mud on his uniform but not a scratch. Gottherd could tell from his blinking eyes that he had been frightened. Gottherd did not want to show that fear. That was what he would remember, that he did not want to show fear at first.

"I am doing this to you, Hauff," said the colonel, "to show you fear is different from panic."

"You have told me that several times, Herr Oberst," said Gottherd.

"Yes. Now I show you. You have seen with your own eyes that the private was not hurt in any way when the panzer rolled over his hole."

"I saw. Your word would have been good enough."

"I wanted you to see because that way you are told by your eyes and your reason that you have nothing to fear."

Gottherd nodded, saluted, and then lowered himself confidently into the hole. He did not want to come out with his eyes as wide as the young private. He wanted to come out and have everyone see that he was more concerned over the smudges on his uniform than anything the tank had done.

Perhaps it was because he felt the tank as he heard it, or because his whole body shook and the walls of the hole felt so close and he was sure he was going to be smothered by the compression, but when the tank reached the hole and the tread made it all darkness, he screamed.

And then the tank stopped. Right above him it stopped, and then slowly backed away and then came over again. Terrified, he knew he could not even put his head out of the hole.

And then there was von Kiswicz's face, peering down at him.

"Good," he said.

Didn't he know that Gottherd had panicked? The colonel had enlisted men help him from the hole.

"I panicked, Colonel," said Gottherd when they were driving back.

"No," said the colonel. "That is just what you did not do. If you had run from that hole, you would have shown panic. What you had in there was fear. Know this if you know nothing else in your life. Fear is different from panic. Fear is what you feel. Panic is what you do. That is the chasm that separates the good officer from the bad. It is not something that can even be seen on the outside. It is all in you."

And of course then he knew. All the words could not equal the sensation of fear in that little hole, believing he was going to be crushed to death. The knowing that he would be killed if he ran and not running was what had kept the fear from becoming panic.

At the breakfast table with his daughter somewhat sullenly eating her breakfast along with him, he reminded himself again quite forcefully that what he was feeling now was just fear. Just fear. She had brought the tanks right over his earlobes.

"I wish you would explain it to Todd, Dad," she said. "I'm a bit embarrassed."

"If you want me to."

"No. I don't. I don't want you to at all. I don't understand your attitude, and I don't see any rational reason behind it, and frankly, Dad, I am disappointed in you."

Her voice cracked and Charles Drobney opened his Boston *Globe* to the sports section. If he stood up yelling to get the young man out of the house now, that would be panic.

Todd came down cheerful, shaved, very pleasant, kissing Sondra on the cheek, asking how Mr. Drobney slept, and got himself a cup of coffee.

He had one of Charlie's books taken from his study.

"I borrowed this last night. It's all right, isn't it. I was surprised to find it in your library."

The FBI man had found a copy of an English book on the German General Staff.

"I do like to keep them in order," said Drobney.

"I'm sorry," said Todd.

"That's all right," said Sondra. She gave her father a cold look.

"You know, this book is somewhat inaccurate. It concentrates on just certain military maneuvers like the undeviating thrust, and the overwhelming force at the point of weakness. It makes them seem like a bunch of bangers. But they were more than that," said Todd.

If the young man knew they were more than that, someone had told him. And someone probably told him professionally. So they had connected, somehow, more than forty years later, that the General Staff was behind this station. The tank had stopped over the hole again.

"Pass the milk, please," said Drobney.

"I also noticed that it was a rather varied library. You had this right next to the life of Mahatma Gandhi," said the young man.

"They are both *G*s," said Drobney. He smiled. He had to be a little friendly. He couldn't be rude.

Sondra came into the conversation. "Oh, Gandhi was a general, one of the great ones. You see, Dad has a theory about understanding objectives."

"Oh, really," said Todd politely, and just as politely added that that sounded fascinating.

"Nothing," said Drobney.

"Dad thinks, and it makes a hell of a lot of sense to me, that most leaders, and especially generals, don't understand their objectives in wars. Basically, why are they fighting it? Gandhi understood his, and figured out the tactics to achieve them. Most generals don't bother with that. Dad used to bore me with these theories sometimes, but I'm so glad he's got you, Todd, to talk about them with," she said, her voice rising, trying to pump some cheer into the conversation.

She turned to her father. "Todd's interested in this. I think you two would just love to really punch around each other's mind. Todd is more sensitive and intelligent and perceptive than even he realizes, Dad. And he knows the military. He was in the Air Force."

"I was a legal officer," said Todd.

"Is the milk fresh?" asked Drobney.

"Why are you so interested in the milk, Dad?"

"I was just wondering."

"I want to thank you for letting me stay here, sir," said Todd.

Should he say no now? Would he say no if Todd were not the FBI? And if he would say yes to another man, why not say yes to Todd? He would stay in his hole. He would ignore all conversations about the investigation as well as he could, and he would openly let the young man into his house, which he would have done if he were anyone else.

The big problem was going to be resisting trying to find out exactly what was going on.

"It seems convenient for everyone," said Charles Drobney, wondering if he had written any comments in the margins of that book.

"She said you wouldn't mind. She said you were always the most open thinker she knew. As a matter of fact, she talks a lot about you, sir."

"He is wonderful," said Sondra, kissing her father hard on the cheek.

Not only had the tank swooped over the hole, but the driver had gotten out and gone on furlough. Charles Drobney held out his cup again for more coffee.

"Do you ever watch the Red Sox?" said Drobney.

"Only when I can't get the Orioles," said the FBI fellow.

"You know, you are going to have to be very careful where you put that gun," said Drobney, "with Brandon around."

"They have experience with that, Dad. I mean, if anyone knows how to make sure a gun is safe, then they do. Dad, Todd is a unit chief in the FBI."

M. Hiram Lederle had called and Charles Drobney refused to speak to him. Bob Goldstein decided that he had to have a little talk with his partner.

"Charlie, do you respect my judgment?" asked Bob, who came up to the little platform in the rear of the store to sit and talk.

"What are you going to tell me that you presume I am not going to listen to?" said Drobney. The question facing Drobney out of the computer monitor was whether he should mass-order screws now, which he would always need, and put out that much cash, assuming the value of the screws would rise more than the value of the cash.

"I know you don't want a boat," said Bob.

"Right." Go for it. Screws always sold. And they never went on sale like a mop or a toaster. A three-quarter-inch screw held its value better than gold.

"Charlie, there are people you fuck with in the world and people you don't fuck with."

"Imitation brick? Next year," said Charlie, looking at the monitor. The computer showed the product was moving slowly this year.

"Condo owners trying to make something from that shit Sheetrock they're putting in. Yes. Imitation brick," said Bob.

"Big?" said Charlie.

"If it's not big, you can't discount low enough. Middle, maybe. We'll give a winter feeling to the front. Brick fireplaces. Charlie, M. Hiram Lederle is one of those you don't fuck with."

"I don't want a boat. How middle on the imitation brick?"

"Charlie, I am not asking you to buy a boat from this man. I am asking that if his secretary calls and asks, you should take a little spin with him out in the ocean for him to show you a boat, Charlie, take a spin."

"You spin with him. You buy the boat. Are we going to do anything with the new model electric broom?"

"Charlie, if M. Hiram Lederle has taken it into his head that he wants to be nice to local tradesmen, hey, what is the harm? That man can help us."

"We're in trouble?"

"Charlie, c'mon. Be reasonable."

"What makes you say M. Hiram Lederle is not to be fucked with?"

"Well, I hear, just hear, that he is somewhat still connected to unpleasant people."

"Bob, how much money do you think he has?"

"Hundreds of millions, I guess. He's finally been accepted to Bailey's Beach. He's self-made, so that was a drawback. He belongs to everything else. I would say hundreds of millions."

"Bob, if you had fifteen million dollars, all right. Fifteen million. Would you still mess around with those sorts of connections?"

"Me? No . . . but . . ."

"I'm asking. Give it some thought. What do you think?"

"About the man? He's an asshole. But that doesn't mean you don't give him his little due. Go out in the boat with him, and then let him go. Let him go his own way. That's what you do with a shmuck like that, you see?"

"Bob, I do not know what this store is worth in exact dollars. But what I have, what I have earned here with you, is that precious freedom to say for one afternoon I will not spend it with an asshole no matter how rich or powerful he is, but at my platform listening to my Red Sox. God bless this blessed land for that. God Bless America."

"Fuck Lederle," said Goldstein. "Are we going heavily inventoried into the winter?"

"I don't know."

"What do you mean, you don't know? Finally don't know?"

"Not yet," said Drobney.

Halfway through the Red Sox game, a Silver Cloud Rolls-Royce pulled into the parking lot. Lederle stormed out. He spoke at the counter with Goldstein.

Drobney went about his books. Goldstein came to the rear of the store.

"He's here," said Bob.

"I know," said Charlie.

"Well? Five minutes? He says he's gone to a great deal of trouble with this boat. Five minutes. I don't think he's leaving."

"Okay."

"And Charlie, if you're going to put in the time with that asshole, why not be nice?"

"You're the shmuck," said Drobney.

"After all these years, you're just finding out?" said Goldstein, and escorted Charlie to the front and stood by the window to stay tuned to a possibly delicate situation. He knew Charles Drobney was invariably polite, and one had to really push him beyond limits to get any sort of rudeness. But Bob Goldstein also knew, for all Charlie's softness and decency, he could be inordinately strong and unyielding.

Mr. Lederle was a good six inches taller than Charlie, and one could feel the wealth in the man even without a Rolls-Royce behind him. But Charlie in his simple chinos and pressed white shirt budged not a fraction of an inch. In fact, he stood quite casually firm where he was. There was no retreating of feet, no bowing of head in agreement, almost rigid, the hands folded. If Bob Goldstein didn't know for certain that Charlie had been 4-F during the war, he could have sworn here was some commanding general tolerating an overly enthusiastic battlefield commander complaining of things he knew nothing about.

Bob had once seen Admiral Ernie King on Guam at a distance, listening to a loud report from a marine officer who had been on the lines too long, just like that. No matter how Lederle moved his hands, grew red in the face, Bob's partner never lost an inner superiority. Bob felt proud of Charlie. Of course, he could not hear what was being said.

As soon as Drobney had gotten away from Bob, he said under his breath, "What is the purpose of this idiot meeting? Would you mind telling me?"

"You're letting things get out of control," said Lederle. His voice, too, was hushed; they were like two prisoners in a lineup talking out of the sides of their mouths.

"You know the FBI was leaving the day you did that insane thing to Mrs. Wheaton?"

"She brought it on herself. She had her warning."

"What are you talking about? Do you think about these things first? Do you run around shooting people like some hoodlum?"

"Watch your life, little man. You watch your life."

"Why don't you just gun me down here? I don't know why you are not doing it. I am mystified as to why you do things."

"Your own daughter is keeping that FBI man here. Break it up."

"I am to break up their romance? That's what you want?"

"Yes," said Lederle.

"And how am I supposed to carry out that order? The first thing the most junior lieutenant learns is never to give an order that can't be followed."

"No. Your problem is carrying it out."

"Hiram, I couldn't break up a romance when she was sixteen. What am I going to do when she is almost thirty? Stop her from going to the movies?"

"Do what you have to."

"Hiram, why are you doing this?"

"Break up that romance."

"Hiram, do you ever think?"

"I have had all I can take from you. If you are dead, maybe the others—and I do think there were others, Charlie—will think twice. Maybe they are dead. People do die in their sixties. Maybe you have nothing, Charlie."

"Anything else, Hiram? Or are you going to choke me again?"

"Remember Elizabeth Wheaton."

Charles Drobney started to answer, but the anger was so strong, the contempt so full, all that came out was a patronizing laugh. The asshole. Lederle still thought that killing was a good defensive tactic.

Lederle's large hand went ramming into Charlie's shoulder. Bob Goldstein, still watching, saw Lederle grab his partner's neck. He was out of the door landing into the parking lot and at the car before the door shut behind him. His own hands were on Lederle's throat and he was screaming, "Keep your fucking hands to yourself, scumbag!"

The force of his charge knocked Lederle into the car, freeing Charlie.

Lederle swung wildly, missing Bob. Bob punched Lederle in the face. Lederle got Bob's shoulder. Charles Drobney lay against the car getting dizzy, trying to tell the men to be reasonable. Lederle announced he wouldn't get into fistfights with someone like Bob. Bob answered Lederle could shove his connections up his ass.

Lederle drove off in haughty fury in his Silver Cloud, and Charles Drobney asked his partner, "What was that, Bob?"

"Fuck him. He has no right to lay a hand on you."

"Are you sure you saw that?"

"I am. He's a bastard and fuck him. He's not the only connected person in the world, all right?"

"Bob, what are you talking about?"

"Fuck him," said Goldstein, watching the car drive up Broadway and throwing an obscene finger at its taillight.

"Let it pass. Just let it go."

"He may do something."

"What is he going to do to someone who didn't buy a boat?" Goldstein thought a moment. "I didn't like his hands on you."

"Neither did I," said Charlie.

"He's crazy," said Bob. "You shouldn't have started with him in the first place, buying a boat from a lunatic."

"I won't mention that it was your idea that he was the good one to do business with in this town."

"I didn't know he was a crazy man. Crazy man. Nobody knew that."

"Keep it that way. I know how tempting it must be when you can't do anything else. Just leave it at that," said Drobney, and he was not joking. His voice was softer, not quiet, but almost ordering. It was very direct.

Goldstein heard the tone and looked at his partner to make sure it was that. Seeing how serious Charlie was, he understood he had heard correctly. He would mention this to no one, not even Charlie. If there was one person's judgment he trusted even more than his own, it was Charlie's. He could go into the store and put it out of his mind because Charlie had asked him to.

But when the time was ready, Lederle would pay for putting his hands on Charlie's throat, a man sixty-seven years old with high blood pressure. Bob Goldstein wasn't sorry that he had engaged in a fistfight in the store parking lot. He was sorry now he didn't get a kick in.

Charles Drobney took an Ismelin and went home early. He was beginning to see a tactical pattern in Lederle. There was no real purpose to the meeting in the parking lot.

What did Lederle expect Drobney to say? "Yes sir?" and then fail? At most, Lederle might realistically find out if Elizabeth's death had frightened Drobney, and if so, how much. That might be worth something. But Lederle didn't bother. He had rushed in to give an order.

Why? This time he pushed. The last time he choked. Twice. It was almost as if the man had to take some action. Arouse him, and he struck.

Of course, it was limited. He obviously was still afraid to kill Drobney. It was as if, feeling helpless, he had to exert some form of control over the object that made him feel helpless.

Yet if he engaged in illegal activities, there must be many who could testify against him like Charlie, and just as unwilling because they would not implicate themselves.

He certainly didn't go swinging away at them every time a situation got tight.

Was it that Lederle feared the unknown spies because he could not control them? Charles Drobney did not know. But he calculated that somehow, someway, Lederle was going to strike somewhere to make himself feel more secure. The Lederle pattern was now clear. That he could survive so long with this impulsive weakness was a testimony to his ferocious skill at dealing with the problems he had created.

It explained now why Lederle had tried to give him the envelope of cash after failing to discover and eliminate the others. He had to try to give it. It was the only thing Lederle could safely do. What an incredible weakness. The man always had to do something.

There was little question that he would do something now, having been thwarted in the parking lot.

Perhaps the man's lust for respectability in society was part of it also, running from morning to night gathering things, influencing things, gaining nothing. Like a worker ant. Like a slave to ambition because he had never thought it through.

One could expect something from Lederle soon.

20

CHARLES DROBNEY had always been able to read Sondra's face. This time it was the eyes that told him she was in trouble. Something was tearing her deeply and more severely than anything in years.

Perhaps it was even more evident because she had been so happy lately. He had seen her banter with her man, agree with him, argue with him, and make those good noises with him that people do when they are in love.

He had seen little caring gestures on the man's part; listening when she spoke—not a small thing—being aware of her, being aware of many things.

Charles Drobney had been very careful to be still around Todd, to make no sudden comments to conceal something, or even to take too much time filtering what he said. He had been so controlled inside his own mind, he had to be careful not to suffocate his own personality, which would be noticeable to Sondra.

He did more reading than normal. That kept him away from Todd as much as possible.

"Dad," she said finally, and in her eyes Charles Drobney saw that something grave had been bothering her. And now she had to tell him.

He's told her that he has found out about her father, thought Drobney. It had to happen. It's here.

"It's about Todd," she said. "I want him to get a divorce."

"Oh," said Drobney.

"I don't know what to do. That's wrong."

"Why is it wrong?" he asked.

"I told myself I would never take another woman's man, I would never break up a marriage. I never would. That made everything all right. And now it's not all right. I don't know what to do, Daddy."

Her eyes were wide and helpless, as he put an arm around her, this twenty-eight-year-old woman who was his little girl. Charles Drobney hugged her because at sixty-seven he, too, knew he needed someone to hug the little boy in him.

"Let's take a walk," he said. "Let's take our walk."

"It's crawling with tourists now."

"Good, then we will be surrounded by people who will never see us again, and therefore it doesn't matter what they think if they overhear."

"There's something wrong with that thinking," she said.

"Yes, but you won't figure it out for a while, not the way you're feeling now," he said, smiling.

He ate a banana and drank a glass of water and then they walked the few blocks up to Bellevue Avenue and then to the Cliff Walk, which began at the Elms.

He remembered the times he had taken her here, like he now took Brandon, to look over the Atlantic and see it churning sometimes on the rocks below, see it slate green and flat on those rare calm days. There had been times when they wore mittens here and felt the sting of the wind on their ears.

But this August it was a glory of a day, with the fog burned off and the wind cooling the warmth to make the very salt air feel like an oxygen massage. The tourists were obvious because they were gawking at the mansions.

He held her hand, like he had done since she first could walk.

"I am not a person who steals another woman's man."

That, thought Drobney, *was who she thought she was until she fell in love*. But he did not say that. In another time with another man, he would have said that. But not now. Not with someone from the FBI.

"I want him. I want him a hundred percent. I want him to get divorced. I want him all the time legally and everything. I have just . . . just become not me. I'm losing myself."

She wasn't losing, of course. She was struggling. But he said nothing.

"The question is do I give up myself, my principles, for my passion. And I am thinking that no matter how hard it would be to give up Todd, it would be easier than giving up myself. It would be easier than knowing I had violated myself, so to speak."

Drobney nodded, but he knew it wouldn't work that way. Her principles would not destroy her relationship with Todd if they already had a good one. Even Sondra's. The human mind did not work like that. She would easily convince herself she had not broken up a marriage but saved both Todd and his wife from a stale death of a relationship. When someone needed something that much, reason was not a granite obstacle but paint. It would cover and beautify whatever she did. It would be like historians who had a point to prove. They never failed to prove it.

"I am, Dad, a free-thinking person. I don't want to lose that. But I don't want to lose Todd. I know what a heroin addict must feel. I feel good with him and live in terror of the withdrawals, if I should lose him. That's all I think about now. I think of him going back to her. And I'm scared. I'm scared to need something that much, and I need him so much I don't give a damn about me, the world, anything."

Drobney guided his daughter past a girl with a camera. They walked down the sloping path closer to the Atlantic, feeling the slow majestic crash of wave rhythms that had started hundreds of miles away, ending on rocks beneath them.

She was asking him whether to break up this affair. If she did so and Todd Oliver moved out of the house, then Agent Oliver moved out of the house and Lederle would feel he had done something, that he had exercised some control over the situation.

It would make it far less likely that he would strike out at Charles Drobney. He wouldn't have to strike out at anyone.

And didn't Sondra need a father? Wouldn't she be as violently torn by losing a father as by losing a lover?

"It does seem very much like an addiction, but I don't want to demean what you have," said Drobney.

"It's totally like an addiction, Dad." The wind had her hair and it lost all semblance of order. Her brown eyes stayed on him with the intensity of someone clinging to a rope for life. He noticed her fingernails were short to the flesh and jagged. She was biting them again.

"It is easier to tell someone to break an addiction than to break it."

"It's an addiction, isn't it? I love him though. I know I love him. I've had addictions. Cigarettes. But this involves another person. I see him happy now. I know he is happy with his work now. I know I make him happy. I mean, when you are good for someone—and I know I'm good for Todd—then it's not an addiction, right? Right?"

"Well," said Drobney. He felt Sondra's hand squeeze his hard, almost to pain. She would squeeze with that much effort when she was little and was scared of falling off the Cliff Walk.

"What's the difference? Tell me so I know. Have you ever been in love?"

"Yes, yes. It's not a 'been,' you know. You don't fall out of love. It changes, but it doesn't end. You can forget at times, yes forget, but it's still there, even if the situation is impossible."

"That doesn't help me, Dad. That's looking back."

"Yes, I have been in love."

"Not Mom?"

"No."

"Before you met Mom?"

"Yes, before."

"Somehow I couldn't see you cheating. I know that's old-fashioned, and maybe a girl's view of her father, but I knew you didn't cheat."

"I did. But not by having sex elsewhere."

"You didn't love Mom, is that it?"

"Yes."

"Never?"

"I thought I would. I thought it wouldn't be hard to fall in love with the right person. I was lonely. And people didn't sleep around as easily then. So it seemed like a good idea. And it was a good idea because you're here."

"What was your love like?"

"What is love like?" said Charlie. He had to smile. They left the path at the lowest point and stepped out onto the rocks where the water was close to their feet and they had to balance.

"It's good," he said and laughed because he knew how inadequate the answer was. "It was good. It was beautiful."

"And what happened to her?"

"She's dead," said Drobney. He tried to readjust his position on the rocks and his right foot fell in. Sondra grabbed his arms and tried to pull him out.

"No. No," he said. He wouldn't let her help him out.

"You're in the water."

"Listen. This is important."

"Get out."

"Shhh. Listen. We all die, honey. Don't be without love, for some silly rule. Don't let the chance go by because you think the world has got to be some way; the person had to be the way you want him."

"Your shoes are wet. Okay? Get out."

"You don't necessarily get the ones you love the way you want them," he said, getting her help to balance so that he could get his wet foot out onto the rocks. "You may never replace him. Don't let him go. Don't let him go, honey. I love you. Don't let that man go."

"Okay," she said, shaking her head at his wet shoe. Some people on the Cliff Walk above them were laughing at his having stepped in the water. Charles Drobney did not mind the laughter. He was talking to young Gottherd Hauff as much as the daughter he loved.

"Did you say yes?" he said, making sure she just wasn't saying something to get him out of the water.

"People are laughing, Dad. Let's talk later. They're all looking."

"By the time we're at the top of the walk no one will know us, and if they do, it doesn't matter. Now you listen, precious, you're not betraying yourself by taking that man."

"How?" she asked.

But he knew it would be easy to tell her how. He did not need the awesome structure of impeccable logic. His daughter needed one small bit of salve, and it didn't have to be as good as he made it now.

"Precious, when you made that decision on not taking another's—"

"Please, Dad."

Drobney stepped out of the water with her help. He ignored everyone but Sondra. They didn't matter.

"First, you are not alone in this thing. Todd is not exactly helpless. You have to be giving him something he needs, and if he needs it, it means something is not working all that well at home, unless he is a philanderer."

"No. No. He's not," said Sondra quickly. "But what about me and my principles?"

"When you made the decision not to take another woman's man, you had never loved. Not really loved. You've already lost the old Sondra Drobney because you are someone else now. You are a person who has found another person, and you are doing the great thing of this world that we are given. Do you understand?"

"I think so." She was still looking around to see who was looking at them on this public walk. But by the time they reached the top, from where they could see the first great mansion, no one, as her father had predicted, was looking at them at all.

"What you lost, dear, was control, because love is so powerful. Well, all right; you are now vulnerable. Welcome to the best thing the world has to offer."

"It's what I want to hear so much, Dad. I am just a little hesitant to believe it. But not that much."

"Just because it feels too good to be true, doesn't mean it's not true."

"You were really in love," said Sondra.

"Very much."

And Charles Drobney wept at the top of the Cliff Walk and his daughter was there to hold him.

Lederle would do what Lederle would do, if he hadn't done it already.

M. Hiram Lederle's secretary understood her boss not because she was afraid he would kill her, but because she loved him. What Harriet Tompkins feared the most in her thirty-eighth year was not that Hiram would strike her, for he had already done that and it had hurt and she had cried. Hiram had a temper that he could only control when he absolutely had to.

It did not include her, because he knew she would always stay with him. She could be struck in fury and it would hurt, and she would cry and be angry. But she would also be excited by this great man.

What she could not bear was what she had seen him do at times to lower-level salesmen. Humiliate the very flesh off their souls and then ignore them. She could bear, she thought, anything but that.

He had returned to the office, smothering an inner anger. He didn't even say, "Don't bother me."

She sensed pressures were building against him, but she did not know from where. He had many business ventures she did not know about. Truly great men had to have great secrets, even from those closest to them.

She was closer to him than his wife, she knew, and treasured that. His wife would get the garden parties and the public yachting trips, but she had him in his office, on his couch, on the floor, even laughing in a closet once. She had Hiram where he lived, and there was no man more exciting in the city.

She could have married very well in her twenties, and even safely in her early thirties. There were always policemen and teachers around, even some lawyers. But none of them, none of them was like Hiram. She had known other men, and each time they had only taught her that none of them was Hiram. They were unsure of themselves, so polite, asking if she had enjoyed herself.

Hiram never asked. He never had to. He was Hiram. But Harriet Tompkins was worried.

He had been there for a half an hour and had not used the open line that went through her office. She tried to think of what could possibly be bothering him. He had made Bailey's Beach at last. His son wasn't doing well in politics but Hiram had accepted that. The boy was not the father, and now it was all but certain he never would be. He lacked the ability to move well in crowds, to make decisions, to let the force of his personality move people like his father. His son was not going to be President of the United States and she was sure Hiram had accepted that by now. The question was how long his father would keep buying him political offices.

Not that Hiram couldn't afford them. Hiram was richer even than almost anyone on the Avenue. And yet he did not move into one of those marble mansions. Not yet. She knew, and no one else knew, that once he was fully accepted and had passed that year of subscription, as they called it, to Bailey's Beach, he was going to purchase the first mansion that came on the market, and if one wasn't ready for sale, he would make sure one would be. That was her Hiram.

She glanced at her telephone. The lights on her lines were still dull, dead, clear plastic. No light. Something was wrong.

She looked at her daily calendar for him. There was nothing there that should have bothered him. But if he were fighting something, that bit of noblesse oblige for the local hardware store owner was probably something he should have passed up. Who wanted to show a twenty-nine-footer when there might be real problems?

If he missed that demonstration of the twenty-nine-footer, there would be an untidy apology due. It was just the sort of thing she could handle herself, and then when he did reappear, tell him it was taken care of. And then he might share with her what bothered him, and if not, at least talk to her, touch her, notice her. Something.

She phoned Drobney-Goldstein. She got Charles Drobney's partner, who said to put Hiram on. He wanted to talk to him.

"I thought I might set up a later appointment for the boat, you see?"

"I do not use the language with ladies I would use on that piece of shit. I use the word carefully and with profound thought, madame, towards that piece of shit who came to my store today. How dare he call me?"

Goldstein of Drobney-Goldstein had hung up.

But the light did not go off on her phone line when she put the receiver back on the cradle. Hiram had listened in. Her buzzer rang. He wanted her.

Harriet Tompkins swallowed hard and smoothed out her dress and entered the office of her boss and lover and shut the door behind her.

"Why did you just call that hardware store?" he asked. His voice was sticky sweet, singing, light. But the face was white, hard as a tombstone.

"I thought you wanted Mr. Drobney to see the boat," she said. "I know they didn't bring it dockside from the harbor mooring, so I assumed—"

"What did you assume?" he asked. There was that sweet voice again. She had heard it once when he had a salesman in front of the whole staff go through all the mistakes he had made in not closing a deal, stressing how the salesman was really helping everyone so they would know what not to do. It was rare, Hiram had said, that one could find someone so ill-equipped to represent M. Hiram Lederle and Son in so many ways. The other salesmen had laughed. But Harriet had not laughed. It was not something one should do to another. It was not even anger. It was what she was getting now.

"I assumed you still wished to see him."

"No," said M. Hiram Lederle, in a note like a bell.

He said nothing else. She waited. Finally she couldn't bear the silence.

"I thought this was important to you."

"I never said it was, did I?"

"No."

"So where would you get that impression, dear?"

"I don't know. I just felt it, Hiram."

"Harriet, would you please run our business with that good mind of yours instead of some womanly instinct. I find women have atrocious instincts. Lousy. So what did he say? Stop worrying yourself. I don't know why you bothered over a hardware store owner."

"I just thought. I didn't know it was silly."

"Silly?" said Hiram. He emitted a low throat chuckle.

"Yes."

Hiram shrugged. "I guess you're right."

Harriet Tompkins felt her own nails dig into her palms. She was as rigid as furniture.

"Take off your clothes."

"Hiram, please."

"Nothing new in that."

"Hiram, please."

"What's wrong?"

"Hiram."

He beckoned with a finger. At first she didn't go, but when he nodded his head with authority, she went to the side of the desk with her head down. His thick fingers, with power defying the age spots, very softly and carefully unbuttoned the top of her blouse.

"Hiram," she said.

"Shhh," he said. Like a slow lazy clerk with a box of candies for a customer who wanted to see the contents, he carefully unwrapped the blouse from her.

Her breasts thrust full over her bra. He unsnapped her bra with one hand.

"Take it off," he said.

"Harry, I've been good to you."

"Shhh, shhh. Off."

She looked down on his scalp, reddened from the Atlantic sun, so elegant under the thinning white hair. He could be so elegant sometimes. He didn't have to do this, she thought. Why is he doing it?

The bra was off. He wanted the skirt off, too.

"Hiram, you better love me."

"Harriet, nobody ever made love with their clothes on."

She unsnapped the skirt, and when he motioned, she stepped out of her panties. He touched her right hip with a fingertip and then ran down it with his finger.

"You could lose ten pounds," he said. He nodded, as though agreeing with himself. "Ten pounds."

"Hiram, finish what you started."

He motioned her to step back. She stayed at the desk.

"Hiram, finish. For Godsake Hiram, just don't sit there looking at me. Finish, Hiram, kiss me, Hiram. Touch me, Hiram," she said, quivering. And on the last words she was crying. "For Godsake, Hiram, fuck me, fuck me."

She covered her eyes to shield herself from her shame, and when she brought down her hands, he was still signing papers, as though this were just a lovely summer afternoon and he was finishing up for the day, alone.

She dressed without moving from the side of the desk.

She tried to ask him if there was anything else he wanted, but her voice cracked and she wasn't going to give him any more of her pain. When she left his office, she knew he had done what she had feared. He had dismissed her, and she could never love him again. That was what he took away from her in his office. She might be wheedled into taking him sexually. He might get her in bed again. But he would never have that special sort of love she had for him, that one that she told herself protected her from his cruelties. She was like the rest of the world now, and what she had desperately feared happening had happened in there. She had found out it had always been that way. She had wasted her life.

Of course, Hiram was shrewd. She couldn't leave. He paid her thirty-five thousand dollars a year and somehow she could barely live on that, and no one else was going to pay a secretary that kind of money. Besides, he had so many good contacts in so many places, he would know immediately if she looked around for another job. And he could hurt her. Hiram knew how to hurt.

She thought briefly of a liaison with a young man that he might find out about. But that might not hurt him, and she had to hurt him without being hurt herself. She had to hurt him without being vulnerable herself. He could never know. He could never even suspect. That would be difficult.

He seemed to know everyone, from the racketeers in Providence to the President's Cabinet. She wanted to hurt him in some way that was humiliating. But where was he vulnerable?

Before the afternoon was out, Mr. Lederle got ready for Bailey's Beach. He always took at least half an hour preparing to look casual. She also knew that he had a picture of the beach with its yellow and gray cabanas lined up next to the tennis courts. He had kept it in a drawer for years. He would not let others know he had this picture. But she knew he looked at it very much the way he had looked at her body when she was twenty-two years old.

Harriet Tompkins knew her perfect revenge. There would be such humiliation. And he could never find out it was she. Of course, she had to be careful. She would use a pay phone. She knew the business office number of Bailey's Beach, the Spitting Rock Association, as it was called. She also knew that, if one checked, there was no proof that an M. Hiram Lederle was born in Madison, Wisconsin. That had come up on some official check when Mr. Lederle bought another bank. It always came up and was always ignored because there was no proof that a Mr. Lederle had been not born there either. Records in the early part of the century were not that complete.

She left the office a few minutes early, as was her right as Mr. Lederle's secretary.

She found a public phone on Bannister's Wharf and huddled into its tasteful canopy.

She dialed the number for Spitting Rock. She said it was long distance calling. She wanted to know how to spell the Spitting Rock name because Mr. Lebowitz was a member there, and they were planning a special honorary dinner for him and they wanted to list all his memberships. They already knew about the banks and insurance company he owned. And, of course, the boatyard.

"I know all the members here, but I am afraid we do not have a Mr. Lebowitz," said the woman on the telephone at Bailey's Beach.

"He doesn't use that name now."

"Oh, what name does he use?" said the woman, alarmed.

"Is something wrong?" asked Harriet.

"What name does he use now?"

"You sound alarmed. Is something wrong?"

"Nothing is wrong. What name does he use now?"

"I think perhaps I shouldn't have made this call."

"What's the name? You said banking and yacht brokerage. Is he a new member? I can help you."

They knew. Harriet Tompkins knew they knew.

"I think I have done something wrong," said Harriet Tompkins. "Goodbye." And she hung up. There was no one around listening to her.

They would never tell him exactly why he would not pass subscription. They didn't operate that way. Hiram might find out why. He was good at that. But he would never know who. Of course, he might go to great lengths to prove he wasn't a Lebowitz, but how great would he make those efforts when he had a son in politics. And would that do any good?

She could imagine them all so polite, more polite even than he had been to her in the office that afternoon, saying something like "You just didn't work out smoothly, Hiram."

What was he going to answer? How did you defend yourself against a charge that they would probably never make openly. They would never say, "You didn't tell us you were a Jew."

They didn't do things that crudely on the Avenue. He would never get there now. Harriet Tompkins should have felt good about doing this. But she did not. She went home that evening and cried and didn't stop crying.

21

No one, of course, was going to accuse M. Hiram Lederle of hiding a past. There were those who said they detected faint gutturals in his talk, quite similar to those found in New York City. Not, of course, the New York of certain places one would consider living in, but rather the rest of the city. That sort of thing.

It was not anti-Semitism. Everyone agreed with that. If Henry Kissinger came as someone's guest, he would be absolutely welcome, as had been the twelve's captain several years before who had either a Jewish mother or father or what have you. Anti-Semitism was for hateful people and there was no hate in Bailey's Beach.

There were just no Jews who would feel comfortable. Besides, they had a beach. They could go to their beach. This was Bailey's Beach. What was troubling about Hiram Lederle was who was going to ask him that question about his lie? Everyone agreed it should be his sponsor. Except his sponsor.

"I am not going to ask Hiram if he falsified his past. I'm not going to do it. No."

"But you sponsored him," he was told.

"And I stand by him."

"Then what happens when he asks why?"

"I will tell him 'You know why.'"

"You will not."

"I will," said Lederle's sponsor.

So, lacking someone to tell Hiram right away, they decided to let it slide, for the season, at the end of which a clerk would just not inform him he was a regular bond holder.

No one would tell him that no Lederles had been found to live in Madison, Wisconsin.

So M. Hiram Lederle found little things changing in his cabana on Bailey's Beach. Pleasantries were just a shade less pleasant, people who lingered near him showed only the minimum of politeness, and he was not asked to drop by other cabanas except by his sponsor.

"Is something wrong?" he asked.

"Not that I know of," said his sponsor. "Unless, of course, my gin is bad. Is it, Hiram?" It was a light laugh, and M. Hiram Lederle knew you were not supposed to grab and lunge at this point. Something had distracted Newport, and she did not want him anymore. He felt a slow anger, and even as he sat in his cabana alone, he put his mind to finding out what happened and what he could do about it. And because it was Newport Society, he thought with a bit more subtlety than usual and began to work out plans. For M. Hiram Lederle, this summer of the America's Cup was becoming hell.

Charles Drobney felt a peace he had not known for many years. He was sure something was going to have to unravel; some little strand somewhere had to break loose. If not by Todd's perseverance, then certainly by something Lederle might do. If it was going to go, it was going to go. And all the worry would have been useless. Until then, it was a good, good world.

Charlie told himself he had been just a guilty bystander. He liked that phrase and would have loved to share it with Bob.

He had more time now with Brandon because Sondra spent more time with Todd. Fortunately, Todd understood he had to show Brandon that having him around meant more than just losing his mother. And he played with him in ways a grandfather never could, with light punching and throwing around and some manly teasing. Brandon could feel free to punch away with Todd. Todd was more a father and more a friend.

Charlie was becoming finally the grandfather, good for problems and an ice cream cone but nothing physical. Charlie interrupted only once when he saw Todd teaching something wrong about how to pick up a grounder.

By some miracle, Charlie's body gave him one last smooth pickup of a baseball bouncing along his lawn, and he threw it perfectly to a very surprised thirty-four-year-old man.

"Wow!" Todd said, and Charlie refused to do any more, because he just couldn't believe he could do it again that well. He also threw a little wrench into his right shoulder and left knee.

Sondra was having problems, and she decided to settle them that night when Brandon was in bed and her father was asleep.

"When are you going to ask Anne about a divorce?"

"That's done. I am going to get a divorce," said Todd.

"You know that. I know that. Don't you think we ought to let Anne in on this? I mean to be fair to her."

"Now, Sondra, since when have you cared about Anne's feelings. She's the last person you care about."

"Todd, that's unfair. That is . . . it's totally unfair."

He was in a bathrobe; she was in hers with pajamas underneath. They had a plate of cookies that only she was eating. Sondra was eating them with venom and also pointing with them. She wanted to get them the hell out of the living room because she wasn't here to eat cookies but to confront Todd.

"Now, when are you going to tell her?" asked Sondra.

"At the right time," said Todd.

"And when is that?"

"Soon."

"How soon?"

"There are things happening! A crucial thing is happening that should break the case within two weeks."

"What?"

"I really can't tell you. But it's a breakthrough, and I would be very surprised if we don't have this guy in two weeks."

"How?"

"I can't tell you. I really can't. I tell you too much already."

"No, everything is going to be solved in two weeks because that will give you two weeks longer not to tell Anne."

"That is really unfair."

"Yes, well, two weeks now, two weeks later, she is still not going to know your marriage is over," said Sondra.

"In two weeks," said Todd.

"There will be two more weeks," said Sondra.

Todd tried to reassure her by putting his hands on her shoulders. She shoved them away.

"No," she said.

"Look, you must keep this absolutely quiet for now."

"Keep what quiet?" asked Sondra. She refused to make eye contact.

"We really are all but certain we are going to nail this guy in two weeks."

"You know it's a he?"

"One of them is a he, and we think there are two at least."

"How do you know that?"

"We have got someone who can identify one of them."

"Why does it take two weeks then?"

"Jesus, will you trust me, Sondra?"

"No."

Todd's voice was hushed. He whispered in her ear. "We have to bring him over from Germany. And that's all I am going to tell you. All right?"

"Then you'll go back to Washington."

"I don't think I'll be based in Washington anymore."

"Are you going to leave Anne?"

"Yes, I am going to leave Anne. I told you I decided that."

"Then tell Anne. Tell her for me. I want it. Tell her now."

"You're pressuring me. Don't you trust me?"

"Don't try that horseshit on me, Todd. I love you and I'm not going to share you. You call Anne or we're through."

She said this very loudly and with fury in her eyes, because she knew it was a lie. What she really meant was that if he didn't she would be angry and then try something else to force the clean break. She didn't want anything, especially not a bad marriage, to hold him from her.

"You know you can be a real bitch sometimes, Sondra."

She knew she had him.

"And you don't have to mention there's someone else. You have a bad marriage, and you are doing what is right. You are ending a marriage that doesn't really exist anymore," she said.

"It's my marriage, I'll end it my way," said Todd, pausing, not ready to make the phone call, his hand hovering near the receiver.

"Good," said Sondra. She wouldn't give him arguing ground anymore.

"I'd really like to do it alone."

"I'm leaving the room," said Sondra, who went out into the kitchen and began finishing the rest of the cookies.

Todd dialed his home, and when he heard Anne on the phone, the room became unsufferably hot and he felt guilty.

"How are you, Todd?" she asked.

"I'm fine," he said. "How are you?"

"We're going to close on three owner-occupieds tomorrow. Three, Todd."

"So it's a good day, then?"

"It's the best day of my life."

"Good," said Todd. "That's really good. Because you know, I've been doing a lot of thinking and I am sure you have from time to time, and, uuh, there really isn't any easy way to ask for a divorce."

"What are you talking about?" she said.

"A divorce. I want a divorce."

"Eight years of marriage, and you phone me asking for a divorce? Eight years and 'Hi, honey,' divorce?" There was no anger in the voice. No shock but a chuckle of amusement.

"Yeah. I wish I knew a better way."

"Try flying down here, asking me to discuss something that troubles you, and asking for a divorce. That is a way."

"Well, yes. That certainly is an option, but I can't leave Newport."

"Who is she, Todd?"

"Our marriage is over, Anne. It has been for a while."

"Is she eighteen?"

"Why do you say eighteen?"

"She is eighteen."

"She's not eighteen."

"Ahhh, how old is she, this flame? Because you know I have had flames, too. I have had men. I have been discreet enough not to flaunt them in your face because this is a good marriage whether you know it or not, Todd."

"It isn't."

"Eight fucking years and you fucking tell me with a fucking phone call? Divorce?" she screamed. "No divorce. You'll get a divorce in hell."

"I can get a divorce and I will."

"And your career?"

"I'll have it."

"Maybe. You'll get a divorce in hell."

"I'm sorry, Anne. It really is a bad marriage."

"It's a great marriage, you asshole."

"How could you settle for so little? I don't love you, Anne."

He had said it and, having said it, realized he had always wanted to say it.

Something was over, and she knew it. Suddenly she was begging, cursing, threatening, and finally just weeping, and he felt awful.

"I'm sorry," he said.

"Say anything but that. For Godsake be a man for once."

"I am sorry. I am sorry for what we didn't have."

There was silence on the phone. Finally Anne said:

"I am getting the house. I am getting the joint accounts. I am getting the property." And then she hung up.

He was still staring at the phone when Sondra came in.

"How did it go?" she asked.

"It went," he said.

She saw his pain and sat beside him. They were quiet together for a while. Then Sondra asked:

"Did you mention me?"

"She assumed there was someone else. She thinks you're eighteen."

"Really?" said Sondra. She couldn't contain a smile. She felt devastating. She did not like herself for it. But she loved the feeling.

"I don't know. I guess she figures she lost me to age. She didn't even ask why. She had her own fears and that was all she would listen to."

"Todd, you sound so much like Dad. Really. You have so much in common." She put a hand on his. Todd put the phone back on its little living room shelf.

"Maybe," said Todd.

"You ought to get to know him."

"I've tried," he had said.

"I know, but realize he only has one daughter. We've been close all our lives, and you are the first real threat of anyone's taking me away. He's got three people in the world, and you've got a line on 30 percent of them.''

''He drifts off.''

''Well, don't let him drift. He likes history. He's got ideas about history. Use them. Draw him out. Let him know he's gaining a son. You don't have to agree with him. Just talk to him.''

''Yes, coach,'' said Todd.

''Am I being too pushy?''

''Maybe,'' Todd said.

''I'm not,'' she said. She went out into the kitchen for a cookie and realized she had finished them all.

Charles Drobney never expected to hear that name on this side of the Atlantic. Todd had asked to use the telephone in Drobney's bedroom because he needed a little privacy.

''I don't know how private that is,'' said Charlie.

''It's private enough,'' said Todd. He had brought home folders in a zippered briefcase because on Monday he said he was going to travel up to Cambridge, and he wanted to take right off from the house instead of going to the field office.

It was bad enough having Todd here. He didn't want the investigation here in the house with him.

''Isn't that risky, taking home sensitive material?'' said Drobney. ''I didn't know your Bureau would allow that.''

''It's not allowed. I would never take out a whole file; that could embarrass the Bureau if it got out. I just took parts of serials that I'll need for Monday. It's not a danger of any sort, unless Sondra's chest of drawers is vulnerable.'' He said that with a chuckle.

Todd took the folders into Drobney's bedroom, shut the door, and dialed.

It was a wooden door, which did not fit snugly. If one wanted snug wooden doors in Newport, one had to keep shaving them all the time because of the swelling caused by sea air. When Catherine was alive, Charlie had all the doors trimmed every year exactly. For himself, however, he had cut several years' worth of swelling in one effort. People who lived alone did not need soundproof doors. He heard every word.

Quickly, he tried to get down the steps and back to his study.

And then he froze on the steps and violated his own rule of ignoring everything Todd might say.

"I may not be pronouncing it right. It's a funny spelling. The first name is Hasso. Hasso von Kiswicz. . . . Right, Professor Tobridge. General Staff. Did Doenitz make any comment on him specifically? . . . I'll tell you why I ask, because you were right. A General Staff officer was the one behind this. . . . Right. . . . We had cooperation from the West German Government. . . . Well, because we were looking at the General Staff this time. . . . Sure. . . . There was the link with Doenitz. We were looking for the links between General Staff and Doenitz. . . . Yes. . . . What? What did Doenitz say? . . . Complained about the General Staff? . . . I would expect so from what we have. . . . What I want is your input on this. . . . I really can't tell you that, sir, this is not a secure line. . . . Yes. . . . How did we miss it in Paperclip? . . . I'll show you when I get there. . . . No. Not crucial. Just a verification of everything Doenitz might have mentioned about the General Staff. Makes a more complete presentation. . . . I am not at liberty to say at this time even if this weren't an open sort of line. . . . Tending his horses? . . . No. Not quite. Thank you, sir."

Charles Drobney forced himself down the stairs and into his study. There was the instant panic at hearing the name on Todd's lips. No, not panic. Fear.

He didn't know what to do. He glanced at the books lining the wall right up the ceiling. How many times had he thought of the colonel here in this room, the General Staff and what it was, its history, its folly. How many times had he thought of the colonel, resenting him, admiring him, feeling sorry for him.

It was the boy who had met him and imitated him, but perhaps the man could come closer to understanding him, even forgiving him.

He had often wondered whether the colonel had fared well during the war. He trusted von Kiswicz, even from the perspective of maturity. Drobney had not been surprised when no trace showed up in the wreckage of the Third Reich. The colonel had promised to protect him, and he expected it. The colonel would be in his nineties now, if he were still living. Had an active officer reached him? Would age rot the rectitude of the old Prussian, forcing him to break his word?

Was Drobney being romantic? The Nazis stood for just about

everything the General Staff abhorred, yet they went along while Hitler won. Maybe even the spirit of the General Staff had been broken by that war.

Maybe the colonel had sold him out for a cup of soup in an old-age home.

It made Drobney sad to think the colonel might do that. But how many had sold out for pieces of metal on a shoulder epaulet. Not all, to be sure. There were those of rectitude.

He sat in his own study looking up now at the books that had helped him understand as well as he could what wars were about, what horrors were about, and how he had gotten into that thing.

He felt sorry for the colonel if the old man had turned him in. Then Drobney wondered how Todd could continue to be so pleasant if he knew who Charlie was.

And what about the colonel? What did they know?

Charles Drobney had already broken his vow to himself to ignore everything Todd Oliver might do, treat it like the tank passing overhead, frightening but harmless.

He was going to look at those folders. It was not survival. He wanted to know what that man he had so respected was doing now. The colonel was the one person he had never tried to contact again, for good reason, and now, hearing the name, he had to know more. In a way, too, the colonel was his father.

All that poor man had was his self-respect. That, too, might be gone in that war. So much was gone for so many; one hardly looked at the losses of the aggressors, at least those among them who knew better.

It had been an odd sensation reading about them after it was all over, with time and distance giving both greater distortion and in some cases greater accuracy.

Charles Drobney himself had come to realize that these great military thinkers had failed to follow through on their thinking, and ultimately ask themselves why they were doing it at all. So simple. So obvious. And never done.

The knock on the door sounded like a cannon. It was Todd.

"Come in," said Drobney.

Brandon's little red head poked in under Todd's large frame.

"We're going to get ice cream. Do you want to come?"

"No. No thank you," said Drobney.

"Do you want us to bring some back?"

"No," said Drobney.

"Anything?" said Todd.

"I'm fine," said Drobney.

"We'll get one for you, just in case you change your mind," said Brandon.

Todd smiled to Drobney. He had caught the maneuver. Brandon, of course, was going to be willing to eat the extra ice cream cone in case Granpa didn't change his mind.

Charles Drobney waited until they were down the street before he went upstairs to do what he had never done since Sondra was five and stopped hiding perishable things. He invaded her private bureau drawers.

A trap? A test to see if, overhearing a name, Drobney would commit to looking at the files. And then would there be someone coming out of a closet saying, "Well now, do you want to explain what you were doing in there?" Was Todd Oliver taking up with Sondra just to lay a trap? Could Todd Oliver really live in his house, sleep with his daughter, and take his grandson out for ice cream as part of a trap? No. It was not the way of things.

Those little touches in the foyer, the looks at the breakfast table, those very small things that could not be disguised between his daughter and her man. It was love.

He was safe. He opened the dresser drawer, feeling in a way somewhat dirty, criminal, dishonest as a father.

But the excitement when he saw the case and unzipped it overrode everything. It was like the Dead Sea Scrolls for an archeologist, but this was his personal history too.

Carefully he slid out the manila folders, making sure they would go back in in the same order. Outside, a heavy car lapped along the smooth asphalt. Far away, someone honked. Charles Drobney could hear his heart.

He saw a German title for an order of the line of Atlantic U-boats. Someone had figured out they had called their station a U-boat.

A good assumption, but not extraordinary. Given a continuing radio contact to U-boats, that could be the only camouflage. The colonel had used that word as they worked out the details of the operation. Later people would call them "covers," but he and the colonel did not know of those things in those years.

Charles Drobney opened the folder and noticed exactly which words on the underlying paper were cut by the overlying ones, even which letters of which words, to show where the page had been. And then he turned the page, knowing where to return it.

The reports were in both German and their English translation, each sharing a side of the page so that one could check on the accuracy of the language if there was a question. Precision in translation was always a problem.

Drobney read the German. It was obviously written by an officer in the Bundeswehr because it had, ironically, that old General Staff ring to it. An officer was an officer was an officer. Drobney read the report in German easily:

> Generalmajor von Kiswicz was responsible not only for liaison with Grossadmiral Doenitz, Commander of the U-boats, but he provided a special service believed to be some form of intelligence. Records of this service, however, were not available to Doenitz by some strict operations established under von Kiswicz. There is evidence of a real respect for von Kiswicz's intelligence operations on behalf of Doenitz. Unfortunately, specifics of this operation were again part of von Kiswicz's strict code, accessible to himself alone.
>
> Generalmajor von Kiswicz took his own life on his estate at Wenksbrücken three months prior to the end of hostilities. He was believed sympathetic to the officers' plot to kill Hitler as was much of old Prussian Generalstab, but special duties kept him apart from conspiracy. See directive GAD-Atlantic (Grossadmiral Doenitz).

Drobney looked up to make sure he was alone. Then he skimmed the admiral's report.

The grossadmiral was complaining that the Generalstab officer had failed to get the maximum use out of U-038 all during the war, and now in these darkest hours was failing the fatherland even more.

> While thousands die daily, the Generalstab refuses to expand functions of U-038 to compensate for diminished U-boat presence in the Atlantic. Request direct intervention by highest authorities Generalstab to give von Kiswicz

access U-038 under command Atlantic where full and more effective use U-038 can be effected immediately.

There was a separate police report.

Geheime Staatspolizei, Wenksbrücken: Generalmajor Hasso von Kiswicz. Body found 8 A.M. by orderly. Bullet in right temple of Generalmajor von Kiswicz. Personal revolver on floor. One bullet fired. Ballistics match. Generalmajor von Kiswicz, death by own hand. All papers and records on estate meticulously gathered, but no evidence of materials regarding U-038.

Extensive interrogation of aide under way. Aide contends the Herr Generalmajor removed all materials U-038 including access codes, in strict violation of orders, the preceding evening to his Wenksbrücken estate. Fireplace in von Kiswicz study contains odor of gasoline, apparently used to make certain all files consumed on U-038.

Charles Drobney returned the folder to the drawer. He did not bother to read the attempt to reach U-038 later in the war with new codebooks. He had read enough. The colonel had kept his word.

"Goodbye, sir," said Charles Drobney silently and very much in English.

In his daughter's bedroom, among the old Barbie dolls and the high school banners, in a Newport August, there was an ever so slight touching of rubber heels. The commander of U-038 had signed off.

Brandon returned with an ice cream cone half-smeared across his face and all over his new blue jumpsuit. Todd knew enough not to waste a mouth wipe and suit change until the rest of the cone was gone.

They were going to the Cliff Walk. Would Granpa care to come? Todd had put him up to asking.

"It sounds like one of the grand ideas of this world," said Drobney.

"Certainly there must be grander one, Mr. Drobney," said the young man.

"Not really. No. I don't think so."

"Liberty, justice, equality?"

"No."

"Are you serious?"

"I've never been more serious," said Drobney, getting a sticky little hand from Brandon, who wanted to be in his arms for security, warmth, and a place to relieve some excess chocolate maple whip.

"I don't understand," said Todd as they left the house. Charlie explained that there was nothing wrong with the aspirations for liberty, justice, and equality; it was just that these things had so often been used to arouse mass movements that killed people.

"All the best hopes we have ever had have become tools to arouse people to hate. And the fears too," said Charlie. He smiled.

"Uh huh," said Todd. And then he added as the conversation sort of drifted away into silence that Sondra had said her father liked to reason without fear and hope. "Do you think that has anything to do with it?"

"With what?"

"With using fear and hope to inflame people. The absence of what she says is your good thinking, so to speak."

"Maybe," said Charlie. "Nice day, isn't it?"

"Really nice," said Todd, and they were quiet all the way up to Bellevue Avenue.

They passed the Elms and lines of sightseers and descended down the Cliff Walk. The Atlantic was queenly this day, dark with rises, not quite waves until they made polite splashes on the rocks below. The Newport mists were out over the Atlantic where the American defender was being decided today. There was an inordinate amount of boat traffic rushing to get to buoys seven miles out around which the twelves raced.

But helicopters were already returning and that meant the photographers were coming home. It was over out there and yet the sloops and yawls and bouncy powerboats plowed out toward the horizon destined to realize their mistake when they saw the twelves towed back by powerboat tenders. Maybe they wouldn't even realize it then.

"Sondra says you know more about the Talmud than Bob Goldstein," said Todd.

"Correct. I read one survey book, and Bob has never read even that."

"I thought being Jewish was very important to him. He didn't seem to think about anything else when the newspapers tried to make the Wheaton shooting into a Nazi scare and some kid painted a swastika on the Touro Synagogue."

"That's something else," said Charlie. "It has to do with who he is, not what he believes. People did not escape the ovens by deciding they rejected Jewish thought."

Todd saw Mr. Drobney's face harden. A small vein in the forehead began to throb. He thought of switching the subject, but he did not want Mr. Drobney to drift again.

"That was in Europe," said Todd.

"That was in Europe, but it happened to Bob. It happened to my friend. It was not exactly some Europeans attacking other Europeans. It was the only case of an attempt to eliminate a people without a scintilla of strategic reason everywhere in the world they might be. No. Not even to steal, or reduce power, or drive them somewhere. It was not just another tragedy, not just another mindless massacre."

Todd could sense the anger in Mr. Drobney and was saved partially by Brandon.

"Is Europe a bad place?" asked Brandon.

"No," said Todd. "It was a place where bad things happened, but bad things happen everywhere."

"Like the shooting of the lady?"

"Well, yes. Yes, that was a bad thing," said Todd.

"You're going to catch the bad men, aren't you?"

"Yes, I will," said Todd.

He smiled at Mr. Drobney. Mr. Drobney was distant. The smile he returned on that was so perfunctory and so without warmth that it came like a slap.

Todd knew that sometimes he had a personality that drove some people off. But since he had been with Sondra, he had found himself more open and more alive to people and found out that they liked him too. He was angry at this man for not liking him, not even responding to him.

But this was going to be his father-in-law, so he pressed on.

"Sondra says you told her once how you thought Martin Luther King, Jr., was one of the great American generals. I always thought he was a preacher," said Todd.

"Just some theories."

"The way she explained it, it made sense."

"Everything makes sense if it's just talk."

"Sondra says you think most leaders don't really understand what they are doing. They just do it."

"Well, most people in most jobs don't understand what they are doing. Why should we make exceptions for our leaders?" said Drobney, pointing out to boats on the horizon. "Look at the tenders. Here they come. Watch the pleasure boats turn now when they realize today's Cup trials are over."

"I don't see Dr. King, though," said Todd.

"A theory of mine. He understood what he was doing," said Drobney. "Maybe I was being too dramatic in calling him a general. Ah, here come the twelves."

Charles Drobney nodded to the horizon over the Atlantic. Two of the twelves with their tenders towing them made their way back toward Newport and the harbor toward the inner side of this arm of an island.

"No, it made sense. It was really intriguing. I never looked on him like that."

"Well, yes. Your job. Any policeman cannot possibly look favorably on a disruption, even one in a cause that we would all have to admit was a just one. You see?"

"How was he a general?"

"I am going to try to use military terms," said Drobney, only because the way he had thought of it was in military terms, and he did not want to go waffling around looking for other words on the spur of the moment and possibly trip himself further. This young man was not going to let it go.

"King's goal was to better the lot of his people in a land where they were a minority. That was his objective. Strategically, he isolated the South from the North and West, made allies there, and only after having defeated the premise of legal segregation in the South with the strength of the people who might otherwise have been his enemies, the Northern whites, he then correctly turned his forces North."

"Okay. So how was he a general? He was born in the South. That was where he lived. Maybe he just started there."

"He certainly knew the terrain. But what he understood about the battle in the South was that it was not being fought in the South but in the living rooms of the North and West. Birmingham was a classic battle in which one general rendered the other general's weapons absolutely useless because he, not the other general, understood what the war was about. The Birmingham sheriff had police dogs, hoses, and guns. When those hoses were turned on King's supposed civilians and the dogs barked and showed their teeth, Birmingham had lost and King had won. He broke them there in that city and then went on to roll up this nation. You cannot legally segregate anything by race in America today."

"You're talking about public relations," said Todd.

"If that's where the battle is, that's where it is."

"Why did you say 'supposed civilians'? He didn't have any troops."

"Look at those pictures again. Those little girls and men in clean white shirts advanced on those dogs and fire hoses in perfect formation. They were trained for a job, and they did it well. Granted, most people have to see uniforms and medals to believe they are watching soldiers."

"I guess," said Todd. He was sorry he had started this. Mr. Drobney's back became rigid. His voice was sharp and cold, his head almost cocked arrogantly. And for some strange reason he was now nervously tapping his left wrist with his right hand.

What Todd did not know was that if there were a pair of leather gloves that went with a General Staff uniform, they would have been in that hand, tapping the wrist with the gloves as a young man had learned, imitating a colonel he had once admired without reservation.

Charlie saw Todd's glance at the hand and thought, *Mein Gott*. He stopped. They were at the bottom of the Cliff Walk now where Charlie had told Sondra not to lose this love. He was still glad he had told her that. But he did not have to make life more difficult for himself than it had to be.

And then Todd, thinking he might open up Mr. Drobney by talking of his own work, bent his own strict rule about discussing work outside the office.

"They were good too. They knew just what they were doing," said Todd.

Should he assume the "they" were the spies Todd was after? wondered Charlie. Would it look suspicious if he didn't assume that?

"The spies," said Todd.

"I thought they were bad," said Brandon.

"Words aren't always that clear," said Todd. "They did a bad thing very well."

"So they'll be forgiven," said Brandon, who obviously was thinking of some incident of clever cookie stealing that diminished the retribution.

"Not like that. You can do a bad thing very, very well, and they did. Which means we have to do some things even better to get them."

"What things?" said Brandon.

Charles Drobney looked out to sea.

"It's a secret, but I can promise you that we are going to catch the bad men," said Todd. He smiled at Drobney.

Charles smiled back.

On the way back up the path Todd commented absentmindedly that "they had this whole section set up. Those submarine nets were useless. They could have brought a submarine in anywhere they wanted."

We did, thought Charles Drobney. What he did not know was that the man on the other hand of his grandson had known this too. For three days now both the FBI and the United States Naval Intelligence, Newport, knew of the submarine landing in Newport on November 18, 1944, and a second one a week later, which they learned from assistance of the Bundeswehr Intelligence.

They had never appeared in any U-boat record, and for good reason. When Todd and the admiral heard what the landing was for, they didn't know whether to laugh or kill.

"The balls of them," the admiral had screamed. "The fucking balls of them. Where the hell was our shit-eating Coast Guard?"

"Wired," Todd had answered, "like the rest of the East Coast. They had the whole coast wired."

"Well, fuck it then. We have him now," said Admiral O'Connell.

"One way or another, I think so. I think we can do it. I think we have him," said Todd, "and probably the rest of them."

"We should have," said the lieutenant commander.

"What brass. What absolute fucking arrogant, spit-on-our-heads brass," said O'Connell. "Looking at those bastards, I'm beginning to wonder how the hell we ever won this war."

"Because people like you, sir, went out to sea again no matter how many times you were sunk," said Todd.

He saw the older man suddenly turn his head away. A small rim of tears filled the older man's eyes. Clumsily the admiral got on to another subject, other than his courage.

"Speaking of spies, you have to wonder why they did it at all, you know. If it weren't for contempt for us."

22

NOVEMBER 18, 1944. Newport was being asked to pray for the boys who would not be home for this Thanksgiving and those who would never be home. The Red Cross and all the churches and the synagogue were collecting clothes for the children of Europe.

Charles Drobney paid for part of his rent with extra meat ration stamps. He could have gotten books of them from Lederle, but he had chosen not to waste the contact on a luxury even though Lederle was insisting he take them, as well as real scotch, prewar, which he had.

Mrs. Goldstein had put up a single starred flag in the window to show Mr. Goldstein had gone off to war. So, too, had iron and steel for rakes this autumn, which were now all wood and bamboo.

Blackout tape for windows was sold at cost, and the last rubber garden hose was hidden in the supply room for either Mrs. Goldstein or the absolutely best customer. And for some reason Christmas lights and decals were in abundance.

Charles Drobney was behind the counter explaining again why the young ensign had to buy three packages of bathroom decals with every quarter pound of tenpenny nails.

"If I don't sell you the decals along with the tenpenny nails, I am stuck with decals. That's how the distributor sells them to me. I can't buy tenpennies alone myself."

"I don't need the decals," said the young ensign.

"Neither do we," said Drobney. "But if we want to buy nails, we have to buy decals. Same thing for bars. Why do you think there's so much damned blackberry brandy around?"

"Well, Mr. Goldstein, I guess someone has to make a profit on this war."

"I am not Goldstein," said Drobney, pointing to the blue star in the window. "Goldstein is not stationed in Newport. He is in the South Pacific flying P-38s."

The young ensign looked at Drobney's face again, as though Drobney might be trying to hide some Jewish identity for the sake of a good riposte.

"Yeah, well, I don't need the decals."

"And I don't need naval transients. How many nails do you need?"

"Ten."

Charles Drobney counted out ten nails, put them in a bag, and told the ensign to keep his money. His phone was ringing. The ensign wanted to pay. Drobney waved him away. The ensign pushed forward a dollar. Drobney pushed a single package of decals at him but the ensign wouldn't take them and the phone was still ringing.

Drobney answered it as the ensign left.

"Mr. Drobney? This Mr. Drobney?"

"Yes."

"I can get you some three-quarter-inch screws at a good price."

"I am always interested in three-quarter-inch screws," said Charlie. "How many for how much? And what else do I have to take?"

"Nothing."

"Okay, let's see your wares. We're on Broadway, just up from the police station."

The caller hung up. It was Lederle. There had been a radio contact. Something was wrong. Harry Lederle had been delighted two months ago when Drobney had told him not to acknowledge any message in the old code. But for some reason the new codes had not arrived, although von Kiswicz must have known that the old codes had been used too often and too long. There were limits to how much a code could be used even though communication was kept to a strict minimum. Twenty-five seconds was maximum.

Every U-boat knew they would not get confirmation beyond that time limit, nor would their messages be received beyond that limit.

They had specific times, too, which varied at a random pattern set back in 1938.

A 1941 Packard with dealer plates and new tires was parked in front of the fishing shack in Little Compton. Smoke was coming from the chimney. It was one of the first things Charlie looked for this lead gray November day.

Lederle had not lived in the shack full-time since June. He had explained that he had to make a living. He couldn't live on nothing. He had hired men to operate the fishing boats, saying this would enable him to have use of them whenever they needed them, and also be safer. It certainly would look suspicious, Lederle had contended, if someone who liked to live as well as he did still hauled fishnets and lived in a virtual shack.

Lederle was inside smoking Camels and wearing alligator shoes and a double-breasted sharkskin suit, with narrowed ankles. A wide-brimmed peach-colored fedora sat on a simple wood chair.

The scotch, cigarettes, and tires were no longer stored here, at Drobney's insistence, because the police might raid the place or, worse, before raiding it stake it out and watch for a while.

Ever since El Alamein and Stalingrad, Lederle had been more amenable to safety precautions.

The fire was going, so Drobney knew Lederle was carrying a message on his person. A fire was by far the most permanently safe file cabinet for paper.

They had been using American shortwave equipment since before the war, equipment that the fishing boat needed. The Argenten had been turned down by Drobney personally because he had not trusted Lederle to destroy it rather than sell it.

Lederle's hand came out of his pocket as soon as Drobney entered. He smelled of sharp after-shave. He gave Drobney a penciled note. It was almost a full page long. A good minute and a half.

"They wouldn't get off the air. They wouldn't get off the air," said Lederle. "I was here at the proper time, and they started all right, but then when the twenty-five seconds was up, I signaled them an end, but they overrode me. They just went on. I took it down for a minute. I thought maybe it was something to do with the new codebooks. It isn't."

"Shhh," said Drobney. He read the message.

A U-boat commander had apparently fallen or been hit on the head by something. He had suffered subdural hematoma, a brain injury. The message went on proving the injury, dilation of pupil on side of head injury, bleeding from the nose, loss of consciousness.

What did they want? Did they think he was a doctor?

He was aware that they did have on board a medical corpsman who could perform operations on any part of the body but the brain. Emergency operations, of course, and only as a last resort before death or permanent injury. But they could not go into the brain. That was far too complicated.

According to the corpsman in this too long message, the captain needed a subdural decompression.

Fine, what's the U-038 supposed to respond? "We will send over our brain surgeon?"

The message ended with a plea for help. They thought they had about five days before the brain swelled beyond the cranial capacity and the captain died.

Drobney looked up. Lederle shrugged.

"Crazy, right?"

"Hmm," said Drobney.

"Right?"

Drobney wondered whether it was one of the new commanders. So many had died. He could tell by the radio traffic. So many were gone. So many and the war indisputably went on longer than the professional soldiers should have allowed it. They had to know there was only the dying now. Where was that wonderful theory about a professional soldier's war limiting useless deaths? But the U-boats were not the hardest deaths for Charles Drobney to see.

Widows were coming into Goldstein's. He knew they were widows because they would start those conversations in their pain, wanting to hear another person's voice, walking around in a daze, young women with rings on their fingers that they would move over to the other hand upon death. Some would mention that they knew they should, but they couldn't.

They were navy wives here in Newport who were going to go home now, wherever that was in America.

There had been one, a very young girl, no more than seventeen, who said she believed that her husband had died for something noble. She couldn't stop crying as she looked for support for this.

"He didn't die in vain, you know. I come from coal country and some of the fellows die because they made a mistake or a support slips or a fire gets going or something. But my man died for something. I'll always have that, you know? Did you know?"

Did he know? He told her yes, her husband's death had meaning. She had to hear that. What was he to tell her, that her husband was an acceptable loss? Everything was so acceptable on maps where grand strategy was planned. The unacceptable ones were the ones you had to face yourself.

And he faced them. Safely looked at the raw pain on the people left behind.

He was so safe. Brilliantly safe. He was safe; Lederle, a black marketeer, was safe, and Elizabeth was safe to enjoy the war among the troops. They were all so safe, and nobody anywhere had ever told him we would have to look at nineteen-year-old widows and assure them their husbands' deaths had meaning.

He could explain away almost anything to himself, until the ones left behind came into Goldstein's with all their worries on their faces, and sometimes their pain. Charles Drobney discovered, to his horror, an ability to share grief.

Everyone else was fighting a war except his unit, made so damned safe for obvious tactical reasons. Charles Drobney thought of this in the fisherman's shack looking at the message. They were all safe and a U-boat captain out in the Atlantic was going to die, because to help him might endanger a useless unit in a uselessly long war, safe to continue being safe.

He despised himself for his safety, even while he treasured it. And he read the note carefully again. And his mind quickly sorted out possibilities and dangers. It looked a hell of a lot more dangerous than it was. Some things were like that.

"Those bastards are crazy, right, Charlie? Want a Camel?"

"No, no."

"I can have a case shipped to your rooming house. Better than money."

"Shhh," said Drobney.

"What?" said Lederle. He waited anxiously on the words like a groom during a wedding ceremony. He reached for the note that was still in Drobney's hands, signaling that he would do the duty of throwing it into the fire.

"Can you get me a car that won't be traced to you?"

"No problem. Gimme the note."

"That I can crack up."

"Sure. What year, what model? Anything for you, Charlie. You know we only have ourselves. Maybe I had some crazy ideas before but I see now you were right, Charlie."

"You will need it by tomorrow. I don't know what time yet, but we need that to begin with."

"Sure. What for? You got to let me know. We're working together now. This is something tricky. I can help, Charlie. I know how the police work. There are police, and there are police. Do you understand?"

"You don't have to know," said Charlie. Of course, there was more that would involve Lederle. He could probably figure it out for himself.

"Charlie, if this is going to be dangerous, you've got to treat me like a partner, not your orderly. Now let me help."

"All right. I need the car so that I will have an excuse if the police will investigate. I don't want them to go further into where the patient comes from, if he dies from the brain injury. We're bringing in the U-boat captain."

It was the only time Charlie could ever remember seeing M. Hiram Lederle, né Otto von Schaumburg, gasp. His mouth opened momentarily. The eyes blinked, trying to understand, and when the brain apparently reaffirmed it had heard correctly, red anger surged up into the thick face.

"You're not bringing some German sailor into Newport? Shit, Charlie. They've done nothing for us. We haven't been paid. All right, fuck it. Let them keep their money. They've probably lost this war already. What we have to do is protect ourselves. Those fucking subs have never done anything for us, Charlie. Never."

Drobney could taste the harsh tobacco on Lederle's breath. The man's large hands were working his shoulders as though trying to make a sale. Drobney answered, "I haven't paid you because I decided against unnecessary contact during the war. Money was not enough of a reason to meet a sub."

"And some U-boat captain is? You're going to get us hung for them? Hey, Charlie, while we had a chance I did everything you asked. I would have done anything. But look, those guys get killed all the time. They take an oath to die. That's what they're there for. Not us. See?"

"He's coming in. Now get me the car."

"I've done everything, but, Charlie, you've got to give me something, something to breathe in. Just don't jam it down my throat now, buddy. I mean, we're partners."

"If I do it and get caught, you lose either way," said Drobney. "I will turn you in."

"What about falling down in the bathroom?" said Lederle. "He could have gotten hurt like that."

"Which bathroom? Where?"

"Any bathroom; the fucking island is loaded with bathrooms," said Lederle.

"Not my boarding house. I can't drag him in there just to drag him out. My landlady knows everything that happens in her house."

"Your store."

"You don't understand, Harry. If someone dies in a hospital from a head injury, the police are going to investigate for a possible murder. They will be suspicious. They may or may not find something. But if there is an auto accident, then they investigate, and if the person dies, they already know. They are not going to reinvestigate."

"Charlie, another fucking U-boat commander who has never done anything for us except make a lot of enemies of Jews."

"What? What are you talking about? What do Jews have to do with this?" said Charlie. Lederle probably had some very big deal going on with a Jewish person.

"Hey, we've got to learn to live with people. That's what this fucking war should have taught us. You know. Live and let live."

"U-boat commanders have nothing to do with Hitler's racial policies, which you at one time agreed with."

"I mean generally, Charlie. The whole fucking thing was a mistake, don't you think?"

It was not a time for a discussion.

"We're bringing him in," said Charlie.

The time, of course, depended entirely on the Coast Guard. And for that, he needed Elizabeth. She was alone in a fine apartment in nearby Portsmouth. All he had asked during the war was that she stay in contact nearby.

He knew she couldn't afford the apartment, and she sensed it by the way he looked around.

"You know I didn't steal to get this place."

"How you got it is your business," said Charlie. He was sure some man had paid for it.

"Even though you have convicted me with your eyes, I am still glad to see you, Charlie. How are you?"

"I need you. I need the Coast Guard."

"What for?"

"You don't have to worry about that."

"I'm still glad to see you, Charlie. Even like this. I met an admiral in the Coast Guard once. At a party. He was married, Charlie."

"I need a rank closer to the working of the base. Got to be here in Newport. A chief petty officer would be fine."

"What for?"

"I need a patrol schedule. That's all. When they change. When they're relieved. Things like that."

"And how do you propose I get it?"

"You know."

"Do you hate me, Charlie?"

"No," he said. "Be careful. Don't ask right out. These things can come up in conversation."

"Charlie, I'm not a fool," she said.

"No," he said. "You're not." She was so incredibly beautiful in just a blouse and slacks with her golden hair long and curly, as it had been before the war, before everything.

At coordinates 41 degrees 43 minutes longitude and 21 degrees and 28 minutes latitude, with the entire coast blacked out for fear of enemy air attacks from an air force across the Atlantic that couldn't even defend its own cities, a large black boat surfaced in the moonless night, like a big fish coming up for air, five hundred yards from the beach.

They had been warned which beach to row in to. They had been told to look for the large white house to help spot the beach in the night.

They had been told the time and the depth of the water where they would surface. They were told there would be no lights to signal them in to the beach, but that at 2 A.M. a man would have trouble lighting a cigarette a certain number of yards south of the beach. At 2:45 A.M. EDT, American, they were to surface and row in on a dinghy. If the beach did not have fencing around it, they had landed wrong and should row the dinghy north to the next beach. That would be the place for a pickup.

On American charts it was called Bailey's Beach.

If they were not met within seven minutes by the contact, U-038 command sub ordered them, regretfully, to return to sea.

U-038 did not explain, other than by saying it was going to handle the captain's problem. Whether there was some base on shore, no one on the U-boat had known. All during the war, U-038 was the boat every captain wanted to reach, because if one could, it would be given the most accurate convoy information. No one knew its captain, but it was believed he never sent any U-boat into the teeth of the growingly effective American antisub forces.

When U-038 ordered something, these spirited captains always listened, and when it returned a terse message to put the captain ashore, none doubted it had arranged something. Where it found a surgeon, they did not know, and when they were to put the captain on an American shore, they did not know. But the captain was certainly dead without help, and there was no lack of volunteers to man the rubber landing boat even though it was possible this was some kind of trap. After all, U-038 had not been transmitting convoy information for months now.

Everyone in the landing party including the captain wore black sweaters, black hats, dark pants. Everyone but the captain covered his face with dark grease as U-038 had ordered.

The captain had moments of lucidity, passing between consciousness and unconsciousness. He knew what his crew was doing for him. He told them they didn't have to.

They were quiet as they approached the shore. Something was wrong. On the dark beach, they saw no one. Were they supposed to leave the captain and row off?

The boat skidded onto the clean white sand in the dark night, and then they saw him, so motionless no one had noticed him until he walked toward them.

He said one word to them. "Go."

The captain was aware of what was happening and was even able to step out of the boat.

He took the captain by the hand, supporting him with his own body, and guided him to a large house. They were rowing back and did not see what happened to their captain after that.

The thing that hit Charles Drobney that cold dark night when he finally got the captain into his arms was how the man reeked, like he had been sleeping in his socks for a month, which apparently was the way U-boats smelled by the time they had gotten over to the American shore.

Elizabeth, who knew her way around this beach, had the door to the vacant clubhouse open. Loose clothes, with American labels, were waiting. The captain remarked that being undressed by someone so beautiful was worth dying for.

"Your accent is obvious. Try to talk as little as possible," said Drobney. He knew the man would speak some English; all U-boat captains were fluent in that language, and some of them thought they spoke without an accent. He might even be one of them. It was a dangerous misconception.

"You have a surgeon here?"

"We have a nationful of them. You are going to be an American patient."

"With an accent?"

"We have many people driven out of Germany."

"Ah," said the captain. "Do you think this will work?"

"Not if you feel some compulsive urge for discourse," said Drobney.

He got the captain into his car and drove out through the gate. Elizabeth would follow, closing the gate. She would dispose of the clothes by burning the little labels and then dropping the pants and sweater and underclothes into a Red Cross war relief bin.

Drobney drove up Ocean Drive to Bellevue Avenue and then left to where a gray Buick was parked. The driver leaned through his passenger window and tossed a wallet into Drobney's lap.

Lederle had gotten him the identification he wanted.

"You are a Mr. Aaron Rosenberg," said Charlie.

"Ah yes. We had a friend who was Jewish. Before the madness. We are an old naval family, as old as a German naval family can be, Mr. Drobney."

"Shut up," said Drobney.

"*Jawohl,*" said the commander.

"This will not be dangerous, provided you do not lose your head and you do what you're told."

The commander nodded.

"Good," said Drobney. He heard a crash down the street. Aaron Rosenberg's car had just had its accident.

There was a good reason to use the name Rosenberg. If the captain should talk in his sleep, they would at first assume it was Yiddish, and if he had to use English, they would think of the accent as that of a Jewish immigrant. If anyone knew the difference, Aaron Rosenberg would be a refugee from Germany.

And he would be Charlie Drobney's second cousin by marriage so that Charlie would have an excuse to be visiting him every day, and if worse came to worst, would be the first one contacted. The cousin had been visiting Newport when the accident occurred.

At Newport Mercy Hospital, the admitting nurse got him to a doctor immediately. The doctor was elderly because the young doctors were all in the service.

He was tired, he was old, he was rushed, and commented that they were lucky they had brought the patient in because the wound seemed several hours old and sometimes people suffering a subdural hematoma thought the symptoms would pass and they didn't, of course.

The wound. Drobney thought quickly. He hadn't made allowances for that. He had never been exposed to the nature of wounds because he had never had battlefield training. The wound.

"I was showing him the way out of town in my car, and he swerved behind me. Just swerved. I stopped and pulled him out," said Drobney. He would let the doctor come to the right conclusion.

"May have had it earlier," said the doctor. "Passed out at the wheel. You're lucky."

"I don't know about anything earlier. I do know about the crash," said Drobney. *Good,* he thought.

"We're going to have to operate," said the doctor. "What he has is a subdural hematoma. It's a brain injury in which pressure builds up and will kill him unless we relieve the pressure. Do you understand?"

Drobney nodded as though hearing it for the first time. He let the danger of the time difference pass. Already the nurse in the emergency room had it listed as an auto accident, which the police were confirming, labeling it an auto accident injury. If the patient walked out, there would be little problem. If he died, then Drobney would be vulnerable . . . possibly.

This was a navy city at war. The entire police department was strained to the limit with the bucket-of-blood bars on Thames Street. Injuries were common. Sailors fought. Pimps fought. Whores fought.

Who knew how much time or energy the police might have to look for a previous injury when they could be rid of this one with a traffic accident and the emergency room report?

Maybe. And maybe not. It was a danger over the horizon, the magnitude of which could not be accurately calculated at this time. It was not cause for despair. Anxiety, if he wished to indulge in it.

All of this Drobney quickly calculated while he heard from the doctor that the critical time for these things was five days.

"But I am optimistic," said the doctor. The patient's head was already being shaved as Charles Drobney gave permission as closest relative for them to operate. Aaron Rosenberg had slipped into a coma again.

The operation was fast, less than three hours, and the captain was conscious in the morning, but he had forgotten his new name. Charlie told it to him again, and again reminded the captain not to speak. He would be out in a week.

Apparently he was the only patient who enjoyed Newport Mercy Hospital food, prompting one nurse to ask where he had been eating. Another nurse, purposely cruel, commented within hearing of the patient about his perfect health and 4-F draft status.

"The only way a Rosenberg is going to get hurt in this war is by falling off his black market food stamps."

The patient was released in a week and Drobney drove him to Little Compton to wait. It would be easier, now that they had less time pressure, to sail him out on a fishing boat at an opportune moment, rather than to bring in an entire submarine again through unpatrolled moments in the coast guard schedule.

If worse came to worst and there were any problems, the fishing boat with the crewman Aaron Rosenberg could always turn back.

"May I talk now?" asked the captain. His head was bandaged and he wore a too large hat. He still had the clothes that Elizabeth had gotten him.

"Yes."

"We have lost the war, you know."

"I know," said Drobney.

"Then thank you and the commander of the U-038," said the captain.

Drobney nodded.

"We haven't been able to get the U-038 that much lately," said the captain.

"Please," said Drobney.

"You are not a submarine at all, are you?"

"If your way of thanking me is getting me killed, then you are welcome, Herr Kapitän."

"My apologies. I just realized this when I was going to be returned to my own submarine and not the U-038. I realize what a risk this was for you. You cannot sail an ocean home, can you?"

"No," said Drobney.

"It is not safe under the ocean either. Still, thank you."

"Compliments of the Generalstab."

"Oh, one of those. Well, it's good to know I am not in the hands of a Nazi, you know."

"You must be lonely as a captain," said Drobney. The man did talk.

"Not as lonely as you. My name is Wolfgang Wankele. Do you have anyone at home?"

Charles Drobney wanted to send a message to Stuttgart to his parents, telling them he was all right. He wanted to do it so badly, but it was not the time and not the place. The war would be over soon. *Then I will try,* he thought.

"If you wish to repay me properly, tell nothing of this to your officers and crew. I don't want a record of this. I am not looking for medals. Thank you."

"What a Prussian. So curt."

"I'm a Schwabian, if you must know."

"So am I. We are kin then, no?"

"Come, come, Captain."

"Jawohl, Herr Feldmarschall von Generalstab. Excuse me, but my good, good man, I am happy to be alive."

Charles Drobney left Captain Wolfgang Wankele off at the fishing shack with another request for discretion, even in his reports.

He did not see the man again until he was watching his kitchen television set and Wolfgang Wankele was answering reporters gathered around him at the U.S. Naval War College.

One of them asked him jokingly, "What does Newport look like from the surface?"

"Please, gentlemen, excuse me," said the former submarine commander. "I am only allowed to make statements through your Federal Bureau of Investigation."

His English had improved.

23

CHARLES DROBNEY caught it all on the evening news with Brandon on his lap, who wanted to eat like a baby again, which he had been only two years before. Todd had come home for supper and Sondra said he would not be home this evening and perhaps not the next day. He was escorting the U-boat commander around Newport and not letting him out of his sight.

"But tonight, Dad, he's even going to stay in the same room with him. God, I hope Todd's all right."

"He's fine," said Drobney. He had taken an Ismelin when the show started and then added a Valium for nerves, which was dangerous, and he found himself drinking too much water. That also could push up the blood pressure. He might need a diuretic.

Sondra's fiancé had executed this campaign to perfection. Charles Drobney felt both fear and admiration. The man knew what he was doing. "He's just fine, dear."

"How can you say that, Dad? What do you base it on? What do you really know? Do you know that Todd cannot talk to the press without clearance, so the Navy had to call the press conference. What's going to happen to Todd's career? I'm worried about it now."

"He knows what he is doing, I think."

Sondra put out the salad bowls. Brandon turned his over. Drobney put it right. Brandon looked for something else to play with. He marched his knife across the table to attack his chewable vitamins. Sondra put the knife back in place.

"Todd's going to catch the bad men," sang Brandon.

"I don't know," said Sondra. "Let's say the Navy calls this press conference and then they don't get the spies, which is possible, you know. I mean, who calls a press conference when spies can run and hide, you know?"

People who know exactly what they are doing, thought Drobney. "Well, I don't know," he said.

"It can make Todd look like a pure asshole if he doesn't get the spies."

"The man mentioned nothing about spies here," said Drobney.

"He had a brain injury," said Sondra. "What did he do? Check in with his Nazi medicare card? No, he had help. Everyone knows he had help. I think the Navy has done something foolish, with only Todd risking his career. I think the spies have got to be long gone by now. Unless, of course, they don't watch television or speak to people. It's awful."

"I think soon, maybe tomorrow, that U-boat commander will announce that he is about to identify the spies," said Drobney.

"Why do you think that, Dad?" said Sondra.

"Because he didn't do it today, dear," said Drobney. He tried to comfort his daughter. He could see in her face that when you loved someone you were at risk; their fortunes and pains were yours. He wondered if Todd could somehow share with her how good a position he was in.

Charles Drobney reached out for his daughter's hand and sat her down next to him.

"Dear, Todd Oliver is a very intelligent, careful, and, I believe, probably thorough young man. I think he knows what he is doing."

Sondra wouldn't accept that. "The Navy isn't risking anything. You don't know what Todd is doing. You don't know what the FBI is like. You've got Bob to work with and he's your friend. Who does Todd have? I worry about him."

"He's not a unit chief, dear, because he doesn't know his way around."

"That was before. He always looked out for himself before. Before me."

"He is a good man. I think he is a very smart one, dear."

"I have faith in Todd. It's the damned world I don't trust," said Sondra.

Brandon wanted to know if Todd was going to be shot, and he was told that wasn't the problem, that Todd was going to be fine. Fine.

"Will he catch the bad men?" asked Brandon.

"We don't know, honey," said Sondra, cleaning a bit of dinner off his face. But Drobney knew. He was all but certain this FBI man was going to wrap it all up. His positioning appeared perfect. He probably didn't even need an identification from former U-boat commander Wolf Wankele, and then Drobney wondered if Wankele could identify him or Lederle, for that matter, who had personally taken the fishing boat out for the rendezvous. It had been a long time ago. On the television screen Wankele did not look like the same man, although undoubtedly he was. Time had worn on him terribly. Even recovering from the operation as a young man, he had seemed more robust than this visitor today, the old man in the ill-fitting suit. Did they all become so old and frail, these warriors of the sea? Was old age the living grave of the brave?

And who was brave and who was not? Did the man feel forced to come here? Did he volunteer?

Brandon splashed potatoes with a spoon in an attempt to renegotiate his age. He had been talking like a baby lately, and Drobney assumed it was to get attention, or the execution of the very rational supposition that babies had a better life.

Sondra slapped his hand. He could talk baby talk but he could not act like a baby.

In all, Todd had been good for the boy. Since Todd had come into the picture, Brandon had stopped seeing men who, he claimed, were his father in passing cars.

"I don't know, Dad, if I can take being an FBI wife. I wonder if I am not selling myself out for love. You know? I spend so much time like a housewife worrying about her husband."

"Mommy worries," sang Brandon.

"No. You're not alone anymore, dear," said Charles Drobney and he kissed Brandon on the head, Sondra on the cheeks, and left them to go into his study and shut the door. Drobney was sure that Todd Oliver had made the *Takt* decision. It was masterful. Especially the television appearance of Wankele. Drobney reviewed the elements.

Wankele may or may not have come willingly, and if he could

identify Drobney, maybe wouldn't. All Drobney knew was that Wankele was here. His body was here.

The good captain might not even remember the hospital he was taken to. The news program had only mentioned an area hospital. Were they going to check out records for every hospital from Providence to Brockton, Massachusetts, records done on paper in the 1940s style, records that might be destroyed?

They probably could get the date he was here. His own U-boat log might tell that. That could help them a bit. But the man had been here so far for three days. And only tonight was Todd staying with him.

The reason why the captain was put on television was not because he had found something, but because he hadn't. And that would be the same reason why he would announce that he had recognized someone or something.

And soon after that he would announce an arrest was imminent. It was going to work because Todd Oliver, his future son-in-law, had recognized the weakness of the group. He didn't have to know the names.

The point of attack was on the person who had ordered the killing of Mrs. Alexander Wheaton. They had correctly assumed that person could not take the pressure and had had to strike. That was why Todd was staying with the U-boat commander this night forward. They probably even had the city sealed off, waiting for some strike somewhere. They were inducing another attack from the killer of Mrs. Wheaton.

And Lederle would not fail them. Lederle had finally met the man who was going to take advantage of his strategic weakness. He was going to demonstrate why this cavalry commander, like Hannibal and Custer, and Guderian, always had to lose in the end.

Good for you, Todd, thought Drobney. And then to further business. There was little question where Lederle would strike. The man had to be wound tighter than a lanyard. Lederle was going to strike at the one danger he knew would cauterize his weak point, which was Charles Drobney, whom he could not control.

He would probably make it so horrible that whoever he thought might be remaining would be terrified out of his mind and not come forward to testify or act. And if they did, Lederle would reason he would handle that too.

But the real reason was that he had to do battle to live with himself. He could not exercise strategic discipline. It was a classic *Panik vorwärts,* and Charles Drobney was dead.

Was there a way to kill him first? Now would be the time to strike. Of course, that would be just Lederle's sort of battle. He undoubtedly was protected in so many ways. Drobney would not be able to get near him now, least of all with a weapon, and without one, the man was just too personally powerful to overcome.

Tell Todd everything? Then what? Live in one of those safe houses the FBI saved for witnesses? Would Sondra and Brandon live in it too? And Bob?

And how safe was it? Lederle might make the compulsive decision on getting to him, but tactically he would probably make the right ones on how. Lederle would still get to him to kill him. How much better would it be for Lederle to show those who he thought were the remaining members of the ring that nothing could protect them.

And if by some chance, Lederle couldn't penetrate a safe house, then what?

No. M. Hiram Lederle, on his way to his destruction, was going to successfully strike out at Charles Drobney, and the only thing Charles Drobney could do was to make sure Lederle got the absolute minimum, which was, regretfully, at long last, Charlie's life.

It was over. The time had come to die. If Lederle had his life, then he would be satisfied for the moment. And after, when they closed in?

Todd would handle it. He most certainly would handle it. Sondra had found herself a good man.

Charles Drobney wondered for a moment if he should say goodbye in some way to those he loved, but he realized as he sat in his study with the cool evening light announcing impending darkness that he had already said his goodbyes in the best of ways. He had loved these people.

He felt himself tremble, and knew he had to do this last thing properly. *Come, come, Gottzy. There's nothing else you can do. This has to be done,* he told himself. There was no way he could save his life.

He left the study and told Sondra that his room was too uncomfortable to sleep in, so he would sleep out on the porch. He helped dry the dishes, got his pillow, and went outside, and turned on the light so he would be seen from the street.

The porch was cool, even for early September, but the air was beautiful and Charles Drobney finally got to sleep before dawn, watching insects batter around a yellow light bulb.

In the morning, the first observable fact was that he was alive. It came with the sunlight and the sound of a horn honking, and Brandon standing by the foot of the porch couch playing with his toes.

Quickly, Drobney got Brandon into the house and dressed and did not even bother to shave.

"I'm going to have a bite to eat in town. Tell Bob I won't be in today," said Drobney.

"Where are you going?"

"Are you all right?" asked Sondra.

"Yes, I am," said Charles Drobney.

"Dad, how many Valiums are you taking now?"

"I am fine. It's a good day, precious. Let me enjoy it."

"Then shave."

By the time he finished shaving, Sondra had a breakfast on the table. She knew her food was safe. He couldn't refuse it. He ate as quickly as possible without appearing crazed.

On a street down to the harbor a car with two young men in their twenties in it pulled up. The motor idled. They looked at Drobney and he wondered if he should turn to them to give them a better shot. He wondered what the first blow would feel like. He wondered if they were going to snatch him off the street and take him somewhere. He felt the breakfast come up in his throat and he grabbed a parking meter for support. It was moist from the morning kiss of the sea.

"Hey, buddy, you know where Christie's Restaurant is?" called out the young man at the window of the car.

"No, I don't know where it is," said Charlie of a place he knew quite well. He just did not want to talk to them. They had gotten more than enough from him this morning, by just pulling up and asking. He owed the strangers nothing, the young men who did not end his life.

His fear made him thirsty, and the water increased his blood pressure, and he knew he was becoming a bomb. If he suffered a stroke, he wondered if Lederle would send his people into a hospital to finish the job. Of course. Possibly with hatchets.

He felt very tired in his fear. It was not an easy thing to die.

Perhaps this walking around might actually make it more difficult for the killers. Finding a person would undoubtedly be the most difficult part of a murder if the person were wandering around.

After all, a fluid defense was always more formidable than a pile of rocks somewhere. The Wheaton mansion had actually, when one thought about it, been a simple target.

It would have been far, far easier to go to Boston, check into a hotel, and let his whereabouts be known. He could tell Sondra and Bob he was seeing plays.

Then again, that would mean leaving town while the U-boat commander was here, and while that might not attract attention, maybe it would. And who knew what Lederle would do to the family if Charles Drobney were actually arrested? How much blood would he need?

Charles Drobney walked the shopping district, saying hello to friends, stopping in a store, sitting down, chatting, answering questions about Bob and Sondra. There were two places he would not go. Lederle's boatyard and the Cliff Walk. He did not want that place ruined for Sondra. He wanted her to go back and remember the good times there, and Brandon too. He was not going to give Lederle any more than he had to. A life was enough.

In the afternoon the fog rolled in and young people went to the bars, and people moored their boats out in the harbor, and the twelves crew, down to two finalists now, polished the hulls of the magnificent boats.

Charles Drobney sat on a bench in the new marketplace watching a gull perched imperially on gray wood piling with all the illusion of wisdom, when all it really wanted was safety and food, a machine designed to do nothing but stay alive.

At times like this, thought Charles Drobney, *one could envy a gull.*

He looked at his watch. It was three forty-five in the afternoon. He did not want to go home, and yet there was no place else to go.

He certainly wasn't going to Bob's house. He wasn't going to trade one person he loved for another. He thought briefly about finding a woman in town, which would enable him to have a reasonable place to stay. But could he really entice another human being into providing him with a place to be killed and possibly being killed with him? In this he differed from the gull, who looked like he knew what he was doing. A gull would do that to another gull if it could think of it, and most generals would have thought that a fine maneuver, a *Takt* decision; taking the punishment in a less precious place.

But Charles Drobney knew he was neither gull nor general. Life was less convenient as a caring human being, but dammit, it did make the moments precious on this earth.

At 4 P.M. he thought he would try something before putting himself in his home. It would not cost more.

He phoned M. Hiram Lederle's yacht brokerage and asked to see the boat Mr. Lederle had wanted to sell him.

The secretary connected him with Lederle himself. Maybe there was a chance? At that point, Drobney needed another sedative.

The phone was sticky in his hand. Lederle's voice even sounded sweet.

"Hello, Mr. Drobney. I'm sorry. The boat has already been sold. It was a great buy when it was available but it's gone. And let me say now perhaps I have made a mistake. I didn't know your situation. But I do now. I know you will do the honorable thing."

"What is it, Hiram?"

"A bit familiar, aren't you?"

"What do you want?"

"Look, you know what the honorable thing is. I am very busy today."

"I don't know what the right thing is. Tell me."

"The honorable thing," came Hiram's voice, very sticky, very sweet. "You know. You were taught. And you'll do it." There was joy in that voice. The phone clicked dead, and Charles Drobney knew for certain there had been joy in that voice. The honorable thing? Did Lederle actually expect him, like some Prussian officer, to put a bullet in his own head? Why would he do something like that? To save Lederle the trouble of killing him?

No, more likely Lederle wanted Charlie to think he had time, a diversion perhaps, to allow him to strike at a better spot. But where? Where could Drobney go for them to end it?

He did not want to return to the house, but there was no other place he could think of at the moment. He had not expected to see it again when he left in the morning.

He found Brandon alone looking at the television.

"Aren't you supposed to be in a school play this afternoon?" he asked.

"I was, Granpa, but I got taken out."

"By whom?" asked Drobney, sitting down, careful as a cat in an alley of large dogs.

Children just did not get taken out of school by strangers. No school would allow that. Someone had gone to the trouble to use a subterfuge, proof of being a relative, a voice like Sondra's over the phone saying she was sending someone over because Brandon had to come home early. Even a note supposedly from her. Whatever it was, they had not only gone to the trouble to do it, they knew how to do it.

"Men, Granpa."

He could have asked Brandon to talk to him directly, but then the fear in his voice might have frightened the boy.

"They took you from school? They took you right home?"

Brandon shook his head.

"What did they do, honey?"

"They got me ice cream."

"And then?"

"Nothing. They like you."

"What do you mean, precious?" asked Drobney. He felt the room get dark, and prayed not to go now. Not yet.

"What, honey?"

"They said you do the honor thing."

"Honorable?"

"Yes, that's it. That's right."

Hiram Lederle had done it. He had found out the absolute most vulnerable point, and then demonstrated it was his. He didn't even have to kill the boy. All he had to do was move the boy to another home, maybe even out of the country to a market for children. At the very moment that Charles Drobney imagined his grandson being disciplined by some stranger for a sex act or some form of slavery, M. Hiram Lederle had won.

If Drobney took another Ismelin, he might pass out. If he didn't, he might have a stroke this very moment. But if he took the whole bottle of Ismelin he would be dead.

That indeed would be the honorable thing Lederle wanted. The Prussian honorable thing ordered by a supposed von Schaumburg. How beautiful. How perfect. How shrewd. The killer would be Drobney himself. There would be no roadblocks, imported killers, no special Coast Guard because the only way Drobney would get to the sea would be to be buried there.

And even better from Lederle's point of view, Drobney would have to make sure that whatever other spies there were had not been set up to turn in the rest of the crew. Lederle had thought this one out. He had thought it out perfectly. He had figured out what Drobney could not afford to lose. Dead or alive. Under extreme pressure, Lederle had managed a tactical miracle.

It removed Drobney from leading to Lederle if there should be an identification. It forced Drobney to remove all links to Lederle in one master stroke.

Charles Drobney looked at his grandson. He knew Todd would be useless. The special agent himself had once mentioned how some agents would advise a family suffering a missing child to learn to bury it in their hearts; so many never returned. In America it was a free and open market in stolen children.

He was numb. So ready to die when he was helpless to stop it, he now had to do it himself.

He phoned the store. Sondra had not known Brandon was missing. She wanted to know how he had gotten home. How had a school allowed that?

"It was a mistake, dear. I guess some male nurses came for a child, it was the wrong one."

"That is outrageous."

"Yes it is, dear. But they had identification. I'm sure. Come home. I'm not feeling well, and I wish you would be with Brandon."

She would never have to know.

"I'll be right home, Dad."

When Sondra arrived, Charles Drobney went into his study with his full bottle of Ismelin and a glass of water. He thought at first water was foolish, since it only made it easier to swallow, but he did not want to be vomiting up his death because of choking. So they had to go all the way down.

He set the glass on a little table, careful that it not make a ring on the wood, and set the bottle down next to it. He looked around his study, where he had tried to find out how all the horror of the world had happened, and he realized what he had realized some time before. He was never going to understand it all. But he understood enough. He had been wrong. He was sorry. But he had found those he loved, and they made his years right, whatever right there was in them.

He aligned the red cap with the arrow on the bottle and got it open. He would take all of them. Just open the bottle.

He did not have to do it immediately; he still had perhaps until evening. Did he want those few hours?

He wanted them desperately. And he wanted the hour after them, and he wanted the morning, and he didn't want to kill himself. He knew everything it meant, and still he did not want to kill himself.

It was different when death was coming, when you couldn't avoid it, when you didn't have to do it yourself. All he had been doing was trying to make the place where it happened be away from his loved ones. This was far harder.

He sat in the den looking at the bottle and the water, using his last hours for nothing but staring. Even his mind did not work anymore.

He was still numb when the light faded and darkness came to his study. What was he waiting for? He took one very big breath, put his right hand on the bottle, his left on the water, and lifted the open bottle to his lips. His hands were shaking.

Wolf Wankele was facing the American television cameras, feigning an inability to speak English. His age and the ignorance of the reporters helped him. Apparently none knew that it was mandatory for every U-boat commander to be reasonably fluent in English because the U-boat was originally intended for a war with England and to defend Germany from the power of what was then the great British fleet.

The harsh lights bothered his eyes, and he sat now with the FBI man. And he was saying what the FBI man had told him to say.

"Yes, I have recognized many places and things. And yes, people."

"Did you face them? Were they the spies? Were they innocent bystanders? What were they?"

"I am sorry, I don't understand. I have recognized people."

"What people did he recognize?" asked a reporter.

"I am sorry," said Todd. "All questions must be answered by the Boston Field Office."

"Do you expect an arrest soon?"

Todd kept his lips shut and he smiled confidently. Wankele did not blink. He had been in this city for three days and only yesterday had they brought in the FBI man to stay with him at night.

He had told the naval people who had brought him around from place to place what he had told his own government.

"I was unconscious. I don't remember anything."

They tried to help his memory. They reminded him that his grandson's naval career could be hurt if Captain Wankele continued to protect spies, spies who had been paid well for their duty, certainly a lot better than a submarine captain.

They said he was misplacing his loyalty. They told him flatly that important people wanted that spy, and if he was so concerned about protecting him, he never should have reminisced with those few other surviving captains about having had an operation on shore in America. If he boasted about the most daring landing of all on the American coast, certainly he could fill in more details. According to his friends back in Germany he remembered so much of his visit, why not remember it now for Germany's allies?

"I had a brain injury. I certainly wish to help."

"We know there was a spy station there. You saw them."

"I saw someone. It was in a car."

"What kind of car?"

"An American car." And so it went.

They took him to a beach and asked if this was the beach he had landed on. He said he didn't recognize it. There were people playing tennis and many gray and yellow cabanas facing the Atlantic. They were not invited inside.

"It wouldn't have had the cabanas in November," he was told.

Did they turn left or right? He didn't know. He was willing to help; he just couldn't.

He certainly was conscious leaving the hospital, however, and he was asked what he remembered about leaving. They crossed a bridge, he remembered. Yes, he was sure of it.

Did his rescuer speak German?

Not that he remembered.

"I told you and I will tell you again, he looked average. Not too tall, not too short. I don't remember the color of the eyes."

And so the days went. On one of the days, the American FBI man, who was less abrasive than the others, put an electric band around his chest and drove him, starting from Bailey's Beach, through Newport, just watching a monitor.

"It's a lie detector?" asked Captain Wankele.

"Just sort of a monitor," said the American. He had a pleasant smile. When they passed Newport Mercy Hospital in their car, the red brick building up Broadway, Captain Wankele turned his head as casually as he could to look at the other side of the street. When he carefully and slowly looked back at the American FBI agent, he saw he was looking at him.

"It might have been a hospital like that?" asked the FBI man.

Wankele shrugged.

"That certainly could lead down this road to a bridge."

"May I ask, quite frankly now," said Captain Wankele, "why all this energy for a war that is over?"

"They didn't surrender," said the naval officer riding in the front seat. "So it's not over."

"When your war was over, what did you do?" asked the American FBI man.

"I tried to stay alive, is what I did. I eventually got a job teaching Latin, and later that provided me a small pension."

"They didn't give you a pension for your service in the U-boats?" said the naval officer.

"No," said Wankele. The two Americans were quiet. And so the week was up, and they had him in front of television cameras one day and the FBI man stayed with him that night, and then the next day, again with the television cameras, telling of course that lie, that he had recognized a person and places.

Captain Wankele was tired. He returned to the house of the superintendent of the Naval War College. It was large, wooden, airy, and beautiful. He knew that the older man with the white hair, Admiral O'Connell, hated him and was only frostily militarily correct.

They told him nothing of what was going on, but had conversations out of earshot. Although an ally now, he was really their prisoner. He sensed that the junior active naval officers felt friendly, but kept it back because of the admiral.

The FBI man was something else. Captain Wankele would not call it cold. Cold was more of an emotion. It was almost friendly. But it was not friendly. It was, if anything, like a sailor treated a sail.

When this man, Agent Todd Oliver, brought him a little glass of schnapps on a tray the evening of the last press conference, Captain Wankele knew it was over. The tall American with the dark eyes was truly warm now.

"You can go home whenever you want. Thank you."

"I am sorry I could not have been more help."

"How much could we have expected from you against a man who had saved your life?"

"Thank you. May I ask, again now, why you pursue this with such vigor?"

"I am a cop. This guy got away with something. I don't think they're bad people or good people. They broke the law. And our law says there is no statute of limitations on spies. They're not getting away."

Captain Wankele drank his schnapps and rolled the hot liquor around his tongue. "No," he said. "You are pursuing this because you are Americans. That is how you fought the war. You came on, and you came on, and you never stopped."

"Lufthansa flies out of Boston. I am sure I can get you on one of those flights within a day or so," said Todd.

"Yes, good. As soon as possible. Thank you."

"I've got to stay with you until then. I haven't seen my fiancée for a few days now," said Todd.

"I know this has been a hard week for you. But I wonder if you would mind coming to dinner with me at my fiancée's."

"I would absolutely enjoy it," said the old U-boat commander, who had spent almost a week in polite but coldly formal commissary dinners. Even though he was among allies, he had undoubtedly killed some of the friends of the older ones, and the forgiveness went only as far as military courtesy. "Perhaps it is age, but it has not been easy on me," he said.

Sondra Drobney knocked on her father's study door.

"Dad," she called in. "We'll have company tonight. I hope you don't mind."

There was no answer. She knocked again. And still there was no answer. She saw underneath the door there was no light on in the room. It was dark.

"Brandon, go upstairs and see if Granpa is sleeping up there," said Sondra.

"He's in the room with the books."

"Are you sure?"

"He went in."

"When?"

"When Captain Amazing went on."

"Dad? Are you awake, Dad?"

There was still no answer. When a person had high blood pressure and suffered his age as badly as her father had recently, there was always that hesitation in the morning, or at the end of his afternoon nap, that period between the first call and the first answer, when despite herself, she felt that moment of anxiety that he would not answer. That this time he was gone.

Not now, she thought. Not with Brandon missing this afternoon and not finding out where he was until the people who picked him up by mistake left him at the house. *Not now,* she thought. *Not now, Dad. I love you, Dad. Not now. For Godsake, not now.*

She opened the door and the foyer light shone on him, sitting rigidly with an open bottle of pills in his left hand, resting on his lap, and the water glass on his knees. He was not moving, but staring ahead.

She froze. She focused on the middle button of his sports shirt, hoping the button was moving.

It is not moving, she thought.

Then it moved. He was breathing.

"Dad?"

"Yes."

"We're having company for dinner."

"Good."

"Are you all right?"

"I am very tired, precious."

"Do you want to rest?"

"No. Later. Later will be fine."

"Todd's coming. He'll be here for dinner."

"Good."

"Do you want dinner? Would you rather rest?"

"I think I will have dinner. Yes. I will have dinner."

"Okay. But only if you feel good."

"I am all right," said Charles Drobney, and he let her shut the door and he sat in the dark. *Even a little longer it could wait,* he thought. *Even a little longer.*

Todd came in with a white-haired gentleman that Charlie recognized from television. And he was sure the U-boat captain did not recognize him right away. Did Todd know? Was this a trap?

Todd gave Sondra a very big kiss and wrestled briefly with Brandon on the couch, as a way of hello. No. He wouldn't be that loving with Sondra. He didn't know.

"This is my father, Charles Drobney," said Sondra. "He is a bit tired. We have to salt our own food here. He is on a salt-restricted diet."

"It looks like a lovely dinner. I can smell it already," said the U-boat commander. He was smiling. When was he going to realize? Was he going to drop a glass? Was he going to ask a foolish question?

"May I get you a drink?" said Drobney.

"Thank you, no. I have had one. At the Naval War College. A beautiful place."

"How does it feel to be here?" asked Sondra.

"Tiring," said Wankele. He stood in the kitchen, not knowing where to sit or go. Drobney got plates for the table.

"The men help serve here in America," said Sondra.

"Yes, I see," said Wankele. Drobney put down the plates at every chair. "What do you plant around here for vegetables?"

"What?" said Sondra.

"I noticed flowers. You plant things here. Which ones?"

"We can't grow roses for beans," said Sondra. "Dad used to garden. What did you plant?"

"Flowers," said Drobney.

"Ah, flowers," said Captain Wankele. "They are a gift in the world. A great gift that should be said 'thank you' for."

Drobney knew the captain had recognized him.

Drobney did not look up. He finished putting down all the plates, and said he was not tired at all. Todd turned off the television and sent Brandon to the bathroom to wash his hands.

They ate chicken in tomato sauce with asparagus, and a light salad with very little oil. They talked of gardening, the chicken, and silverware and flowers in Germany and then light bulbs and the hardware business. And the weather. The weather was very important. It was nice in Newport.

"Because of the Gulf Stream," said Wankele.

"Yes," said Drobney.

"I would like to visit a third time under different circumstances."

"You must," said Drobney.

"You say you have problems with roses," said Wankele.

"I don't. I don't try them," said Drobney and they all laughed very hard. Brandon thought the man spoke funny. Brandon was corrected for being impolite.

"In Germany you speak funny," said Wankele. And they all laughed again. Todd had his eyes on Sondra and noticed nothing. Sondra had her eyes on Todd, and noticed less. Brandon escaped eating his asparagus.

"Well, I am sorry I cannot stay longer here, but I am going back tomorrow," said Wankele. "I am not at liberty, of course, to say what—"

"Enjoy your flight," said Charles Drobney.

It might all be over. Over for good. Over in ways he would never fathom. The tank had passed and there was a chance to put this one away finally.

He didn't even have to hear Todd telling Sondra he would be going down to Washington in two days to know the investigation was over.

The one advantage about taking his own life was that Mr. M. Hiram Lederle had to wait to find out whether he had committed suicide. And in that time there was something he could do.

"You know, I will have a glass of brandy tonight," said Drobney. The U-boat commander said he would have one, too, before he left. They clicked their glasses and toasted each other to a long life.

hat very reason-
s loaded with
Everything
dly with a
of one
busi-
you

24

CHARLES DROBNEY entered through the side entrance and waited in the kitchen of the large house off the Avenue. In any other city in the country, it would be a mansion. In Newport it was a large house off the Avenue.

He wore a light gray windbreaker over a green sports shirt, and a pair of fresh chino pants. He held his hands folded in his lap.

He looked more pitiful this morning, more humble. He would probably be asked to leave by the butler. He was prepared for that. It would have been lovely to believe that because the U-boat captain was leaving, Lederle would feel safe. But Lederle never calculated safety factors by themselves. If that were the case, Elizabeth would be alive.

And knowing that, Charles Drobney saw something he could do that just might settle this thing long enough to call it forever.

He couldn't even calculate the odds anymore. But he knew one thing. He knew M. Hiram Lederle now. Lederle just might take something other than Charlie's life.

The man obviously had not gone around killing in every situation, but in every situation he felt endangered. He had to make a move. It was an almost sexual tension, a sense of dominance the man had to have.

If there was a way Charlie could give him that, Lederle might let him live. But M. Hiram Lederle had to be in control; he couldn't

even suspect Drobney had dared reason with him.
ing could still be a goad.

The kitchen was smaller than the Hickories but wa
new gadgets. It was an electronic marvel of cooking.
money could buy to make cooking better, and undoubt
great chef who didn't need them.

"I am sorry, sir," said the butler with the smooth resonanc
with a certain place in an orderly world. "Mr. Lederle handle
ness matters only at his office. Please do contact his secretary i
have any problems."

"No," said Drobney.

"I beg your pardon," said the butler.

"I'm going to see him."

"That's just not possible, sir."

"You don't understand, he has forgotten this appointment," said
Drobney. He was in what had to be the safest place in the world for
him, Lederle's house, the one place in which he would be least likely
to have anyone killed, although knowing Lederle that might not be
impossible, just least likely.

"Would you be so kind as to bring this matter to Ms. Tompkins,
his secretary?" said the butler.

"No," said Drobney, and the butler left. He sat there hoping a
stroke would not take him. When Lederle came into the kitchen, the
cook almost stood to attention. The butler was not with him.

He said nothing to Drobney. He was in lounging clothes, and
when he marched outside, his shimmering dark green robe flew
behind him like some loose spinnaker.

Drobney followed. Lederle was leading him to the main garage,
fifty yards from the house past statuary and hedges.

Lederle opened the door and went in first. He shut the door
behind Drobney; his face was white with rage. Lederle waited near a
green Bentley. There were several cars in the garage, all polished.
The place smelled strangely clean, like a schoolroom or a cafeteria.

Lederle tapped a foot on the cement floor. He folded his arms.
The garage was very big and very quiet. Drobney said nothing.

"You know, I have tried to be decent with you. I just don't see
what the problem is. What are you going to force me to do? To you?
Your grandson? Is that what you want?"

"This afternoon they went to Logan International Airport in Boston," said Drobney. They had won.

"They *were* bluffing!" said Lederle with a yell on the "were." It arrived along with a star-ringing smack at the top of Drobney's head. He felt himself bang onto the hard cement floor. He had been hit for joy.

"They were, they were! I thought so. I thought so," he heard Lederle say.

Drobney stayed on the floor. He felt a slipper tap his ribs.

"Get up."

"Don't hit me again, please," said Drobney.

"I am not going to hit you. Get up."

Drobney reached up for a handle on the Bentley and pulled himself to his feet. Lederle wiped off the hand smudges with a handkerchief.

"Who were the others?"

"There weren't any."

"I thought maybe so. Yes. Were you an officer? A Prussian?"

"No," said Drobney.

"I didn't think they'd make you an officer. But you acted it."

"Yes, sir."

"Stay on your feet, for Godsake," said Lederle.

"Yes, sir," said Drobney.

"Do you understand that I can kill you?"

"Yes, sir," said Drobney.

He could feel Lederle calculate. The man was shrewd. He was not running into this one wildly.

"And you understand your life is in my hands. You understand that now?"

"Yes, sir."

"You understand you live only by my grace?"

"Yes, sir," said Drobney.

"All right. If you understand that, you understand I can call on you for anything."

Drobney nodded.

"All right. This is the way it should always be. And I will tell you something, Charlie. If you have problems with your store, you come to me now. All right?"

"Yes, sir."

"And Charlie, don't call me 'sir,' for Godsake. You're not in the Army. It's 'Mr. Lederle.' "

"Yes, Mr. Lederle."

"All right. I don't have any desire to kill you. I never really wanted to hurt anyone. You know. These things get forced on you. But look, you're in a lot better position than others. You know who I am now. Some never found out. Too bad for them."

He gave Charlie a little pat on the back and that meant he was dismissed. Charles Drobney knew he was now as safe as he was ever going to be with that man. Lederle had him where he wanted him. He was no longer a danger to Lederle physically or emotionally. He was subdued.

Lederle might yet kill him at some convenient point down the road. But if he did so, he would not make it especially brutal and, most importantly, he would not harm Sondra or Brandon or Bob. It was not perfect, but it was the *Takt* decision. At best, a good chance, while M. Hiram Lederle felt he was on top.

Admiral O'Connell would not leave the car. He would not enter a German plane to see that U-boat commander off. He waited until the FBI agent returned to the car.

"Well, where do we stand?"

"I've got another day."

"What are you going to do?"

"As much as I can. We've proven they had the spies here. It was a spy network. You got that."

"I knew that. I knew that before you came here."

"You believed that. You didn't know it," said Todd.

"None of them made a move," said the admiral.

"I thought they would," said Oliver.

O'Connell was quiet. He was quiet through the tunnel that led to the Southeast Expressway to Rhode Island. They could cut through the edge of Boston and not be tied up by any of it. They would be back in Newport within an hour and a half. O'Connell was staying in Newport for the ball honoring the finalists in the America's Cup, which would be in a few days. The Navy would be represented at that one.

"That sonuvabitch was laughing at us," said O'Connell.

"I don't think so. I think he was scared."

"I don't give a shit. Where do we go now?"

"I have today and tomorrow, and then I am due back in Washington."

"It's over," said O'Connell.

"It's over the day after tomorrow."

"It's over," said O'Connell. "I thought we had them. I really thought we had them. If we were Nazis, we would have gotten the information out of him."

"They did lose, you know," said Todd.

"Wasn't there anything else we could use on him?"

"The West German Government already used more than we would. His grandson's career was threatened. That's why we got him over here in the first place. We couldn't do that if it were going the other way. We do not visit the sins of the fathers on the children. It's biblical and constitutional. And it ain't bad."

"Would you say this was tougher or easier than your normal spy case?"

Todd Oliver thought long before he answered. He was very tired from a very hard case. And he knew every word when he finally let them out.

"This is my first E-65. That's our code for espionage."

He did not look at O'Connell. The car drove past the outskirts of Boston where a golf course rose on a hill hiding the vast Atlantic. Todd noticed someone had put out cigarettes in the ashtray a long time ago. Then he looked outside again, and the golf course was gone, and there were wooden homes and telephone lines and washing hung on lines.

With stark suddenness, he felt an arm around him.

"Son, you fight wars with who you got, not who you wished you got. In my book, you did okay. You did damned well. And I'd go into battle with you any day. I'd sail with you any day."

"We have an RA, resident agent, who has worked on them, assisted the Providence Field Office, and he said I was doing the right thing."

"We gave 'em a scare. We sent a charge by their bow. I would have liked to have sent it up their ass. You leaving the FBI?"

"I don't think so."

"You like your work?"

"I think I do. Yes."

"That's good. Because if you don't, it can be hell. I don't think there's any worse torture than spending your life waiting for retirement. We have some in the Navy, poor bastards. You know, it can be a curse. Sucks the joy right out of the job."

"I know," said Todd.

Brandon became virtually hysterical when his roller cart was broken by the cleaning woman who came once a week. Sondra knew it was not the roller cart that had bothered him. He had come to rely on Todd's presence, and when Todd was gone for two days and then returned for an evening, not only didn't Brandon get Todd back, he lost his mother, too, and Granpa.

So Brandon needed some time and attention, and the broken roller cart became the worst crime of the century, done by the worst person of the century, the cleaning woman, and tolerated by the traitor of the century, Brandon's mother, who didn't think the cleaning woman should be kept out of the house forever.

The boy needed time. Unfortunately, Sondra Drobney needed time also. She had been taking care of Father, grabbing only snatches of good time with Todd, and trying to give Brandon a mother. She had not been to a Renaissance League meeting since June and had discovered that as she had feared, fully half the projects they were supposed to support were being ignored. Even worse, as she discovered, no one else seemed to mind except the poor man who had taken her place and was now doing 80 percent of the work and wanted her back.

There hadn't been time to think, to let her feet dangle in water somewhere, to read a novel, to visit friends, to complain, to worry enough and hope enough and all the things one did when one looked after oneself.

The good and the bad of it, she didn't have enough for herself and the agenda from now on was going to be Sondra Drobney taking care of her own needs. The rest of the world would either contribute to that end or stay out of her life.

But not now. She spent an hour with Brandon repairing the cart. Now she made sure Dad, who was looking awful, took a nap before supper as she brought him some herbal tea. Something quite wrong had been happening to him. He was not reacting to the world like the man she knew.

It was not the hour he spent in the dark alone. He liked to think alone, and sometimes he would let the world get dark around him without turning on the light. The night before he had been worrisome because he had looked so bad.

What was really strange was the way he treated the guest from Germany. Sondra had expected probing questions. Very few people knew how intelligent his questions were when he met someone he was interested in. On the other hand, when he thought the person a fool, he would just be quiet.

"It is lucky we live in Newport. I am awful in elevators. I just can't make conversation," her father had once said.

"I can. I tell them my life story between the third and fourth floor," she had answered.

Last night with the German visitor, he had made the polite elevator kind of no-contact, no-thought conversation for the entire evening.

Son and father taken care of, Sondra Drobney turned that evening to her lover. He lay on his back, asking only that she keep her arms around him. Several times he said he loved her. Out of nowhere he said it. Out of the silence, he said it. And when she tickled his stomach gently with a fingertip, he said he wasn't interested in sex. But she was.

She moved the finger down into the pubic hairs and then down the length of his flaccid organ, tracing the outline of the head, and then leaving it for the base, almost grabbing with her palms, but not quite.

"Not tonight," he said.

She moved his organ back with a finger, and then forward with a finger. It was hers now. His, but hers. And when he didn't push her hand away, she turned her playing to teasing and teasing to arousing.

Todd made sudden, almost violent love to her, a far more powerful act than she had expected. It was as if both were seized by it, and she wondered if possibly their bodies were making a baby. It was so powerful. He withdrew his mind, again, while she held his body.

After a while he said, "You know, you can't second-guess your life all the time."

"You are," she said.

"I mean, you shouldn't."

"What would you do differently?"

"I would have married you first. No. No. That's wrong. If I didn't have Anne, I might have always wanted her."

"Did you always want me?"

"No. I didn't know I wanted you till I loved you. I didn't know I would love you. I didn't imagine someone like you would be someone I loved. I—"

"Can it," said Sondra. Later she asked him if he thought they would have liked each other as children. But he wasn't even listening. He was holding her and falling off to sleep.

At the Touro Synagogue Robert Goldstein left the rabbi's study. He was, as Goldstein had said often, the last rabbi he would go to. He had seen two others that day and only ended up at the Touro because the others had not given him the answer he wanted. At the Touro, he was asked another question.

"You have got to tell me the nature of the crime before I can help you with your obligations, as to whether you are obliged to turn the person in. Offhand, I would say yes. But what law are you talking about? There are many laws."

Very carefully Robert Goldstein chose his words so as not to make his revelation irrevocable. He knew this was not a priest in confession bound by laws of silence. This was a rabbi bound to other laws, most of which Robert Goldstein did not know, and the others he didn't all that much believe in. But for this, he needed a rabbi. He needed a rabbi to tell him what he couldn't tell himself.

After an hour, the rabbi apologized and said Robert Goldstein had to be more specific, especially about the nature of the crime. And why come now, when after so many years, Robert Goldstein had not even attended shul during high holy days?

"No reason, Rabbi," Bob Goldstein said, leaving the third and final rabbi without the answer he wanted. The next morning he told the salesmen and the schlepper to take the day off. Drobney-Goldstein was closing for the first day, the first business day, since its founding more than forty years before.

25

"WHAT'S WRONG, Bob?" asked Drobney.

No one else was in the store and Bob Goldstein looked like a man facing death. It was 10 A.M., a half hour after opening.

"Let's go into the back," said Bob.

"A surprise? What's going on?" said Drobney.

At first he thought perhaps it was a surprise party, and that everyone was hiding in the other room to jump out and wish him something or other. But it wasn't his birthday, and Bob Goldstein would not unnerve him like this for a party. Bob had more sense than that.

"Is something wrong?" asked Charlie. "Is the store all right?" He didn't think it was the store.

"Probably not."

"What's wrong, Bob?" Charles Drobney dropped the paper bag with the muffin on the checkout counter. Goldstein locked the door behind him.

"Are we all right?"

"No," said Goldstein.

"Is someone after us? What's wrong? I forgot to get rid of your dynamite. Right?"

"I don't know," said Goldstein. "Fuck the dynamite."

"I don't need suspense for my blood pressure, Bob."

"That's not why you've been sick, Charlie."

Goldstein shut the storage room door behind them and turned on the harsh yellow light bulb, bathing khaki cardboard boxes in enough light to read the mailing labels. Stacks of crushed cartons were bound and waiting on a solid yellow galley truck with the paint chipped. The lawnmowers that hadn't moved on discount, even through August, had been stored under cloth in the rear, ready to resume full spring prices after the winter.

Goldstein stood beside two small cartons of RCA bedroom television sets. He leaned against a round steel beam set in the gray concrete floor that supported the metal ceiling.

"Why did you do it, Charlie? Why?" Goldstein's face was heavy and his eyes dark. He hung on to the steel roof support as though he had done fifteen rounds with an opponent that had not missed one shot to his soul.

"What?"

"Spy for the Nazis."

"Bob, you know me."

"Yeah, I know you. That's the problem. Why did you do it? Tell me. Make the world make sense."

"Obviously there is something that has led you to believe—"

"Charlie, are you going to have Lederle kill me too?"

Charles Drobney did not answer. He found a carton to sit down on and slumped there.

"The Wheaton estate returned these. Both the broken one, the one that didn't work, and the one you delivered to replace it. Neither of them were opened," said Bob. He went on.

"M. Hiram Lederle, who has more money than I can imagine, gets in a shoving match with you over a boat you won't see. The total cost of that boat is maybe less than he earns in interest on his money in a day. But look, I figure it is some ego thing. The man is not unknown to get heavily involved in ego things. And you ask me to forget it.

"Now what do Charles Drobney, Elizabeth Wheaton, and M. Hiram Lederle have in common? Well, for one thing they were all here during World War II."

Drobney took a deep breath and did not move. He did not answer either.

"And guess who all arrived at the same time in this area, roughly the same time. And roughly the same area. And when we go into the past, we find that according to your job application with me, your previous employer had gone out of business, and you were born in Racine, Wisconsin. Well of course records weren't that good then.

But when you are friends, like you and I are friends, Charlie, you remember little things about your friend, like I remember your telling me how proud you were when your father finally got a telephone in his house. Well, if you had a phone and you were proud of it, Charlie, then of course you had your name in the phone book. They still keep old phone books at the phone company and never anywhere was there a Drobney in any phone book in Racine. It was trouble, but I took the trouble to find out.

"But look, I'm not turning on an old friend because of coincidence. There's Lederle, or as the whole city seems to have heard by now, Mr. Lebowitz, also from a small town in the Midwest. Now here in Newport, it's possible we didn't know he was passing for gentile, but certainly in the town Mr. Lebowitz was supposed to come from the Lebowitzes would know. And they didn't. So what kind of business do you have with some blond cunt on the Avenue and M. Hiram Lederle? You got spy business with them is the business you got."

"She was the woman I loved, Bob. I never told you about her."

"Wonderful. Tell me about the gas ovens, Charlie. Tell me about dragging women and children into ditches, Charlie. Tell me about rounding up people and burying them alive, Charlie. Tell me about throwing babies off of rooftops, Charlie. Tell me about it, Charlie. Did she love it too?"

"She didn't know what she was doing."

"Tell me about lampshades of human skins, Charlie. Tell me about cutting off a man's testicles without anesthesia. Tell me about the cattle cars, Charlie."

"You knew how I thought they were animals. You knew that." Drobney was rising now, his hands out, reaching for some bridge of reason he knew had collapsed when the first cameraman followed the first soldier into the first concentration camp and every living Jew saw what could have been himself.

"But when you said they were animals I didn't think you meant you. I thought you were talking about them, Charlie," said Goldstein, and then the life returned to his face with pain. The eyes screwed tight, the teeth bared, and Robert Goldstein slammed his bare fist into the steel pipe holding up the roof.

"You drove us into ditches like animals. We couldn't even surrender," said Goldstein. He slammed his fist again into the pipe with more fury.

Charlie tried to get him to stop, but he broke free and hit his fist again, with great agonizing pain. Goldstein screamed and then took his other hand, with Charlie hanging on, and hit that, too, into the pipe, but without as much force.

"Stop it! Stop!" yelled Charlie.

"You burned us alive. You rounded us up. There was no crime we committed but being born."

"Stop it!" screamed Charlie. "Hit me if you've got to hit someone."

Bob Goldstein slammed his head into the pipe. "I'll never hit you. I'll never hit you. I'll never hit you. God, I'll never hit you, Charlie."

"Idiot," yelled Drobney, and got his body between Bob's head and the pipe. There was a reddish bruise swelling there. His right hand was bloody. A bone stuck out of it and he was crumpled there on the floor, sobbing, the former P-38 pilot who would not lift a hand to strike his friend.

Charlie tried to bandage his hand. He told Goldstein to get himself to a hospital.

"You've got to go on living, Bob."

"What for? You're the only friend I've got, Charlie. I don't have anyone else."

"You're the only friend I have, Bob."

"I can't . . . I can't, you know. I can't ever be your friend. I'm not going to let you have the store. You're not going to get a store out of this."

"I don't want the store," said Charlie.

"Neither do I," said Bob Goldstein.

"Can I drive you to the hospital?"

"I'll walk, Charlie. It's close."

"No one was more horrified than I by what they did, Bob."

"Didn't you read *Mein Kampf?*"

"After the war, I read it. After the war I read a lot," said Charlie.

"Why did you do it, Charlie? You're not like them."

It was a question that did not have a good answer. But if there was someone he wanted to have an answer for, it was this man.

"I was trapped. I didn't know better. Maybe I was so trapped I didn't want to know better. I can lie to myself you know."

"Not you, Charlie."

"Oh yes," said Drobney. "And once I was in it, I did it because, dammit, I was in it. I was in it."

"That's a reason?"

"That's not a grand reason. It's not a logical reason, but, Bob, for Godsake, it's the reason most people do most things."

"You're not most people, Charlie. And it wasn't most things. Why you?" sobbed Bob. "Why in hell you, goddammit, Charlie Drobney?"

"Bob, I was not part of those horrors. I was not even reporting to people who were part of those horrors. They looked down on those kind of people. Down on them."

"I know you wouldn't do it. That's one of the things that's so hard."

"I would never do it. I didn't do the killing here."

"I figured it wasn't you. It was too stupid. You ran the thing, didn't you? Or was there someone else?" asked Bob. He cradled his right hand on his thigh, wincing. Charlie tried to help him up but he shrugged away his hands.

"I ran it," said Drobney.

"Lederle went off like an asshole because he's got a few bucks and he can get people killed."

"Yeah," said Charlie.

"You're lucky they didn't put him in charge. You would have lasted a week," said Bob.

"They were, in their own limited way, smart."

"Yeah. Smart," said Goldstein, his face screwed in pain.

"Goodbye, Charlie."

"Goodbye, Bob. I love you."

"I fucking know that," said Bob Goldstein and hid his face with his tears.

The partnership was over. Charles Drobney left the door open as he left because Bob might have trouble with the key lock. There was no danger of someone's coming in and doing harm to the unprotected shelves. There was nothing more to lose there.

Charles Drobney squeezed between the tourist buses lined up on Broadway. He walked slowly away from the store in which he had spent much of his life. If he had been shot the other day, he never would have gone through this. It would have been cleaner.

It was not the sort of day he wished to live for.

He went home and did not know what he would say to Sondra about the store and Bob. He would figure something out. He did not go into his study, but went up to his bedroom. He was very tired, and even Brandon's noise did not cheer him.

He was sure in some way this was bringing his death closer, and if he closed his eyes and did not wake up, it would be, after all, an easy exit from this world.

But the world reached for him. M. Hiram Lederle called with a command. Charles Drobney was to appear at his brokerage, immediately.

The weathered wood and carpeting of the office of M. Hiram Lederle seemed an island of quiet in a fuming tourist sea, which packed the Newport docks, crowding the last two contenders in the America's Cup, jostling the crews as they set out for another run at each other.

Lederle was banging around his private office like a man on a leash, wearing the yachtsman's virtual uniform for the race, the blazer, Top-Sider shoes, and white pants. He pointed Drobney into a chair.

"I heard from your partner. An obscene phone call. What does he know?"

Drobney lowered his head.

"He called me a Nazi. Does he know?"

Drobney thought a moment.

"Well?" said Lederle.

"He knows," said Drobney.

"Wonderful," boomed Lederle. "How did he find out? When did he find out? Where is he now? Did you tell him?"

"I didn't tell him. He found out today because of the invoices on televisions to the Wheatons. I made a mistake. Ordinarily I would handle the invoices and returns, but I've been sick. So one thing led to another."

"Who else knows?"

Charles Drobney paused. He let his gaze wander around the room as though he were thinking. He noticed how all the boats in black and white pictures were sailing boats. A title deed to land from King George III hung on the wall between pictures of two sloops.

"To my knowledge, no one else knows, or cares, in my family."

"Including that FBI man?"

"He cares but there is no way he could know. At least not so far, and all we need is until tomorrow. He is leaving tomorrow. He has failed, you know."

"Of course I know. What else does Goldstein know?"

"That's it."

"You can't really be sure he won't talk. While I am sure I could keep us out of jail, some way, the embarrassment would be too much for me. I am not going to stand here and let the world find out who I was, someone hired and bought by another government."

It hit Drobney very hard that moment that Lederle had not killed out of fear for his life so much, but to protect his social standing. He had never felt his life threatened. He did kill so easily, this man, thought Drobney.

"Yes, sir," said Drobney.

"But we are not going to allow it."

"No, sir."

"Will he go to the police?"

"I don't think so."

"Why not?"

"Because he gets the rest of the store," said Drobney.

"Good," said Lederle. "Good. Wonderful. He has got his little store, and it will take him a day or two before he realizes he is on to something even bigger, bigger money."

He cupped Drobney's face in his large hands almost tenderly.

"Your wonderful friend there is not so much a friend," said Lederle. His grin sparkled with pure joy.

It was the nature of the Lederles to be more comfortable with the cunning of the world than with the good. Germans acting out of decency, which had happened, was a threat to Lederle and his kind. It was the nature of the man. It was a given factor in the situation, thought Drobney.

"The partnership worked."

"Until, of course, he wanted it all. Yes. Well, so much for your dear friend."

"I misjudged our friendship."

"How long can you keep him satisfied with your half of the store, so that he doesn't go creating problems for me?"

"Forever," said Drobney.

"Only dead is forever."

Drobney nodded.

"Ahah," laughed Lederle. "You want your store back. You little bastard. I love you. I love you. You want your store back. Well good. Good for you."

Lederle kissed Drobney's head and laughed again.

"Have you ever killed a man?"

Drobney shook his head.

"Well now, that's not a surprise. Why should you, eh? All you knew was how to maneuver Prussians. Never a match for a shrewd Schwabian. God, I would not put one of those Junkers in charge of a hot dog stand, Charlie. Not your fault at all. But here we are with a problem."

"I am suggesting it, Mr. Lederle, because of the quieter way it could be done by me. I don't want to kill anyone, but I have access to so many things that could be so natural to him. He is not a young man."

"He's no older than I am," said Lederle. "But, you're right. As you know, and well know, we can take him in any way at any time. But who needs more attention now?"

Drobney nodded.

"Without writing anything down, gather your thoughts on what he does, and what his health is, and what natural dangers he exposes himself to. He gambles a bit, so if worse came to worst, he could be killed for a gambling debt. But something more natural is better."

"I think I need an evening to get it all."

"Good, because today we are heading out to the Cup buoys. I have important people as my guests. I have another problem in my life that I am getting settled. The dumbest thing. Do you know that I have found out, and no one would tell me to my face, that they think I am a Jew. What should I do, Charlie, show the members of Bailey's Beach my party card? I should have saved my *Marmeladenplatte* for them. Of course, they don't like Germans all that much."

"I will have everything tomorrow. But it may take a long time to work something out."

"Usually it just takes minutes."

"Well, you know you are dealing with someone inexperienced. We have to get the right thing. I couldn't look at someone and kill him, you know. I am just a hardware store owner."

"All right. We need isolation. I don't want people thinking I spent hours in business with you unless of course we do go into some business, and as you can understand, I really don't have any great desire to buy a hardware store. Okay. You are the little man I have taken under my wing to sell a boat that is right for him. M. Hiram Lederle and Son brokerage takes great care in matching the person with the vessel. We are not interested in dumping any boat on anyone because we have been here a long time and will be here a long time. We are Newport. Tomorrow at ten, we watch the Cups final together. That should be enough time, and who is going to plan a murder in view of two thousand other boaters? Also, tomorrow the FBI man is gone. Good. Done. Go."

Drobney got up and gave a little bow before he left.

Todd Oliver was painfully aware of the morning. How the sun burned away the fog, how the shingled boards of houses bowed to their wood-braced ends, and how the people seemed to float down toward the harbor, where the action was, the center of the world for that day and those people who had bused to Newport for it.

Todd headed in the opposite direction, up Broadway, past the closed Drobney-Goldstein hardware store toward Mercy Hospital.

He wore Bermuda shorts, a T-shirt, and a blue windbreaker to hide his shoulder holster. He had a notebook and one readout from the polygraph he had attached to Captain Wankele. He had not expected the man to tell the truth, but he thought his body might.

Todd could have stayed in the field office fiddling with the report. But he had one more day, and he was going to give it one more day of work. Of all the hospitals he had passed with Wankele, Newport Mercy had registered the highest pulse rate. Although it was probable that the man didn't even remember what the hospital looked like.

But it was possibly this hospital, and he did have the dates from the sub's log, and he had one more payday to earn on this case. And he was going to earn it. Resident Agent Wannaker helped make it easier. With one phone call to the Newport police, he found out that the records department was not the place to ever find out anything about the records. There was a retired hospital clerk who had handled the records before computers did. She was the one who could guide him through the maze of boxes where they were now stored.

Todd wondered, as he now sensed the very air itself, something he had not done before, whether he had done the right thing. Whether he could have even done something better to find these spies.

But now he had someone to tell his fears to, and someone to mourn with him when he failed and feel joy with him when he triumphed, and he was not alone anymore. He wasn't even alone in that one-man office. He could trust Wannaker.

He had to admit, for someone who felt awful about how this case had turned out, he was feeling rather good, better than he had all his life. Not happy. Good.

And Agent Oliver knew the difference now as he met a white-haired woman in a print dress who, the police had assured Wannaker, was the only one who could make sense of the war records.

"I am looking for a brain operation that occurred on or after November 18, 1944. That week," said Todd.

"What are you looking for?" asked the woman.

"Everything," said Todd.

"Good," said the woman. "Then you'll be glad you are not using a computer. Because you couldn't ask a computer that. Nobody is interested in everything anymore. They don't treat patients anymore. They treat cells and blood samples. I can give you everything about a patient. I know files, paper files."

Contrary to his fears, she did not mind the labor of going through the records. She loved to be needed again. The records brought back memories of the war and shortages, and how everyone worked together, she said. Maybe she was getting old, she said, but she longed for those times when "we all felt like one."

After a lunch break, about 3:30 P.M., when Todd's lungs felt like a musty record, and when his eyes were bleary, and this seventy-eight-year-old woman was still fresh, he pulled out a record sheaf that she pointed to, after they had tracked through several years and several departments.

The manila folder was dry as crackers and just as brittle. The old blue-lined paper was filled with scratchy ink. The ballpoint pen wasn't in use yet.

They got the right date. They got the right operation. And even though there was a Jewish name attached to it, Todd Oliver was sure this was it.

"Can we get the admitting ledgers?" asked Todd.

"Yes" said the woman, beaming.

Todd took an old box onto his lap. The old paste on the label crumbled as he removed the lid.

Large sheets were folded like a snake on top of each other.

"I'll have to go through by date first and then match the name. That's the only way," she said.

"Sure," said Todd.

This was the hospital. This was the operation, and now, he thought, he might just get his man. He wondered why he wasn't more excited. Perhaps it had been so long and so hard that there was no more excitement left, just a will to push through.

He was sure his man would not do something so foolish as to dump a brain-injured man into a hospital and then leave a phony name. What if the man died? There would have to be a police investigation, and if the name proved phony, police throughout the state would be looking for a homicide suspect who fit the description of the man who had given a phony name.

Anyone who could have pulled off bringing the U-boat captain in would have the nerve to keep everything under his control. At that time, Oliver was sure, this "enemy who thinks" would understand the differences between apparent danger and real danger. He would have given his correct name.

What he felt sure of now was that after a span of time greater than Todd's entire life, he was going to find the name of the man who thought he had escaped at the end of the war.

Beaming, the woman gave Todd Oliver the admitting ledger sheet for the emergency room on that date. She pointed to the Jewish name, Rosenberg. It matched the injury. It matched the doctor's name who had performed the operation.

The man who had delivered Mr. Rosenberg and paid for the operation, the closest kin to be notified, there being no closer kin readily available at this time, was . . .

Todd's mouth was suddenly dry. His fingers somehow made a decision for him. They kept moving through the box of ledgers. He was numb. He didn't want to think. Most of all he didn't want to think about that. He didn't want to know what he knew now and kept telling himself.

Charles Drobney had stayed back as 4-F. But there had been so many civilians here at that time. Unfortunately, now it was narrowed to one.

The man who understood the tactical impossibility of a high tower on Bellevue Avenue being a Viking fort, who could see strategy in a civil rights leader, a man who was reluctant to discuss his theories of war with a prospective son-in-law, the man who had taught his daughter that most people feared what they did not have to . . . the man who had in his way by that helped him to this day, and this place. The Enemy who thinks. The Enemy. The Enemy. God help them all. The Enemy. The name on the ledger was Charles Drobney. . . . Todd asked for another date, and the woman happily gave him another box of ledgers. He went through that, too, just to divert her. At 4 P.M., Todd left Newport Mercy Hospital, went to Tuesday's Restaurant, ordered a bourbon, even though he was carrying a gun, excused himself from the bar, waved to a friend of Sondra's who was sitting at a table, and entered the men's room, where he shut the black toilet stall door behind him and into the somewhat fresh, white bowl threw up his lunch and his breakfast.

Sondra Drobney was not going to take "nothing was wrong" anymore.

She had gotten "nothing wrong" from Uncle Bob, who had hurt his hand in an accident and therefore had closed the store; and "nothing wrong" from Dad, who had to rest and was not resting but calculating something in his study; and then Todd came back with stains on his shirt looking as though he had seen his own grave, and he said, "Nothing was wrong," and she said something obviously was wrong and he begged her to give him some more time, which, of course, she had to say yes to.

But when Brandon returned from school with something inside his shirt and he said it was nothing, Sondra Drobney unleashed all her anxiety on that poor child and that poor shirt as though it were the crime of the century.

There had been a frog hidden in that shirt.

"You get that frog and you get that shirt out of this house, and then you come back here, Brandon Drobney, because you are in trouble."

He was so frightened by the fury, he did what he was told immediately. Seeing his fear when he returned, she hugged him, and then he began to cry, and she felt ashamed, and Todd, who could have been of some help in this situation, was inside the study with Dad. And they didn't even come out right away for dinner.

Charles Drobney had been making a little chart when the door opened to his study. Without being obvious, he covered the paper.

It was Todd.

"Excuse me, Mr. Drobney, I've got to see you a minute."

"Later, Todd, if you would. I'm busy," said Drobney. He smiled. *What a good man,* he thought. Sondra had done well. She would be fine.

"I am afraid this will not wait," said Todd.

Drobney turned over the chart and put it between himself and the armrest of his chair.

"Please be brief," he said.

He shut the door behind him. "I know who you are," said Todd.

Charles Drobney did not move. He did not move his leg, which was crossed over the other leg. He did not move his hands. He did not even move an eyelash.

"Oh," he said.

"You are the guy I am looking for. You're the spy," said Todd. That simple.

Done, thought Drobney. *At last, done and done.*

"Well done," said Drobney.

"Yeah," said Todd. "You have a right to remain silent, to retain a lawyer—"

"Todd, I am going to tell you everything. You've won. Congratulations."

"—to retain a lawyer. I must warn you that anything you say may be used against you. You are under arrest."

"Would you care for a drink, Todd?"

"I don't drink on duty," said Todd.

"I am going to get a brandy," said Drobney, and he went in the kitchen and came back with two glasses and a bottle.

He poured a drink into each and raised his in salute. Todd took out a notebook.

"Who are the others?" asked Todd.

Drobney could see how pale he looked, how tense. The fingers clutched the pen as though squeezing its life.

"Todd, take the drink. You need it."

"Who are the others? What have you been doing? How did you arrange the Wheaton killing?"

"Dear boy, son," said Drobney. "I am going to give it all to you. Do you think I would resist you now?"

"You ran a very successful scam while I was in your house, sir," said Oliver.

"You mean you're mad because I didn't surrender at the first breakfast?"

"I slept in your house. I became engaged to your daughter. I was like a father to your grandson."

"And who was that hard on, Todd? You ran this campaign perfectly from day one. You've got a brain. Who was the one who suffered by that?"

"Jesus. Why you? Why you?"

"A question I have asked myself for a long time."

"Are you a German?"

"No. I am an American."

"Were you a Nazi?"

"God no!"

"Why did you do it?"

"Ah," said Charles Drobney. His shoulders were very heavy. He took half his drink.

"Todd, there are several problems that we have now and I think I can help you get through all of them."

"Uh huh," said Todd, with no belief in his voice or on his face.

"There's Sondra, you know. I am happy that she has found you. I am not happy that you have found me. It is not in my interest that she hates you for arresting me. Let's avoid unnecessary casualties."

"I am not letting you go now, Mr. Drobney," said Todd. He had come too far and worked too hard and suffered too much fear to do anything but his job. He was numb. It was combat of his soul and he just wanted to get through another day doing his job right. He was not going to play exotic games at this point. He had his man. He was going to nail his man.

"There is no place for me to go or any reason to go, Todd. It's over."

"Is that why you killed Mrs. Wheaton?"

"I didn't."

"You mean to tell me that her death had absolutely nothing to do with this investigation, is that what you're claiming, Mr. Drobney?"

"No, her death was a tragic mistake. Tragic because I loved her, and a mistake because it was something you could not let pass. You are here now because of that. In fact, you ran your whole campaign on that, didn't you?"

"You were lovers?"

"I loved her. We hadn't made love for a long while. She was married after all."

"She had her affairs."

"She was a good woman," said Drobney. "I have often thought about love, and I think it happens. When you are right for each other, it is a blessing, and when you are not right for each other . . . it is a troublesome blessing."

"Did they teach you that in the General Staff?"

"No, that was the one thing I believe they lacked. . . . I know you knew about my teacher, Hasso von Kiswicz. I took a look at your briefcase. I'm sorry," said Drobney, realizing that he had run an espionage network during an entire war and now was apologizing for looking at other people's correspondence. He was not an officer in the General Staff. He was a spy. And here was the policeman to arrest him for breaking the law.

"So, it was Hasso von Kiswicz, Brigadier General of the General Staff, who was your teacher, not Dr. Martin Luther King," said Todd.

"Obviously, if it were King, I would be mayor of Atlanta, not facing arrest. King did achieve his objective, von Kiswicz did not."

"I am sure Goldstein is not upset by that."

"You must know the General Staff was not Nazi."

"Does Goldstein know about this?"

"No," said Drobney.

If he had told Todd that Bob was aware of his committing a crime, Bob would be liable for arrest as an accessory.

"Let's get on with the Wheaton homicide," said Todd.

"There were three of us, including me, in the ring, all German-Americans who for one reason or another returned to Germany and for one reason or another agreed to spy. Elizabeth Boswell Wheaton was one of those. Her name . . ."

Charles Drobney paused as her name became very hard to say. He remembered how he had held her the last time he saw her.

"Her name, I will put down on paper. You're going to get everything. Another spy did the killing, or was behind it. Today he is very rich, very powerful, and shrewd. You are going to need a good case against him."

"Who is he."

"M. Hiram Lederle."

"Never heard of him."

"I guarantee the head of the Justice Department has heard of him, and probably has been at a dinner or two with him. Everyone in Newport knows him. You are going to need what I give you, and I guarantee I will give you everything you need, not only for him, but for Sondra. It is not in my interest to destroy her future marriage."

"I see. And what do you want?" said Todd. There was bitterness here. He was sure that the old Todd Oliver would have had no problem with any of this.

"Yes, I will give you the entire situation in my handwriting. The names, dates, places, the irrevocable proof signed, signed on every page, which will give you a solid case and an intelligence debriefing. In other words, what happened and how."

"And I am supposed to take the word of an officer of the German General Staff? Is that what I am dealing with?"

Charles Drobney wanted to tell him that the word of an officer of the General Staff had far more worth than most contracts in the history of the world, but there were things that had to be done.

"What I want is tomorrow morning to myself, until the afternoon. To be able to move about, away from surveillance."

"No way," said Todd.

"You think I am going to run, Todd?" said Drobney incredulously. "How can I run? I am sixty-seven. I have a blood pressure of 200 over 110. I have been put in the hospital just an eyelash from a cerebral hemorrhage. Do you really think I am going to ruin your career, my grandson's future father, my daughter's life, for another few weeks, months, maybe a year on the run? And what sort of life would that be? Think. All my life I have arranged things with places for them, with loved ones, with time to think and smell the flowers in the morning. I am not going anywhere."

Todd did not answer.

"You think I wouldn't be able to stay out of jail for the few years I have left once I am charged with espionage? I didn't murder civilians. I didn't commit atrocities. I am not some old Slavic sadist unleashed upon his fellow citizens by a chicken farmer in a black uniform."

"Chicken farmer?"

"Heinrich Himmler of the SS. You might have been better prepared for this case. You should have known that."

Sondra called in asking if everything was all right. She had heard raised voices.

"Everything is fine," said both men in unison. Only Charles Drobney appreciated the humor of this.

"You'll write up everything?" asked Todd.

"Yes," said Drobney.

"Let me see it and then I'll decide."

"That's fine. I know you will." Drobney dared not tell him everything, but he would give him what he promised and then some. He offered the drink again. Todd refused.

"Please," said Drobney.

Todd stared at the drink. And then he looked at the man's eyes. It was as though he were asking for the courtesy of a last cigarette before being shot. He took the drink.

Mr. Drobney toasted him, and then began to talk, and Todd did not stop him. There was still that inner boundary in the man but the aloofness was gone. It was a beaten general talking about life, a father talking to a son-in-law, it was Gottherd Hauff talking about baseball, loving, and a young man being impressed with the thinking of the General Staff.

It occurred to Todd at this moment that he was the only one this man had been able to discuss things like this with since he had left America in his early twenties.

Mr. Drobney told him that strategic concepts and the thinking was something that came easily to him. Left alone after the war with all that training, he began to apply those methods to trying to explain to himself how all the horrors had ensued from the noble art of war.

"Of course, I had learned almost everything about war but the killing."

"And the General Staff kept that from you to get you to go along?"

"I'm not sure. It was just that when you begin to think like they do, it becomes a grand, noble game with rules. I guess they recognized a shrewd games player. Of course, none of them, I believe, ever really asked themselves why they were doing any of this. I once asked the colonel, von Kiswicz was a colonel then, whether he was happy."

"Was he?"

"He said that was unimportant, but really that is the strategic question of anyone's life. I was twenty-two at the time. I didn't know better. We got on to what I thought was business."

"Are you happy? I don't mean now."

"I have been. Very. I am happy that you and Sondra have found each other," said Drobney. "She is very special. I think you are too."

"I am puzzled about one thing and curious about another. Why did you save Captain Wankele?"

"Captain Wankele, whom you used to pressure Lederle into overreaching again?"

"Yes."

"It was near the end of the war, I knew. It was over, but I felt a responsibility to those boys out there. Yes, I was a traitor. I understand, I am an American. God bless me, I am. But he was out there, and he was going to die, and dammit, I knew I could pull it off."

"You didn't, Mr. Drobney. I got you for that."

"But I did. I've had a wonderful life. That one thing was what I was proud of all during the war."

"Why did you choose Newport for the base? I am sure the Navy will want to know."

"That will be in my report to you. But initially we came here because this is where America plans its naval wars."

"One more thing. Why didn't you turn yourself in at the end of the war? They weren't executing spies."

"I didn't want to go back to Germany. I am not a German. I'm an American. And Lederle was already successful and he didn't want to go back, and poor Elizabeth always tended to drift towards what was most pleasant. You will read it all."

Charles Drobney stayed in his study until 1 A.M., writing in longhand the report to Todd, which he signed at the end.

And he was done, but for a few more details on the little diagram he had been organizing. He looked around the study for the last time. The books were still there, some read several times, some he suspected he did not really understand. They were there and what had he learned?

Among other things, he thought, perhaps his father, whom he had seen the last time in Stuttgart, actually understood everything Charles Drobney had fought a war to find out. Charles Drobney would never know. He had never really talked to the man.

He collected the glasses and the bottle, turned out the lights with his shoulder, and pulled the door after him with a foot.

It was hard for him to go to sleep, but he had already said good-bye to his study and did not want to go downstairs again. He picked up a *National Geographic* and read in more detail and drama than he thought necessary about the hardy struggles of the South Arctic emperor penguin.

26

An eighteen-knot southwesterly carved swells into the Atlantic. The offshore Gulf Stream mellowed the crisp September air under a bright yellow sun. The American entry could finish it all that day.

People had slept the night on the open piers, some with stale dead drinks still balanced on the warped gray planking. Guards this year stood in front of both the British challenger and American defender.

Police had ignored young couples grinding in doorways, provided they were out of sight of Thames Street. But there was no loving in the morning. There never was. Loud snores, hugging for softness, but no loving in the morning.

The Coast Guard and the New York Yacht Club Committee were seven miles out in the Atlantic setting the buoys to accommodate the best wind and tide for the sharpest test of the twelves.

M. Hiram Lederle ate breakfast alone in his morning room, and it was a good morning. The burrs of his life, past and present, seemed worn smooth at last. He had just heard that the Spitting Rock Association, which legally owned Bailey's Beach, had ever so matter-of-factly sent the forms for him to become a bondholder, which meant he had passed subscription, and he just as casually sent back the forms. It was the way it was done in Newport.

Nobody had to mention that a proper birth certificate had appeared, with proper testimony, from a minister no less. All quiet. All serene. It was just one of the many things that Newport people just didn't have to mention.

But even the pinnacle of Bailey's Beach was not quite as satisfying to M. Hiram Lederle this morning as a very old insult done restitution by the remorseless leveling of time.

When the word "sir" had come out of the mouth of Charles Drobney, almost a half century of personal exclusion and ridicule came to an end.

It was a hidden wound he had lived with so long that when it was healed, he had to keep reminding himself the sting was not there anymore. It didn't have to be swallowed or avoided. It was gone.

It was not even Drobney who had made the wound, but the man who had selected him, that General Staff officer.

When he called himself von Schaumburg, when he was trying so hard to get on in the world, trying to get that first foothold, he had taken that opportunity offered by the General Staff. He knew they were the old school, but so much was changing in Germany. It was the new order. He thought they would have to give him a chance to command. He had so much to offer. He tried to explain it to that Prussian colonel. But the colonel dismissed him with a contemptuous little smile; there was a little laugh back there in the throat when he said, "We do not exactly select commanders this way."

It was as though his very best was just a joke. And to set the sting even deeper they selected a younger man, a boy, a little shitter with pink cheeks and the same self-assured arrogance they had. But it was that light laugh that Lederle remembered with the most annoyance. And when the hardware store owner dared laugh just like that while presuming to talk down to him, Lederle had not been able to control himself. He might have killed him there in the parking lot at the hardware store with his own hands and worked out the details later.

But now the world was right, and everyone was where he was supposed to be. And so having Charlie on his knees, M. Hiram Lederle had the whole General Staff there also. Drobney might have to be gotten rid of later on, of course. But today, the Prussian's choice would be there taking orders on how to kill his best friend. The orders would have to be simple, something a hardware store owner might be able to do.

M. Hiram Lederle ate his breakfast alone that morning in great joy. His son and wife would eat later and see the race from someone else's yacht. They seemed to like each other anyway. M. Hiram Lederle was secure enough now in Newport to extend noblesse oblige to a local tradesman wanting to buy a little powerboat. Besides, the main party of the America's Cup Ball, not the race itself, was the real event to attend.

For this good morning, Mr. Lederle ate a double portion of eggs with small sausages, shirred potatoes, and sweet rolls glistening with sugar and cinnamon glaze just baked by his chef. All of this was washed down with three cups of dark coffee, each laced with his private stock of brandy.

Charles Drobney had two Ismelins for breakfast, put on his neatest white pants, and then shined his brown shoes immaculately. He put on his finest white shirt, which he had bought on sale from a local clothier, and combed his hair with the same part he had used since childhood. He brushed and flossed his teeth, steadied himself by the basin, and then went downstairs to see if Todd had finished the envelope he had handed him the first thing in the morning when he heard movement in the hallway.

"Everything seems fine. Okay. You'll be back when?"

"I will be back here, right after the race," said Drobney.

"Okay," said Todd. His lips were tight.

"Everything will be all right," said Drobney.

Todd was making breakfast for Brandon. Sondra was asleep. Drobney was not hungry. He kissed Brandon and shook Todd's hand, telling him to say good morning to Sondra for him.

"Okay," said Todd. He did not look up from the eggs.

On the day that could be the final race of the Cup, there was no way he was going to maneuver his Buick through the traffic, so Charles Drobney walked to the store. In every other year they had closed the store and rented the parking lot spaces for the day.

But today, the lot was filled, unattended, unroped, unprofited. The store had been closed only a day, and already it had that sense of faint mustiness. The sadness of it helped, Charlie felt. He wanted to say goodbye to the store, too, but could not.

He would never say goodbye to it, anymore than he would say goodbye to Sondra or Brandon or Bob, and now, even Todd Oliver.

No, he would not say goodbye. He took two sizes of Playcool

thermos boxes for picnics to the back room and searched out the rear corner of the storeroom facing the driveway. The three small wooden boxes of dynamite were stacked separately, still waiting for return, along with other construction material Bob had ordered while Charlie was in the hospital.

The invoice had listed blasting caps and a blasting machine to set them off. Dynamite itself was relatively stable and had to be set off with another charge.

He remembered ordering the schlepper to put the blasting caps themselves at the other end of the storeroom, and the blasting machine itself in a locked closet on a shelf.

The blasting caps were the touchy things. They came in sealed metal cases, almost like the thermos cases he was carrying. He brought them to the dynamite and very carefully put their boxes to the side. The dynamite sticks were packed in soft excelsior sponge and were yellow. Each was no wider than an inch in diameter. He took five and let them sit out in the open, and then very carefully he opened the container of the caps. They were brass, hardly bigger than his thumb. He took the diagram he had been working on the afternoon before Todd interrupted him, and reread his configurations. When a paper seal at the end of the yellow dynamite stick was opened, the brass blasting cap could be pushed through. He did the first one with his mouth dry and his hand shaking. It went in like soft earth. Good.

He did it to four more, then even more gently, using more excelsior to keep everything in place, he put them all into a Playcool lunch box. Then he inserted wires into the five blasting caps and secured them with black electrical tape very carefully against the waxy dynamite skin. And he shut the Playcool box.

He opened the smaller box and then tore the cardboard wrapping away from the blasting machine. Inside the wrapping there was a metal box. He took the machine out of the box and brought it out into the empty store to an electrical charge tester in the auto section of Drobney-Goldstein. It worked.

He could have built one if he had to. He wasn't the best mechanic in the world, but he had learned these things with the business. He packed the blasting machine into the smaller thermos box with its wires taped together also.

Then he cleaned up, packing everything away. The store was so very, very quiet. The Red Sox were playing, he knew. In Newport one felt this day that the world watched the Cup races and that this port was the center of that world. But it wasn't. The world went very much on its way. As it had for a very long time, as it would to-morrow.

Charles Drobney left the store, locking up, and joined the buzz of tourists. He knew no one could see anything connected with the race from the harbor, and yet they were here, packed in like Times Square on New Year's Eve. They wanted to be where the action was even when it was seven miles out beyond the harbor.

If they went up to the Cliff Walk they might see the pleasure boats surrounding the races' course being herded back into formation by the Coast Guard, which by now had to be desperately trying to avoid collisions and drownings of children overboard and some power-boats getting in the way of the course itself.

At the harbor itself now there were only the tourists telling them-selves they were at a great event. Charles Drobney made his way through the people drinking in the streets to the piers, and the Lederle brokerage. He carried the thermos box close to his body, and made his way at some crowded points by knifing the other hand through the packed bodies.

At the end of one pier, he saw what he wanted.

Lederle was at the wheel of the small powerboat, booming with joy. Even the half-cabin boat caught the bounce of the day.

He spotted the cooler box right away.

"What's that?" he said.

"I have to have special foods. I have high blood pressure," said Drobney.

Lederle smiled tolerantly and helped him down into the boat. Charles Drobney knew he was thought of as frightened and there-fore safe for Lederle, at least for this day when the older man was going to give him orders.

He put the Playcool box in the rear and realized his hands were wet with sweat. His mouth was dry, and he nodded as Lederle talked. He nodded very politely.

He told himself that that was the *Takt* decision even as he edged away from the white and red cooler box with the death inside it. He would never have a better chance. It was a thing he had to do. He didn't have many years left anyway.

But he did not go near the box in the harbor, because he might injure others if he set off the charge in such a dense pack of ships, he told himself. Out past Fort Adams into Narragansett Bay, he told himself that he might fumble while the boat was moving, and Lederle might overpower him. So he stayed away from the box then. He told himself all these things until the Lederle motor launch reached the pack of ships set around the race buoys. And then the sea was calm. And there was nothing more he could tell himself. He could not get himself to move to that red and white box no matter how much logic was on his side. He ordered his body to move and it wouldn't move. He cursed himself. And the curses did not work.

The salt air was sweet and the yellow sun pure over the Atlantic and he could not get himself to move to that Playcool box. Lederle waved to people and smiled.

Charles Drobney thought of the people he loved. He thought very hard about them. He shut his eyes for a moment. Lederle assumed it was the tension of planning Bob Goldstein's death. He enjoyed Drobney's weakness.

But when Charles Drobney shut his eyes, he saw the faces of Bob and Sondra and Brandon and even the FBI man who was now part of Sondra's life and Brandon's life. It was good. It was all good.

It is good, Gottzy, Charles Drobney told himself. He did not have to say anything more.

He went to the rear of the launch, claiming he was getting some food. And when Lederle turned to wave to some other people he knew, Charles Drobney attached the detonator.

When Lederle turned again, he knew in an instant what had happened.

"What are you doing, you crazy little man?" he snapped.

"Do you really think I could explain it all to you now?" said Drobney. What was he supposed to do, begin lectures in *Takt* decisions? He couldn't help it. Lederle's insufferable rage seemed so inappropriate, Drobney had to laugh. It was a pitying laugh.

Drobney had no way of knowing that little laugh carried the same contemptuous tolerance that so seared the man now lunging at him with the anguished cry of a child. He did not know it was the laugh of a Prussian colonel hearing from a barroom bouncer that the bouncer instead of a General Staff–trained man should be in charge of a mission.

There was no more time for thought. It was over. He set off the charge.

The Lederle powerboat went up like a thudding geyser of water; the concussive effect first flattened the waves like a giant hand slapping the water and every boat in it, sending two helicopters into almost uncontrollable dips. An adjacent yawl caught the full force of the blast in its sails and tipped like a kicked toy.

Windows imploded on ketch and sloop alike. Tables shuddered on the great yachts. The two twelves, just starting out, both with great captains, tried to take advantage of this thing they didn't expect.

For hundreds of yards around, waves flattened white, then bounced up again.

The blast could be seen from the crowded Cliff Walk, just about the only clearly observable part of the race from that distance.

Todd Oliver knew immediately what it was. *Shit,* he said to himself. Sondra and Brandon immediately looked to him for safety.

27

TODD OLIVER stayed with Sondra the entire afternoon until the phone rang and she screamed, "No." He stayed with her into the evening when she cried and wanted to know why something that horrible had happened. Wannaker called Todd and told him that his future father-in-law had probably been killed in a mob rubout. Word was that Lederle had amassed part of his fortune through some very gray areas of commerce and had been connected in some ways since before the war. He was not the only Newport fortune like that.

"Made a few in the black market while everyone else went off to war," said Wannaker. "I kind of hoped to get him some day."

Brandon did not know what the tears were about, and finally Todd had to tell him about Granpa.

"There was a terrible accident out at the race and Granpa is dead," he said.

"Gone away?" said Brandon.

"Yes," said Todd. Brandon thought a moment and a single tear spilled over the wells of tears in one of his eyes.

And then the boy cried and Todd held him. If ever there was any question about pushing through all the difficulties to marry Sondra, it ended this day and this moment with this boy in his arms. It ended with Sondra's grief, because he was not going to leave her ever while his body could stay near her.

This was his son. He always suspected he could love a child and in so doing he was more a man than he had ever been. He was more a person, which was what he had learned here in Newport.

He wanted to share what he knew about Drobney and Lederle and Wheaton. He wanted to share it with Wannaker. He trusted the man, but once Wannaker knew, Wannaker would be as responsible as him for prosecuting this. Of course, what was Todd going to do? It was killing him.

Sondra made a few phone calls to close friends. She didn't know what she was going to do about the funeral. There was not a body left.

"He died instantly, honey," Todd said when she had winced at the thought of no body being left.

"He's gone," said Sondra, and a sharp thin wail came out of her soul as her body jerked in spasm in Todd's arms.

She sobbed silently, crying without tears. He would never let her go. She was not alone. He would never let her go.

Brandon came into her bedroom, where his mother was sobbing, and climbed into her lap and was held. And Todd held them both.

Brandon eventually went to sleep, and with another sedative Sondra, too, terminated her conscious pain for a few hours. Todd went down to the study to think.

He reread Drobney's long handwritten note, signed, dated, and, of course, delivered earlier in the day. He had the three members. He had what they did and when they did it, and even the reasons for doing it, why certain limited objectives were chosen as opposed to others. As suspected, he had gotten maximum use of a submarine fleet against a supply line the General Staff had hoped to diminish sufficiently to effect their solution to a European war.

There was even Drobney's last comment on Hitler, how in retrospect the General Staff had to know that should one war have been won, he would have been off on another. What Drobney had eventually realized was the man was chasing his own ghosts and own fears and sold them to enough of a nation to follow him. One never caught one's ghosts in the outside world.

Nations, Drobney concluded, were often led by salesmen, not administrators. He doubted that his colonel, Hasso von Kiswicz, who he thought would have been a fine administrator for any country, ever could have gotten elected or intrigued his way to becoming a dictator. He would have liked to write about this and other things, but of course Todd could understand why he didn't want the publicity of a book.

The last thing noted in the five handwritten pages was that Charles Drobney was Gottherd "Dutch" Hauff, who batted .188 for the Kinston, North Carolina, Aviators in the old Piedmont League. And of course he didn't stand a chance because the man right behind him was named Wee Willie Carter.

Todd Oliver looked at his watch. It was eleven-thirty at night. He could say he found this in the morning. He could find it just about anytime.

Admiral O'Connell called the house to share his sympathies with Todd. And he wanted to see him.

"Does it have to be tonight?" said Todd.

"No. But I think we ought to talk about something right away."

"I could use a friend, Admiral," said Todd. He was numb. If he felt better, he would hurt. But he was tired and numb like men in combat he had seen pictures of.

There was a pause on the other end of the line.

"Maybe," said the admiral.

Todd let the older man into the house quietly and shut the door behind them in Drobney's study.

"There is a rumor in the town that the two men killed today, including your girlfriend's father, were either spies or killed by spies . . . among other rumors," said Admiral O'Connell.

He was in a sports jacket and a pair of white pants. Todd hadn't seen so many white pants in one place since he accidently stumbled into a gay bar for a drink in Washington once.

Todd shrugged.

"Do you think the rumors are just connecting the tragedy to the spies, or what?" said O'Connell.

"You got them," said Todd. "Okay. They're dead. You got 'em. You won, you fucking won."

"They *were* involved," said O'Connell.

"Celebrate. . . . I've got a fiancée upstairs asleep and I care about her more than anyone. I love that woman. And she has just lost her father. And the boy who will be my son has lost a grandfather whom he loved. And I am grieving, too, now . . . so take your fucking victory and do your celebration. We got 'em."

He gave O'Connell Drobney's handwritten statement with the signatures on every page, very neat and very conclusive.

O'Connell skimmed down the lined pages.

"Marcus Hiram Lederle," he said in awe. "He wasn't just a victim. Do you know what that man really is, Todd? I've been to dinners with him. I would have had him on our board of directors. No wonder they got away so long."

"He wasn't the tough nut. Mr. Drobney was. It was always him. The enemy who thinks," said Todd, and he nodded his head toward the books in the study. . . .

Admiral O'Connell saw the tiredness beyond tiredness in the young man's eyes. He had seen it before. Too much tension too long. Battle fatigue was around the corner.

"What are you going to do with these?" said O'Connell, holding up the lined yellow pages with the neat inking, each one numbered precisely even to the paragraphs.

"What do you care? We got 'em, right?"

Todd expected the admiral to get angry, raise a flag, give a lecture. Todd didn't care. He was surprised at how his anger didn't seem to bother the admiral.

The admiral went back to the statement. When he got to the part about which convoys were chosen, a part Todd did not quite understand, O'Connell nodded.

"Of course," O'Connell mumbled. "Yup. Yup. Yup." He finished the statement and then asked again what Todd Oliver was going to do with the statement.

"What do you care, Admiral, your ass will be protected."

"Todd, you did a hell of a job. We got the bastards. As you said, we don't visit the sins of the fathers on the sons. Am I the only one other than you who knows this?"

Todd nodded.

O'Connell threw the papers back into Todd's lap.

"Buddy, if I saw those things, as a lawyer, what would you advise me to do to protect myself if something goes wrong?"

"Not to see them," said Todd.

"That's what I thought."

"I don't even want to see you burn them, Todd."

"I don't know if I should. I don't know if I shouldn't. I don't know what to do," said Todd.

Admiral O'Connell took back the written statements, asked where the liquor was, and went outside to the kitchen to get it. When he returned with two full glasses of liquor, Todd could smell the smoke from the little fire of burning papers.

"Who was Wee Willie Carter?" asked Todd.

"A lousy bush-league ballplayer who did well during the war until the real major leaguers got back. Played second base. Anybody who lost out to him had to be real lousy."

"I saw Charles Drobney pick up a grounder once. It looked great to me."

"Sure, you never played major league ball, I was pretty good. Never wanted to be a ballplayer, though. I wanted to be a G-man."

"Why didn't you?"

"Couldn't afford it. Annapolis takes care of everything and pays you to boot. I could afford that," said O'Connell.

Brandon came downstairs, rubbing his eyes because he said he smelled something burning and he was afraid the house would go on fire.

"Bill, thank you. I've got to say goodnight now, and put my son to sleep," said Todd.

"Good night, Todd. And thank you," said the admiral. On his way out, the admiral mumbled something about Wee Willie Carter and how bad he was. "Thought I'd never hear about that bimbo again in my life after we all got home from the war."

In the morning, Sondra had decided what would be done for her father's funeral. They wouldn't go through the mockery of putting fragments into the ground in the cemetery next to her mother. It was not the way her father should be remembered.

She wanted his close friends to meet in his study, and they would all tell what they remembered about him and what they thought they had gotten from him. She did not want a minister because her father in his lifetime had not come to a definitive conclusion on God. He said there wasn't conclusive evidence either way to prove that the logic that we perceived in the universe was not some variation of randomness.

He personally believed in a God, but only suspected that God was benign. There was even less proof for that.

The ceremony had to be held quickly because Todd was being transferred from his special assignment. Apparently, Bob Goldstein was so stricken by his friend's death, he did not want to attend. But as he said, he could deny Sondra nothing when she pleaded.

He had hurt his hand and it was in a cast. His son also was there. Bob did not want to speak, but Sondra begged him to, so, quite embarrassed, he searched for words as everyone stood around in the small study.

"I don't know," he said. "I don't know. He was my friend."

Everybody thought he was done, but then, staring very hard at his son and wife, he said, "The thing about my friend was that he was wise, he had seykhl. They didn't give out degrees for that. He didn't write any great books about which people said, 'Hey, this guy knows what it's all about.' He just used his head. And it's not a small thing in this world. And I know he loved me. Okay, that's it. Goodbye, Charlie."

Everyone had made sort of a circle in the study and when Bob stepped back into it, he couldn't cover his eyes because of his bad hand, which was in a cast, and he couldn't bury his head in a friend's shoulder, because his one friend was not there anymore.

Mrs. Charlotte Goldstein, in formal black with a single strand of proper white pearls, declined to speak, as did her son, Professor Nathaniel Goldstein, whom Sondra had known as "Puggy" a long time ago.

Brandon stepped forward into the center of the circle with a big step like a march.

"Goodbye, Granpa," he said. "Thank you. Thank you for all the things. Some of them I liked."

Sondra began crying when Brandon said that and kissed him on the head, and then she stepped into the center of the circle and tried to talk. She was crying too hard to speak right away, and Todd stepped in with her and put an arm on her shoulder. Outside in the garden, he could see the Newport fog hide the house across the street. Cars moved with their lights on at midday. The garden needed tending but probably wouldn't get it. The house was going to be sold.

Finally Sondra spoke. "I had thought that I had something so good to say. You know. Something so meaningful, and something that would sum up so many things. I don't. All I feel is that I had the smartest, bravest, most loving father in the world and now he's gone."

She stood there awhile and then surprised Todd by asking him to say something. He, too, did not know what to say, but it didn't really seem to matter. He was thinking about something and it wasn't Drobney.

"Sondra often told me that her father claimed she saved him by his loving of her, that loving, caring, was what made you not alone in the world, and that is true. The world is a scary, lonely place, and you'd better not be without someone to love in it."

Years later, in a very good marriage with this woman, he would come to suspect that perhaps his knowledge of Drobney was wrong. That indeed his daughter, innocent of what he had done in the war, really knew him because all Todd had unearthed were some facts.

Love knew someone else. It was the only way to know. The rest were just some incomplete facts.

Sondra kissed him hard in the study, right then, and the funeral for Charles Drobney was over.

Todd was being transferred to Austin, Texas, and Sondra and Brandon were going with him. He didn't know whether he was going to stay with the Bureau or leave. They would decide that together. Sondra, who had thought she could never leave beautiful Newport, found she had no trouble. It was a beautiful place with beautiful memories, and, if she could return, it would be nice. But it was not the necessary thing it used to be. She had Todd.

The service was over when everyone left the room.

The empty brass coffin of M. Hiram Lederle was put into the earth in one of the more exclusive cemeteries of Rhode Island. Two hundred people attended the funeral, including the press, which was rife with all manner of speculation about the man.

The minister spoke of the resurrection they could all be sure of, with the deep spiritual conviction of a corporate lawyer reciting the minutes of incorporation.

Mrs. Lederle wore black and a new twelve-carat diamond she had purchased. She was surprised by her own lawyers when they told her how rich Hiram had left her.

"Isn't that nice," she said. "What a pleasant, pleasant surprise."

She planned to move back to Providence because she had never felt really accepted in Newport.

Her son waited through the ceremony, occasionally looking at his watch. He didn't even bother returning the messages of sympathy from around the country. As far as he was concerned, if he never saw another politician again, it would be all too soon. The psychiatrist who had been treating his severe depressions agreed it was a good move that he get out of politics, but it was going to be a lot harder and longer to get rid of the other damage his father had done to him.

Lederle's secretary cried. The gossips said she had had an affair with him. Used to be a beautiful woman, everyone said.

In Newport society a good obituary was an important thing and M. Hiram Lederle had one of the absolute best, astounding considering where he had started.

No one, of course, asked where he had thought he was going all along.

It was, all in all, everyone agreed, one of the cruelest America's Cup summers in memory. It certainly would be talked about during the winter at Palm Beach and elsewhere. The American defender, of course, won despite protests from the British yachting club. But it was ruled that the unseemly explosion affected both twelve-meter yachts equally.

Six months after Sondra had donated most of her father's books to the sort of charities she thought he would approve of, several books came back to her with an apology. The Newport League of Retired Naval Officers felt it was inappropriate to stock so many books making a former enemy appear so noble. They were referring specifically to one segment of the German war machine that was portrayed almost like helpless knights in a brutal society. Specifically, they referred to passages about the basic rectitude of the German General Staff, and how important their word was to them. It made them sound like George Washington cutting down the cherry tree and admitting it, saying he would not tell a lie. While the respondent was sure some of them did keep their promises, they were after all helpers in the worst horror the world had ever seen. And so the books were being returned herein, "Regretfully, Commander William Farley McFeester, USN, Ret."